" 'One,' murmured Hayes.

'Two,' said Lubbock.

The baskets were lowered quickly past each of the galleries by an elaborate pulley system fixed into the roof.

Hollis Jackson grinned and glanced below at the table. 'Three,' he said. Shouts went up which turned into a roar as the croupier stopped and indicated clearly the three gold coins remaining on the baize table-cloth. Immediately all bets on the side of the square marked 'three' were paid and delivered to each gallery in a winners' basket.

'Real money, Silas. Remember it, Eli? What are you two playing with?'

'Prospects,' growled Silas Hayes. Eli Lubbock smiled and raised a glass containing merely coloured water. 'All the tea in China,' he said."

FOR ALL THE TEA IN CHINA

Stephen Sheppard

Tudor Publishing Company
New York and Los Angeles

ISBN: 0-944276-28-8

Printed in the United States of America

First Tudor printing—November, 1988

FOR THE THREE MOTHERS IN MY LIFE,
LADIES WITHOUT
WHOM . . .
ELLEN MARY WHO HAD TO SUFFER ME;
WINKY WHO CHOOSES TO;
ANNIE WHO WILL . . .
ONE FROM THE HEART

PROLOGUE

On the Chinese Bund, in a murky twilight of the summer solstice, the evening bustle of Shanghai's waterfront had already begun. Beneath torches, lamps and lanterns, blazing into the growing darkness, rickshaws clattered across cobbles. Phalanxes of coolie porters, bent beneath back-breaking loads, thrust between crowds of dockers, sailors, merchants bellowing orders, clerks come to take instructions and employees rushing to do the bidding of their masters. Gangways led to junks berthed at the wharfside serving the larger ships, mostly heavy-tonnage steamers moored in the channel where the deeper water of the Whampoa, yellow with mud carrying the soil of another, mysterious China more than a thousand miles away, sluiced past the greatest treaty port in the Far East, on into the night and down to the sea.

Beside a Customs office, next to a barber's shop where an élite team, in poor lantern light, were expertly preparing sailors for their night on the town, going to their task with a will and cut-throat razors which were dangerous only if they brought a lump to the throat, the Navigator Bar sported a terrace with the best view of all sea-bound river traffic. Its advantage was that the old wooden balustrade leaned out from the first floor, precariously suspended over the confusion below. A flurry of activity, as dockers directed arriving wagons and carriages towards a sleek but ageing windjammer tied at the quayside, brought two men to their feet. For several minutes they leaned on the rail, sipping whisky, content to say nothing. As loading of the ship began, they identified the cargo as tea.

Both men were unshaven and unkempt. One wore a creased and grubby white suit, the other a dark seaman's jacket and grey flannels, but beneath a peaked cap the sharp glint in his clear blue eyes indicated a strength and intelligence that belied the disreputable impression.

Silas Hayes glanced at his friend Eli Lubbock, knowing what was in his mind. His own swarthy good looks and slight Scottish burr were a contrast to Eli's knotted chestnut hair, pale complexion and seemingly innocent expression. Only a blunt voice with a Cockney accent conveyed Eli's authority to command. Gypsies had brought Silas from Glasgow to London, where, barely in his teens, he first encountered Eli Lubbock. Thus, the two men were now long-time friends, but for the first time on this distant shore, had been washed up and become landlubbers for a period neither enjoyed remembering.

Rumours abounded about both of them, which they took care neither to confirm nor deny. But they had been forced by well-meaning friends to discontinue their dubious exploits. The facts were simple. The law knew of their whereabouts but had never assembled sufficient proof to charge either of them with what, if the truth were known, would certainly have led to their execution. Morally, as Silas had often pointed out to Eli, they were doing no more than the major trading houses had engaged in when they first began to exploit the Chinese coast. Words like 'opium' and 'slavery' were often brought into the conversation in the bars these two men frequented, but they would only smile and murmur 'tea and silk'. For, after all, both of them had reputations in the very respectable business of world trade, having traversed half the world in laden clipper ships to that other great port, which both friends still called home – London.

Above all the noises from the mêlée on the harbourside, an old sea-shanty began to emerge. The words, sung plaintively, accompanied by an accordion, brought back images of teak decks, straining masts, a surging ocean and a following wind. The trades had taken these blue-water sailors to the excitement and adventure that, as boys, they had only dreamed of, but now it was already history. Steam had dispensed with the romance of windjammers. Speed had become the important requirement. The world was changing too fast for men like Lubbock and Hayes. Their expertise was gradually becoming redundant. Clewing canvas or choosing the exact moment to run out studding yards to take full advantage of a north-east blow was no longer one of the considerations an owner bore in mind when selecting a captain. 'Tin kettles' were now manned by sea-going 'plumbers' and tall funnels that belched black smoke had replaced graceful hulls beneath tapering masts and billowing sails.

> Not for all the tea in China
> Would I ever leave the sea
> For I know of no sight finer
> Than on tail ships sailing free.
> So blow you stormy weather,
> To bear us o'er the sea,
> Wash the rail and fill the sail
> 'Til England's on our lee.

The accordion player stopped beneath the balcony and looked up. Silas and Eli recognised him as a shipmate they had sailed with on different clippers and numerous routes, to the Western Isles and the Antipodes. He looked even worse than they did. Times were hard for them all.

> 'Til England's on our lee my boys
> 'Till England's on our lee.
> I know of no sight finer
> Than old England on our lee.

The two men listened as the accordion player continued and Silas grinned at Eli's long face and began to sing along:

> We'll set the sky sails soaring
> To a wind that's strong and free
> Sail her tight till land's in sight,
> 'Til England's o'er the lee.

Eli had grown home-sick for Limehouse, the London dockland where Chinese immigrants had made their own community. He stepped back despondently to the table and poured the last of the whisky into his glass.

> To be the first to Dover
> The first ship they will see,
> Night and day we'll sail away
> 'Til England's on our lee.

Silas was now singing with gusto. Swallowing his whisky, Eli joined Silas at the balcony rail and made a chorus with him and the accordion player:

> Till England's on our lee my boys
> Till England's on our lee,
> I know of no sight finer
> Than old England on our lee.

The words and music below were suddenly cut off as another group of laden porters pushed the man aside. He fell heavily on to the cobbles, only just managing to squirm from beneath the wheels of a carriage whose driver was forcing a pair of horses through the crowds. Eli and Silas reached into their pockets, but it was merely a gesture; neither of them had even a single coin or note in any of the currencies that circulated in Shanghai.

The passenger sprawled in the back of his open

carriage was dressed in finely tailored clothes. He glanced up at the two men on the terrace and, knowing them well, could see in the flickering light from torches set at each end of the balcony rail that their condition had deteriorated rapidly since they last appeared in public. Attempts to avoid their many creditors were obviously becoming more difficult. Jacob Hollis Jackson smiled to himself at his fortune. He remembered all too well that he came from the same background as these men, and had endured similar privations. It was then with pleasure and great self-satisfaction that he smelt the polished wood and felt the soft leather of his hand-built barouche. He ignored the stony expressions of Silas and Eli, reached into his waistcoat and cursorily threw four glittering coins on to the cobbles in front of the accordion player. With barely a murmur to his driver, a whip cracked on instruction and the horses continued to force a passage along the Chinese bund.

The first explosion took everyone by surprise, then came a second and a third. The cascade from the first rocket's zenith created shouts of anticipation in the milling crowds. More fireworks soared into the sky, indicating that the Festival of the Lost Souls was not forgotten. The wandering dead who had found no place in Heaven or Hell were to be prayed for, and with some luck they might find a resting place.

Silas and Eli watched the spectacle for several minutes then, charming further credit from Chung Lee – whose expression only changed if he actually saw money – they descended the stairs and stepped out into the throng. Silas paused in front of the barber's shop, but the sign for closed in both English and Chinese was rapidly presented at the door. He peered through a window, only to be confronted by a belligerent face and a waving razor, both stating quite clearly that credit had its limitations.

The two men walked on, and only when several young boys began to shout 'Lucky, lucky,' did they pause beside a creek which led on to a slipway. One of the young boys presented two paper boats, each containing a candle. It was tradition, especially among the many people who had lived upon moored sampans, to celebrate the festival as their ancestors had over the centuries before them. Both Silas and Eli shrugged and showed empty pockets, but one of the small boys offered them boats and candles, bowing seriously. 'No b'long plopper. You b'long Shanghai side good. You savvy box, I learn piecee.'

Silas smiled ruefully and ruffled the boy's cropped hair. His mother was an amah he had employed for several years, but been unable to pay in recent months. Loyally she had remained. The boy's fascination for the sea always brought him to the dockside. Silas had been no different at the same age. Ships offered other worlds and another life of adventure.

Captain Hayes saluted the boy, who came to attention and gave them each a paper boat and candle, then lit a match. Silas and Eli knelt on the slipway, presented the wicks carefully, then, as was tradition, placed the paper boats on the unruffled water of the small creek. The men and boys watched as they moved away towards deeper water. As they were caught by the current they began to bob, the flames sputtering for a moment when a first breeze caught them.

The boy grinned. 'They lightee still, good joss. Velee good joss.'

The two paper boats turned suddenly and, swept by the current, began to move towards the sea.

'You wishee makee,' said the boy, and prodded both men. 'You wishee makee – good.'

Silas and Eli stared at the boats, so frail and now moving quickly, until they disappeared into the darkness. More rockets exploded above them, and for a moment the two men were lost in thought, prompted by the boy's trust in tradition.

'My wantee go too,' he whispered. Eli looked at the child, who seemed to have read their thoughts, and put out a hand. Maybe the boy was right – maybe he'd bring them luck, good *joss*. After all, everyone was a gambler in China.

'I go Englandside?' asked the boy, with hushed excitement.

Silas grinned and nodded.

'Can puttee book?'

Eli began to laugh. The two men stood up and lifted the boy into the air. He squirmed between them with excitement at the prospect of leaving. If they went, he went – and if he believed, then they would. . . . They shook hands and struck a bargain.

Walking away from the river into the crowded streets and through the Chinese market, the two men remained silent and oblivious of the rockets continuing to erupt. As both men knew, the beginning of anything started with a wish. How that wish was turned into a dream and made into reality was a familiar mystery. All those years ago and so many thousands of miles away, as ragamuffins they had stared out at the dark waters of the Thames and wished desperately to leave. Now, almost four decades later, they were on the other side of the world, looking at a yellow river, the adventure and excitement they had sought behind them. All they now wanted was to go home, they thought, and all they had to do was believe they could get there and, perhaps with luck, they would. . . .

If the two men had been absolutely honest with themselves they would have admitted what real sailors learn quickly: that home is only a destination – life is the sea.

1

An open eye, painted on the prow of a Chinese junk seemed to glimmer with an expression of apprehension, caught in the torchlight from the shore. River water purled at the bow as all hands on deck brought the junk's stern around and threw first lines on to the wharf, where they secured the junk against the current. Shouting instructions, the leader of the group disembarked quickly and began leading them immediately into the crowds filling the streets of the old Chinese city.

Though many recognised their headbands, few were willing to acknowledge the group as they moved purposefully towards their destination. High in the sky, a spectacular display of fireworks illuminated sections of the city momentarily. In the streets, masked faces abounded, drums beat, musicians played, cymbals clashed and men, forming the heads and bodies of dragons, cavorted. Only the dull red characters on the dark headbands, which matched the loose-fitting cotton suits, showed a smudge of colour amongst the group as they turned a corner to be swallowed by the darkness of a narrow street.

As one, they broke into a run and, snaking through the throngs beneath the awnings of the seedy tenements, began making their way towards the mouth of the rainbow, as the Hong Kew district was known – although the many Europeans in Shanghai acknowledged that because so many imposing buildings had been erected by those who had come to live and work here it could more properly be called the American settlement. Emerging on to a wide boulevard, each man in the group continued to move quickly and remain in shadow, once more reminded of the European presence in their country.

At the corner, the leader slowed and held up a hand. Lying against a stone wall, they waited patiently for the meandering crowd on the bridge spanning the creek to disperse, then at a signal they ran quickly across the boulevard, over the bridge and on to another wide street, where several rickshaws and numerous vehicles – both horse-drawn and horseless – rattled on the cobbles. One by one they traversed tramlines, then squatted in the darkness against a high wall where spikes were set into each coping stone, and awaited instructions.

A rickshaw appeared and slowed. The Chinese coolie stopped and nodded towards the group. The leader raised his hand into the night, then began to concentrate on what must be done. They had been given plans of the great house and gardens and instructed to wait only for one light to be turned off.

The leader signalled to the man at the rear of his group. Instantly he was on his feet, staring up at the wall. He selected a spike six metres above, and threw a loop of rope unravelled from his waist. The loop fell on the spike, the rope was jerked taut and moments later, having pulled himself hand over hand, the man was peering towards the large house. In the distance open french windows spilled light across a wide terrace and into the garden. Every downstairs room was glowing from within. Lamps and lanterns hung above rattan chairs outside. The man on the wall could see the large dinner party now assembled in the spacious drawing room. As yet, only the landing lights were on upstairs; all the bedrooms were unoccupied. He glanced below and shook his head.

The man froze as he heard barked commands at the gatehouse fifty yards away. He could just make out the

15

guard changing and heard laconic banter between the several Marines. As the sergeant-at-arms marched back to the great mansion and up the steps the man's eyes followed him then he looked above the upper floors to the roof. In front of a large clerestory, atop a tall flagpole, the American Stars and Stripes hung limply, indicating the residence of the United States Consul to Shanghai.

Purple velvet curtains were pulled apart brusquely, revealing a heavily made-up face which thrust between them. Hands pushed back a bowler hat over slicked hair, and painted lips broke into a grin.

'I'm the *turn* of the century,' came the voice, and a man stepped through the curtains towards improvised footlights. His garish checked suit, cane, frills, ruffles and bow tie were a sharp contrast to the refined dress of his audience, who had left the dining room and assembled in the even larger drawing room in anticipation of the show they had been promised by their host. The entertainer stopped dead above the lights, grinned again at his audience, took two steps back and a pace to the side, pointed his cane at a small group of Chinese musicians in European dress and introduced the song already made famous in Europe by Hurley and Hanley:

> She's got 'er mother's blue eyes
> Yer humble's beautiful thirst.
> Me and the missus is proud of 'er
> She's our first.
> When Maria's a cartin' 'er out,
> Fol-de-roll'd up so smart,
> There's a look on 'er chivvy that seems to say –
> 'Ow's this for a start?

There was some polite applause. From the other room came the noise of Chinese servants clearing the long

16

dinner table still cluttered with liqueurs and coffee cups. It was a hot night and many of the ladies were fanning themselves. The English entertainer could already feel sweat on his back, then as it began to emerge through his powdered make-up he wiped his forehead with a silk handkerchief. Maybe there were too many Americans in the audience. 'This might be more difficult than I imagined,' he thought to himself, and realised he'd have to pull out all the stops.

'Stanley Grace is the name. Entertainer extraordinaire! Freshly fallen but not yet landed. After ten weeks in a steamer, travelling from Gravesend to Gibraltar, Suez to Ceylon, Singapore to Hong Kong and on . . . to this 'ere tahn of Shanghai, I feel more like an old boiler.' There was a murmur of approval and some laughter of appreciation at the problems and discomforts during a long sea voyage.

Rockets exploded outside, suddenly illuminating the night sky and startling some of the ladies. Stanley Grace played off it well. He dropped to his knees, pointing his cane as if it were a gun, mimicking shots.

Jacob Hollis Jackson shifted uncomfortably in his seat. Although he appreciated the English humour, he felt he had grown beyond its coarseness. He longed for a cigar and to be able to relax with the men, as he had business with the American Consul and wanted a quiet word in the man's ear. It was undeniably hot, even for June, which was why he had limited himself at dinner merely to a single glass of chilled wine. He was frugal in his habits as he was careful with his figure. He carefully readjusted his brocade waistcoat and re-crossed his legs, smoothing the creases in his pale cotton trousers. Hollis's thoughts were disturbed as, oblivious of the entertainer, he saw the girl beside the American Consul rise to her feet. She kissed her father then, quickly murmuring excuses about the heat and a

17

headache, made her way discreetly from the group and stepped out into the large hallway.

Anticipating her mistress's early arrival, a Chinese maid waited at the top of a long flight of stairs, which the girl ascended lightly. The maid curtsied and followed her mistress to the bedroom.

With the door closed, the Consul's daughter, Adèle Morgan, who was barely twenty, disrobed thankfully. The maid assured her mistress that the windows were open. Adèle accepted the thin cotton nightdress, which she slipped over her naked body. A rocket bursting outside illuminated the pretty young woman for a moment, emphasising contours usually hidden by her fashionable but restricting clothes. Climbing into bed beneath the mosquito net, she pulled a single sheet over her body and bade the maid goodnight. She gazed towards the lightly billowing curtains for a moment, then turned down the lamp wick on the bedside table. Ignoring distant noises from the Chinese district of Nan Tow as celebrations of the festival continued, and the applause and laughter from the drawing room beneath her, she fell into dream-filled sleep.

The man on the coping of the consulate wall hissed to his comrades below in the darkness. Immediately they assembled themselves and one by one leapt on each other's shoulders, forming a human ladder as if part of a circus act. Grasping the metal spikes tightly, the strongest took the full weight as each man climbed over the other, reached the coping and dropped down into the garden. They had been warned of patrolling guards and moved silently, fully prepared for trouble at any moment. They stopped once and hid amidst the lush undergrowth. Two young Marines sauntered past, more intent on finding a quiet place to smoke than seeking intruders. There was a wide strip of lawn beside the eastern wall of the house, which was illuminated from the terrace. This could be dangerous, as the crouching Chinese leader saw and indicated to his men. They waited patiently, eyes searching the darkness for movement. Sounds of laughter and applause came from the great house. The leader signalled and flitting shadows crossed the lawn, safely reaching the wall of the consulate building. Above, a balcony protruded and again, with practised ease, the men formed their human ladder. The leader secured a rope around the balustrade. He smiled to himself; the window had been left open, as he had been assured it would. He said two prayers under his breath, one to the god of night, the other to the god of chance, hoisted himself up and stepped on to the narrow balcony.

He was the first man through the open french windows and he quickly crossed the large room. He stopped beside the bed, hearing the comforting sound of a distant song finishing to much applause. Withdrawing his knife from its sheath, he silently slit the mosquito net. Instantly two of his men stripped back the top sheet over the sleeping figure. Adèle's eyes opened briefly, mistaking reality for a nightmare. She had not even the chance to scream. The leader seized her neck, pressed with fingers and thumb, and immediately the girl was unconscious.

Two men ripped the thin cotton nightgown from her body and, pulling the limp weight from the bed, dressed her naked figure quickly in the same dark Chinese coolie clothes they wore themselves, then carried her to the window. The leader hesitated a moment longer to carry out final instructions. The men holding the girl froze for several seconds on the balcony, as bursting rockets seemed to turn night into day. Darkness returned, and they lowered the Consul's daughter to willing hands below in the garden. The leader was last to leave. He loosened the knot of the rope, climbed the balustrade and swiftly began to descend. His weight detached the rope from the balcony. Expertly, he turned in mid-air and dropped lightly on to the lawn. The rope followed him; he caught it then threw it to one of his men. Supporting the girl between them, the group crossed the lawn, merged once more with the vegetation and, moments later, were at the wall. Negotiating it as before, they hoisted the girl's body over, then gently let her down to the wide pavement. They ran through shadows to the rickshaw waiting between the trees. The Consul's daughter was bundled in and immediately the small vehicle began to trundle off. The group followed, running in escort with ever increasing speed, towards the bridge which led over into the 'mouth of the rainbow'.

On the Chinese bund, the painted eye on the prow of the junk stared patiently at the men, and the extra passenger who was carried aboard. Lines were cast off and respectful congratulations were exchanged. Once out into the current, the swirling yellow river began to convey the Chinese junk downstream. It was fourteen miles to Woosung on the Whampoa, from there to the mouth of the Yangtse it was another forty. With some luck, as the leader knew, they would be at sea before dawn.

Loud applause greeted the end of Stanley Grace's act. Several people began to leave, amongst them the American Consul, who excused himself to his elder daughter, nodded to Hollis Jackson that he would return and slipped out into the hallway. He decided, before preparing papers in his study for Jackson's examination, to kiss his daughter goodnight. His early morning departure to the southern province for several days would deny him a proper farewell.

He paused at the top of the long stairway to catch his breath, determined that if the increasing trouble in China could be solved – which might prove a feather in his cap and allow him to stay on – he would install a lift. The maid outside Adèle's room curtsied to him as he entered. Treading softly, he reached the bed and then with a shock realised his daughter was not there. The mosquito net was torn, as was the thin cotton nightgown his daughter had worn to bed. There was no blood, only four coins glittering in a shaft of light streaming across the room through the open door.

Suppressing panic, the American Consul stared about him for clues, anything. . . . The tall windows were still open. Below, the English entertainer was introducing his encore:

'And now for something mysterious. All Chinese are gamblers, as you know; they'll take a chance on just about anything.' Stanley Grace began to sing 'In the Fan-Tan Dens of Old Shanghai'. Tears appeared in the Consul's eyes and his fists clenched. All the security around him, and what did it do? A silk scrap which lay between the coins had created both fear and helplessness in him. Clearly marked on it was the symbol of the Triads.

'Damn China!' he growled.

In the drawing room, Stanley Grace continued with a will, encouraged by his remaining audience.

> . . . A game is played with stakes so high.
> I know of fortunes lost and made,
> By chance or luck, on wagers laid.
> Men take the risk to live or die
> In the fan-tan dens of old Shanghai.

In his daughter's bedroom the American Consul strode to the door, stepped out and quickly made his way to the stairs. His anger was building at the inefficiency of his staff, his men, the Marines and Shanghai itself. All around, China was being incited to rebellion, and no longer were they safe even here in this European haven.

The Boxers, as they called themselves, and the Triads could run amok as they pleased. What hope was there, what future? The West, he thought to himself, had come here to civilise a barbaric people – and how were they being repaid? He ground his teeth in fury.

He could hear the entertainer still continuing with gusto, and began to descend to the great hallway, his anger increasing at every step.

> On the green baize table the game is set
> You choose a number and place your bet.
> From one to four you have the choice
> Or ask of fate the best advice.
> Money's placed to the dealer's call
> From three floors high the baskets fall
> As tier on tier the faces peer
> To see if luck or fortune's near.
> In the fan-tan dens of old Shanghai.

Stanley Grace had written the song aboard ship, cosseted in the luxury of a first-class passage. He was quite proud of it and had spent most of the afternoon schooling the musicians into playing just the right mysterious notes. Judging by the faces of his audience, he knew it to be already a success, so with his best expressions he began the big finish.

> The dealer turns the pot of gold
> And starts to count as all behold.
> Till four or less are left to stay
> As four by four he takes away.

'Yes, that was rather good,' thought Stanley Grace as he paused to create an expectant hush. After all, he was actually describing the game in the song. He raised his eyebrows then bent to peer at the audience.

Gamblers gaze with frenzied stare
Their 'opes, their fears – all laid bare.
Until at last the pile is down
And winners smile, as losers frown
In the fan-tan dens of old Shanghai – tahn.

The music finished and he raised his arms to accept applause. The American Consul thrust open the doors of the drawing room and, with apoplectic face, bellowed: 'Enough!'

There was instant silence. Stanley Grace visibly crumpled, all the confidence he had built up ebbing away rapidly. It was, after all, his first show in the Far East.

'Blimey!' he thought to himself, 'Ow's this for a start?'

2

A small polished brass bowl was upended on a green baize table-cloth, spilling glittering coins which formed a pile. Instantly, the Chinese croupier, using ivory sticks between his fingers, began expertly to take four coins at a time from the pile. The table was surrounded with expectant faces; three tiers above, more crowds peered over from the narrow galleries.

The fan-tan den was not over-large, but was acknowledged as one of the best, which really meant that the croupier was faster than elsewhere, allowing more bets to be placed during the course of the night. Fans revolved in the high ceiling and young women on each tier, supervised by burly guards, collected bets on slips of paper, placed them in baskets and lowered them to the table where they were quickly taken and laid out before the process of counting had finished.

The pretty Chinese girls knew their customers as they worked within sections of the galleries. The lights were low and even the ornate painted woodcarving was not a distraction to any of the gamblers, who gave full attention to the swiftly diminishing pile. The game was simple – the winners were whoever bet correctly how many coins were left after they had been taken away four by four.

On the top gallery, seated comfortably, Jacob Hollis Jackson blew smoke across the narrow space to the opposite side. In the turmoil created by Adèle's abduction, the evening at the consulate had dissolved and he had decided to try his luck in a familiar haunt. To his pleasure, he had found his two old friends. They had done what little they could to smarten themselves up since he saw them earlier.

William Silas Hayes and Henry Eli Lubbock absently acknowledged drinks placed quietly between them on a table by a pretty waitress, as nervous shouts interrupted the hushed concentration of the entire building. The *click-click* of the ivory sticks reduced the pile of coins until every gambler in the house was prepared to make a guess in his own favour.

'One,' murmured Hayes.

'Two,' said Lubbock.

The baskets were lowered quickly past each of the galleries by an elaborate pulley system fixed into the roof.

Hollis Jackson grinned and glanced below at the table. 'Three,' he said. Shouts went up which turned into a roar as the croupier stopped and indicated clearly the three gold coins remaining on the baize table-cloth. Immediately all bets on the side of a square marked 'three' were paid and delivered to each gallery in a winners' basket.

'Real money, Silas. Remember it, Eli? What are you two playing with?'

'Prospects,' growled Silas Hayes. Eli Lubbock smiled and raised a glass containing merely coloured water. 'All the tea in China,' he said.

Jackson had left his polished and shining barouche amongst many others, his driver waiting patiently on his master's whim as the attendant boys outside fed and watered the horses. He had resisted the impulse to order a horseless carriage, as society remained old-fashioned and they, as yet, were deemed only a novelty. Besides, he thought, he looked so much better riding smoothly at the rear of an open carriage than juddering along the cobbles in a machine that sounded at all times as if it was about to explode. He had endured the private and painful experience of learning to ride as if he had exhibited himself on horseback all his life, and he maintained his physique and health with morning outings on a fierce-looking but essentially docile stallion which preferred to snort loudly rather than gallop fast.

From London poverty in Pennyfields to luxury in Shanghai was a story he regularly embellished. Having left the sea and its universally acknowledged attendant discomforts, luck had given him opportunities which industry had rewarded with fortune. As a merchant trader he had been accepted into the very heart of one of the world's major cities. The more dingy, less attractive and downright damning parts of his past he could discount with words honed surreptitiously at elocution lessons or, alternatively, by a small bill of exchange presented to a business associate who knew a little more than society might accept.

If he had clawed his way up, his now manicured nails were most certainly an indication that he had arrived. He had most of the things his contemporaries envied – wealth, a large house run by many servants, a flourishing business, the freedom of having remained a bachelor, pleasant features, his own hair and an attractive smile, all of which had lured many eligible young women literally into his hands. Fostered restraint and developed manners had won their approval and gained the admiration of their parents. Unknowingly, these poor young women had merely been the rungs by which he had climbed higher. Privately he had established a very different life and was known as an extremely good customer to numerous madams of dubious houses where anything was possible, for a price which ensured discretion.

The winners' basket arrived at the gallery rail and one of the Chinese girls took out the notes and gave them with a bow to Jackson. He held up the money, showing the wad to the two men, who found it difficult to keep envy from their faces.

'Luck,' said Jackson, 'is an attitude of mind. Some of us are winners' – he leant on the rail and blew smoke across at the two men, glancing below as again the croupier began his expert task – 'and some of us, gentlemen, will always be losers.'

Silas grunted; in his present state of mind he found it very difficult not to agree with Jackson, but Eli was about to reply facetiously when there was a tremendous noise below. The three of them peered down to see men in uniforms who had forced an entry, along with numerous excited Chinese merchants Silas and Eli had taken advantage of, rain glistening on their shoulders. Jackson indicated them with his cigar. 'Your creditors?'

Eli and Silas were already on their feet. Having successfully avoided detection for so many days, they were unable to believe that at this late hour they had been discovered. Both men had run out of promises weeks before and knew in their hearts that accounting had arrived in shouts, pointing fingers and running feet. For a moment there was confusion as the Shanghai police began to climb the steep wooden stairs to the top gallery, pushing aside all who got in their way. Eli and Silas looked about and realised that they were trapped. If the place had caught fire, they would have been burned to a cinder. There was no way down but by the steps where the first policeman emerged, shouting and waving his truncheon.

Jackson shook his head sagely. 'I don't want to appear discouraging, my old mates, but no white man can hide for long in Shanghai.'

Silas leapt to the stairwell and kicked the policeman, who fell back on to his companions with a scream. Silas spun around and saw Eli staring at the large, multi-coloured glass window which reached from ceiling to floor. He groaned as Eli shrugged. There was no alternative except incarceration, but neither of them was young and Jackson murmured with astonishment when he realised what was in their minds. He actually stood up.

'Three floors?' he said. 'At our age?!'

The two men continued to hesitate, until the Shanghai police emerged from below, filling the two stairwells either side of the gallery, bellowing threats, and confirmed Silas and Eli's single course of action. Gritting their teeth, the two men ran straight at the window. Jackson grimaced as the delicate tracery shattered and coloured glass exploded all about the two disappearing figures.

The police inundated the gallery and thrust Hollis Jackson against the rail, where he put up his hands and grinned.

'Not me.'

The fact that it was already dawn came as a surprise to both Silas and Eli. The window had been more flimsy than either had hoped and, as if time had stopped, for a moment the two men, surrounded by slivers of glass, seemed to be suspended by an unseen hand. Then each was falling separately.

They hit the first roof together, tumbling from it to fall directly through a second, which turned out to be merely extended guttering above a third roof, where each cracked the tiles beneath his body before rolling off to fall on to yet another, steeper than the rest and nearer the ground. They slid slowly and helplessly off the edge. Eli tried to straighten himself, seeing the cobbles fast approaching, but fell hard on his side. He lay on his back in a pool of water, moaning. Silas, who had at first grasped a loose tile, watched it break under his grip and he too crashed heavily on to the wet cobbles. Groaning, he glanced towards Eli and realised they had no time to assess their bruises. The two men stood up shakily.

'We used to land on our feet,' murmured Eli, and he began coughing.

The door of the fan-tan den burst open. Shouts came from the creditors and police uniforms appeared. The two men took to their heels, raced across the wet cobbles, skidded to a halt in front of a large entrance and plunged into what was a Chinese theatre.

They spotted the door beside a distant stage, where an astonished troupe had frozen mid-scene in attitudes depicting a farmer's displeasure at his wife's unfaithful behaviour whilst he had been travelling to a shrine to beg forgiveness for his evil suspicions.

Ignoring shouts from the director, who was concerned that the rehearsal of his eight-hour extravaganza was being interrupted, Silas and Eli stepped through the door and bolted out of the back of the theatre exactly as the Shanghai police entered at the front. Running together and already breathing hard, each man reached a separate conclusion as to his best destination. They paused at an intersection in the old town, which they would have to penetrate deeper to escape.

Sucking air into his lungs, Eli rasped, 'Are you going my way, Silas?'

Silas shook his head, 'Not this time, Eli.'

Shouts from behind prompted the two men to move. Pushing through early-morning crowds in the narrow lanes between overhanging balconies, the two men began to run in different directions for freedom.

The Chinese bund had been rebuilt six years before, in 1894, after a fire had devastated the area. Squalid tenements led back from waterfront shipping offices and several dockyards. The most imperious buildings in the area were the guild houses, one of which Eli Lubbock knew well. He quickly negotiated the narrow street to a lane at the left of the building for the wood merchants from Chu Chou. He entered quickly, bowed to several of the guards who recognised him, crossed two open courtyards, took a turning to the right, avoiding a theatre, and bowed respectfully towards the temple where several gods were represented. One, being Lupai, brought a rueful smile to the now sweating features of the Englishman. The god was one which merchants referred to for settlement of any dispute. Eli could hear the Shanghai police and creditors, having divided their numbers, arguing at the outer door, so he ran across to an archway set in a large whitewashed wall. It opened on to a square where a fairground had been erected. Western machinery and music intermingled with Chinese stalls and stands.

Eli made his way to a small market beyond, where vendors were already laying out fresh food on marble slabs. He dodged between a fishmonger and a flower stall as he heard whistles close behind. Curious eyes were staring. People pointed. He had one ace which he was now forced to play. It was stepping into the past, which was both disagreeable and dangerous, but he had no alternative.

He ran out of the market, along Jade Street and turned sharply into the forecourt of one of the most magnificent guild houses in Shanghai, built for timber merchants. The Mosang Way Kway contained a huge temple lacquered in red and gold ornamentation, with pewter stalks, incense burners and chequer-patterned walls. Eli had done business for these merchants, years before, which had required great courage and little conscience. He stopped, hearing his breath sawing in his lungs. The priest, standing beside an effigy of a god, was dimly lit and his narrow eyes glinted at Eli. He beckoned.

Although the room was spacious, it was oppressive. The heavy ornamentation was stepped towards the roof. An array of candles at several altars picked out the gold amidst flickering shadows on the red lacquer. The incense made Eli cough.

Whistles and angry voices came from the forecourt, proving pursuit was close behind. Now he could only trust a sworn oath.

Standing beside the robed priest, Eli felt suddenly uncomfortable, dishevelled and soaked with perspiration. He knew in his heart he was relinquishing a great deal to gain his freedom, but he followed the priest through a small door and across a courtyard. At the centre was a bubbling fountain which seemed to murmur warnings to Eli.

They reached the entrance of a large building where huge gates stood closed before them. Set into either side were two pilasters inscribed with Chinese characters which Eli recognised. The priest knocked and waited silently. Water bubbled in the fountain and noises beyond the temple signalled the approach of the pursuers. Nervously Eli looked over his shoulder then turned back to the gates, which slowly opened. The priest pointed. Eli stepped forward, and the gates were closed, separating the two men.

Eli found himself in a large covered courtyard. Coloured glass set into a huge clerestory above threw strange light upon lush vegetation growing all about. A tall Chinaman wearing a long, simple silk robe, walked out of a red-lacquered doorway, down some steps and paused several yards from Eli, staring quietly. His thick black hair was tied at the back and a fine moustache drooped from a striking and angular face. His expression was blank, but his slanted eyes were cruel. Eli did not have to turn to know that others had appeared in the courtyard.

'Why have your eyes bloody veins?' asked the man in a whisper.

'I've been playing fan-tan all night,' Eli replied, and

31

felt the Chinamen behind him move closer. The tall man's eyes narrowed even more. Eli realised for the first time that Kin Sang's irises were unusually blue.

'Why is your face so yellow?'

Eli wiped sweat and, still out of breath, greedily sucked air. 'Because I'm not up to this any more.'

The Chinamen behind him where almost breathing on his shoulder when he conceded an answer to the original question, which as he well knew was a Triad code.

'Because . . . I was born under a peach tree,' he whispered.

Kin Sang smiled slowly and nodded. 'This is the festival of Poo Too, when the gates of Hell are open to receive those roaming souls who have given up hope. We here,' he gestured, 'can save them, as you know from old experience.' He bowed. 'Welcome.'

Outside in the temple courtyard where the fountain bubbled, the police and creditors arrived and immediately began hammering at the entrance. Eli looked around nervously then bowed to Kin Sang.

'Thank you,' he said. Oblivious to the noise, which was muted by the thickness of the great gates, Kin Sang gestured again, now towards the red-lacquered door. The two men climbed the steps together and entered the main house. It was exquisitely decorated and lit only from lamps which glowed amber. Eli followed Kin Sang between a pair of large, superbly carved dragons into a room which smelt of perfume. Two young girls, wearing little but loincloths, bowed and proffered towels either side of a steaming bath set in the floor. Someone closed doors to the enclosed courtyard and the noise outside was suddenly shut off. Eli took a deep breath.

In a dark ante-room he could just make out several kneeling figures who started to move as music began to play softly. Kin Sang gently placed a hand on Eli's shoulder, which was unspoken instruction for the girls to disrobe the guest.

'Police. Creditors. What are they?' smiled Kin Sang, watching as Eli's filthy clothes were dropped in a pile beside him. The girls were gentle, unobtrusive and efficient. They slipped the old English brogues from Eli's feet with practised ease. He stared at the steaming bath with longing. The perfume in the room was making him heady. He glanced at Kin Sang, who, although a contemporary, showed few of the signs of ageing common to Western man.

'You will be at sea, Mr Lubbock. We have watched you. We need you again with us. . . . You have been reluctant to make contact, but we are patient.'

Suddenly Eli understood; Kin Sang had informed on both him and Silas, put pressure on the creditors, forced them to bring in the police. But perhaps it was only his imagination. Eli stared at the steady gaze from the blue eyes.

'Did you . . . ?' he began.

Kin Sang's expression was unchanged when he spoke. 'All life is a test. Above all things there is only loyalty.' He smiled again. 'Where else was there to turn? You have come back to us – by choice.'

Eli was now naked. Kin Sang took a pace towards him and lightly touched the small tattoo on the white flesh of his shoulder, created in the sign of a dagger.

'Only death could ever take you from the Triad brotherhood,' he whispered. At an unspoken command, the two girls led Eli with smiles of encouragement to the edge of the bath and guided him down steps into the steaming water. As his groin touched the surface he took a sharp intake of breath. The two girls giggled.

'Just like the old days,' murmured Eli as he sank into the hot water. 'Out of the frying pan. . . .' His head went under and the words were cut off.

*

Clouds of steam pouring from the presses either side of the walkway through the Chinese laundry made it difficult for Silas Hayes to judge his footing as, sprinting between startled women, he made for the distant door which he had glimpsed at the far end of the building. Sheets, clothes and large pieces of laundered silk in a myriad colours hung all about him as desperately he slid on the metal walkway where it turned sharply to the right. The door, he could see gratefully, was unlocked. There was no need to look behind as shouts of surprise from the women became alarm. The Shanghai police and creditors had entered the building. Whistles blew loudly. Silas kicked open the door at the back of the laundry, fell down two steps, rolled on the wet cobbles and lay winded against the far wall of a narrow lane.

Helped to his feet by several well-wishers in the crowd who seemed to find his predicament amusing, Silas muttered his thanks quickly in Chinese. He turned quickly left, running into the huge market where already hundreds of fishermen, farmers and butchers had laid out their produce.

The roaring babble from those buying and selling all around seemed to Silas as if he had plunged into a typhoon at sea. The noise enveloped his senses, submerging him in a welter of humanity. Only his size allowed a passage through the bargaining crowds. Even at the crack of dawn they had come to buy live duck, lobster and the thousands of *walkie-walkie* fish thrashing about in a huge tub, dragged out when purchased and cleavered to death in the blink of an eye.

Silas shouldered between queues before miniature mountains of fruit and vegetables, and was thankful when he emerged from the crowds. He dodged between several rickshaws in a narrow street, then made for the more elegant section of the city.

He emerged from an alleyway on to a wide boulevard

and cut his run to a brisk walk in the hope he would not stand out from others taking early morning strolls. Tree-lined pavements, laid out between imposing mansions, indicated the residential part of the European settlement.

Whistles and renewed shouts as Silas was spotted by his pursuers brought him back to the run. Ahead he saw six marching British Marines turn into the boulevard and began moving towards him. He hesitated, then ducked into a tree-lined lane. He ran across to the Shansee bankers' section, took the steps two at a time, saluted the guard who recognised his face, and entered the elaborate Chinese building. Silas had been asked to bring many of the materials for the construction of the building, some years before. The owners had never asked, and Silas had never revealed, how they had been obtained.

He made his way across the familiar courtyard. His breathing was heavy and with his legs ready to give out, he knew he had had enough. If he was going to be taken, it might as well be in the one place to which he often came. With the permission of the guild members, he had been given access to the theatre. Sprawled in the auditorium he would look up at the curiously shaped dome above, where in the highly polished mirrored glass it was possible to see oneself completely upside down. Silas always found this a sobering image, consistent, as he maintained, with the conditions of the world into which he had now fallen.

He heard running feet outside the theatre, prayed to fate and closed his eyes. The door was flung open and boots sounded on the marble floor. Silas turned his head and opened his eyes to see six British Marines at attention.

'Hello, boys,' he said.

The Sergeant-at-arms nodded and grinned. ''Ello, Captain Hayes. This is a funny coincidence, in'it?'

Silas stood up. 'Why?' he asked.

'Well,' the sergeant started, '*we* was just comin' to find *you*.' He beckoned and Silas joined the Marines. They formed up around him, the sergeant barked the command 'Quick march!' and, with Silas in step, the group marched out of the building and towards the Garden bridge.

The Shanghai police spotted Silas amongst the Marines and, exhausted, halted the creditors, who had long since been unable to shout and were almost resigned to the fact that their quarry had escaped. Several of the policemen, in frustration, blew their whistles towards the marching Marines, but were ignored. At least they would now be able to make an official protest, and they knew exactly where Silas would be held.

The Marines marched steadily across the Garden bridge, where plants entwined themselves around girders, giving it its name. On the other side, which was the official Bund, to the left of a miniature park, was the British Consulate. Silas was escorted through the gates to the front steps, where four of the men remained, and only the sergeant and one other Marine continued with Silas through the entrance, down a long corridor and into a grand ante-room. An aide stood up from behind a desk and took over from the sergeant, whom Silas thanked quickly, before being ushered through into a beautifully proportioned room.

The ornate office belonged to the British Consul. Hands behind his back, he was staring out of a tall window towards the front gates of his consulate, where he could see police and creditors protesting to his guards. He heard a cough and glanced behind to see the familiar Captain Hayes. There was no need to ask questions, the man's condition said it all. Silas smiled genially.

'I was just coming to see you.'

'For what?' asked the Consul, tersely.

Silas coughed again. 'Sanctuary?' he suggested.

'From what?' asked the Consul. Silas hesitated to answer.

Outside, the noise and commotion at the gates increased. The Consul observed critically the efficiency of the guards at the gate. Chinese passers-by appeared to have joined the hue and cry as Silas had cut a swathe through the old town. With a frown, the Consul realised the scene had the makings of a riot. The previous year, throughout China, there had been demonstrations against foreigners culminating in violence.

Silas Hayes joined the Consul at the window.

'Trouble?' he asked innocently. The two men watched the gates of the consulate close as more and more people joined the group, shouting with mounting aggression, barely controlled by the few exhausted Shanghai police, presenting a disturbing threat to the Marines within the consulate garden. The British Consul took a pocket watch from his waistcoat, snapped it open, then glanced at Silas.

Physically he was a sharp contrast. Of medium height with a florid complexion, he was clean-shaven but had allowed thick, whitening hair to grow at either side of a bald pate. He was dressed in a full morning suit, which was unbottoned over an ample girth covered by the single flamboyance of an intricately patterned silk waistcoat. If there was any similarity whatsoever between him and Silas, it was in the firmness he conveyed with a steady gaze. The deep blue eyes demanded respect and obedience, showing a strength that came from wielding power. Silas stared out at the gatehouse, analysing the ugly situation as if he were examining his set of sails in a change of weather. More Marines came running from the building as the noise level from the consulate entrance reached a dangerous pitch.

'That is more than your creditors, Silas,' murmured the Consul. 'That is China today . . . unfortunately.' He shook his head and replaced his pocket watch. 'I've been up since before dawn and, by the look of it' – he surveyed the man before him – 'so have you.' He paused. 'All night?'

Silas nodded ruefully.

'Same problem, I suppose,' snapped the Consul. 'I wish to God you could learn to handle your own affairs.'

'At sea, sir, I have no problem in that regard,' answered Silas. 'The weather dictates my actions.'

The Consul's harsh expression softened.

'Well, I've always found a brandy good for the digestion at this hour of the morning. What will you take?'

Silas grinned, 'Rum sir.'

The Consul led Silas away from the window, around the desk and towards the library. They entered a room which was a strange combination of exquisite Chinese workmanship and European taste. It was spacious, panelled and plush, yet comfortable. An array of books which covered the entire wall opposite the closed door added to the peaceful, insulated atmosphere. The Consul crossed the thick pile carpet to an ornate lacquered cabinet containing many bottles. Silas turned to examine a large oil painting in a gilt frame. The Consul glanced over his shoulder as he poured the drinks.

'*Serica*, and *Fiery Cross* in '68.'

'I know,' muttered Silas.

'You were on *Taiping* in the old days, weren't you?'

'*Ariel*,' whispered Silas, realising the artist had got it just right, although perhaps he would have put out more studding sails; but then he had no knowledge of how long the wind conditions in the painting had held. Long curling waves indicated that the two great ships were before following trade winds. The clouds, softened at their edges, looked to be travelling in tandem.

'I wonder where they are?' mused Hayes quietly.

'What's that?' asked the Consul as he arrived with the drinks.

Silas accepted the rum without taking his eyes from the picture. 'I was just wondering. . . .' His voice trailed off.

The Consul looked cursorily at the picture. 'Off the Paracels, more than like.'

Silas shook his head and sipped the rum. 'There's no running ocean in the China Seas like that. They're through the Sunda Straits and beneath the Southern Cross.'

'Wherever they are, they're not in China,' said the Consul. He swallowed some brandy and grunted, 'Do you know, in all the years I've been out here, and God knows that's been long enough, this is the first time I want to leave. Things used to be so different. We developed this coastline, created trade.' He paused, watching Silas sip more rum. 'Great heavens, I've been bailing you out since before I like to remember.'

Silas raised his brows.

'Well, man, I can say that in this room. As this consulate is sanctuary for you, this room is for me.' He breathed deeply. 'The fact is, things are bad. I hardly have to tell you that. All around us the Chinese are beginning to feel their power. Open rebellion has actually been condoned by the Empress herself. It is the very root of Western influence which they wish to stamp out and I must confess I am quite perplexed. After all, we've done our very best – '

'I've seen our sort of influence,' interrupted Silas.

The Consul cleared his throat. 'Well, we may not have been the perfect masters, but our trade has given and . . . and continues to give. . . .'

'Give?' snapped Hayes. 'We have only ever *taken*

39

ruthlessly. We have used and abused the people here with a moral hypocrisy that has been, and still is, astonishing to behold. We have given opium to the people, then sold them into slavery, and now the Chinese have turned against us. What did you expect?'

'Yes, yes,' said the Consul, 'I know your views and I've heard the argument many times before. Your liking of the race,' he continued cynically, 'still seems not to preserve you from their wrath.'

Silas shrugged, 'It only takes the lack of money to make a creditor from a tradesman.'

'Then you are successful at least in one thing?' suggested the Consul, pointedly looking Silas up and down. 'Although I can hardly say the same thing of your tailor.' Silas was about to speak. 'Or barber,' went on the Consul, and glanced down at the broken boots. 'Or cobbler.' His clear eyes looked Silas in the face, noting his hollow cheeks. 'Idealism does not buy a meal, Silas. Try it some time.'

'I have sir.'

'I'm a little older than you, Silas, but you seem not to have changed in all the time we've known each other. If I may be permitted to give you some advice, don't you think it's a little unusual for a man of your age to continue to live a life which is already part of another era? You have been a vagabond and adventurer too long. Settle down, make a family. You have memories.'

'And no money, sir.'

'That has never been my problem, Silas.'

'Obviously,' said Silas, his voice hardening, 'and I tried the land once before and I liked it as much then as I do now. But in California, however ill-advised, it was at least my choice and, as for a wife. . . .' He stopped himself, then went on, 'I do not choose to be here in China now, sir.'

'Force of circumstances, Silas?' suggested the

40

Consul, happy that Hayes was playing right into his hands.

'What circumstances?' asked Silas wryly. The Consul actually smiled. If he liked Silas Hayes it was perhaps because, although the man was an antithesis of himself, he was honest about his views even if they were misplaced. He had lived and apparently continued to endure the kind of life the Consul wished for himself on sunny afternoons after pleasant lunches, but was more than glad he did not have to suffer on dark nights when lashing rain on a howling wind was the harbinger of a typhoon about to hit the Bund. A warm bed and a soft mattress then was proof that he was quite content to allow the rest of the world to turn elsewhere — especially at sea.

'So *you* were coming to see *me?*' said the Consul, and smiled, 'And *I'd* sent out to find *you*.'

'Yes, sir,' nodded Silas. 'Curious, isn't it?'

'Not on my part!' the Consul snapped, and became officious. 'You've worked for us before and you will again . . . now. Over these past twenty years, perhaps because of some of your dubious exploits, you have developed an intimate knowledge of this coast.'

'Is blackmail part of British diplomacy?' cut in Silas.

'Call it what you will,' said the Consul. 'You might be distressed to hear that Miss Adèle Morgan has been abducted by what I gather are Triad pirates. For ransom.'

Silas ground his teeth at the news but said nothing.

'I'm surprised at your lack of family feeling, Silas. To a man with any sense of responsibility, a sister-in-law should provoke some sense of concern.'

'I *was* married in San Francisco. . . .'

'Yes, Silas, you have no need to continue. That is also a subject we have discussed in the past.' The Consul turned and crossed to a small bureau where several letters were laid out. He picked up one of them

41

and extended it towards Silas, who approached warily. 'You, Silas, I have always deemed luckier than myself. Compatibility is never an easy thing and, although we have shared the same problem, you were able to alleviate it; I unfortunately, because of my position cannot even entertain the thought. I still have a wife and,' he smiled, 'so, I find, have you.'

Silas took the letter, 'We are no longer . . .' began Silas apprehensively.

'Read the letter, Captain Hayes. It's from her lawyers. Perhaps there are complications,' said the Consul with relish. Silas read the letter and swore. The Consul began to laugh.

'The Morgan girls always had minds of their own, Silas. You knew that when you married Cornelia, and she almost bearded you.'

'What do you want me to do?'

'If you wish me to put it this way, I shall: on my direct instructions you will work for the British Government, serve under the captain of a man-o'-war and find the American Consul's daughter. I have ships and Marines, but to send them – where? You will decide.'

The two men finished their respective drinks, then the Consul led Silas Hayes back into his office and glanced out of the tall window. The crowd was thinning but the creditors remained.

'You see, Silas, how loyal the Chinese are to their own money. How much do you owe them?' Silas shrugged; he had actually lost count. 'If you are successful, they shall be partly taken care of from these offices.' The florid face beamed at Silas Hayes. He indicated the letter. 'Oh, yes, I'd almost forgotten, your wife is actually here in Shanghai, staying with her father at the American Consulate.'

Silas Hayes' expression changed. The Consul pressed a bell. Instantly the door was opened and an aide stood with two Marines, awaiting orders.

'I think you'll need an escort back to your hotel, Captain Hayes. At the request of the American Consul, this matter must be despatched immediately.' He shook hands with Silas. 'Pack quickly.'

Silas paused at the door and with an almost Chinese acceptance of fate, smiled.

Shanghai police, at the gatehouse of the consulate, were signing a document declaring an official protest as Silas Hayes was escorted through the gates and past his creditors by the same formation of six British Marines. After some heckling from the irate Chinese traders, which brought only a grimace of irritation mixed with an apology from Silas, the marching group was soon far along the wide boulevard. Silas suggested taking a tram, which brought a sharp rebuke from the sergeant-at-arms and smirks from his men. The sun, already high in a leaden sky, accompanied by the familiar, uncomfortable humidity, had them all in a sweat after almost half an hour. Passers-by stepped quickly to one side as, to order, the Marines wheeled about, crossed into a small street and made for the entrance of what once had been an elegant small hotel, but now, with its four-storey façade peeling paint, its unhinged signs between shutters at the large windows, had become a seedy temporary haven for itinerant travellers. Silas Hayes had stayed longer than most, merely because he dared not leave and be faced with a bill he could not pay. The Marines halted at a shallow flight of steps where the sergeant-at-arms allowed Silas to lead the way.

The reception lobby was probably the best room in the whole place. The wood was seldom polished, the upholstery never cleaned, all the carpets were worn and the large chandelier, illustrating pretensions to a grander design, was dulled with dust. But there was an overall atmosphere of a greater past and, if it did not exactly suit Silas Hayes, he had to admit ruefully in his present circumstances he could certainly expect no better. There were a number of groups, individuals and couples milling about, examining brochures, wandering to and from the dining room. Breakfast had begun soon after dawn to allow sufficient tourist hours before the heat of midday.

Silas approached the desk and smiled with charm. The long-faced clerk, an ageing Anglo-Chinese in a severe suit which had not been laundered since brandy stains had spattered its lapels, grunted as he handed Silas a sheaf of letters and only smiled with suspicious, patronising eyes as he saw the Marines assembling behind his client. Pleased that at least one person he knew was worse off than himself, he awaited Silas' reaction.

'Somebody loves me,' grinned Hayes.

'Bills,' stated the clerk, 'to be paid.'

Silas nodded at the man, and handed the sheaf back.

'Keep them for me,' he said, then strode towards a flight of steep stairs. He noticed, in passing, a group of young boys, well dressed but sprawling amongst sofas gathered around a Chinese table. Most of them were listening to a single voice which rose with a plaintive insistence, grating to the ear. Silas paused to observe the boy in velvet and ruffs. He knew the type, the spoiled brat of a wealthy merchant, no doubt. The familiar expression of arrogance met Silas' steady gaze. Discounting the cocky boy, he took the steps two at a time. Three floors above, he reached the corridor and a door which led to his rooms, where he waited out of courtesy for the first Marines to appear. Breathing heavily, the sergeant-at-arms stopped before him, blowing hard. Silas smiled.

'You wouldn't last long at sea, Sergeant, with shrouds to climb in heavy weather.'

'I ain't going to last long at all, sir, 'iffen you stays

in Shanghai much longer. I've had more exercise in one morning than I've been forced to take in a month.'

'Wait here, if you would,' said Silas and entered his rooms.

The suite matched the lobby and could be described merely as furnished, but the woman who waited anxiously at the window, staring out beyond the small balcony, certainly did not match anything in her accommodation. That she was beautiful was obvious; that she was in love was equally transparent – her blue eyes shone with joy. Silas was beside her before she had risen, seeing tears of happiness and concern appear instantly.

'Emily,' he whispered, and kissed her tenderly. Her lips were soft against his and although his stubble was uncomfortable, his sweat was an aroma she had missed. She clung to him, pressing her body against his, and without withdrawing his lips, Silas slid a hand down to her belly and gently spread his fingers over the fabric of her dress. Emily pulled away and stared into Silas' eyes.

'What is it?' he asked.

'Good morning,' said a woman's voice. Silas Hayes did not have to turn around to recognise the contrived dulcet tones. He had fallen in and out of love with them and then suffered and endured for several years the honed and polished skill he had actually grown to admire. Inexorably his wife had attempted to change him into someone he knew he would never have chosen to meet. Silas took a deep breath and turned to look at Cornelia Morgan. She was seated confidently in the corner of the lounge, both hands placed atop her folded parasol, as if she were about to be photographed for posterity.

She was undeniably beautiful, but knew it. She was exceptionally intelligent, but always thrust her sharp wit down other people's throats. She was not humble, but compassionate when it suited her. The impression she had always left with Silas, who knew intimately the extraordinary figure she concealed beneath voluminous but couture clothes, was of a unique woman who was not merely satisfied with entrapping the admiration of all and sundry about her – worse, she was extraordinarily satisfied with herself. Others, of course, did not see her this way – this was only in the eyes of Silas Hayes, who had enjoyed what at first was real love, but quickly turned into a war of attrition. With Emily, it was different. Where her face was soft and open, Cornelia's angular beauty constructed a host of calculated expressions which Silas had grown to know as if he were staring at familiar constellations in the heavens. She smiled at him and indicated Emily with her parasol.

'So,' she said, 'I see you've decided to start another family.' The tone in her voice was supercilious. 'How on earth will you keep us all?'

'Cornelia,' began Silas, 'we are not – '

'Yet divorced,' she cut in, and held up papers. It was a triumph, Silas knew. If it was a fact, only lawyers could solve the problem, so he said nothing. A knock on the door heralded the Marine sergeant, who leaned into the room.

'Will you be needing any help, sir?'

When Silas broke the news of his departure to Emily, she fell into floods of tears. Cornelia's reaction was more unexpected. Discounting obvious concern for her sister, her expression remained cold. Silas suddenly realised he had checkmated her. The divorce and final papers were, no doubt, to have provided a cabaret of final humiliation, skilfully arranged. A moment's panic in her face was quickly suppressed then replaced with studied malice, while she appeared to be trying to help in the bedroom, packing essentials into a small trunk, aided by two of the Marines. Silas asked her to leave the room. She retired eventually to the doorway and pointed to several suits.

'I bought those,' she said. Emily held them in front of Silas hesitantly, eyes questioning, embarrassed at the situation.

'Do you want them?' she asked.

Silas shook his head, glanced at Cornelia and then said softly, 'No, they haven't worn well.'

Cornelia, affronted, strode across the room and seized the suits.

'They're as good as new!' she snapped.

Silas took the clothes from her.

'Hardly,' he said.

'You're no different, Silas, are you?'

'I'm older,' he answered, 'and wiser.'

The Marines closed the trunk and Silas followed, them into the lounge. Cornelia remained for a moment, absorbing what she regarded now as competition, evaluating this younger woman.

'So young, and so naive.'

Emily blushed and strove to remain pleasant against her better instincts. 'I believe you have a child with Silas?'

Cornelia showed her teeth in an attempt at a smile.

'You are positively correct, Emily – isn't it? But *I* was a married young woman and my *son* was legitimate. Good day to you!' Cornelia sashayed out of the door past Silas and the Marines.

If truth were to be admitted by Cornelia, as she walked down the corridor to the top of the stairs of the seedy hotel, having actually seen Silas Hayes after so long, her emotions were confused. His physical presence had reminded her – as she had never allowed herself to recall – that their relationship had not been all bad. But she consoled herself, as she descended to the lobby, that his torrid past had never fitted into San Francisco society.

'Thank you, James,' she said, staring across at the group of boys sprawled around the lacquered Chinese table. Conversation stopped and, in respect, the boys rose to their feet. Cornelia smiled and gestured that they should all sit. Only one remained standing, seemingly reluctant to move. The ruffles beneath his chin, together with curling blond hair, framed a face proving him to be his mother's boy; but curiously penetrating and seemingly wise pale blue eyes with black lashes and dark brows indicated an inner strength, and an already firm and wiry body beneath the velvet suit confirmed that at thirteen years old he was fast developing qualities of his father.

'Mother,' he began. Cornelia extended an arm and would have no argument. Behind her she heard Silas, accompanied by Emily, reach the bottom of the stairway, followed by two Marines with the heavy trunk.

'I'll be back, lassie,' murmured Silas. He kissed Emily quickly and was about to stride past Cornelia when she spoke loudly to her son.

'Your father.'

Silas stopped, turned and looked the boy up and down. James was astonished at first, and then embarrassed as the boys behind him began giggling. One glance from Silas stopped them instantly.

'You haven't shaved, sir,' began James pompously. 'In San Francisco, sir, a gentleman would consider it improper to venture out – '

'This is Shanghai, boy,' growled Silas.

'Silas, please,' Cornelia interposed. 'James had been taught manners and is receiving the very best education afforded him by. . . .' She stopped, seeing Silas' expression. There was accusation in his eyes. She felt herself blushing.

'Well, what could *you* have done?!' she snapped.

'What have *you* done to him?' countered Silas harshly. 'Velvet and ruffs?'

'Sir, I must ask you to stop immediately,' stuttered James.

Silas turned his complete attention to the boy and stared down into his face. 'What's your full name, son?'

James hesitated, intimidated by the stern gaze of his father.

'Captain Hayes, sir,' began the Marine sergeant, 'we have to go – orders.'

'His surname, if you wish to know it, Silas,' stated Cornelia, 'is now Morgan.'

Silas Hayes nodded, glancing at his wife. He looked again at the boy.

'Then you'd better be reading about stocks and shares, *Mr* Morgan.' He turned away, anger in his heart.

'I read about pirates, sir,' his son blurted out.

'Jamie!' exploded Cornelia, 'You do not!'

Silas turned back, seeing suddenly a totally open, bright and enthusiastic expression on the boy's face. He looked up at his father with a smile and almost conspiratorially whispered, 'Are you a pirate, sir?'

The rush of emotion in Silas Hayes took him by surprise. He winked and ruffled the boy's hair. 'No, Jamie,' he said, 'I hunt them.'

The Marine sergeant coughed and Silas began to laugh, waved to Emily, bowed his head to Cornelia, shook hands quickly with the boy and strode out of the hotel with the Marines, roaring with laughter.

3

'Halt!' barked the sergeant-at-arms. His men took one pace, stamped their feet and were still.

Silas shifted uncomfortably amidst the six British Marines, then glanced behind him at a Chinese coolie transporting his trunk. Now shaved and in British naval uniform bearing merely the rank of lieutenant, Silas squinted against the suffusing light of the heavy day and looked beyond the dockside, out into midstream where the imposing British man-o'-war lay at anchor. Already a wisp of smoke from her smokestack indicated that the boilers had been stoked and she was ready to be underway. Silas checked his pocket watch, taken from a new dark flannel waistcoat. He could see the Whampoa was high, and knew that the swirling currents would facilitate a passage down to the sea for the iron-clad. Below the dock, with its engine still churning, a cutter waited, presumably to take him out to what he had been told was the *Leviathan*.

Whistles sounded loudly as a carriage approached. His curiosity was quickly satisfied as he saw a familiar figure step on to the cobbles and cross to a gangway which led down to pontoons. Polished brass buttons shone brightly, a sharp contrast to the blue naval jacket.

Captain Van glanced up at Silas and briskly saluted. With no response from Silas, his florid face hardened with anger and he stepped down into his own private cutter. Engines churned in the yellow water and took the commander of the British man-o'-war into the channel. The sergeant-at-arms barked another command and the British Marines fell out, forming up loosely at the head of the gangway.

'Just my luck,' murmured Silas.

'Well, you're not bringing us any, sir,' said the sergeant-at-arms. 'I was due for leave in seven days. Now the Consul thinks it would be good for us to see some action.' He tapped his belly. 'We're getting too fat, he says.'

Silas nodded and smiled grimly. 'Yes, these are not easy times.' He stared out at the man-o'-war. 'You never know, when we come back there may not be a Shanghai. If the rebellion takes place in our absence, it'll be difficult even to find an anchorage.'

Two shrill hoots sounded loudly from the steam whistle of a second cutter waiting below.

For the first time in many years, Silas felt like a pawn in someone else's chess game. All he had been told on his return to the consulate were the few details available about Adèle Morgan's abduction. The Triads had been seen leaving in a junk, soon before midnight: they had been spotted also at Woo Sang, crossing the bar, well before dawn. Although she could have been hidden in the city, it was assumed she had been taken to some other place. Silas had commented that assumption was always dangerous when dealing with the Triads, relying on his past experience.

A carriage containing a last passenger pulled up and stopped. Silas shook his head, watching Hollis Jackson, elegantly dressed, step on to the cobbles. Two Chinese servants carried a large trunk to the head of the gangway, then, together with the smaller one belonging to Silas, it was transported down to the pontoons and put into the naval cutter. Jackson paused and looked Silas up and down.

'Well, this is an improvement: bathed and perfumed, and actually working.' He smiled and drew on a long cigar. 'You surprise me as, indeed, does the British

Government. To my knowledge you spent so much time working against their interests, I am astonished that you have now been accepted by – '

'Society, Hollis?' Silas cut in.

'That,' smiled Jackson, '*you* will never be.'

Two further hoots from the cutter's steam whistle prompted the Marines, with slung rifles, sweating in their full kit, down the gangway and on to the pontoons. Silas and Hollis Jackson followed them down together.

'Why are you here?'

Jackson's expression lost its joviality. 'Enough of my ships have been raided to fill a treasury. I'm coming along to identify what is mine.'

'If we find them,' murmured Hayes.

'Adèle has grown into a young woman almost as beautiful as your wife. You know these Triads and what they might do,' Jackson went on. 'We must find them.'

'Ex-wife,' he said.

Jackson nodded and stepped onto the rocking gunnel. 'I'll remember that,' he said, 'for the future.'

Loaded and fully boarded, the naval-cutter swung around in the swirling yellow water and churned out into the channel towards *Leviathan*, one of the biggest British men-o'-war of the Chinese squadron. More whistles sounded to herald the new arrivals. Tabor drums beat briefly to welcome the Marines from the consulate, who were merely a small addition to many others already aboard. Stepping on deck, Hollis Jackson extended a hand to Captain Van, whose slight speech impediment, through thick lips, seemed unfortunately perfectly to complement his large features: protruding eyes, fleshy hooked nose and almost totally bald head, concealed by a peaked cap. The heightened colour in his cheeks emphasised that this seaman was if competent equally so with a bottle.

'Welcome,' said Captain Van.

Jackson smiled. 'I understand that these abductors have been identified as belonging to the same group of pirates who have been pillaging up and down this coast for some years?'

'Yes,' nodded the Captain, 'we have come by that information from Woosung, and now in a telegraph from our men in the lighthouse at the mouth of the Yangtse.'

'Is she aboard?' asked Jackson.

'We have no way of knowing,' answered the Captain. 'But in truth, it is only one consideration. The naval authorities have been looking for an excuse to pursue these blaggards for some time, and now fortune has given us pressure from the American Consulate. We have free rein to seek them out and, should we find them, by God they will be destroyed!' He glanced over Jackson's shoulder to see Silas Hayes waiting patiently with an expressionless face. He stepped forward and gently pushed Hollis Jackson to one side.

Whistles sounded about the ship and its loud horn indicated imminent forward passage as the gangway was winched up. As the cutters were secured on their derricks, Captain Van spoke quietly.

'Is it not in your nature to salute a superior officer?'

'It is,' answered Silas, without moving, 'I am also a Captain.'

Hollis Jackson coughed. 'You know each other, I presume?'

Silas moved not a muscle but Captain Van glanced at Jackson and nodded with some relish.

'Oh yes, Mr Jackson, we know each other of old.'

Hollis drew on his cigar again, feeling a shuddering in the deck as *Leviathan* began to nose forward downstream. It was late afternoon, and if they could be in the estuary of the Yangtse by dusk, they could make sea room at night, which would be a safeguard against the regular Chinese blows that occurred at this time of year. There was a slight breeze building, and on that first vesper Jackson thought he could already smell ozone and brine.

'This,' he said, 'might even be enjoyable.'

'It will be,' stated Captain Van. He turned and strode up to the bridge.

'Well, Silas,' said Jackson.

'Well, what?' replied Silas morosely.

Churning the silt-filled yellow waters of the Whampoa, *Leviathan* made way through other river traffic towards Woosung and the China seas.

By nightfall they were at the mouth of the Yangtse and from *Leviathan*'s open bridge a seaman, on instruction communicated by morse-light with the lighthouse. The message returned was no more encouraging than the weather. No further information had been acquired. The British man-o'-war was now on its own and steaming, as Silas could quite well see, into heavy weather. The prospect did not trouble him, as it was nothing new, but Hollis Jackson looked apprehensively at the dark clouds towering towards the stars.

'Typhoon,' murmured Silas Hayes.

'Rubbish!' snapped Captain Van, 'It will only be thunder and lightning. We'll go north and hug the coast.'

'I would suggest,' said Silas quietly, 'we go south and give ourselves plenty of sea.'

Captain Van grimaced and rang on the telegraph 'Full ahead', bellowing to his second officer, 'Hard to port!' and 'Full steam!'

Spray whipped over the bridge as *Leviathan* came about, for a moment wallowing in the troughs of waves that were increasing in size. Although it was not cold, Hollis Jackson shivered. Silas folded his arms and leant against the bridge wall, above all things, happy to be back at sea.

'So it might be enjoyable, eh?' he said, repeating Hollis' words.

'If we find the girl it will at least have been worthwhile,' replied Jackson, swallowing first bile he could taste in his throat.

'You actually mean Cornelia's sister, don't you?'

'I do.'

'As I thought, Hollis.'

'Have a care, Silas Hayes. I admire the lady.'

'*I* was married to her.'

'Then you have lost something I continue to regard as precious.'

Silas smiled, 'One man's meat, Hollis . . . ?'

'How dare you?!' hissed Jackson. Silas stared into the night sky where the stars were almost obscured by vast clouds. In the air there was a sound as if a distant choir was increasing its volume and approaching rapidly.

'How dare Captain Van!' murmured Silas.

'How dare I what, Hayes?' asked Captain Van with irritation.

Silas smiled. 'Thunder and lightning,' he said and nodded, 'I hope you've got good sea-legs, Hollis.'

*

The typhoon blew itself out in three days, when it did become merely thunder and lightning, rain, heavy seas, then spume and spray as *Leviathan* despite her extensive metal-plate armament, emerged battered and still buffeted as she ran, well out from Chu San islands. A further day in relatively calm weather, with scudding clouds travelling in convoy with the man-o'-war, and high cirrus obscuring even the sun, enabled them to plan both a course and course of action. It was real grey China Seas weather, as Silas recognised only too well. Circumstances had brought him aboard; the weather had forced Captain Van to listen to him; and now his knowledge of the Chinese coastline and of the

Triad bastions secreted amongst the islands, dictated that, albeit with reluctance, the commander of the British man-o'-war comply with instructions issued by 'Captain' Hayes.

The watch had sighted nothing at dawn on the fifth day when Silas, newly risen, arrived on the open bridge to taste the salt in the air, squinted into the haze beneath the bright clouds and murmured to the First Officer, 'Up ahead.'

Captain Van came on deck and followed the pointing fingers with his eyes. The watch, having now also seen a small junk labouring in the running sea, tried to evaluate whether it was of any interest. Cursorily raising his telescope, Captain Van merely identified the junk, from several flags fluttering at the masthead, as probably out from Ning Po. He noted that it was crowded not only with men, but women and children, and scoffed at Silas' interest.

'It's nothing,' he said. *Leviathan*'s armour-plated bow threw out foaming waves into a dismal, choppy sea and, approaching rapidly, began to tower over the junk. Captain Van merely glanced at the passengers aboard then crossed to the other side of the open bridge.

Silas Hayes reached out and pulled the telegraph lever to 'slow ahead', then rang 'dead slow' and 'stop'.

'Lower the gangway!' he growled, and began running.

Captain Van's face darkened with anger. 'Well!' he exploded to his First Officer. 'Secure alongside!'

Sailors and Marines had formed up and were already shouting belligerently to the occupants of the junk, who stared up fearfully whilst a single voice from one of the elders pleaded that they were merely returning to Ning Po. His words were unintelligible to most of the men aboard the man-o'-war.

Silas stepped between the naval uniforms, thrust several of the Marines aside, descended the gangway and crouched on the platform just above the choppy sea. Several aboard the junk hauled the vessel closer, using ropes thrown from the deck of the British man-o'-war. Silas beckoned to the elder to approach the rail and talk. Hollis Jackson, at the top of the gangway, leaned against the bulwarks, looked down and strained to listen.

Silas' Chinese surprised the old man, who bowed in respect. The children aboard lost their fear, hearing familiar words from the foreigner, and they began to laugh, shouting above each other and pointing to the south-west. The Chinese elder spoke patronisingly to the white man who conversed so well in Mandarin. Most of the women gathered close, with furtive eyes, as if he alone could protect them. A wave splashed against the gangway's platform, drenching Silas' tunic, which brought gales of laughter from the children. He smiled at them and even the women began to relax. The elder continued describing their journey, which had been from one of the distant coastal villages, revealing that they had had to lay up in a small bay for several days to avoid the passing typhoon and had prayed to the gods for help. Silas glanced at the mast-head, and amongst several pennants that flew there, he saw what he had first noted. He smiled again engagingly before asking the elder if he was protected against all things at sea. The old man's eyes narrowed.

'Why is your hair so long?' murmured Silas. The old man said nothing. 'Is it the Star God of longevity?' suggested Silas. The old man's lips did not move, but they whitened. 'Why is your mouth awry?' Still the old man refused to answer. 'It is the sign of the character *wo*,' said Silas and inscribed it with his fingers in the air. 'Your pennant, old man, carries the character *shau*, but your belly is not large.' Several of the younger men holding the ropes now showed fear in their eyes at Silas' accurate testing of the old man with familiar

Triad exchanges. He stared Silas in the face, suddenly fixing him with narrowed eyes.

'Why do you look so pleased?' he asked. Silas smiled. The old man was wily. It was a good test. It could be an ordinary question.

'Heaven has sent the kilin, unicorn. The appearance of this rarely seen animal is the prognostication of good times coming,' he answered.

The old man took a deep breath and his respect for this white man increased.

'I am no threat to you,' said Silas, 'or your people. Your pennant, amongst others, will protect you. I have drunk tea for many years with brothers of yours.'

'They are brothers no longer,' said the old man.

Silas nodded. 'Your pennant is an old one. The mark of *shau* is that only of a friend. You told the truth, old man. Now I ask again for a girl, as I have described – European.'

The old man shook his head. 'We have seen no girl who is European aboard any ship we have passed.'

'The children say something else,' said Silas. 'Explain if you wish to reach Ning Po tonight.' Tradition sealed the old man's mouth and again he bowed his head, but the women around him began to babble and, once more as if it was a game, the children laughed and shouted, pointing as they had done before. Silas absorbed the information, listening carefully, then silenced them all and respectfully thanked the old man. He climbed up the gangway as it was winched back to the deck, and waved his goodbyes. The ropes were released from the junk and gathered in by the British sailors. *Leviathan*'s engines created the noise of thunder in the sea, which brought awestruck looks from the children on the junk. As the two vessels parted, Silas went up to the bridge, followed by Jackson.

'Well?' snapped Captain Van.

'A Triad barque,' Silas stated simply, 'course south by south-west, maybe six hours away.'

'How do you . . . ?' began Captain Van angrily.

'I don't *know* anything,' interrupted Silas. 'I can only guess.'

'And if it's nothing?' asked Van.

'It is not *nothing*,' murmured Silas, and he stared ahead towards the horizon from the open bridge. His emotions were mixed at other information he had gathered but was not prepared to divulge. Captain Van grunted and, together with his First Officer, stepped back into the chart room.

Jackson lit a cigar. 'You speak the lingo pretty well.' He grinned at Silas. 'So do I.' Silas stared silently as Jackson blew out smoke, which was whipped away as *Leviathan*'s speed increased. A glint came into his eyes which caused most men who knew him to be wary, as Jackson went on blithely, 'Those coolies described a barque with Triad flags and a full crew of Chinamen.'

Silas nodded. 'As I said,' he grunted.

'And,' continued Jackson, 'an Englishman with chestnut hair and a pale complexion. A real white man who waved to those Chinkie kids.'

'So?' challenged Silas.

'He was helming the ship,' said Jackson, and drew on his cigar. 'Now I wonder who that could be?'

Sunlight began to break through patches in the blanket of cloud as Silas tried to ignore the implications of Jackson's remarks, feeling uncomfortable because all his instincts told him exactly who the information described. Why the hell had *he* become mixed up with the Triads again? Silas thought angrily. There was always an alternative, as he had found, but then he and Eli were different, even as best friends. Jackson leant on the rail next to 'Captain' Hayes and stared up ahead, following Silas' gaze. When he spoke the words were almost lost on the wind.

'Auld acquaintance – eh?'

Eli Lubbock stepped from the helm of the Triad barque, giving the wheel to one of the seamen who, on the whole, were adequate but not exceptional, being distinctly unhappy when they were out of sight of shore. He opened a mahogany box and took out the beautifully polished brass sextant. Holding the frame and the limb, he checked the index bar was moving freely, adjusted the mirror and found the level of the horizon. Telescope to his eye, he calculated the measured angle to the sun, which shone briefly through breaking clouds as it sank towards what would be a glorious sunset.

Shouts from up ahead distracted him for a moment. He glanced the length of the ship to see through the rigging, not a league away, riding in the grey swell, a junk *going large* – her lug sails turned to take the wind abaft the beam. The barque's timbers groaned and ropes, rat-tails and shrouds chafed loudly; Eli had insisted 'all sail' be put up on both the barque's masts. She'd been Dutch built and acquired by the Triads, who by some miracle had managed to sail her to a safe haven. She already needed a refit but would do well enough with Eli's expertise.

His instructions from Kin Sang had been to navigate to a familiar destination. Both he and Silas knew it well from the old days, but few others had ever found the old Portuguese fortress built amidst heavy vegetation in a small bay. From the sea it was difficult to find and actually required tacking to enter. The anchorage protected any vessel moored within from both detection and any heavy weather.

In the small captain's cabin where Kin Sang waited, Eli made adjustments to his chart, calculating time and distance. He had measured their speed on the knot line and was debating whether to come over, taking full advantage of the lee-shore wind to head the barque through outer islands before entering the bay at dusk. After nightfall it would be difficult, although, as Kin Sang revealed, a rocket was the signal to light great fires either side of the entrance. More shouts came from above, and Eli Lubbock, having heard the sailors' exclamations, looked questioningly at Kin Sang.

'One of ours?'

Kin Sang nodded. 'A rendezvous,' he answered. 'They must have been delayed by the storm. Come,' he indicated, 'this might interest you.'

On deck, Eli quickly barked out commands to a burly Chinaman who had been designated his first officer They were carried out with some efficiency. The barque overhauled the junk quickly, slowing as topsails were furled. Eli looked up to the foot-ropes where Chinamen were securing the canvas, then ordered a lie to, counter bracing the yards. A rope was passed across to the junk. Several passengers were quickly helped aboard the barque. They wore dark cotton tops and trousers, and all but one, seemingly a boy, had an armband bearing dull red characters. Even at a cursory glance Eli could see that this indicated they were members of the Triad brotherhood. All of them appeared to be extremely fit and were ushered below decks. The junk cast off. Kin Sang bowed respectfully to Eli and with his usual inscrutable expression suggested that they make for home with all possible haste.

Eli issued instructions to his first officer and within minutes the barque, her sails filled, was driving into the shallow waves, throwing up light spray over the rails. Eli took the wheel, and as he checked the course against the position of the descending sun, which was now casting a myriad colours of blood and orange amongst the breaking cloud, he allowed himself a moment's exhilaration despite his circumstances. He had once more been accepted into the bosom of the Triad brotherhood, from which it was never easy to travel far before incurring their displeasure.

As the sun dipped below the horizon, Eli barked orders and fore and main sails were furled quickly. Under top gallants alone he nosed the barque between the shores of two islands he now recognised. They rose out of the sea steeply, granite cliffs and gnarled pines creating an eerie landscape.

Kin Sang nodded and a rocket was sent soaring into the sky. As it exploded, an answering rocket burst in a cascade of green and Eli saw flame ahead as great fires were lit on the two promontories that formed the small mouth of a hidden bay. He smiled to himself. 'Home,' he thought.

Kin Sang touched Eli lightly on the shoulder and smiled, which altered the contours of his face so that, together with the glint in his eye heightened by the firelight his expression reminded Eli of a tiger about to leap towards its prey.

'You are indeed a navigator, Mr Lubbock,' said the Chinaman.

'I was a captain,' he replied.

The Triad leader bowed in respect. Eli spun the wheel hard over and the barque entered the bay. Judging the depth of water in the fast fading light, Eli shouted rapid commands. Sails were furled and anchors let go. Immediately several cutters were rowed out from the shore, where great torches lit the beach which skirted the thick woods, broken only by the pale walls of the Portuguese fortress whose turrets were crumbling. Music played from within and, peering over the rail and into the open doorway of the gatehouse, Eli could see more lights and lanterns, and hear the sounds of a host of people.

'They have been expecting us, Mr Lubbock,' said Kin Sang. Commotion sounded below the barque's decks and the Triad passengers emerged. Two women came aboard from the first cutter, now moored alongside. Without instruction, they crossed directly to the group and took the young boy in charge. He immediately pulled away. Kin Sang watched Eli Lubbock's reaction with amusement. The group approached and the young boy stopped before Eli Lubbock, looking him in the eyes. Suddenly Eli recognised the face. He reached out and took off the boy's cap. Long hair fell on to tense shoulders and, for a moment, Eli was dumbfounded. With a sweet smile, Adèle Morgan extended a hand, which Eli took and bent to kiss. She hit him hard across the face and her expression changed to pure hate.

'You are a dead man in the eyes of God and the law,' she spat. The two Triad women, at first surprised, now grasped Adèle, whisked her away to the rail, over the side and into the cutter.

Eli turned to Kin Sang angrily. 'What is she doing here?'

Kin Sang's geniality left him. 'You may have cause to ask yourself the same question, "Captain" Lubbock. If you do not remember that you are here on an invitation at present.'

Eli stepped to the rail and his eyes followed the cutter as it was rowed the short distance to shore. Rockets soared from the courtyard of the old fortress and he could hear singing.

'Come, Mr Lubbock,' murmured Kin Sang, 'you have brought us safely to our destination and proven that you are, as always, a man of the sea. As a loyal friend, accept the rewards.'

Eli glanced at Kin Sang, who indicated the waiting cutter below and the distant fortress glowing beneath the stars.

'With pleasure,' he said.

*

Old instruments played ancient music as voices rose in unison, evoking the mysteries of another culture which Eli Lubbock had never really come to understand. Hearing it all, as he stepped on to the white sand beach, he realised in his heart how far from 'home' he really was, and was doubly reminded as he walked through groups of men and women surging across the beach, greeting new arrivals and transporting plunder brought in from the barque.

The blackened corpses of several men, hanging upside down over smouldering fires, made him shudder. A cruel death meted out by merciless judgement. Nothing new, he remembered. He entered the bastion through the open doors of the gatehouse. A huge banquet was laid out on a large marble terrace set above the courtyard floor. Lanterns and torches created flickering shadows. Servants waited for the guests to be seated. Adèle was already in place, as Eli could see, her face stony, her guards either side, alert.

'I'm impressed,' said Eli, looking about him, 'I knew this place as just a ruin – uninhabitable.'

Kin Sang gestured to the table. 'We have given it life.'

Dinner was served from large dishes. Eli ate with chopsticks from a small bowl and surveyed the long table full of Chinese faces. Only Adèle, looking pale even in the light of the glowing lanterns, provided any amusement for him. Obviously hungry, she attempted to eat with chopsticks she could hardly hold, unable to convey food to her mouth with any expertise.

'You are the only foreign man here,' said Kin Sang. 'It is an honour to be so privileged.' He swallowed rice and reached for a small cup of wine. Here, at the head of the table, voices were more muted, perhaps out of respect for the leader's presence. The far end was loud with music, singing and laughter. Kin Sang wafted a hand. '*They* have earned their joy, Mr Lubbock. Others of us who were here before are . . . no longer.' He raised his eyes a moment. 'I hope they have found their peace.'

Eli chewed then swallowed some rice, saying nothing. He glanced at Adèle, who was staring at him.

'And you, Mr Lubbock,' went on Kin Sang, 'where are you?' He held a pause, then smiled. 'The answer is – with friends. Think – how long have you been a friend of ours? The answer is, since your days running opium from one port to another. Think – where might you now be without us, our help, our protection? The answer is, Mr Lubbock, you would be dead.'

Eli gestured towards Adèle, 'She tells me I am, already.'

Kin Sang lost a measure of control and looked quickly from the woman, back to Eli. 'She knows you?'

Eli nodded, 'She knows me.'

Kin Sang sighed. 'That is unfortunate,' he murmured.

'It could be a problem,' said Eli.

Kin Sang shook his head almost imperceptibly. 'We will kill her.' Adèle heard the words and Eli could see that her expression changed. The confidence seemed to ebb away and Eli's admiration for her courage turned to sympathy – she was, after all, only a young woman.

'You would lose the ransom,' stated Lubbock.

Kin Sang nodded at the expected reply, stood up and straightened his long robe.

'Come,' he said, and told the two women guards, 'Bring the girl.'

Led by Kin Sang, Eli Lubbock, the girl, her guards and a group of Triad pirates stepped down from the banquet, walked across the courtyard and entered a large room at the back of the bastion, lit by torches secured to the walls. Two of the young Triads ran ahead and removed a padlock – directly from the floor, it seemed to Eli – then pulled open two marble slabs to reveal a wide stone staircase leading below into darkness. Men carrying torches, and several others with lanterns, descended ahead of Kin Sang, who followed gingerly, pausing only to beckon Eli down into a huge cellar full of caskets and chests. Eli had prepared for the unusual, having in the past dealt in contraband, but the vast array of plunder presented to him literally took away his breath. Kin Sang nodded to one of his men and at random a chest and a single casket were opened. Eli examined the contents. In one was gold; the other contained a selection of jewellery, sparkling brightly in the light from the leaping flames of the torches. Kin Sang smiled, amused at Eli's reaction.

'You see, Mr Lubbock, we have no need of ransom. This young woman has been taken only to show that it can be done as, one day, China will show to all the world what we can achieve – alone.'

Eli nodded, looking about him, reminded of the time when he had first discovered the islands, the two promontories, the hidden bay and this crumbling Portuguese fortress.

'In the old days we stored opium here,' he said, 'but never as much as – '

'We?' interrupted Kin Sang. 'There are others who know of this place?'

Eli bit his lips. Censoring further information, he remained silent. For a moment no one moved, only shadows leapt about the caskets as flames sputtered on the torches. Kin Sang's face appeared carved from stone.

'When you first came to us you offered this place as a secret known only to yourself.'

'There were,' Eli began hesitantly, 'those who sailed with me.'

'But you are the navigator, Mr Lubbock. Could *they* find us without *you*?'

Kin Sang glanced at Adèle then looked steadily into

Eli's eyes as the English man answered slowly, 'I came to you for protection, not to be discovered.'

'You answer well, Lubbock,' said the Triad leader. 'I am merely a small part of a huge brotherhood. You are one man amongst us. Your loyalty is admirable and your safety dependent upon only one thing – my trust in it.'

Eli knew when to say nothing, and remained still.

'You will be sought out and beheaded with the rest of your friends, Eli Lubbock!' shouted Adèle Morgan loudly, tears in her eyes. She had broken away from her guards and stood before him, ignoring the warning in his eyes. 'You have known my father for many years. You have worked for him and he has helped you. I ignored all the stories I ever heard about you and, as a fool I – admired you.'

'You are now a grown young woman, Miss Morgan. You should respect your circumstances.'

'Respect?' she screamed. Her hand raised to point at Kin Sang. 'For him?' Eli grasped her arm and slapped her hard across the face. She sank to her knees, whimpering.

'She is very young,' murmured Kin Sang. 'Do you want her?'

Adèle, hearing the words, cried out, 'No!'

Kin Sang nodded and the two women guards dragged her away up the wide stone staircase.

'She appears to hate easily, Mr Lubbock, even though she knows you, but then appearances are always deceptive.'

'Coincidences are deceptive, Kin Sang. You need have no fear of me.'

Kin Sang smiled, pleased at the way Eli had slapped the hostage.

'Which would appear to be the truth, Captain Lubbock.' He indicated the wide stone stairway. The two men went up, followed by the entourage as torches were extinguished and the great marble slabs were once again closed over the treasure.

Before midnight half the table was empty. Eli, having eaten sparingly and drunk the rice wine with restraint, was content, now the hot night was relieved by a soft breeze, to lie back beneath the stars. Kin Sang had retired so, eventually, Eli left the long table and stepped up to the walls.

He negotiated the walkway until he was leaning on a parapet overlooking the white sand beach which led down to lapping water. It was a beautiful picture, framed between tall trees and thick undergrowth which had grown even into the walls. Years before, with Silas Hayes and other friends who were sadly long gone, he had stood as he did now and dreamed into the future – which had arrived without the great rewards he had felt sure would be his to enjoy. He looked up to see a crescent moon suspended in the clear night sky, set amidst the familiar stars. A reflex caused Eli to traverse the heavens, naming the constellations. At least he had forgotten nothing of ingrained seamanship and, in that moment, longed to be at the helm of one of those great sea-greyhounds, windjammers, clippers. As a boy, he had worked his way up until eventually as acting captain he had transported cargo beneath the Southern Cross to the greatest docks in the world – London.

'England.' He spoke the word softly. It sent a shiver down his spine. Staring out at the moored barque amidst numerous junks on the glittering water, he felt a sudden urge to be gone from these people, this place – China itself. He wanted to leave all this behind and step into the life that had always promised itself – again to be Captain of a clipper. He realised he had entrapped himself. He swore. Memories of lost ambitions created an increasing canker which was slowly destroying his spirit.

A door opened somewhere below, and he heard

laughter then, carried on the air by a vesper, he detected a familiar aroma which had occasionally been a friend. Somewhere drums were beating, elsewhere voices sang together. There were few guards patrolling and, as far as he knew, no watch had been set on the ships. The Triads were confident. Here they were safe. This was their secret haven.

Eli Lubbock stepped into the opium den and the door was closed behind him instantly. Men and women sat around a large, central fire contained and damped down by clay bricks. Surrounding this were several marble slabs where clay pipes were laid out, constantly filled by servants who presented them to everyone in the room. It was through this fog that Eli saw Kin Sang and then, between her two guards, Adèle Morgan. To one side, several musicians played languidly on Chinese string instruments. On bunk beds, men and women lay in a stupor, dreaming away their lives, knowing the joys of fulfilment without achievement.

Eli joined Kin Sang and sat beside him, next to one of the women guards. He glanced at Adèle; she was affected by the very air, which was thick with opium smoke and pungent trails of incense curling through the fog towards the roof, and began to slip sideways, her head lolling. Eli looked at Kin Sang, who nodded unspoken permission, and immediately the Englishman was on his feet. He bent down and took the young woman into his arms, feeling with surprise that she was hardly any weight at all. Her head fell against his shoulder, eyes already closed. Securing her firmly he stepped towards the door. It was opened, allowing him to pass out into the fresh air.

He looked into the slumbering and now relaxed face of young Adèle Morgan and remembered the precocious girl who had doted upon him during holidays from her school in San Francisco. It had started as an amusing indulgence to better his relations with her father, for whom he had worked. It had only become a problem when she matured. A general worsening of his situation – specifically, a fall from the graciousness of money, a general knowledge of his increasing creditors, increasing dissipation and seeming inability to find work he was best suited for – cut him off from even his former friends. He reached the nadir of his life in company with the only friend he could call upon. Now, he and Silas Hayes had gone in different directions.

He was striding through bastion gates towards a white sand beach, holding a beautiful young daughter of the American Consul in Shanghai cradled in his arms as if she were a child about to be put to bed. He smiled towards the pale flesh of her face as the crescent moon softly sculpted the now fully formed, almost perfect features. He began to laugh quietly. Years ago *this* would have been his dream; now it was a physical and emotional burden, and provided a morally dangerous position. In time to come, if there was the luxury of a court of law, he knew what the verdict would be even as he now paced the white sand towards the lapping waves. Justice was harsh on the China coast. As the Empress had declared all foreigners enemies of the people, to be put to death, so the European treaty ports had developed a policy of unmerciful retribution towards criminal activity. Thieves were punished, pirates incarcerated but, as abduction had become commonplace, anyone connected with the kidnapping of a single soul was ensured of instant justice which was inescapable and meted out ruthlessly – beheading.

Eli stopped at the prow of a dory and gently laid Adèle between the seats, then pushed off, waded into the water, climbed over the gunnel and began rowing quietly towards the barque. Half-way out from the beach he saw the two women guards crossing the sand, shadowy figures making for a second rowing boat. By the time he had shipped oars, taken Adèle in his arms once more and begun ascending the narrow slung gangway, the two women, together with a crew member of the Triad barque, were rowing out towards the moored ship. For a moment Eli wondered if Kin Sang had actually thought he would, in turn, abduct Adèle and attempt to sail the barque back to Shanghai alone. It was an amusing idea, but hardly practical. As he went below to the cabin, he heard the women guards come aboard.

He put Adèle's limp body on the bunk against one side of the small captain's cabin then, hearing the women guards positioning themselves outside, he turned back and closed the door. From a drawer beneath the bunk he took out blankets and laid them lightly on the young woman, then lit a single candle at the centre of a polished table. He poured himself rum from a decanter which still bore Dutch markings and placed it beside the candle. He lay back on the banquette seat, opened two of the stern windows to allow a passage of air and lit a small cheroot. Oblivious of the girl, he began to remember other times and other places.

Several hours passed as he smoked numerous cheroots and drank almost half a decanter of rum. Outside, above the hidden bay, stars glittered, but the moon was waning. Still a reflected sheen on the water, stirred by a breeze, together with the flickering light of the candle, illuminated a painting on the cabin wall, depicting a clipper in full sail. Eli sighed and turned to Adèle as she opened her eyes and spoke, her voice intruding on his thoughts.

'You hit me.'

'Then we're even,' said Eli quietly.

Adèle pushed the blankets from her body, feeling the

warmth of the soft night. 'You're not going to . . . ?'
She hesitated.

'You're only a girl,' murmured Eli.

'And what are you, Mr Lubbock, a kidnapper?'

Eli blew out smoke and watched the candle sputter.
'I did not take you, Miss Morgan, but I will try to
ensure your safe return.'

Adèle swung her legs from the bunk and tried to take
a step, but opium vapours, still in her head, caused her
to stagger. She reached out for support. Instantly Eli
was on his feet, holding her hands. She looked up into
his face.

'You will protect me?'

He nodded. 'If I can.'

'You always did, Mr Lubbock. Do you know what
thoughts I used to have about you?' Eli smiled. 'I used
to imagine. . . .' she stopped herself.

Eli nodded. 'We all dream,' he said.

'I wanted – '

'Different things,' Eli interrupted softly. 'You're still
very young.'

Adèle leaned against him for a moment. He was
taller than she, so his expression was lost, unseen as her
fingers touched the fabric of his clothes with something
more than passing curiosity. Eli had always acknowledged that there was something between them; it had
started with stories about the sea, told to a beautiful,
wide-eyed child whilst he waited in ante-rooms for her
father. He had been a friend of the family Silas had
married into, and Adèle had 'taken a shine' to him, as
her father would remark with a smile. Trusting Eli
implicitly, he had allowed him to act as surrogate father
and bodyguard on numerous occasions when it
coincided that his daughter and the 'captain' were in
Shanghai at the same time. Adèle had seemed to pass
through adolescence quickly and from pretty she had
become exceptionally beautiful.

Now Adèle looked into his face with wide and knowing eyes. She reached up on tiptoe, put her arms round his neck and murmured softly,

'I am not *so* young.'

She deliberately kissed him lightly. Eli, with difficulty, remained still. Her cool eyes looked into his and smiled.

'Perhaps,' whispered Eli, 'I am too old.'

Adèle kissed him again, now passionately, and Eli found it impossible not to respond. Eventually their mouths parted and they began laughing. He picked her up and held her within an inch of the cabin roof. They had always known it was inevitable; the circumstances merely emphasised their feelings. Adèle, with female courage, trusted her instincts, but Eli, with masculine wariness, did not. He shook his head releasing her.

'What is it?' asked Adèle. She reached up and seized his face between her hands. 'Look at me, what do you see?'

'A young girl with a big mouth and a sharp wit,' answered Eli. 'In pigtails.'

Adèle moved closer. 'Look again, Eli,' she said huskily.

'It's difficult,' murmured Eli. Adèle sighed, having found in his eyes exactly what she had been looking for.

'Love is never easy, Mr Lubbock,' she said, and the softness of her lips touched his mouth. If Eli was ever to review his history, it was at that moment that he truly lost his heart.

Only at dawn were their conversation, laughter and kisses interrupted. A sharp knock on the cabin door heralded Kin Sang, framed by the two women guards. Eli swung his legs quickly from the banquette, buttoned his shirt and reached for his jacket. Kin Sang watched silently as Eli dressed. Already he could hear, from above, orders being shouted in Chinese. Lines were being cast off and the anchor pulled from the sea bed.

73

'Information has come to us,' said Kin Sang, glancing at Adèle before looking Eli up and down. 'Besides, it will be good discipline to go to sea again so quickly, for both my men and – ' he paused – 'for their new captain. You will see some action shortly, Mr Lubbock.' Eli indicated Adèle as he felt the barque getting underway. 'Too late, Mr Lubbock. She stays.' Kin Sang's eyes glittered. 'Guard her with your life.'

As the barque nosed through the two promontories, Eli took the helm and, with the mainsail set, top gallants being clewed to the yards, guided the ship through choppy water, catching a first breeze from the islands. In minutes they were out into the open sea and running before a north-easterly exactly as the sun appeared over the horizon. Eli's expression was grim as he saw the Triads on deck oiling their guns and honing wicked-looking swords and cleavers. There would be no escaping; today there would be a fight. He touched the Remington .32 pistol he always kept at his belt beneath his coat for small comfort. Kin Sang smiled.

'They are merely slave-traders, carrying a quantity of both opium and gold.'

'How do you know?' asked Eli.

'The news was brought to us in the night,' replied Kin Sang. 'They left a village near San-Mun bay this morning, sailing north-east.'

'I don't like the girl being aboard,' murmured Eli.

Kin Sang indicated his men on deck, as barbarous a crew as Eli had ever seen.

'I do not think we have to fear, *Captain* Lubbock. We shall succeed, of that I have no doubt, and,' he smiled, 'she may even be allowed to watch.'

Adèle emerged from the cabin and stepped on to the poop deck, followed by her two female guards. She was bleary-eyed but soon became exhilarated by the wind and sea. She stood beside Eli and watched silently for several minutes as he steered the ship, constantly examining the sail plan with a seaman's gaze. For a moment she believed Eli's promise of rescue had already come true. Perhaps he had even negotiated some bargain with this man, Kin Sang. She seized his arm and he turned to look into her eyes.

'Are you taking me . . . home?' she asked.

Eli shook his head and indicated the deck, where the Triads continued to prepare for battle. Adèle's face whitened and she understood. A shout went up from the bow and Kin Sang, with a speed that surprised even Eli, took the telescope from its watertight chest beside the wheel and peered ahead. He nodded in satisfaction.

'We have them,' he said.

Closing on the large old trading schooner in the running sea took several hours, by which time the sun had risen high and the combination of heat and humidity was intense. At a distance of half a mile, Eli began to bark orders to his first officer, then sent Adèle below, escorted reluctantly by the two women guards.

Panicking, several of the crew on the schooner fired shots in the direction of the barque from the small-calibre armament they had aboard. The explosions went wide, foaming in the sea, but brought shouts of expectation from the boarding party of Triads, who began to jeer at the apprehensive faces they could now see lining the rail of the schooner. Kin Sang and Eli consulted briefly, and Eli decided to come about and cross the stern of their obviously heavily laden prey. As they did so, the fixed armaments aboard the barque thundered a broadside which raked the schooner; holes appeared all over the aft section and tore through several of the ship's sails.

Spinning the wheel hard over, again bellowing orders, Eli began to nose ahead of the schooner and, ignoring sporadic fire, he took the schooner's wind. She slowed immediately, which was a signal for Eli to close hard. Grappling lines were thrown and, moments later, the screaming horde of Triads leapt from rail to rail, instantly attacking anything that moved. As the two ships wallowed side by side in the water, Eli took one last look at his set of sails. He turned to see that aboard the schooner it was more of a massacre than a fight. Slaves, released from below, came on deck in broken chains and, despite their condition, began to claw at their former captors and masters with bare hands. From the forward hold, Eli saw a Triad pirate leap up shouting excitedly. There was blood on his tunic, but in his hand, gold. Kin Sang, who continued to direct the fight from the poop deck, drew his sword from its sheath with a hiss of triumph, then glanced at Eli, who shook his head.

The Triad leader joined his men aboard the schooner as Eli descended into his cabin and poured a large rum. He drank the first glass in one gulp, then poured a second as he heard Adèle shouting from the small dining room adjacent to the captain's cabin. He opened the door and beckoned her to join him. He poured a small rum, which she sipped, then she coughed, but eventually swallowed it. By the time Eli deemed it safe to go up on deck, the noise had died down outside and Kin Sang stood in the doorway. Paeans of victory sound loudly from his men. There was blood on his robes, his eyes were burning and he smiled cruelly.

'You no longer have a stomach. They are only slave traders with opium and gold – which was *once* your business.'

Eli nodded. 'I was also once a trader who took tea half-way around the world beneath clouds of canvas, for old ladies to drink over gossip on lazy afternoons in England.'

'Paid for with opium!' snapped Kin Sang. 'Your British morals have no place here in China. You have brought more than an unwanted religion to our country. You have presented us also with the great gift of – hypocrisy.'

Eli poured himself another rum, refusing to be drawn into argument. Kin Sang prowled across the small cabin, ignoring shouts from above which sounded to Eli very much like alarm.

'Western governments,' began Kin Sang, 'have degraded the Chinese people long enough. Aboard the schooner we found – what? *European* men but *Chinese* slaves, *Chinese* opium, *Chinese* gold. The time has come for our revenge.'

'I am only a sailor,' said Eli, 'who uses the winds.' He looked at the small picture of a clipper ship on the wall.

'Then I must find you a steamship,' smiled Kin Sang.

Eli grunted and stepped to the banquette, where he leaned forward against the window frame and looked out through the thick glass. From behind he heard Kin Sang invite Adèle, 'Come and you shall see what we have done.'

He was about to turn and insist that the girl remain in the cabin to save her the sight of blood, despite her curiosity, when his eyes narrowed. Across the shimmering water, almost two leagues away, he thought he could make out smoke. He spun around and ran to the door, leapt up from the cabin on to the poop deck, took the telescope from the chest and examined the dark smudge he had seen in the distant haze.

'Damn!' he whispered to himself and, with a sinking feeling in his heart, repeated the word, 'Damn!' He replaced the telescope and his mind began racing as he watched the Triads slowly crossing the rail and returning to the barque. He examined his set of sails, felt the wind on his face, grasped his First Officer and began issuing orders. Kin Sang, who had now joined him on the poop, was puzzled at Eli's behaviour. He was commanded to get his men and all moveable plunder off the schooner immediately.

'Why?' asked Kin Sang. 'Time is our friend.'

Eli pointed into the haze where black smoke was now quite distinct.

'And there is the enemy,' he said. 'A British man-o'-war.'

All grappling lines were released and both Captain and Triad leader conveyed a sense of urgency to all their men. Dead and wounded were left aboard the schooner, those still conscious crying piteously for help.

'Come on!' growled Eli to himself as the barque slowly disengaged from the schooner. Adèle, who had pulled away from her guards, stepped out of the cabin and ran across to Eli as he spun the wheel and shouted for the top gallants to be clewed in.

'But you can't just leave them,' began Adèle, seeing the men on the schooner, which had begun to list to port.

'Take her below!' snapped Lubbock.

'Eli!' pleaded the young woman. He ignored her and she was dragged back into the cabin just as two Triad pirates hurled bombs in an arc on to the schooner's decks. One of them fell directly into the hold. The first exploded, creating a sheet of flame on the deck. Eli looked up as the wind cracked his canvas, and with a prayer of thanks he realised they were out and away from the stricken vessel. A noise like thunder came from her hold as it was gutted by the second bomb, which had clearly found munitions. Several pieces of her yards fell on to the poop deck. Eli narrowly avoided them, giving the wheel to his First Officer. He grunted and with pursed lips watched the schooner settle deeper into the China Seas. Kin Sang continued to look anxiously towards the man-o'-war closing on them.

'It's a cruiser,' murmured Eli. 'It's old, so we might have a chance, but the China squadron keep their ships

Bristol fashion, so if her engineer knows his stuff, it'll be, as Wellington once said, "a damn near run thing".'

'Can we elude them, Mr Lubbock?' Kin Sang's voice revealed his fear. Eli shrugged and quickly examined his sails which were filling rapidly. He realised that they might even have to be double-clewed.

'If the wind holds we might lose them amongst the islands. If it freshens, and they don't sink us with their guns, I'll guarantee it. I know this coast, and it's tricky.' He stared at Kin Sang, who seemed to accept his decision as fact, bowing his thanks. Feeling the increasing movement in the barque, Eli was at least grateful they had a chance. After all, what else could he say? If they were caught. . . . He censored his thoughts; the idea was unthinkable.

'Piracy I accept,' he said, 'but kidnapping the daughter of an American Consul. . . .' He stepped towards Kin Sang. 'One thing you must understand about the *Western* mind is that when *you* go too far, *we* also seek retribution.'

'We, Mr Lubbock?'

'You damned fool. Because of her they have sought you out.'

Kin Sang smiled. '*Us*, Mr Lubbock.'

From the corner of his eye Eli saw a distant flash, as a fisherman might see a leaping marlin caught in the sun, but it came from what was now dark shadow beneath the rising smoke. Eli counted seconds, heard the whistle and whine, and half a mile from the barque's starboard bow a huge geyser of water erupted from the sea. Cries of apprehension came from the crew on deck who, although bloody, and moments before ruthless, rushed to the rails to see the approaching battle-cruiser emerge from the haze.

'Do you believe in fate, Mr Lubbock?' asked Kin Sang.

Eli shook his head. 'No,' he said, 'luck.'

4

The first shot from *Leviathan* had been deliberately placed as a warning. Binoculars had shown the distant barque was flying Triad flags, identified by both Silas Hayes and, astutely, also by Hollis Jackson, who was proving to Silas to be more than he seemed. The effete merchant trader, who had absorbed so many of the manners of society to further himself, seemed to have lost none of the grit from his ocean-sailing days.

The view from the bridge of the British man-o'-war allowed them all a hundred-and-eighty-degree panorama, from horizon to inshore, where many small islands jutted from a shallow sea, dangerous for vessels with any draught. Silas stepped out on to the open for'ard flying-bridge then glanced back into the enclosed bridge, where a sailor manned the wheel. He nodded to him through the glass, hearing Captain Van, who was standing beside the helm, already bellowing into the telegraph for 'all speed'. Bells sounded throughout the ship as Silas, leaning on the rail, stared ahead. Feeling the wind at his back, he swore loudly as Hollis Jackson joined him.

'He's ordered "full and by".'

Jackson nodded, 'Yes, he's close hauling. Could a Chinaman keep full sail that close to the wind, do you think?'

Silas did not reply. The bells continued to clamour as Captain Van came out on to the open bridge and slammed his fist against the brass rail.

'We'll have them!'

'Not yet,' muttered Silas.

'I've ordered "full ahead",' snapped Van, 'and

brought all forward guns to bear. They'll fire on command.'

'Aren't we going to stop and see if there are survivors from the schooner?' asked Jackson.

Captain Van looked at the man with a supercilious expression. 'And lose our prey? Are you mad? You saw the explosion; if anyone survived they've already been consigned to Davy Jones' locker.' A flash in the sky ahead disturbed him, and for a moment he thought it was gunfire, but the barque was still too distant for anything aboard her to have reached *Leviathan*. Captain Van smiled with pleasure as he recognised only a flash of lightning, content to feel the surge of his battle-cruiser as the engines forced it to maximum speed. Silas could see that the heat of the day, temperature and humidity combined, had forced a change in the weather. Already the sea was picking up and the air had become heavy despite the following wind. Light dulled as huge clouds began to move out from the land seawards, obscuring the sun.

'We're in for a "Chinese blow",' said Silas.

'Do you think so?' asked Jackson, genuinely apprehensive.

Silas nodded, 'It's the time of the year.'

'We'll have them!' repeated Captain Van, again slamming his fist on the brass rail, as if to convince himself of the fact.

'I wouldn't put money on it,' stated Silas. Captain Van, grasping his binoculars, peered ahead before handing them to Silas, who adjusted the focus and smiled to himself as he watched the barque scud between two islands, and disappear for a moment into a rain squall.

'Where's *he* gone?' shouted Captain Van.

'Fire!' he bellowed.

'Wait a minute . . .' hesitated Jackson, 'are those islands inhabited, do you think?'

A roar of the forward guns absorbed all other sound. Silas counted as the shells made an arc but fell short to the starboard side of the barque as it emerged from the squall.

'If we sink them,' he said, 'you'll learn nothing of either the girl or their home port.'

Captain Van snatched the binoculars and peered towards the shore. The barque seemed to have disappeared. Swearing, he turned and led his First Officer back into the enclosed bridge in the hope that further invective to his engineer might produce an increase in speed. 'God damn it those blasted yellow faces aren't sailors!' he cried and slammed the door.

'*He* is,' murmured Silas to himself.

Rain spattered the open bridge and the forward movement of *Leviathan* became suddenly very apparent in the building sea swell. Jackson grasped the brass rail, feeling the queasiness in his stomach.

'An Englishman perhaps?' He looked at Silas, who was staring into the increasing gloom. 'And quite a sailor,' he murmured, in turn.

'It takes more than a pretty set of sails to make a sailor,' Silas answered.

The elegantly turned-out merchant trader could feel the bile rising in his throat. 'Sails are not necessary at all, *Mr* Hayes – that world is finished. This is a steamship. Are you trying to tell me we cannot catch that little yacht?'

Leviathan was closing fast on the islands, her thundering engines thrusting the sharp bow into the grey sea, causing spray to lash the deck. Silas ignored the question, realising suddenly that there was cause for concern. He could see the dark cloud mass and pouring rain already shrouding the coast towards which they were heading.

'We'd better stand out to sea,' he said. 'We're too near the shore.'

'But he's going in!' Jackson pointed out.

'He can,' Silas explained. 'We draw more water.'

'Are you trying to tell me the British Navy can't navigate?'

'I'd never try to tell you anything,' Silas replied, turning and walking back into the wheelhouse to make suggestions to Captain Van. All Jackson knew at that moment with complete certainty was that he wanted to be violently sick.

The course was altered and, after a brief consultation with Silas, bells were rung and, gritting his teeth, Captain Van gave the order, 'Slow to half.'

With some amusement, Silas watched Hollis Jackson step in from the flying bridge, wiping his mouth.

'He's gone,' he said.

Rain had saved them, providing a blanket, most of the pirates agreed, behind which they had hidden. Dutch timbers and resilient canvas was how Eli Lubbock put it. He relinquished the helm to his first officer by late afternoon, seeing open sea ahead. Already, familiar islands were several miles to seaward, and in the backing wind Eli felt safe to go below to his charts and the waiting Triad leader. Kin Sang bowed, knowing better than his men, or than Eli was prepared to admit, that their escape was entirely due to Captain Lubbock.

'You are indeed a seaman,' he said, and glanced at Adèle Morgan lying asleep on the bunk. 'It seems you are indeed many things. Thank you, Mr Lubbock.' Kin Sang stepped out of the cabin.

Eli leaned over his charts, feeling with instinct the movement of the ship. He had noted the wind direction, checked their speed with the knot rope and begun calculating time. He estimated arrival if conditions held, wrote it down in the log then crossed to the bunk. Adèle's eyes opened and she touched her forehead. The rough weather and fast movement had taken their toll, as Eli could see. He smiled.

'Even Nelson was seasick, young lady,' he said, and quickly took the bowl placed on the floor as she began to retch yet again.

At twilight, the dark sky began to clear. The heavy weather lessened. Rough seas calmed and a breeze from the north-east filled the few sails Eli set on his main mast and, as if with a guiding hand, the barque slid past the outer islands and entered the concealed bay between the two promontories, where beacons blazed a welcome. Anchors were let out and lines cast to a large buoy chained to the seabed. Kin Sang, a recovered Adèle Morgan and a tired Captain Lubbock, stood on the poop deck and watched boats come from the shore, where torches and lanterns illuminated the old Portuguese fortress.

'Home, Mr Lubbock,' said Kin Sang. 'And safely, thanks to you.'

'I hope so,' grunted Eli. Kin Sang stepped into one of the first boats as a babble of news began to spread from the crew to those who had come from the shore. Eli leaned on the wheel and stared out towards the promontories, where the fires were being extinguished. Adèle followed his gaze.

'Will they find us?' she whispered.

'They might,' Eli answered, lost in thought.

'Will they let me go if my father pays a ransom?'

'They might,' Eli repeated, his face hardening. Adèle, suddenly feeling rejected by her protector and weak from her ordeal, burst into tears. Eli reached over the wheel and held her face in his hands.

'Years ago, I used to run contraband out of here, with a friend. We knew it as a safe anchorage.'

'A friend?' Adèle sobbed.

'Silas Hayes.'

'But isn't he in Shanghai?' Adèle asked.

'I doubt it,' Eli said quietly.

* * *

'Eli Lubbock?!' exploded Captain Van.

'Well, the description fitted perfectly,' said Hollis Jackson, shifting uncomfortably on his chair at the captain's table. 'Tall, red-haired, bearded, unshaven probably. Pale complexion. . . .' He looked across the polished mahogany at the impassive face of Silas Hayes, who leaned back against the panelling to allow a steward to clear his place.

'Those Chinese in the junk told you that, Hayes?' asked Captain Van incredulously.

'They did. I heard them,' smiled Jackson.

The Captain fixed Silas Hayes with a look demanding an answer. 'Do you think it's him?'

Silas took his time lighting a cheroot before answering slowly, 'I doubt it.'

'But the description fits,' spluttered Captain Van. 'And if it's Lubbock . . . well, damn it, no wonder we lost them.' He reached for a half-full crystal glass, swallowed the contents, then, as a steward moved in to re-fill it, he frowned at Silas Hayes. 'I never liked him.'

'You've never liked me,' stated Silas.

The First and Second Officers were puzzled. Jackson, despite his increasing queasiness, explained, 'They're friends.'

'They were once rivals,' stated Captain Van, indicating to one of the stewards that liquors and cigars should be brought. He had agreed to remain in the vicinity where it was calculated the barque must lay up. Silas felt sure it would not have risked running on where it would be easily exposed in open sea beyond the island chain. *Leviathan* had ridden out the rough weather which had passed on over the horizon leaving that most uncomfortable of things afloat – a heavy swell. Now the man-o'-war at 'slow ahead', merely wallowed where before it had laboured in the dark sea.

Dinner had been served in the finely appointed cabin, where gas lights and candles gave a warm glow to highly polished wood panelling and brass fitments.

'During the great Tea Race of '66 you were on *Ariel* under Captain Keay, weren't you?' questioned Captain Van.

Silas nodded, 'In the old days,' he said, 'I sailed with him quite a while.'

'You won, didn't you?'

'Ask him,' said Silas.

The naval captain looked at the British man-o'-war's other 'guest'.

'You, Mr Jackson, were aboard . . . ?' began Captain Van.

'*Serica*, under Captain Innes,' he answered. 'I was a 'prentice, like them.'

Silas glanced at Jackson with some distaste. 'Eli, on *Taeping*, serving under McKinnon, beat us both.'

'Keay lost by a trick,' Jackson explained.

Silas shook his head, drew on his cheroot and spoke laconically, knowing the truth full well.

'He lost by design, Jackson. The owners had already agreed who would arrive first. They had their publicity and split the profit. McKinnon shared his bonus with Keay.'

'That surprises me,' said Jackson in disbelief.

Silas shrugged. 'It was the owners' decision. All three were Scots captains, about that there is no doubt.' For a moment the Glaswegian accent was marked and pride obvious in the voice. 'After one hundred days at sea we hit the English Channel only twenty minutes apart. That, gentlemen, is seamanship, in any race.'

'Who entered the "Downs" first?' Captain Van asked curiously, referring to the narrowing waters of the English Channel generally acknowledged to be the real end of the race to be first home with fresh tea from China.

Silas Hayes smiled. 'We did,' he said, 'Keay on *Ariel*. That I'll never forget.'

The steward began to pour drinks.

Jackson belched and apologised. He could already taste the familiar bile as his stomach, feeling the sway of the cabin, hesitated to accept the meal.

'Times have changed,' he said quickly. 'Now we have conquered the winds and command the sea – with steam.'

'You should know better, Hollis,' murmured Silas. 'The sea will always claim the foolhardy, no matter what size or power of vessel carries you. You must have – respect.'

Jackson nodded, took a cigar and began to light it – which was to prove a mistake.

'I have respect,' he said, 'for the ingenuity of mankind.'

There was a knock at the door and a young officer entered, saluting. 'The boilers, sir,' he said, 'the engineer is having a problem with – ' Captain Van wafted a hand angrily, watching the young officer trying to steady himself in the doorway as the ship moved quite markedly to one side. Jackson stood up and swallowed. The young officer remained in the open door, seeing a guest about to leave.

'Are you all right, Mr Jackson?' asked Captain Van. Hollis Jackson shook his head, not daring to speak, crossed the cabin and went out.

'What's the weather report?' demanded the Captain.

The First Officer coughed and replied, 'Well, it's thought to become heavier after midnight, sir, but should blow itself out before dawn.'

'Good,' replied Van. 'We'll go in then – if you can find us a channel, Mr Hayes.'

Silas hesitated to answer, watching the Captain take a decanter of port perched precariously on a silver tray held by a steward.

'May I remind you of your duty Mr Hayes, and what is fact. There is a girl and there are pirates who have plagued us for many years and, if what you believe is correct they are not two leagues to starboard. On the charts what is a fact,' continued Captain Van, 'is that there is a bay and there is a sufficient depth of water to enter and what is also fact is that I have guns and Marines to ensure the outcome of any battle.'

'Then at first light we will find out,' said Silas quietly.

'Indeed, we will, sir,' grunted Captain Van.

The man-o'-war lurched in the building sea and the sound of the increasing wind force became quite audible in *Leviathan*'s quiet dining room. Captain Van poured for himself then slid the decanter across the polished table towards Silas.

'Port?' he asked.

Silas nodded, 'In any storm.'

Action stations sounded throughout *Leviathan*. At first light, as her bow nosed slowly through a calm sea within sight of the two promontories, the British man-o'-war emerged from the heavy morning mist like a ghost ship. Silas Hayes had successfully negotiated the channel where the only deep water allowed the battle-cruiser access to the bay. In fading starlight then, as dawn began to show, with mist obscuring visibility between the islands, Silas had judged from swirling currents and deeper colours in the water where the channel led. Ordering 'cut engines', he had several sailors put up sails on the fore and aft masts so that the final approach, although slow, would be silent. A breeze had begun to disperse the mist as if an unseen hand were wiping condensation from a glass. The Marines, on full alert, had been checking their weapons; now they ran from below to assemble on deck. All guns were loaded and with hydraulics greased and oiled, each of the t targets as ordered. Starin bridge, Silas Hayes waite in the distance Triad pira promontories. In the stilln he could hear them screami which as yet was hidden doubt in his mind; everythi

The sailor at the wheel, enclosed bridge, watched as and opened his fingers twice in this fashion for some tin degrees to port. He flattene course, and several seconds w from a promontory and explo sky, cascading a red warning t bay. Captain Van and Jackson Silas at the open rail.

'We've found them, by God Van, sipping hot tea.

Jackson was equally impresse 'Save your praise,' growled Sil Sporadic rifle fire was comi promontories but Silas held cour water foaming against the two r they plunged sheer into the sea. as there was no longer need for silence.

'Hard over, now! Start engines!'

Captain Van glanced behind him as his first officer pushed the telegraph to 'full ahead'. *Leviathan*'s engines thundered into life, steam pressure having been maintained for some hours, and with a sudden movement the British man-o'-war surged forward. A bow wave appeared and the ship began to glide between the promontories towards the Triad's hidden bastion.

Alarm bells rang loudly to indicate enemy action, immediately causing the Marines to kneel behind the iron bulwarks. In devastating volleys they fired upwards at the Triads assembling atop the two cliffs. Several bullets whined past the heads of Captain Van, Silas and Jackson, and only Silas remained on his feet, as the others crouched to protect themselves. He knew where they would have to stop before the shallows and the last thing he wanted was to go aground.

'Full reverse!' he bellowed. The telegraph bells rang and a great rumbling sound began as Leviathan's twin screws went into reverse.

'Stop!' ordered Silas. The engines slowed. 'Drop anchor!'

The British man-o'-war was within the bay and almost a mile from the shore as Silas heard clearly the rattling of anchor chains. Further volleys from the Marines silenced remaining opposition on the promontories, and all attention turned as the heavily armed turrets traversed towards the distant shore. Already Silas could see, beyond several junks and the moored barque, the familiar walls of the old Portuguese fortress. Now action was about to begin he felt the exhilaration and energy which always came to him and made decisions easy. He grinned as he saw both Captain Van and Jackson stand and peer towards the thick woodland that came down towards the beach.

'We're here,' he said.

Captain Van began bellowing orders.

'Prepare the cutters!'

Marines were already clambering aboard them even as the large craft were being winched down into the water.

'Major!' he shouted. 'Board your men and let's get this done!' The Marine Major on the foredeck saluted and moved quickly amongst his men.

Silas, leaning on the rail at the port side, examined the barque with binoculars. 'There she is,' he muttered.

Jackson uncorked a flask of rum, took a gulp and smiled. '*He*, don't you mean?'

Silas ignored the remark and handed Jackson the glasses, but knew that he was right. Eli Lubbock was trapped.

'Ranging shots; all guns; select target; fire at will!' shouted Captain Van. Immediately his first officer, in the wheelhouse, echoed the orders to all parts of the ship. The roar of guns resounded throughout the bay, momentarily deafening everyone aboard *Leviathan*. The first salvo from both heavy and light armaments fell between the moored ships and the shore. Plumes of water rose and cascaded around the barque and several junks, one of which received a direct hit. A second salvo thundered out from the British man-o'-war, and this time shells fell on to the beach and into the fortress, gouging sand and rock from the ground and throwing them high into the air. Silas could see panic everywhere on the shore, figures running to and fro – surprise was complete.

As the shells of a third salvo from the battle-cruiser whistled overhead, Kin Sang stepped quickly from his quarters in the main blockhouse of the fortress and went up on to the flat roof. Buttoning his long robe, he stood calmly above the screams and confusion. He winced when the shells exploded on the walls surrounding the courtyard. Beyond, a view across the bay revealed the enemy clearly. The Triad leader's eyes narrowed as he assessed the situation. His men were running to create some order and establish opposition to the approaching cutters full of British Marines. He grunted with an acceptance of the truth: this might well be a battle he would lose. He realised with increasing anger that their discovery could not have been an accident.

'Betrayed!' he hissed.

5

In the Captain's cabin on the Triad barque, Eli Lubbock stirred in his sleep, disturbed by thunder which seemed to come from the sea beneath the ship's timbers. He opened his eyes to the sound of sporadic gunfire and distant bells. He glanced from the banquette across to the bunk, where Adèle Morgan slumbered still. The thundering faded. Only then did he recognise ship's engines. The distinct sounds of rattling anchor chains snapped him awake. He swung his legs from the banquette, guessing the horrible truth. It was immediately confirmed by the first roaring broadside from what, as he leapt out of the cabin door on to the poop deck, he could see for himself was no dream. *Leviathan* dominated the bay. The bastion had been found by the British Navy and, as Eli realised, it was by no accident – only one other man knew where the forgotten fortress had been built.

'Damn you, Silas!' exploded Eli, then shells hit the sea, forming huge plumes of white water all around, drenching him even as he began running. Ignoring the odds, Eli was determined, from sheer anger, that battle would be joined.

Six three-inch breech-loading guns, made in a Shanghai foundry, had been secured to the deck of the barque, converting her effectively from a Dutch trading ship to an instrument of war. A first broadside from three of these guns fell short of *Leviathan*, but certainly indicated a willingness to fight.

Eli went among his Triad crew, who were already reloading and had begun firing more out of panic and confusion than bravery. He snapped out orders, and the three guns on the opposite rail were swung full around and aimed through the rigging to fire across the deck, doubling the weight of each salvo to come. Eli quickly estimated the distance, bellowed instructions and commanded, 'Fire!' Each of the six shells whistled over *Leviathan* and fell into the sea fifty yards beyond. Already the pirates were reloading, and Eli squinted to revise the trajectory and ensure greater accuracy for further salvos.

Again he snapped out orders and the guns were re-set. He could see that the cutters, laden with Marines, had begun their approach. The men were crouched and looked dangerous – as Eli knew them to be. The small motor which powered each of the cutters moved each one in turn away from the ironclad's side and towards the shore.

Eli glanced over his shoulder towards the bastion and again commanded, 'Fire!' almost exactly as the British man-o'-war, in turn, fired another salvo. The two bombardments crossed above the bay; the lighter one from the Triad barque falling all about *Leviathan*, but scoring no hits; the heavier one from Her Majesty's Navy exploded with great effect in and about the old Portuguese fortress. Eli saw part of the main wall blown to rubble, and amidst the deafening noise he could detect high-pitched wailing from the women and screaming from the wounded. What had once been a safe haven he knew would now, for so many, prove to be their burial ground.

The first volley of rifle fire from the leading cutter ripped into the masts, rigging and rails all about the Triads manning the guns on the port side of the barque. Eli ducked and grasped for one of the pirates, who fell back gurgling blood, shot through the throat. He dragged the man to comparative safety between the hatches, then bellowed for the guns to be fired yet again. Adèle appeared from the door which led down to his cabin.

'Stay inside!' he commanded, but she remained on the threshold, so he ran across to her as, once again, the guns fired. Eli fell against the wood, instinctively squatting, as another volley of rifle cut into the barque, tearing at wood, severing lines and ricocheting about the deck. His salvo, as he had calculated, again fell all about *Leviathan* but scored no hits. It would, he thought, at least keep some heads down and perhaps give him some time to get away, but if one of the breech-loaders hit a Marine cutter, well, that would be fate. He could certainly not be seen to give up without a fight for, if he was to get away, he would need Kin Sang's help.

'What is happening?' asked Adèle.

'We've been discovered,' said Eli.

'Have they come for me?' asked Adèle.

Another roar sounded from the British man-o'-war and what seemed like the noise of a huge vehicle passed overhead and landed once more amidst the bastion. A pall of smoke rose from the burning buildings. More rifle fire came from the cutters, and Eli pulled Adèle down to her knees, only then noticing the two women guards close behind her.

'If they have come for you,' he said grimly, 'they don't appear to be too concerned about your welfare.'

The girl's face paled but Eli could see that she was game for anything, with as determined an expression as he had ever seen.

'We shall be saved, Mr Lubbock.'

Eli smiled. 'Indeed, I think you will be, Miss Morgan. Although you do seem to have a problem which we must first dispose of . . .' He could hear distantly across the water orders being shouted by sergeants and officers to their Marines. The Triad men at the guns on the deck of the barque had begun firing independently and, as Eli saw, some of the shells were

94

falling dangerously near the cutters, which were now approaching fast. If there was a time to get away, it must be now, as he knew – but first the girl.

As more rifle fire spattered about the barque's deck, the two Triad women guards, shouting fearfully, pushed Adèle out on to the deck and began to move towards the starboard rail where several of the crew were lowering a dory.

'Eli!' shouted Adèle. One of the women grunted and prodded her with the flat of a wicked-looking knife. Eli saw that it would be a near thing if the crew got the dory away before the first cutters arrived. Most of the pirates who had been sleeping below were now on deck, running about confused whether to fight or leap overboard. Others, who could not swim – and there were many of them – were releasing the other dory. For them, Eli calculated, it would be too late. Again rifle fire raked the barque, now with some accuracy, dropping several of the Triads where they stood.

'Eli!' screamed Adèle again from between her two guards. Eli stepped towards her. It was all up now, and time to move.

Leading cutters, full of Marines from *Leviathan*, had proceeded as ordered towards the north and south ends of the beach where it became rocky and difficult to land. The idea was that if there was opposition, a pincer would be formed and the Marines would approach along the sand, pushing back the Triads to the centre, where another force would land, having taken care of Triads aboard moored junks and the barque. Sporadic rifle fire and shots from the breech-loaders aboard the barque had ensured most of the Marines kept their heads down, and as yet they had been lucky – only a few bullets had found their mark. None of the men had been killed and the most serious injury was only a bullet in the shoulder of a nineteen-year-old boy, who would merely end up drunk on the rum rations that were being issued to alleviate any pain.

The regular broadsides from the barque had stopped but, perhaps more dangerously, at point-blank range the remaining pirates had begun firing directly towards the cutters in the centre of the bay; only panic, which caused the Triads to shoot wildly, had saved the Marines from anything more than the sea water which cascaded over them from near misses. The Major, aboard *Leviathan*, was supervising the launch of his last cutter, knowing that, once ashore, his Marines might face greater opposition from knives and swords, when their advantage might be lost. For the moment, the might of the British man-o'-war was quite apparent.

A salvo from all guns brought to bear on the Portuguese bastion again thundered from the British battle-cruiser, resounding throughout the bay and up into the thickly wooded hills behind. Captain Van, watching through binoculars, saw that his gunners had been trained well as the bombardment fell exactly as aimed: into the fortress, where a huge flash beneath the dense smoke rising into the sky indicated that a shell had found munitions. With jubilation the British Captain slapped his thigh.

'By God, we've got them – caught like the rats they are!' Silas Hayes traversed the shoreline quickly with binoculars, then turned his attention to the Triad barque, under fire from the leading Marine cutters.

'The girl,' he murmured.

'Damn the girl!' exclaimed Captain Van. 'We've been after these pirates for years.'

Hollis Jackson and several of the other officers, who were unaccustomed to accurate retaliation, regained their composure as return fire had apparently ceased. Jackson smiled.

'First they're too long,' he said, 'then too short, and

having straddled us they have scored no hits at all. And now' – he indicated cascading water near the cutters approaching junks beyond the barque – 'they are proving that they have no accuracy at all. I would have thought, Silas, from your description of these pirates, they would have put up a better show.'

'The fight's not over yet,' said Silas Hayes, and focused the binoculars to the poop deck of the barque. He traversed the starboard rail, where he saw Eli standing beside several crew. They had successfully lowered what, he guessed, would be a dory on the lee side of the sailing ship. Then he recognised Adèle.

'You son of a bitch!' he said to himself.

'Who?' asked Captain Van, then he too found the barque through his glasses. 'By God, it's a white man! We'll have him!' he bellowed.

Silas had begun moving. At the top of steps leading down to the lower deck, he shouted, 'Wait, Major!'

'You will remain here aboard!' snapped Captain Van. 'I order it!'

'They'll kill the girl!' shouted Silas.

'I command it!' said Captain Van.

Silas paused only to establish his weight on the deck then hit the British officer squarely on the chin. Captain Van swayed and slumped into the First Officer's arms, his bulk taking both of them heavily to the caulked timbers.

'Silas,' began Hollis, and reached out a hand, 'have a care, you are aboard a British Navy ship. . . .'

Silas Hayes spun around, glaring at Jackson, brushed away the man's hand and raised a fist.

'Not us, Silas,' faltered Jackson.

Silas Hayes grinned, 'Why not?' he said and swung a punch. Reflex or expertise dragged from Jackson's past saved him and he managed to block the blow, but a second caught him glancingly on his cheek. He responded with a straight left and cracked Silas on the forehead as he attempted to duck, which put him in the perfect position for an upper-cut. He connected heavily, throwing Jackson backwards. He staggered to regain his balance. Silas stepped towards him as he raised both fists. A thundering broadside from *Leviathan* distracted the attention of both men, then a shout went up from the Second Officer, who pointed towards the barque. She was engulfed by huge plumes of water as the British man-o'-war's heavy armaments, having changed target with deadly accuracy, straddled her entire length. Jackson seized Silas by the shoulders with both hands.

'It's Eli, isn't it?'

Silas nodded in answer.

'Well then let's get him out of there.'

Silas made a grimace. 'We came for the girl.'

Hollis Jackson was already tearing off his coat. 'Old friends,' he said.

Silas and Jackson ran down the steps to the foredeck, crossed quickly to the bulwark and stepped through the open metal gate. They descended the gangway and jumped into the cutter, which was half-full of Marines. The Major signalled and a chugging engine roared into life. The cutter, picking up speed, moved inshore towards the continuing action. North and south, the first Marines were already jumping into the shallows and wading on to the beach. Other craft were engaging what little opposition was presented to them from the moored junks. A number of the pirates had leapt overboard and swum back towards the fortress, or were drifting on anything that could float. Some had been picked up, manacled and thrown into the bottom of the large cutters. With satisfaction the Major realised the operation was going well and would now, with some luck, prove ultimately successful. A last salvo roared out again from *Leviathan*. Water cascaded around the barque, directly ahead of the fast-moving cutter. The Marine officer could see that a shell had carried away the fore-mast, which groaned against its stays then slipped from its footings and fell across the starboard side, into the sea. A cheer went up from several of the Marines, echoed by others across the bay. Still, several guns continued to fire from the barque. Explosions appeared some way to port as the Marine commander's cutter moved in to the Triad ship. The sergeant at the tiller turned hard to starboard and, although his intention was to escape further shots from the barque, Silas knew he was presenting a perfect target. He grabbed the tiller.

'The barque, man!' he shouted. 'We go straight in!'

'Where's the girl?' shouted Jackson.

Silas, swinging the cutter hard over so that foam creamed along the rail, pointed. 'She's there,' he said. Jackson took a small pair of binoculars from the Major, who was ordering cutters to converge on the stricken barque. Jackson focused and saw for himself.

'Adèle!' he said. Silas nodded grimly, leaned forward, seized the handle of the accelerator and pushed the engine to maximum.

Shouts from the Chinese crew on the lee of the barque told Eli that they had successfully launched the dory and were about to cast off. The two Triad women guards reached out to Adèle Morgan, intending to lower her into the small vessel now floating at the water-line of the barque. Eli was quicker; he grabbed her, spun her around and thrust her behind him. Immediately, the first of the women guards raised her honed dagger, which glinted in the morning sun. Screaming at Eli, she plunged towards him, twisting the dagger at the last moment in a slashing movement. Eli side-stepped and kicked her hard, his boot contacting muscle, causing her to gasp in pain. A punch, with all his weight, whipped her head to one side and, by the sound of the impact, broke her jaw.

The second woman flew at him, hands extended. Her nails found the flesh of his cheeks and ripped downwards, causing blood to flow immediately. With a roar of anger, Eli swung his forearm and hit her in the throat. She gagged and sucking for air, then fell sideways against the rail. He stepped towards her, but with practised skill she kicked sideways and her foot snapped taut against his fist. She turned, fighting for breath, and threw two blows at Eli; one caught him squarely in the chest, the second sank into his diaphragm, knocking all the wind out of him. For a moment he could see nothing and only instinct forced him to step back. He felt the point of the woman's knife slice air beneath his nose and reached out, as she slashed a second time, to seize her wrist firmly. With a seaman's grip he twisted outwards, but the woman leapt into a cartwheel, regained her footing and crouched, having forced Eli to release his grasp. She thrust the knife again. Eli stepped in close and smashed his elbow against her jaw. The woman crumpled but seemed conscious still, so he kicked her face hard, hurling her against the rail. Feeling blood on his cheek, he picked up the woman and threw her into the water. He spun round to see Marine cutters very close. A combined volley of rifle fire from all of them effectively silenced the remaining port guns. With screams, the Triad pirates at the breaches were hit by the fusillade of fire. Eli dragged Adèle to the deck as the bullets whistled over their heads.

'They really care about you,' he said, but his words were lost – the young American girl was sobbing. Having seen Eli attack the two guards, she had been shocked by his ruthlessness.

'How could you be so cruel?' she said, tears welling, her breast heaving. Eli shook his head and again ducked as another fusillade sounded from the cutters, now barely fifty yards from the barque.

'Can you swim?' he asked. She nodded. The noise of approaching engines had become louder and Eli could hear commands in distinctly British voices being barked to the Marines. Answered responses told him that they were about to be innundated by disciplined troops who in the heat of battle might well shoot first. They had obviously been instructed to seek and destroy – if they found the girl, well and good. Perhaps, thought Eli, she had merely been the excuse for action against the pirates.

'I thought they'd come to save me,' whispered Adèle.

'And so they might,' said Eli.

'What will you do . . . ?' she began. It was a good question, thought Eli, to which he had not yet established a satisfactory answer. If he could find Kin Sang, perhaps there was still some way out – a hidden route into the hills, where he could join the lucky few and escape the authorities. Remaining crouched he took Adèle quickly to the starboard rail. The first dory had already gone and the crew on the foredeck, in their panic, had dropped only the prow of the second dory into the water, suspending its stern on a rope from its derrick. They were shouting and arguing amongst themselves; several seemed ready to continue the fight with a vengeance. One of them stepped out of a hatchway from the quarters below, holding a large bomb, which a second crew member lit. Firing from the Marines had stopped – *Leviathan*'s cutters were almost at the port water-line.

'Oh, my God!' murmured Eli. British voices sounded all about, but his eyes remained on the crewman with the bomb, which was thrown in an arc. It fell through an open trap into the hold.

'Nooo!!' bellowed Eli – but it was too late. Powder, ammunition and guns stored below were a perfect target. Seizing Adèle's clothes, he lifted her on to the rail, leapt up, pushed her and jumped. Their bodies hit the water and sank beneath the surface as the barque exploded.

Grappling irons were blown high in the air above the cutters, torn from the grip of Marines who had thrown them to the rails of the sailing vessel as they themselves were hurled into the water. The force of the explosion ripped through the cutters beside the barque, tearing at timbers and swamping the boats so that the Marines suddenly found themselves thrashing in the sea or rising to the surface. Coughing salt, Silas Hayes turned several times to establish his bearings. Other heads bobbed in the water beside his. Marines who could swim grasped others who could not and the Major, beside Jackson, proved himself worthy of command by shouting the standing order that his men should swim inshore as fast as possible. Already the hulk of the barque was settling in the shallow bay and, amidst flames that became quickly extinguished, came the staccato sound of ammunition exploding at random.

'God in Heaven!' spluttered Jackson. 'What happened?'

'She's gone,' answered Silas. 'Major, get your men away from here or they'll be sucked down!'

The Marines, the Major, Jackson and Silas swam away from the sinking barque. Other cutters approached quickly and picked up the stunned or struggling. Silas began to swim powerfully towards the shore, and only then did he recognise the familiar, tightly curled chestnut hair, forty yards away, swimming beside a young girl whose long hair spread behind her on the surface.

'Jackson!' shouted Hayes, and pointed. Hollis Jackson saw the couple and immediately began swimming beside Silas. They began to close on Eli and Adèle.

Eli Lubbock found his footing in the shallows and,

pulling Adèle Morgan after him, dragged her from the sea. She fell on to the dry white sand. Eli, breathing hard, looked out into the bay and recognised the two people who were rapidly approaching.

'Give yourself up!' panted Adèle.

Eli shook his head. 'You're on your own now.'

'*Please*, Eli!' implored Adèle. Eli shook his head again.

'Be lucky,' he said, turned and began to run.

Adèle stood up shakily and tried to follow, but once more fell into the sand. Marines leapt from the first cutter to the beach. Silas Hayes and Hollis Jackson emerged beside the craft, strode out of the waves and reached Adèle. Silas knelt and smiled into her face.

'It's all right,' he said, then looked up at the Marine sergeant beside him.

'Miss Morgan,' began Jackson haltingly. 'I cannot tell you how – '

'Take care of her,' Silas interrupted, addressing the sergeant. 'It's the girl we came to find.' The large British Marine's hard face softened and he attempted a winning smile.

'You're in good 'ands now, miss.'

Silas Hayes slapped Jackson's shoulder hard, already on the move.

'Come on, Hollis.'

'Excuse me,' Jackson said to Adèle, as if he were retiring from a dance floor, and at the run followed Silas, who had spotted Eli Lubbock in the distance. The sergeant shouted orders for his Marines to follow the two men, then crouched beside Adèle.

'That Mr Jackson's got wonderful manners, 'swat I always say, miss. Even amidst shot and shell, you've gotta 'ave an attitude to things. S'wat makes us British, what we are.' The Royal Marines surged past their sergeant, racing up the beach.

'I'm American,' stated Adèle quietly.

'Well never you mind that, miss,' said the Marine sergeant, 'It's all over now, you're safe.'

Adèle smiled pleasantly. 'Can I tell that to the Marines, Sergeant?'

'Very good, miss; Charles the Second, that's the origin; loyalty and trust.' The Major arrived and saluted the young woman as the sergeant helped her to her feet.

'I'll have a cutter take you out to *Leviathan*, ma'am.' he said.

'No, Major,' said Adèle. 'I wish to go in the other direction.' She pointed towards the bastion, where sounds of heavy fighting had broken out.

Eli Lubbock leapt up from the beach on to the flagstones of an old road constructed by the Portuguese. It was overgrown but gave a better footing than the soft sand and soil all about. Knowing his pursuers were close gave him impetus and it took only a short time to reach the damaged gatehouse and enter the fortress. Flames continued to lick at several of the buildings. Smoke hung heavily above, darkening the bright morning. Several sections of the thick walls had been totally destroyed, and what had once been the blockhouse had received two direct hits, so that it was now roofless and on fire. Braving the flames, Eli stepped in and crossed quickly to the rear area. Here it was dark, cool and peaceful, like the inner sanctum of a temple. A single torch guttered on the wall but it was enough to show that Kin Sang and several of his immediate followers had retreated to the only remaining safe place.

'Treachery,' said Kin Sang quietly. 'The girl was right, you are a dead man.' The Triad leader motioned his men to move towards Eli, who wafted away the threat, disbelieving Kin Sang's intentions.

'You're wrong. How could it have been me? I have done nothing but defend – '

'The girl,' said Kin Sang, 'is still alive?'

'Your instructions to me were that I should guard her.'

'Therefore you have exceeded your orders by returning her into the bosom of the enemy.' Sounds of fighting came from the courtyard. Sporadic rifle fire met disciplined volleys from platoons of Marines who had formed up.

'How do we get out of here?' asked Eli.

'That no longer concerns you, Mr Lubbock,' answered Kin Sang. Knives gleamed dully in the torchlight as the Triads stepped closer towards Eli.

'I had nothing to do with any of this,' stated Eli. 'There must be a way out.'

Kin Sang nodded. 'Our paths are from henceforth to be in different directions, Mr Lubbock. We shall simply melt into the forest, but you. . . .' The Triad leader paused, staring at Eli with hate in his eyes.

'Well,' snapped Eli, 'what do you expect me to do?'

Kin Sang smiled, 'You, Mr Lubbock, will die. Kill him!' he ordered.

The Triads rushed Eli. He stepped back, reached beneath his waistcoat and from his belt pulled out his Remington .32. Praying that despite the sea water it would still work, he cocked, aimed and fired. The first pirate coughed and fell to the stone floor, causing the others to hesitate. Eli backed away. In front of him the Triad pirates, behind him the British Marines. His feet found the two huge flagstones which, when pulled, cantilevered from the floor and led below to the vast cellar. With his pistol traversing the approaching group menacingly, he reached down and with all his strength pulled at one of the ring handles. As the flagstone slipped vertically into place, revealing the entrance to the treasure trove, the pirates ran at Eli again, screaming. He fired twice. The first man died instantly, the second fell at his feet, groaning, which prompted

105

Eli to move and, taking a deep breath, he turned and plunged down the stairs into the darkness.

Spinning round at the foot of the stone stairway, Eli peered above, seeing dark shapes silhouetted in what little light penetrated the depths of the fortress. One of the pirates brought a torch, and for a moment, presented a perfect target. Eli fired. With a scream the pirate collapsed amongst his comrades, dropping the torch, which rolled down the steps. Eli seized it and, using its light, found refuge behind the stacked caskets and trunks. He could hear Kin Sang shouting to his men, inciting them to take every risk to finish him off.

Three pirates together ran down the steps, brandishing knives and swords. One with a gun fired wildly towards the torchlight. Eli, aiming accurately, fired twice, then a third time, but the loud click, confirming an empty chamber, made his heart sink. One of the pirates lay sprawled on the stairs, the second groaned, with a stomach wound, but the third man, with a large sword, now grinned and with a shout of triumph began to approach Eli, who thrust the torch towards the man several times. The first hefty blow from the heavy sword split a casket at Eli's shoulder and pearls erupted from it, then spilled over the flagstones. Eli backed away, his heart sinking further. He could hear the battle raging outside, but could see only the malicious eyes of the large Triad pirate, who wanted the glory of killing this Englishman. Suddenly Eli felt the cold dampness of the cellar wall and knew that he was literally boxed in amongst the stacked plunder. The Triad barked a challenge as he raised his sword in one hand and spread the other arm, pointing a kris. Eli braced himself, having decided that if he was to die, he would die fighting. The Triad pirate saw defiance in the Englishman's eyes and his grin widened. Again he barked a challenge and stepped closer, the sword raised above his head.

Eli was about to move, determined to throw the

torch at the man's face and plunge towards him, when a woman's voice shouted from above, 'Eli!' The shout took the Triad pirate off guard and he actually glanced over his shoulder. With one thrust, Eli put the lighted torch hard against the man's head and swept several caskets from the top of two large chests with his other arm. Eli smelt burning flesh as the Triad screamed, then fell heavily. A first then a second casket hit his body, bursting on impact to reveal precious stones and jewellery. Eli swung the torch mightily and with a crack knocked the man senseless. He looked up to see an array of Marines peering down from the upper room. Then Silas Hayes and Hollis Jackson, who were both bruised and bleeding, having fought their way across the courtyard, descended with Adèle Morgan between them.

Eli leaned back against the cases, trunks and caskets, with resignation. He began to laugh. Light appeared as Marines with torches and lanterns quickly followed the trio down the steps.

'Eli, are you hurt?' Adèle shouted into the gloom.

'No, I'm shipshape and Bristol fashion!' came the reply. Then Eli was surrounded by a ring of Marines, torchlight and a glow from swinging lanterns causing shadows to dance in the darkness.

'Have you ever read Robert Louis Stevenson?' asked Eli, and indicated the treasure.

Hollis Jackson was already examining several of the large cases. 'They're mine,' he said.

Eli stared into Silas Hayes' eyes and his laughter grew.

Adèle stepped towards him.

'So, in the end,' said Eli, 'we get the treasure and the girl.'

With a Marine escort, Eli Lubbock was led above, then marched out into the courtyard, where the Marine Major saluted him.

'Mr Eli Lubbock?' he began. Eli nodded. 'You are under arrest, sir.'

Eli shrugged. The Major turned his attention to Silas Hayes.

'And it's my unfortunate duty, sir, as I have just been informed from *Leviathan*, to state that you, Mr Silas Hayes, for striking a superior officer in the course of action, are also under arrest.' Silas' face fell. Hollis Jackson coughed, unsure of whether to laugh or protest.

'I've a brother in the Marines,' said Eli to the Major.

'Gentlemen,' said the officer, and indicated the way down to the beach. The group began walking. The battle was won and sections of Marines were merely mopping up as others, having been given news of the treasure, were organised by several corporals to begin moving the plunder from its store. Silas Hayes glanced at Eli as they stepped on to the beach, seeing waiting manacles in the hands of Marines guarding the cutters.

'You should have sunk us,' he said.

Eli grinned. 'How could I? You were my only ticket out.'

6

Bilge rats fared better; at least they were used to the conditions in the hold of *Leviathan*. A single hurricane lamp placed on a hook in the ceiling swayed wildly as the British man-o'-war bucketed around in a heavy sea. Peering at a metal wall, Silas and Eli squatted on a low iron bench, manacled by their feet and hands to a sturdy bar inset into the floor. Loose chains allowed them to avoid cramp by occasionally raising their legs above filthy water that sluiced about the cell where they had been incarcerated for almost five days. The constant background noise of roaring engines obliterated even the sounds of the storm which they had been riding out for more than forty-eight hours. Other prisoners in cramped compartments nearby screamed and wailed, banging on the metal walls, fearing their fate as pirates would not be an attractive one. The slop and stale bread both men were fed had made them sick. They had a bucket for excrement and urine, and had succeeded in keeping their spirits up with humour, each deferring to the other with ornate manners, before lowering their trousers, as to who should fill the bucket first.

The Marine guards had been persuaded by Adèle to allow her within sight of the barred door, but the First Officer arrived with strict instructions from Captain Van that neither of the men should see even daylight until they returned to Shanghai. Hollis Jackson used all his charm, at each meal suggesting to the Captain that Silas should be released and argued that Eli had, after all, protected and saved the poor kidnapped girl – which was immediately corroborated by Adèle herself.

Captain Van would not be turned. His dislike of both men was apparent and he was content to allow them to suffer until they were transferred into the hands of the proper authorities. In all his years as a naval officer he had never received a blow from a subordinate, and any man who disobeyed orders in action would be, as he put it, punished according to the book. He had declared his position and stuck to it.

Silas Hayes had expected no more, knowing Captain Van as a pompous bigot, malicious whenever he had the opportunity. He accepted his position more readily than Eli, who seemed always to expect the doors to be flung open and their release declared. He glanced at his companion, examining his condition. Welts on his cheek beneath thickening scabs, bleary eyes and continuous sweat from the intensely humid surroundings, complemented the torn and sodden clothes. Each man had long since given up any thought of the niceties of life, other than to dream beyond the all-pervading stench. They had not been the first, nor would they be the last, to be clapped in irons.

'How do I look?' asked Eli.

'Do you really want me to tell you?'

'Tell me.'

'You'd be frightened.'

'I can't look as bad as you.'

'Five more days in this iron bucket,' grunted Silas, 'with a captain at the helm who seems to want to slide sideways in heavy seas, and what difference will it make to either of us how we appear to anyone?'

'Look on the bright side – things can't get worse.'

'You think so?'

'Of course.' Silas looked at Eli as if he were mad and watched his friend make an expansive gesture. 'What do *you* think?'

'About what?' snapped Silas dourly.

Eli indicated their small, dank cell. 'Modern sea travel.'

'It has its drawbacks,' murmured Silas.

Eli began to laugh and lifted his manacles. 'And what about us?'

'I try not to think about it,' answered Silas.

Eli dropped his chains and conjured brightness when he said, 'Well, I'm optimistic.'

Bells rang throughout *Leviathan* and her engines reverberated. As instructed from the telegraph on the bridge, the engineer changed down from 'half ahead' to 'slow' then, as the Captain negotiated the channel east of the Bund, the screws went into reverse, churning the silt-laden waters of the Whampoa into a yellow foam.

Hollis Jackson, bathed, perfumed and smartly dressed, observed the city, gloomy under a pall of cloud from which drizzle floated on to wet rooftops. 'Shanghai in summer, Miss Morgan. Who would ever want to leave?'

More bells rang and sailors began to run to lines, hawsers and anchor chains. Safety brakes on the derricks holding the Captain's private mahogany cutter were released, and Captain Van waved impatiently at his men, issuing orders before coming back to the flying bridge and the wheelhouse.

Hollis pointed to the Chinese quarter, where smoke hung in the air, penetrating the low cloud. 'Trouble,' he said.

Captain Van dismissed the possible implications. 'If they keep their riots to themselves, we'll sleep better at night.'

'There's enough problems up north,' said Hollis, 'to cause concern. There's talk of open war.'

'We already have open war!' snapped Captain Van. 'You just haven't seen it here in Shanghai yet. If they continue to fight amongst themselves, we'll survive.'

'And if not?' asked Jackson.

Captain Van looked at Adèle Morgan and raised his chin to release the pressure of the tight collar around his neck.

'That's a prospect I prefer not to consider. If they were united, Mr Jackson, the odds would not be in our favour. That is all I can and will say on the subject.'

Leviathan dropped anchor. Hawsers carried by the pilot's small tug secured her stern to one of the large buoys anchored in the channel, and the British man-o'-war was moored amongst others of her squadron, in line ahead. A morse lamp flashed ashore was answered from the Naval and Marine Authority building and immediately several large vessels began to chug out into the muddy river water towards the battle-cruiser. A gangway was let down and a colonel of Marines, together with several liaison officers from the consulate, was boarded, met and shown up to the wheelhouse. Taking off wet outer garments to reveal their splendidly laundered uniforms, the officers were welcomed with port, rum and, it being midday, offered lunch.

To Hollis Jackson's surprise, Adèle accepted the invitation, even though she had been complaining for some time that the clothes packed for her were neither of the style nor cut she would have chosen. The mood at the Captain's table became one of growing excitement as those who had come aboard were told exactly what had happened. Orders were given for the prisoners to be brought on deck for trans-shipment to prison, where they would await justice. Adèle immediately excused herself from the table, followed by Hollis Jackson. She stared down from the open bridge, protected from the rain beneath a large umbrella held by Jackson, to see the pitiful sight of prisoners being led out from the forward hold, bullied and cursed by Marines and sailors alike.

When Silas Hayes and Eli Lubbock stepped on to the deck, directly in front of the forward gun turret, they screwed up their eyes against the light, having become accustomed only to gloom during their incarceration. The fine, warm drizzle was at least refreshing. Their condition, bad enough below in the hold, appeared worse in the harsh light of day. Adèle was unable to control an intake of breath as she saw Eli standing patiently beside Silas, holding the weight of his manacles and chains with both hands. Then his eyes found the bridge and Adèle. He could not see the tears in her eyes, but could feel the welling emotion in himself. All the ebullience he had been nurturing so successfully began to ebb from him and his shoulders sagged. Then Captain Van arrived on the bridge with the newly boarded officers, all replete after a splendid lunch, flushed and smoking cigars, holding their brandy glasses and staring curiously. Defiance stirred in Eli as he saw them spread along the rail beside Jackson and the American Consul's daughter, then descend to the deck.

Silas glanced at his friend. 'Watch it boy,' he murmured, and peered up at Hollis Jackson, who remained with Adèle on the open bridge a moment longer before following the officers down on to the foredeck. Silas grunted to himself. 'The sooner we're out of public show, the better.' From the corner of his eye he examined the group of Marines around them, professionally placed at a distance, rifles and bayonets at the ready. Some of the Chinese pirates were already being loaded into one of the prison boats, but Silas and Eli had been detained, perhaps for cabaret after lunch. Captain Van swaggered up as the officers from shore sauntered behind with guffaws and shrill laughter. Sailors held umbrellas above the well-laundered and beautifully tailored uniforms. Resplendent in full dress with gold braid, the group stopped before Eli and Silas.

For a moment everyone aboard was distracted by a

booming noise which resounded across the river. It came from a bridge connecting the Chinese section to the European quarter of the Bund. Following a flash, flames appeared, then smoke, and distantly there was a sound of rioting crowds. They had not been away long, thought Silas, and things were changing fast. Perhaps, like the northern cities, Shanghai too was now about to suffer from the hordes determined to wipe out white influence in China.

'So,' began Captain Van, 'here we have them, gentlemen. Lubbock and Hayes. The one knowing exactly where to find the other. I think their reputations in the city are well enough known. The one was employed to seek out the Triad pirates with whom, no doubt, he has consorted in the past; or else, I put it to you gentlemen, how else would he have known of their whereabouts?'

Silas Hayes' face darkened, but he said nothing, merely glared at the wide girth of the British Captain, hoping he could control his actions. Eli moved not a muscle and seemed not even to breathe, which worried Silas, who stepped on his friend's foot as a warning; in so doing his chains rattled.

'You see, gentlemen,' murmured the florid Captain, eyes gleaming with malice, 'they are now both where they should have been years ago. Their kind have long since disappeared from this coast. I have personally stamped out many of them. They have been parasites, opportunists and villains. Their time is over. The era is gone. Their life now is finished. That one,' he pointed to Silas, 'struck a superior officer of the British Navy then blatantly disobeyed orders under fire. I do not, gentlemen, have to tell you more; British Naval law will establish the rest and justly incarcerate the man at Her Majesty's pleasure.' Silas said nothing. The Marine Colonel shouldered through his companions and stood in front of Silas.

'Where are you from?' asked the well-turned-out officer.

'Glasgow,' growled Silas.

'And how did you travel East?' asked the officer, examining the object before him with obvious distaste.

'I was a 'prentice on a clipper.'

'Indeed,' murmured the officer. 'Then your present predicament might give you cause for some reflection as to the wisdom of that decision. See where it has brought you – not merely to Shanghai, but to the very depths of degradation.'

Silas, taller than the Colonel, broader and fuller in the chest, grinned and for the first time spoke with pleasure. 'The opportunities were irresistible.'

The Colonel drew back, noting that some of the Marines had changed their expressions. Captain Van saved him embarrassment by intruding. Stepping forward he pointed a finger directly into the face of Eli Lubbock.

'And you . . . are a dead man!'

'Everyone keeps telling me that,' smiled Eli. Several of the surrounding Marines coughed then regained their composure.

Captain Van's face turned scarlet. 'If I had my way . . .' said the naval officer, snarling.

'You've had it long enough,' interrupted Eli quietly.

Captain Van stared at Eli a moment longer, then hit him hard across the cheek, causing the healing welts from the Triad woman's nails to open and bleed. He backhanded Eli across the other cheek and watched him bow his head.

'How dare you talk to a captain of the British Navy in such a fashion!'

Eli felt blood trickling down his cheek and coming from his mouth and nose. A hush came over the group and although the Marines raised their rifles and bayonets, Eli ignored them as he looked up slowly. Silas closed his eyes, groaning inside.

'A dead man doesn't choose his words,' said Eli.

'You are already a condemned man – you will *not* speak *at all!*' bellowed Captain Van, saliva dribbling from the corners of his mouth. There was a murmur from the group of officers as distantly, from across the water, another explosion sounded in the Chinese quarter. Captain Van turned for a moment, examining the faces of his entourage to assure himself that they appreciated his illustration of authority. He looked back into Eli's face.

'Scum like you,' he said, turning back, 'as scum does, always finds its level. I shall personally thank the hangman.'

Eli lowered his eyes. Captain Van mistook it for submission and an acceptance of guilt, which was a mistake – it was merely a last attempt to control raw hate and, unfortunately for Captain Van, Eli failed. With both fists together Eli swung his chains against the Captain's head. The crack of impact sounded like timber splitting, and the naval officer was hurled against the Marines, then sprawled with blood gushing from a deep wound above his ear extending on to his bald pate. On reflex, each of the Marines stepped forward, loading their rifles, their bayonets poised inches from Eli's body.

'Halt!' bellowed the Major in command.

The Marine Colonel took a pace towards Eli. Indicating Captain Van, he said, 'You have condemned yourself, Lubbock.' He turned around and gestured to the group beneath the umbrellas to return to the bridge. Van's First and Second Officers were already lifting him slowly from the deck.

'March!' bellowed the Major. As best they could, Eli Lubbock and Silas Hayes shuffled to the bulwarks, descended the gangway and joined the other manacled

116

prisoners. The wallowing vessel gunned its engines and moved away from the ironclad, taking its complement on the first part of the journey which would lead to incarceration in the feared prison of old Shanghai.

Adèle was in tears as she watched the prison boat chug across the sluggish yellow water towards the quayside. She stepped to the bulwarks, where sailors had closed the gate on to the gangway, and seized the rail with anger. She looked up at Hollis Jackson, who continued to protect her from the fine drizzle with the large umbrella. His eyes had hardened but there was compassion in his voice.

'Justice, my dear, must be seen to be done.'

'This is not justice,' said Adèle. She sobbed, burying her face into a perfumed handkerchief which exactly matched her buttoned gloves.

Hollis Jackson touched her shoulder. 'They should have left the sea years ago,' he said, 'and invested, become respectable. . . .' He was interrupted by the quiet voice of Adèle Morgan.

'My father shall hear of this!'

Jackson nodded. 'Indeed, Miss Morgan . . . he should.'

Rumours abounded and gossip carried almost faster than the telegraph, that was generally agreed. Shanghai may have been a sprawling cosmopolitan city, but when fresh information was available it became merely a village. Thus, even as Eli and Silas were being roughly handled as they disembarked on the quayside amongst other prisoners, familiar faces had assembled to welcome them. Their creditors were already besieging the outer ring of Marines who awaited the new contingent for prison. They waited beside long, enclosed, metal-sided horse-drawn vehicles which would convey the captives the short route to their own particular hell.

Silas, now manacled directly in front of Eli, shook his head and looked back at his friend. 'Optimistic,' he growled.

Eli, wiping blood from his face, smiled. 'Things can't get worse.'

The prison was old and solitary cells had been built for smaller men than either Silas or Eli, whose large frames paced from wall to wall with barely three steps. A singular concession had been allowed, unofficially; they had been placed next to each other with the mere inconvenience of a two-foot wall separating them.

Nightfall had brought revelations. Howling, wailing and abuse thrown across the square exercise yard from open windows in the five floors of cells, combined with the animal smell, reminded both Hayes and Lubbock of nightmares they had long since forgotten. It was not difficult to imagine the anguish of wild beasts caged in a zoo. Clouds across the moon flung shadows into the cells. Both men came to the bars of their respective windows.

Silas!' hissed Eli.

'I'm here.'

Flashes in the sky, then the rumbling sound of explosions from the Chinese quarter, several miles distant, illustrated that violence was increasing in the city. Clutching the bars, Silas and Eli, their faces pale in the moonlight, then obscured by cloud, stared out grimly from the third tier of cells. Although they could not see each other, they had been friends long enough to know they were sharing the same feelings. After twenty-one days of incarceration, allowed barely thirty minutes of exercise, fed on bread, water and gruel, they were losing not just strength and energy, but hope and purpose.

Since the glory days of sail and the great races across the world, even their grounding in China had always

118

provided opportunities for adventure and reward. But at sea, Silas reminded himself, he was his own master, answering only to the elements; now with the great days of sail gone, steam firmly established and the Suez Canal considerably reducing the voyage back to England, his expertise had been relegated to coastal waters when there was a job available. Like Eli, on both sides of the law, he had plied the China coast, but more and more had come to feel chained to the country, even as he was now physically restricted by the loose manacles on his ankles. He longed for that world elsewhere, one of sea spray and blue water sailing.

'The good days are over here for the likes of us,' he said to Eli. 'If we could get to the American Consul, I'm sure he'd listen. I know the British authorities might protect – '

'There won't be *any* authority here soon,' interrupted Eli. 'If the Boxer rebellion takes hold throughout China and the violence gets worse, they'll have a holy war and we'll all be dead meat. They'll massacre every foreigner. We've already been declared fair game.'

There was a moment's silence between them. Perhaps it was their age, but they were both thinking of home. 'England,' said Eli quietly. More flashes lit the sky and rumbling sounds of explosions came again from beneath drifting smoke, lit by flames in the Chinese quarter.

'Did you ever see W. G. Grace play?' asked Silas. 'Once, between ships, one summer day, I watched the cricket at Lords and saw him make a century.'

'I hope we do,' muttered Eli.

'What?' asked Silas.

'Make the century,' came the quiet reply.

The morning was bright, but it was wet underfoot and the prisoners' feet slipped on the cobbles, their manacles scraping over the stones as they marched out and formed up against the wall at one side of the exercise yard. Numerous guards, some of whom were Chinese, knelt, took sections and unlocked the metal braces. Normally this was a signal for those men to rub their ankles and wrists and take painful, awkward steps around the circular area marked out amidst the cobbles. Today was different. Rifles remained trained on the assembled prisoners. Four of the Triad pirates, two of whom Eli recognised, were led out to blocks placed in the centre of the exercise space. They remained manacled and were forced to crouch, then kneel. One began crying; two of the others were screaming hysterically; only the fourth crossed himself, which surprised Silas. Christianity had obviously made its mark. Something was read out in Chinese, which Silas did not hear as the light breeze blowing snatched away the words, but from fifty yards he could clearly see the prisoners' terrified eyes. All the men in uniform in the centre area were Chinese, even a massive guard who leaned nonchalantly upon a lethal-looking sword. Within the prison, which had been used for some time by both Chinese and foreign authorities, it was accepted that Chinese law was harsh and swift.

An order echoed high above the courtyard where other captives peered down through the bars of their cells with a mixture of horror and curiosity. The first man was pressed to the block, the sword raised in the executioner's hands, and Eli closed his eyes as the distinct impact of steel on sinew and bone made him wince. A pace, and the guard repeated the process a second time, then a third. Only the fourth man, who was actually praying, as Silas noticed, gave the guard pause; from respect he waited, and as the man himself placed his head unaided on to the block, the massive executioner nodded approval. But God did not provide any miracle – the blade flashed as it had done for the

120

other three, and four decapitated bodies lay slumped and bleeding against the blocks. Eli opened his eyes and swallowed, glancing at Silas, whose teeth were gritted.

'I hope we don't get the heads,' he muttered.

Barked commands and pointing fingers selected prisoners from the group to cross at the double and lift the bodies on to a cart, which was wheeled to the centre of the courtyard. Silas was prodded and found himself holding the Chinese Christian by what hair remained after his pigtail had been neatly cut in half. The man's eyes stayed in Silas' memory for several days. There was an innocence and acceptance of his fate, and he could have been no more than twenty. His crime had been admitted and at least he had not been summarily executed on the spot by Chinese captors or bounty hunters, as was often the case. Perhaps in his last days in prison he had found inner peace, thought Silas, and deposited the head with others amongst the bodies.

'Two men! The flag!' bellowed an officer. He pointed to two prisoners against the wall, who ran across, stood at attention and saluted, as was the custom, and accepted a rolled flag from a corporal in British Marine uniform. They crossed to the tall flagpole in the shape of a mainmast with a yard-arm towards the top. Silas noticed that it was set back a short way from the high outer wall. The two men released what reminded him of ships' stays, threaded the flag and ran it to the top of the pole. A bugle echoed throughout the courtyard. All men were forced, as instructed, to stand at attention. The flag was saluted and civilisation returned where barbarism had intruded. Silas and Eli began to pace out the familiar circle.

'We've got to get out of here,' Eli said grimly. Silas did not reply, but paused beside the flagpole and looked up towards the flag cracking in a breeze it caught from above the wall.

'When,' he mused, 'were you last up in the top gallants?'

'Why?' asked Eli. Silas grunted then reached out and touched the loosely knotted rope looped together at the base of the flagpole. His eyes absorbed the expression on Eli's face as he craned towards the flag, examining the strength of the yard-arms.

'Will it hold us both?' he asked quietly.

'We'll find out,' answered Silas.

'When?'

'Soon.'

An officer, seeing the two of them standing still, shouted for them to move and Lubbock and Hayes joined the others shuffling around the courtyard.

The following day, continuing well into the afternoon, it rained so heavily that all exercise was cancelled. Staring gloomily from their respective cells, Silas and Eli watched the flag raised reluctantly by prison officers, cursorily saluted to the strains of the bugle, then left to hang limp and sodden until it was brought down at dusk. For forty-eight hours the rain continued and it was only on the third day after the execution that Silas and Eli saw the first prisoners being led out from 'A' block for exercise in a fine drizzle. It would be touch and go whether the flag was raised whilst he and Eli were out in the yard. The first batch of prisoners were re-manacled beneath a lean-to against one of the walls. Then Silas heard the lock turning in his cell door and voices shouting the length of the tier for prisoners to step out. He took one last look at the naked flagpole and hanging ropes. 'Today', he thought.

'Ready?' he asked loudly, through the bars.

'Ready', came the reply from Eli.

The prisoners lined up on the narrow metal balcony and waited. An order was shouted. With manacles grating on the metal floor, the prisoners shuffled to the head of the stairs and descended gingerly. Audible groans came from many as they were marched into the courtyard to encounter the drizzle and they began to huddle together along the side of the wall, seeking some kind of protection. Silas and Eli and a few others greeted the air gratefully. It was not fresh, but warm and moist and so enervating that Silas consciously braced himself for what was to come. The guard with keys to the manacles approached, unlocking all those who wished to take their exercise out in the rain.

Far across the courtyard, Silas saw the door of the guard room open and several officers peer out. One held the rolled flag, another carried the bugle. Silas nudged Eli. Ropes hung loosely knotted at the base of the flagpole. Across the courtyard, the guards began moving. An officer at Silas' shoulder shouted, 'Two men! The flag!'

Silas and Eli, free of their shackles, stepped forward.

Striding ominously towards the outer gates of the prison, Captain Van, together with a consular official and several British Marines in escort, halted only to show papers, then was ushered beneath an archway into an outer courtyard. The drizzle, fast becoming rain, spattered their long topcoats and it had already created a film on their caps. Captain Van led the group across the courtyard, following a prison guard.

Beside him the consular official played nervously with a briefcase tucked beneath his arm. This was the third time he had been entrusted with such responsibility from the British Consul himself, but whenever he visited Shanghai's house of correction he felt decidedly uncomfortable, as if he too had been sucked into its maw, detained and incarcerated for an indeterminate period of time. The briefcase contained sealed instructions which were to be executed immediately. Captain Van's grim face seemed to make the matter even more grave. The group stopped before another archway, smaller but wider. At the centre there were double doors, with guards either side.

'Hayes and Lubbock,' murmured Captain Van. One of the guards stepped back and snapped to attention.

'Yes, sir, the Governor's expecting you.'

The Governor, a grey-haired man with fine features, stood up as the two men were ushered into his office. He nodded briefly and indicated seats. He took the papers, examined signatures then read the contents.

'As distasteful as this is to me,' said Captain Van, 'I have been given orders regarding Lubbock and Hayes.' He paused. 'To be executed immediately.'

The Governor glanced at Captain Van over reading glasses, said nothing, coughed and continued to absorb the instructions.

'This is unfortunate,' he said slowly, and turned again to the last page, which was signed at the bottom by the British Consul, 'but this signature ensures that it is law. Personally I would have preferred merely to recommend clemency.' He shook his head and looked directly into Captain Van's face, with clear eyes. 'Yes, it is most unfortunate.'

Silas Hayes, with the Union Jack tucked underneath his arm, followed Eli Lubbock across the courtyard to the base of the flag-pole, set no more than four metres from the outer wall of the prison.

'Scotch mist,' growled Silas and, indeed, the rain swirled with a gusting breeze and obscured different parts of the coutyard, giving every reason for other prisoners to remain huddled and the guards reluctant to comply with what was both tradition and instruction. Even the bugler was determined to remain beneath the lean-to until the last moment. The officer in charge, protected by the sloping roof, hung back and waited for the prisoners to thread the flag.

124

Silas jerked the loose halyard, looking up at what, at sea, would have been the cross trees. He was attempting to estimate the strength of the yard and prayed the carpenter had learnt his trade. Rain spattered his face as he pulled on the rope again, lifting from the ground, feeling his muscles tighten in anticipation. A shout from across the coutyard, urging the two men to hurry, prompted Silas to unfurl the flag. He and Eli threaded it, then began to haul the limp colours to the top of the pole. The flag took some life as gusting rain caught it. At the top of the pole it actually cracked once, then the cotton weave sagged.

'Now!' whispered Silas.

From the distance a voice bellowed, 'Attention!' and the bugle plaintively announced British control of the shared prison.

Reaching up then pulling hard and quickly, Silas heaved his body from the ground. Grasping the rope hanging from the other yard, Eli too was climbing as rapidly as his muscles would allow. A shout of alarm went up from one of the officers. Silas let the momentum of his body sway the rope, then he added to it by jerking his feet in front of him and throwing them back. Eli followed suit and, with a prayer, both men hit the wall with the soles of their feet. Absorbing the impact in his legs, Eli pushed off hard and swung back, in tandem with Silas. More shouts came floating across the courtyard through the rain. It was difficult to climb the ropes, which had become slippery, but they seized hard to the wet fibres, knowing they were committed to escape. There could be no turning back now. Hand over hand, the men climbed higher, and on the second swing were only several feet from the top of the wall. They both pushed off again and heard the distinct groaning of wood as the yard took the strain of their combined weight. Below, running feet advanced to the centre of the courtyard and Silas heard a final warning yell. Rifle bolts thrust cartridges into breeches and Silas and Eli prayed bullets would not find a way into their breeches in the next second.

The last swing took each man to the top of the wall. The spikes came as a surprise. A shout from Eli alerted Silas as their bodies rushed towards the coping stones. Only reflex saved them from being snagged and gaffed. Both Silas and Eli found themselves with knees locked over the coping stones and a hard metal spike pressed against their genitals. A volley of rifle fire came from the rain and several bullets smacked into the wall between them.

'Let go!' bellowed Eli and both men relinquished their hold on the ropes. Grasping the spikes between their legs, the two men pulled themselves up, twisted, then hung on the other side of the wall as another volley of bullets chipped the coping stones. Shaking the rain from his face, Eli grinned. 'We're out.'

Silas nodded briefly, knowing there had always been a difference between the two of them. Their physiques and abilities were similar, but Eli's exuberance always contrasted with Silas' caution.

'But not down,' growled Silas, and watched Eli's hands slip from the spikes. With a cry of alarm, Eli plunged towards the ground. Silas, having seen Chinese acrobats, used their trick – he let go and immediately turned in the air, picked his spot and landed heavily in the shallows of the river. Both men were able to wade to the first jetty and climb from the mud and silt-laden waters. They mounted corroding metal steps on to the rain-drenched timbers of an old wharf.

'I thought . . .' began Eli with a pale face, and glanced back at the high wall.

'What?' asked Silas.

'I didn't know there was a creek . . .'

Silas raised his brows. 'You would have jumped from forty feet on to hard ground?'

Eli grinned and nodded. 'We're out, aren't we?'

Silas smiled slowly, knowing they must run if they were to elude pursuit. 'And away,' he said.

The Governor finished his examination of the papers brought to him by Captain Van. The consular official indicated a space for the Governor to sign, next to the British Consul, at the bottom of the third sheet. Pen poised, the Governor checked the last paragraph, which stated quite clearly the fate of the two men. He looked for a moment into the face of Captain Van, which was grim and angry.

'I will comply and execute as instructed,' he said, and paused. 'But be clear that this is certainly not my wish, and knowing the facts, is against all personal judgement I might bring to bear against these men.' If there was any expression that the Governor would remember for future reference in the naval officer's eyes, it was that of a man who had been cheated. The Governor signed the paper with a flourish.

'So be it, then,' he said, took up the sheaf and handed it to the consular official. 'Silas Hayes and Eli Lubbock are pardoned.'

7

The mouth of the rainbow was the agreed destination for both Silas and Eli. The Hong Kew district was so named because it was bounded by a creek in the shape of an arch. The two friends' dishevelled appearance became noticeable to the increasingly more elegant pedestrians who had the advantage of sheltering beneath umbrellas. Trams passed by which, even although almost fully loaded, the two men might have boarded had they any money; however, they had no choice but to trudge the wet pavements, past a series of imposing buildings. Already weary from lack of exercise and meagre prison rations, they had barely enough energy left to walk; running was out of the question.

Silas nudged Eli and pointed. The two men reached a rickshaw stand, where Silas reacquainted himself with a tall, thin Chinaman who had once been a crew member on a ship he had captained. Min Ho had been a bad cook but a good friend and Silas had decided to claim a favour.

'You're losing your muscle,' he smiled. Min Ho's teeth had gone the way of most of his hair and his spare frame belied the fact that once he had been a well-built seaman. He bowed on seeing Silas, then again to Eli. Being of unusual stature, he was called 'Run Lick' Min Ho, so named by an American who declared, 'He goes at quite a lick.' Fallen on rough times, he was still making a living and known even amongst his contemporaries as one of the best.

In very little time the tough and wiry Chinaman had brought both men across wet cobbles to the gates of the American Consulate. Two US Marines blocked the rickshaw, and Silas and Eli were ordered out. One of the Marines came to attention, then saluted, which took Silas and Eli aback. Their condition hardly required respect.

'Mr Hayes, Mr Lubbock?'

Silas nodded, as did Eli, slowly, apprehensive of what might follow. An officer stepped out of the guard building, saluted leisurely and smiled. The warm American accent was comforting to both men, though his words surprised them even more.

'The Consul was expecting you.' The officer took out a pocket watch and cradled it to protect the silver from the rain, and declared, 'but not quite so soon. . . .'

'Expecting?' said Eli, perplexed.

'I wonder if you would . . .' began Silas, with as much charm as he could muster and indicated the rickshaw and Min Ho, who bowed with respect. One of the Marines paid Min Ho, then Silas and Eli were ushered into a large marble hallway, out of the rain and back into sophisticated civilisation. Both men felt decidedly uncomfortable as they squelched across the marble behind the smartly turned out officer, noting some evidence of confusion about them. Crates, boxes and personal possessions were stacked not only in the hallway, but in corridors leading off to both administration and private quarters. The officer knocked on double doors, which were opened by a consular official who took over, examining the bedraggled and unshaven arrivals with distaste. He too checked a pocket watch, noting that it was almost eleven-thirty, and was surprised that prison formalities had taken such a short time.

'And where are Captain Van and my British colleague?' he asked, with a look which Silas identified as being pomposity with a Virginia strain.

'Who?' asked Eli.

'Well,' snapped the man, readjusting his lapels, 'I

129

suppose you want me to believe you released yourselves?'

Eli glanced quickly at Silas, who although he had not plumbed the mystery, decided to bluff it out.

'I'm sure they'll be along in a minute,' he smiled, then sniffed the air. 'Now what on earth is that?'

The dapper little consular official dropped his chin and glared across half-glasses at the two men, 'Brunch,' he said.

'Then we're not too late?' smiled Eli.

'On the contrary,' said the little man; readjusting his tie he stepped to the two doors, 'you are too early.' He turned the knob and ushered the two men into the consulate dining room. It was large, ornate, with two chandeliers hanging over a long table. Tall windows allowed sufficient light into the room to make it bright and attractive and despite the time of troubles there was the luxury of flowers, beautifully displayed with a woman's touch. The sideboard groaned with everything from eggs to kedgeree. The assembled group, Hollis Jackson, Cornelia, Adèle and Jamie amongst them, looked on in some surprise as the Consul, checking his pocket watch, rose in astonishment. 'How the . . . ?' the Consul began loudly.

Silas decided to rescue the situation and snapped to attention with a salute. 'Rickshaw, sir!' he said.

'What?' asked the Consul, not comprehending.

'Damn it, Jackson, speak to these men!' he barked impatiently.

Hollis Jackson smiled, stroked a clean-shaven chin and examined the condition of his old shipmates. He leant back in his chair, spreading an arm behind Cornelia, whose eyes seemed to be inflicting actual bodily harm on her ex-husband.

'We,' began Hollis Jackson, 'obtained a release for you both.'

The words penetrated the minds of Silas and Eli like

130

hot knives and, not daring to look at each other, each man swallowed mightily. Noise outside at the gates prompted the Consul across to one of the long windows where he peered out into the rain and saw some confusion as both British Marines and prison guards, together with Shanghai police, were being refused entry at the gates. A crowd had already gathered about them. The men looked in a sorry state, as if they had pursued with hue and cry a quarry which had escaped them. In the spacious room there was complete silence. The Consul's mind may not have been fast, but it went about its tasks with some efficiency, therefore in the space of several seconds the American Government's representative in Shanghai turned slowly with the glimmer of a truth he would have preferred not to have guessed.

'Anticipation, gentlemen?' asked the Consul. He shook his head, unable to pass judgement against either man. He had known Silas as family with great affection, and Eli Lubbock had never been more than a scoundrel, but. . . .

'Well, God damn it!' exploded the Consul, and pointed in the direction of the groaning sideboard, 'eat!'

Jamie was curious to see how much his father could get on the sizeable Wedgwood platter, but even he would have lost a bet as he saw Eli return to the table carrying his plate with two hands. Silence prevailed at the dining table as almost twenty guests watched the two grown men consume their victuals as a lion might devour its prey. Tearing a strip of ham from his mouth, Eli, partly satisfied, nodded at the boy whom he recognised as Silas' son.

''Allo, Jamie. How old are you now?' he mumbled, swallowing.

'Don't talk with your mouth full,' said the boy, with laughter in his eyes.

'Jamie!' hissed Cornelia.

131

'That's what you always tell me, Mother,' said the boy righteously.

'Manners maketh the man, Jamie,' retorted Cornelia. 'And a man knows just when to say nothing.'

'Or keep his mouth shut?' suggested Jamie. 'That's what you used to say to Father.'

'Jamie!' Cornelia seized the boy's shoulder and shook him.

'Leave him alone!' growled Silas, 'Let the boy speak.'

Cornelia's head turned slowly towards her ex-husband and yet again she felt a shiver down her spine as she recognised all too well the power of the man and reluctantly remembered some of the more pleasant occasions they had shared.

'You are hardly an example to give advice, Silas Hayes.'

Silas nodded and leaned forward on the table. 'The wonderful and comforting thing,' he said, 'as I have always told you, my dear Cornelia, is that in having a conversation with a paragon of virtue, you always know instantly that whatever advice you may give, or opinion you may hold, it can only, if it is opposed by that paragon, be wrong.'

Cornelia blushed distinctly. 'How *dare you* speak to me . . . ?'

'I was not, of course, madam referring to you, although your reaction lends itself to a suspicion that perhaps I have described a category into which you might find a way.'

Adèle giggled. Eli shook his head, genuinely impressed. 'You always had a way with words, Silas.'

The American Consul, seeing the strain in his daughter's face, coughed to gain attention. He introduced Silas and Eli to the refugees from the northern provinces who made up the majority of the table. The conversation turned to the eroding of law and order in Northern China. The refugees gave examples of

132

outright aggression, brute force and violence. They declared themselves lucky to have escaped with their lives, having lost most of their possessions fleeing south. Others of their acquaintance had not been so lucky and tears were shed amongst the women.

The Consul reassured them that, so far, Shanghai had escaped extensive damage, but the pall of smoke that hung over the Chinese quarter gave him grave concern that the situation might change.

An explosion sounded distantly. Riots had begun again in the Chinese quarter. The moment distracted the table and lost the Consul's concentration.

The Consul resumed. 'Gentlemen and ladies, we are here for one reason. Some of you have been given accommodation in this very consulate because of the circumstances which have arisen. What ships are available are either fully loaded, over-booked, or have been seconded for our navies for transport duties up north. Some of us will remain; others wish to go. Destinations will vary. If you wish to leave it is my duty, a responsibility which I have accepted, to at least attempt to find you berths.'

He coughed, feeling the oppressiveness of the summer humidity and the irritation in his throat. Outside, drizzle and rain became a downpour which gusted against the glass on a wind blowing in from the distant sea. Suddenly he felt exhausted. China was sapping his energies, and where he had once taken a pleasure in his duties, he now performed them with an inner reluctance which he found disturbing. Perhaps he too had run his course and this ancient country would, indeed, destroy all that modern development had attempted to create. He nodded across the table and sat down as Hollis Jackson stood up.

'Ladies and gentlemen,' he began, 'the situation in China is now critical, as we are all too well aware. We have been given time to consider the possibilities.

Many of us have large investments here. Some of us have already lost them, but what is most valuable – our lives – we must protect as we defend our property. There are some who are duty-bound to remain. Others can choose to be removed from Shanghai.'

He cleared his throat, like the Consul, feeling the oppressiveness as he looked at the faces staring towards him, some impassive, others with hope that he would provide a solution and – better – transport. He felt a film of sweat on his brow and even though the fans in the ceiling spun lazily, felt uncomfortable in his starched shirt, dark brocade waistcoat and tailored suit.

'I'll come to the point,' he said. 'I have here three large vessels which I am prepared to put at the disposal of all who wish to leave.' There was a murmur at the table and, certainly amongst the women, eyes brightened. 'Many berths have already been taken. Others have been sought for some time. But if you are prepared to endure a little suffering in the interests of safety, those who wish to return to Europe may well be there by the turn of the year.'

There was some spontaneous applause at this; Hollis, now in command of the table, waited patiently for it to cease.

'I have, as I said, three vessels, but only one captain capable of navigating what is essentially almost half of the world.' He glanced at Silas and Eli, who were staring at him, awaiting his every word. Yes, he thought, I have them now; so he paused and looked at the Consul. 'I believe . . .' he began.

The Consul nodded. 'Yes,' he said, 'the first of several American Line ships will be here in only a matter of days to take out those wishing to leave for San Francisco. What must not be forgotten is that every day the danger of a blockade on the Yangtse grows. If the rebels are able to sink one large vessel in the channel,' he shrugged, 'I think the results would be self-explanatory.'

Silence fell. Rain spattered the windows. The fans spun. Another distant explosion rumbled amongst the buildings bordering the Chinese bund. Silas Hayes shifted in his seat and looked at Hollis Jackson.

'What is the condition of your . . . ships?' he asked quietly.

Jackson stepped behind his chair and leaned nonchalantly on its back, staring at Silas with a face empty of expression.

'Two were built in Scotland forty years ago.' He saw Silas desperately trying to control his excitement and went on smoothly, 'They are square-rigged and weathered, but sound. Their "condition",' he enunciated the word clearly, 'has been maintained carefully. They are a recent acquisition of mine, being unwanted by a merchant friend who, sadly, went bankrupt.' He smiled, 'With the twentieth century fast approaching, the poor man seemed content to live with the ideals of the eighteenth. Times are changing, Silas, and in trade, at least, one must go with them, or sink.' The word was chosen carefully and he saw both Hayes and Lubbock wince with a seaman's fear at its implications.

'What are they?' asked Eli.

'Tea clippers,' said Hollis. 'Built for racing.' He watched Eli glance at Silas.

'And what do you want?' growled Silas.

'I simply need two men of experience to sail them,' stated Jackson.

Eli wiped his mouth nervously. 'And you can't?' he asked.

Jackson stood erect and smoothed his long jacket. 'I have a captain for my ship, as I have a driver for my carriage. My business now is commerce, at which I am proven successful and, frankly, I have no desire to sail in anything unless,' he added hastily, 'I am a passenger

in pleasant and, I might add, modern surroundings.'
He looked at Cornelia for a moment and Silas detected
more than he had imagined in the relationship.

'Well, well!' murmured Silas.

'Are you interested?' asked Jackson.

Silas began to laugh. 'You know damn well. . . .'

There was a sharp knock at the outer doors. All eyes
turned as the British Consul was shown in. He nodded
curtly to the group.

'Good morning,' he said.

His American counterpart was already on his feet.
'Please excuse us for one moment, ladies and
gentlemen. May I introduce you to the British Consul?'

'Please don't get up,' said the new arrival. 'Mr
Jackson, would you bring Lubbock and Hayes with
you.'

'Yes, sir,' said Jackson, and motioned to Silas and
Eli.

The five men went into the large panelled study which
was the American's private workroom and sanctum.
Jackson closed the door and looked the two ex-prisoners
up and down.

'My God,' he murmured, 'you two smell as high as
dead rats!'

The British Consul also examined the condition of
the two men. 'You're a disgrace to your nation!' he
exclaimed. 'Before you do anything else, after this
meeting, I want you to clean yourselves up.'

Eli nodded. 'Merely the effects of a month of British
hospitality, sir.'

'I think that's quite enough!' snapped the British
Consul. 'I've come to say what I must. In different
circumstances you, Lubbock and Hayes, would at best
spend the greater part of your lives – if,' and he looked
directly towards Eli, 'you were allowed to keep them,
something which your associations makes certainly to

my mind, very dubious – you would spend them,' he repeated, 'in Her Majesty's prisons. As it is, you may thank the Dowager Empress-Tsu-Hsi's condoning the Boxer rebellion for your. . . .' He paused.

'Pardon?' suggested Eli.

'Release,' countered the British Consul, and glanced at his American colleague. 'Have they agreed, Mr Morgan?'

Jackson answered, 'Yes, sir, they have.'

'Then you have three weeks to crew up,' said the British Consul. 'You will be underway by midday of 22 September, or Captain Van has clear instructions for your rearrest and incarceration.'

'But our – ' began Silas.

Morgan interrupted. 'Your effects are being brought here. You will be provided an escort until you sail.'

The British Consul nodded and sighed wearily. 'This morning reports confirmed that the rebellion which has erupted throughout China has now taken hold everywhere. Reinforcements to the meagre troops we have here will, unfortunately, be slow in coming. The British Empire itself, which has guaranteed peace throughout her spheres of influence for more than half a century, is threatened. In South Africa there is already war. At the present time our resources are stretched to their limits.' He shook his head and stepped to the door. 'Thank you, Mr Morgan. I am pleased at least that we have that settled. If there had been any other choice of captains for these ships, believe me they would have been recommended.' Grudgingly he glanced at Hayes and Lubbock and said, 'Good luck.'

The two men nodded, then, following Silas, Eli too snapped to attention. The British Consul opened the door.

'Here we are on the brink of the twentieth century,' he said, 'and what have we? Turmoil.' He sighed again.

'God help us all! Goodbye, gentlemen.' He stepped out and closed the door.

The spacious study was silent but for the ticking of an ornate clock on the mantelpiece above a large fireplace. Rain on the windows drew the American Consul to look out. Even though it was almost midday, the sky was dark and the atmosphere dismal.

'There'll be a storm before dusk', murmured Silas, joining Morgan.

'I want to thank you,' stated the Consul, and held out a hand.

'For what?'

'*You* found her.'

Silas nodded and glanced at Eli, who was talking to Jackson.

'*He* kept her alive,' said Silas, 'and what thanks do either of us get?'

'Mine,' smiled the Consul. He turned from the window and looked back into the room. 'Adèle seems to be quite taken with Eli.'

Silas pursed his lips and said nothing. The Consul's eyes examined Silas and, dishevelled as he was, still acknowledged him with admiration and affection.

'It seems to run in the family, Silas. My daughters, for all their pomp and circumstance, find the likes of you . . . interesting. I wonder why, when they could have any man?'

'He's not *any* man, sir,' said Silas.

'Neither are you,' said the Consul quietly. 'I'm only sorry that Cornelia. . . .' He lowered his head a moment, then recovered his composure. 'Jamie's a fine boy. He's been spoilt by his mother and needs. . . .'

Silas turned away and stepped closer to the window. Staring out, he saw not Shanghai and the rain, but that other life he had once led in the boom town of San Francisco. It contrasted with society's attempts at sophistication in Chicago and his wife's aspirations in

New York, where he had lost her as she had lost that wild spirit for which he had fallen, so many years before.

'How could I help him?' muttered Silas.

'You might, one day,' said the Consul, 'Don't reject him. Remember, somewhere inside him he has your spirit.'

Silas looked at the man he had liked as his father-in-law. 'We were always friends, weren't we, Henry?'

'Always will be, I hope.' The older man coughed.

Silas Hayes smiled. 'It was you got us out, wasn't it?'

The Consul nodded and began to chuckle. 'When you have a daughter who for almost a month babbles into your ear ludicrous stories of the heroism of two men incarcerated on her behalf . . . what else could I do but get you out? Jackson provided the perfect excuse.'

'Thank you,' said Silas.

The Consul's eyes assumed an alert sharpness. 'I hope you can still do it, Silas. It's been some time since you were blue water sailing.'

The sea captain's face hardened. 'If I have sound timbers, strong canvas and the stars are still where I remember them to be, by God I'll chart a course that will make the fastest wake you've seen leave the China coast.'

'I'm pleased to hear it,' said the Consul, 'because it is my intention to entrust you with a life I hold dearer than my own.' Seeing Silas about to speak, he went on quickly, 'She has expressed a wish to be in New York, but to travel first to England.'

'Who?' asked Silas, concerned with the possible alternatives.

The Consul hesitated and in that moment Eli shouted across the study, excitement in his voice, 'Hollis tells me they were both cracks in their day.'

All three men looked at Hollis Jackson, who nodded. 'They were fast, if they were sailed with experience – so I hear.'

'Well, let's see them then,' growled Silas.

Jackson grinned. 'You shall.'

Silas and Eli were escorted into upstairs rooms which they were to occupy until departure. Eli fell straight into a bath which had already been run for him and actually fell asleep for almost an hour, until the hot water became merely tepid. He had lost all of his clothes during the Triad adventure. As he examined the clothes provided for him, some in a large wardrobe, others still packed, newly delivered from the tailors, he realised some perception must have gone into the selection. In fact, as he was forced to admit, the clothes were probably better than he would have chosen for himself. A short note from Adèle on the bedside table cleared the mystery, and he lay back on the bed, smoking a cigar from the box she had left him, now shaved and perfumed like some toff, as he murmured to himself. He began to laugh from the pure pleasure of knowing that, perhaps for the first time in many months, he might have landed on his feet.

Silas telephoned Emily with genuine concern. Of course there were tears; she was pregnant, a young woman alone, in love and hounded by creditors since Silas' embarkation aboard the British man-o'-war. On his arrival in Shanghai she had been informed that he was a prisoner, but she had been unable to visit him, despite going to the prison gates and telephoning many times. She had borrowed money from several friends who had now returned to Australia. When Silas' bags had been sent for and the bill authorised paid from consular funds she had collapsed on the sofa and into further floods of tears, thinking herself now destitute, rejected and abandoned. The hotel porters were already at the door with instructions to throw her out as Silas' voice came on the line.

With new self-assurance, she had her bags and trunks taken to the lobby and placed in a carriage, and instructed the driver to take her to the American Consulate.

Silas was half-naked and shaving when Emily arrived in their suite. He smiled a greeting through the soap on his face, stemming her tears of happiness as he pointed to the full bath.

Emily undressed and slid into the warm water as Silas continued to scrape the heavy stubble from his firm features. Only when he was clean-shaven did he kneel beside her in the bath and kiss her tenderly.

She stepped from the bath, as the water gurgled away and Silas gently rubbed her lovely body dry with a large, soft towel supplied courtesy of the American Consul. Silas bent and kissed her naked belly and she drew him to her, releasing the towel at his waist, holding his lean body tightly.

'You've lost weight,' she murmured.

'And you're putting it on,' whispered Silas in her ear. She began laughing. Silas picked her up and carried her into the bedroom, laying her gently on the quilt. She stretched and sighed, believing everything that had happened to her in the last few hours was perhaps a dream from which she did not want to wake. Silas gazed from the window, looking beyond the small balcony across the gardens to the shrouded city, where he could see the bund through the sheeting rain.

'Silas, is this real?' he heard Emily ask.

He nodded to himself. 'It's real enough,' he murmured, and thought of the last time he had emerged from the Sunda Straits into the vast open ocean with a roaring north-east trade wind prevailing. Then he had both eyes on his full set of canvas, marking each clew and yard. Thrusting through following waves under a clear tropic sky was a heady experience but the responsibilities of speed at sea in a sleek wind-jammer could never be discounted. One gust and the top-gallants might go, the yards snap, the braces fray or the stays unravel. It had been too long, thought Silas, feeling a surge inside as he remembered other days standing beneath the stars lashed by spray, dreaming of exactly what was now a reality. He turned and crossed back to the bed and the beautiful woman who was to bear his child. He stared at her silently.

'Silas?' questioned Emily. He kissed her – that was real, but lying beside her, his eyes closed, he saw billowing canvas over blue water. Emily sensed his excitement and he told her what had been offered by Jackson. They slipped beneath the quilt and renewed their acquaintanceship, talking and loving as lovers do. His hard, weathered body was a sharp contrast to her soft, white, yielding flesh, and only as they dozed beneath the slowly spinning fan, in a bliss they had created for themselves, did the sun break through the cloud, flooding the room with light.

A servant politely knocked at the outer door to leave tea in the lounge. Minutes later the telephone rang.

'No, you're not disturbing us,' answered Silas. 'What time is it? Thank you,' he said and replaced the receiver. 'I've got to go. We have thirty minutes.' He swung his legs from the bed and stepped over to the large wardrobe where, with silent efficiency, his clothes had been hung by a servant whilst they had been in the bathroom. He began to dress.

'Where are you going?' asked Emily.

He grinned. 'Down to the sea.'

A carriage was waiting for both Silas and Eli, and now that the rain had stopped, the hoods were dropped. Leaning back, smelling the freshening air on a gusting wind, the two men enjoyed the city streets in the unfamiliar luxury fortune had provided. Reaching the bund, they passed through several check points guarded not only by Marines, but also by Customs officers and police. The added security meant, quite obviously, that real trouble was brewing in Shanghai, worse than was being declared and possibly greater than had been anticipated. The sight of several burnt warehouses sobered both men as they realised exactly what might happen if the insurrection in China took hold here, in a city where Europeans had created perhaps the greatest testament to Western culture, architecture and diplomacy throughout the Far East.

The two men alighted from their carriage in front of an open door at the centre of a tall warehouse which concealed a gantry and cranes on the quayside.

They were met by a clerk, ushered through a hallway, along a corridor and up some steps into a chartroom, where a huge window overlooking the bund gave a view across the river.

Jackson turned from a map, blew smoke into the air from a cigar and smiled.

'Welcome, gentlemen. My, my how much better you both look.' He crossed to double doors which opened out on to a balcony. 'I can't say my offices are humble, because they are not. I have sought success and achieved it. All this is but a small part of what I own, but it does represent ambition hitting the mark.' Jackson opened the doors. 'Think – we all began together – how different we have become.' He smiled at them genially. 'Where we were once equals, now *I* am to employ *you*.'

'We were never equal,' growled Silas. Eli said nothing, merely gritting his teeth, as the three men stepped out on to the balcony. Jackson leaned on the rail and wafted an arm.

'Well, boys,' he said, 'what do you think?'

Two square-rigged tea clippers, bowsprit to

bowsprit, figureheads gazing at each other, lay high in the water against the wharf. With practised eyes, Silas and Eli absorbed the lines and what condition they could detect at a distance.

'You'll find them in good order,' said Jackson. 'Have no fear of that.'

Silas peered and Eli squinted against the sudden harsh sunlight. Clouds had parted, illuminating both ships so that braces glittered and brass shone. Their names were clearly written above the anchors slung at their respective bows. Each captain decided, as perhaps each ship chose.

'*Chantril*,' whispered Eli.

'*Vesper*,' mumured Silas.

'They are yours, gentlemen,' stated Jackson. 'You are now in command.'

Neither of the two vessels was over a thousand tons, nor were they more than three hundred feet long, but each was undoubtedly a ship, in the term used both correctly and affectionately by seamen who understood the requirements of the name. On each of their three masts the yards carried square canvas, which was furled and therefore concealed the condition.

'Well, they look bonny,' grunted Silas, trying to hide his excitement.

'They've standing crews,' began Jackson, 'but you'll have to find your own mates and any addition you wish to add to their complements. You've two sets of canvas and, I'm told, enough spare wire, cable, rope, spars and tools to jury-rig either ship across any open ocean before a full force gale.' He smiled. 'All you require is the expertise to do it.'

Silas turned slowly to face Jackson. 'Are you doubting our ability?' he asked quietly.

'I doubt everything until it's proved,' replied Jackson.

Silas nodded. 'When you come up the Thames, we'll be waiting for you.'

'Both of you?' asked Jackson, glancing at Eli.

'Both of us,' answered Eli.

Jackson pursed his lips, took out a cigar from his leather case and, keeping his eyes on both men, lit the tobacco slowly.

Wind gusted about the balcony, bringing noises from the bustling harbourside. Cupping his hands, Jackson allowed the match to go out and blew smoke, which was whipped over his shoulder, curling to the window where it disappeared amidst the reflections of the two sleek clippers.

'Do you want to make a bet?' he asked.

Silas and Eli remained silent.

'First home to the Thames,' went on Jackson, and indicated the two ships with his lit cigar. 'Those hulks and your earned salary to keep against. . . .' He paused and smiled, watching the studiedly impassive faces of the two men.

'Against what?' asked Eli.

'Why, nothing at all,' said Jackson.

'You mean you want to take three months' hard-earned money from us?'

'You have nothing else,' said Jackson. 'And you're both gambling men.'

'And when we win,' said Eli, 'we are to keep both ships and wage?'

Jackson nodded and drew on his cigar again. 'If, Eli . . . if.'

Silas looked at his friend and was about to stop Eli reaching out impetuously, but too late.

'The Thames,' declared Eli. Jackson took the hand and both men shook. Silas' eyes narrowed. Instinct told him to be wary, but Jackson's supercilious smile prompted him also to extend his hand, and the bet was sealed.

'The Thames,' grinned Jackson.

'You call them hulks,' said Silas. 'What have you, that your captain's so proud of? New canvas and a caulked bottom?'

Jackson began laughing and threw back his head as he turned and again pointed with his cigar.

'I have no canvas, unless it be awnings over the sun deck where we dine in clement weather.'

Silas and Eli could see, beyond the two old clippers, the brand new steamship, polished, painted and moored some way out towards the channel. No words were necessary. As both Silas and Eli knew, Jackson had bought himself two captains for nothing.

'She's called *Otranto*,' stated the steamship owner proudly. 'She was commissioned in Birkenhead and made her way out here in no time at all, as I'm sure she will return.' He wafted a hand expansively and indicated the door back into the large office. 'So, you see, it won't be her maiden voyage, she will be travelling with experience.'

Silas smiled wryly, taking his eyes from the smokestack in the distance.

'Like your women,' he growled, and stepped through the doorway before Jackson could respond.

A world chart took up most of a large table. When the three men were grouped around it, Jackson, having given orders that Eli's and Silas' logs and personal charts be brought up, stayed the two men, offering tea and indicating with some relish the two different routes from Shanghai.

'My first bunker port will be Singapore, where we will take on coal before crossing to Ceylon, then' – his finger traced where he already imagined the wake of his ship – 'up the Suez Canal, into the Mediterranean.' He looked at Eli and Silas, whose eyes in turn were already tracing what they knew to be their route, dictated by the best winds. Jackson's finger drew it with a sweep. 'You, gentlemen, of course, must go the long way, around the Cape of Good Hope.' He put the cigar in his mouth and puffed, as tea arrived on a tray, served by an ageing Chinaman. 'Wind against coal,' stated Jackson, and held out a small cup of hot tea as if in a toast. 'Good luck,' he said. Eli shook his head.

'It's *bad* luck to propose a toast unless it's been poured from a bottle. You know that, Hollis.'

Jackson examined his teacup for a moment, exuberance ebbing. 'I forgot,' he said flatly.

Silas smiled and glanced across the room, where numerous bottles were on display in an open cabinet. He crossed to it and quickly poured three tots of rum, which he offered. Lifting his, he waited until all three glasses were touching.

'You see, Hollis,' he said, 'in days gone by people didnae trust each other, so even though a bottle was broached they would pour a little from one glass into the other.'

He watched the two men – Eli amused, Jackson disturbed – comply, spilling rum from one glass into another. Silas waited until they all again had equal amounts. 'Do you get the point, Hollis? If there was poison present, it would be shared by all.' He nodded that the men should drink. 'An old custom, with quaint reasoning, don't you think?' He glanced at Eli, lifted his glass and proposed, 'The winner!' Both men took their shot of rum in one gulp. Hollis Jackson drank slowly.

With some of the larger charts rolled under their arms, and others, together with their logs, in sizeable briefcases clutched in their hands, Eli Lubbock and Silas Hayes retraced their steps through Hollis Jackson's offices and went out to their waiting carriage. Although there was again rain on the wind, Silas ignored it and leaned back against one of the lowered hoods. He stared for a moment at the sombre expression on Eli's face, and instructed the driver to take them around to the quayside. Negotiating the cobbles and pressing through the crowds of dockworkers, officials and passengers, the carriage halted opposite the clippers' bowsprits, where the figureheads gazed upon each other – both mermaids, one with a torch, the other a lamp.

'At least we'll have the north-east monsoons behind our backs before we hit the trades off Java Head,' consoled Silas, watching Eli gaze gloomily towards the ship he had agreed to sail half-way around the world. The excitement had been taken from both men by Jackson's revelation as effectively as wind from a sail. The prospect of a race had been dashed and, although the two men would indeed be captains for the duration, on arrival in England they would be left with nothing.

'Nothing at all,' said Eli quietly, repeating Jackson's words. 'Either of us could beat him and win. For myself that would have made me content for the rest of my life.' He looked at Silas and shook his head. 'Can you imagine . . . I thought for a moment we had both fallen on our feet good and solid this time.'

'You made the bet,' Silas reminded him.

'Which is lost before it's begun,' Eli finished angrily. 'Damn Suez!' He slammed his fist against the carriage. 'I've a brother of mine who made his way to a commission, who's stationed in Egypt, on the Frenchy's* canal.'

Silas nodded. 'It'll take us a minimum of one hundred days to get back. In a steamship he will make it in a maximum of seventy. With the Mediterranean sluicing into the Indian Ocean, he's got all the time in the world.'

Rain began falling heavily, forcing them to lift the hoods and secure them at the centre, leaving only two

*It was designed by the French engineer Ferdinand de Lesseps

apertures to peer out of as the driver took them away from the harbourside. The two men had decided to eat together at their old haunt, the Navigator Bar, where they could pay several of their smaller bills with money given them as expenses by Jackson. They were silent as wheels clattered over cobbles, oblivious to the noises surrounding the carriage and horses. When the driver shouted 'Whoa!' and halted outside their destination, neither Eli nor Silas moved. Both men had survived many years on their wits and, even in the face of what seemed to be an insurmountable problem, they were reluctant to concede defeat so early in what otherwise, each knew, would prove to be the race of a lifetime.

'Suez,' said Eli softly.

'Bunker ports,' muttered Silas. 'We'll have the wind, God willing, but he's got to buy his coal in each bunker port where he *must* stop.' Each man had begun thinking aloud.

'What we've got to buy ourselves is time,' murmured Eli, 'The question is, how?'

'Not how,' said Silas, 'why? The answer is *Chantril* and *Vesper* will be ours.'

Eli suddenly brightened at the thought and grinned wickedly at Silas.

'Then there's the question of you or me. There's only one winner in a race, Silas; you want to make a bet?'

Silas clasped his friend's hand and, as they shook, he smiled slowly.

'You know, Eli, I think I've got an idea.'

8

It took a week to establish some order on both ships, which were not exactly as Jackson had described them. It was a fact that they looked 'bonny' as Silas had observed, but upon close examination, canvas had to be replaced, as well as numerous braces and, in all, three of the yards on both ships. Ropes had been tarred and oiled over where they had already gone rotten, but the brass shone and the decks were clean.

'If we had carpets,' Silas said, 'we'd have found all the dirt beneath them.'

By the end of the second week both *Vesper* and *Chantril* were at least Bristol fashion, although not ship-shape. Silas and Eli had put out the word, interviewed several additional crew at the Navigator Bar and found their respective mates, one of whom had come down the coast from Peking with horrific stories; China appeared to be disintegrating fast. Only in Shanghai was the European influence managing to cling to a semblance of law and order.

Riots were a daily occurrence and the increasing mood of tension between the Chinese and their self-declared masters had begun to make even Eli and Silas apprehensive. They studied their charts, becoming familiar with their elected routes into the South China Sea and out into the Indian Ocean.

The weather, in those weeks, remained heavy. Lowering cloud and occasional rainstorms during the day maintained the humidity and as the motley crew of Chinese and Europeans bent their backs refitting both clippers, their sweat was testament to the effort involved. Tempers occasionally ran high and several times Silas and Eli were forced to stop knife fights and, aboard *Chantril* one late afternoon of the third week, Eli proved to be too late on the scene. He lost his Second Mate with a bowie knife embedded in his back; the Chinaman escaped on the waterfront, over sampans and disappeared into the Chinese quarter. This served as a disturbing reminder to Eli that, as he had heard, the Triads considered him their enemy and, despite his protests to several envoys sent by Kin Sang, he knew they were not convinced that fate had delivered up the secret haven and Portuguese fortress to Silas Hayes. Now that Kin Sang had resorted to threats, Eli Lubbock began to count the hours he must remain in Shanghai, knowing each one of them increased his danger. The Marine guard he and Silas had at their disposal merely served to protect each man from his creditors, who hung around at the gangways in the hope that their protests for payment might succeed.

News of the imminent departures had created speculation, not merely among the seafaring community, but also among the Chinese, and once rumour became gossip that it was to be a race, bets were made and a book quickly formed. There were many takers at all odds for each ship, but betting was heavily weighted in favour of *Otranto*, although some – perhaps more courageous or foolhardy – suggested that the steamship might break down or even sink, and laid their wagers on the windjammers, favouring Silas Hayes initially until the last few days, when it was thought Eli Lubbock had the edge.

Hollis Jackson was content merely to examine his passenger list, ensure that steerage was not too overcrowded, accept tenders for cargo and wind up his business, delegating authority to the few he felt he could trust. Neither Silas nor Eli had found much time to spend in their accommodation at the American Consulate. What meals they had been allowed to attend

151

were formal and stuffy and merely confirmed for each man that this was not a world to which they belonged, but Cornelia thrived, as Silas could see clearly. She loved the environment and seemed, as he quietly observed, to be getting on famously with Hollis Jackson, whose attentions were a form of amusement to him.

Cornelia only ever spoke to Silas to remind him that the lawyers' papers would shortly be in her hands and everything had been prepared for signature, officially ending an epoch in both their lives. Silas saw little of Jamie, and then he was almost always in his velvet and ruff, beside his mother. Attempts to catch him on his own, or, as he had suggested on one occasion, bring him to the harbourside, were met with polite rebuttal. He had better things to do, Silas was informed by Cornelia, and must prepare himself for his further education back in the United States. She remained adamant and icy. The veneer Silas had grown to dislike was no longer merely a façade of sophistication. If fools like Hollis Jackson wished to pander to her, then Silas was grateful he had escaped her allure.

On the morning of 20 September, the two first mates, Billy Williams from *Chantril* and Hughie Sutherland from *Vesper*, reported to their captains that although not everything was at its best, in their opinion the two clippers were sound and seaworthy for the long voyage ahead. Apart from 'greasing the water-line', which would allow them a few extra knots, Hughie had grinned, they were ready to take on the steamship. It would have been an exaggeration to say that the entire bund now buzzed with talk of the declared race, but certainly in the Navigator Bar there was talk of little else.

What started at midday as a cloudburst, turned into a downpour and drove all those fortunate enough to be able to choose off the streets. Only dockers and porters continued to trudge across the quayside, slipping on the submerged cobbles, drenched by the warm rain and often unable to pick their way beneath their huge bundles without shouts, commands and, as the day lowered, swinging lamps in the hands of overseers, to indicate their direction.

Silas and Eli had agreed to halt the final loading of their own cargoes, preferring their men to work at night in the hope that the rain would stop. A dry cargo had always been essential in the old tea days and remained a habit both men found difficult to change. This, if an excuse was necessary for the history of what happened that afternoon in the large upstairs bar room, was why so many of each crew who were not on duty found themselves in the Navigator. The men had been paid money in advance and some, at least, were aware of the privations of a long sea trip. Perhaps it can also be said that the large whorehouse to the rear of the bar was convenient. Certainly the stream of men traversing the narrow alley, exchanging their stools and seats with other shipmates who emerged with grins, indicated that not all their money was being spent on drink. Nevertheless, as was generally agreed amongst the Chinese, the prime culprit was the rain which fell from the heavens, and therefore the whole incident must have been God's will. It was also agreed that perhaps if the crew of the steamship *Otranto* had not been allowed to mix with the clipper crews . . . but, as Silas Hayes said later, 'Speculation is easy after the event. History records facts.'

The fight started as a disagreement; a 'skirmish' as Hughie Sutherland put it, when the two captains, Silas and Eli, stepped up to the first floor, expecting to cross to the sheltered balcony beneath the eaves where they had reserved a table. Loud oaths were a prelude to fists. A seaman hurtled the length of the bar, clearing all the glasses at one end before sliding off and landing

153

in a heap. Numerous Chinamen scattered from tables in the immediate vicinity. The second man was hit squarely, directly in front of Silas, who braced him as he fell backwards.

'Hughie!' he exclaimed. Hughie Sutherland straightened up, ignoring blood flowing from his nose.

'Afternoon, sir. Billy, Ben and meself was just making a bet, sir. Who's to be home first. Everyone's talking about it, sir.'

The fight halted, the crowded bar began to reassemble around the new arrivals. Amongst them were a number of conspicuously large men dressed in distinctly cut uniforms, unlike the clipper crews. One of them, followed by his shipmates, approached as beers ordered by *Vesper*'s second mate, Ben, were raised Brief greetings over, Silas proposed a toast to 'auld acquaintance'. The men drank then refilled their glasses. The large man in uniform grinned at Silas and Eli.

'So you're the new captains of those windbags?'

Silas ignored the man and continued drinking.

'Steamship *Otranto*,' said the man, and pointed to his shoulder flash with the name clearly written. Ben glanced at him apprehensively, which was why he lost his beer. A silence fell throughout the Navigator Bar as the man took Ben's glass from his hand and emptied the beer on the floor, where it ran amongst the sawdust at Silas Hayes' feet.

'We were having a disagreement,' said the man. 'These scum you employ believe they have a chance to win.' There was some nervous laughter from behind him. 'Me and the boys, of course, rightly disputed that, what with all the money at stake. Now, seeing you two, well. . . .' He began to laugh.

Eli and Silas said nothing; the bar owner lay back against his bottles and mirror, closed his eyes and began to whine to himself as the large man in uniform continued with a grin, 'You two don't look as though you could float a bucket across a creek, let alone have a boatload of scumbags blow you out of the harbour.'

Eli coughed, knowing that Silas was only completely still on two occasions, one was when shaving with a cut-throat razor. . . . 'Are these friends of yours?' he asked. Eli shook his head. The uniforms grouped either side of their leader. Silas smiled slowly, 'You take the high road,' he said softly, 'and I'll take the low road and I'll be in Scotland before you.'

There was argument afterwards about which was the best punch thrown. Some said it came from Silas, others from Eli; but the first one, as Silas Hayes exploded with a roar of anger, let out all the tension of the previous weeks, breaking the large man's nose with a definite snap. The force of the Scotsman's full body weight shoved him through his companions, across a table and against the wooden wall at such a velocity he split two of the planks before crumpling to the floor. Eli cracked the Second Mate of *Otranto* so hard that he staggered backwards to the top of the stairs, slipped and disappeared, his body slamming down the wooden steps and out into the street.

Then it was mayhem.

Cudgels were pulled, knives drawn and bottles smashed into jagged weapons. Chairs, tables, stools, glasses, plates, buckets, feet, fists and teeth all served admirably to persuade each of the two sides – steam and sail – that their way was more valid. Heads cracked, bodies were hurled across the bar-room, knuckles, bone, tissue, limbs, sinew, joints and tendons split, broke, tore, wrenched, ripped twisted and snapped. Blood spattered everywhere; after several sustained minutes of fighting, the wreckage of human flesh swayed or lay conscious or oblivious, breathing air as if it was their last – only the drunken Dr Murphy in a corner of the Navigator Bar smiled slowly and mentally began to add to his small fortune.

'How opportune,' he murmured to himself, and sipped the dregs of his whisky.

Silas Hayes surveyed the devastated room and, tasting salt, spat blood on to the floor, where it was absorbed by sawdust. Eli Lubbock, fists raw, his forearm bleeding through lacerations in his coat where he had hastily blocked a thrown bottle, lay against the bar and groaned.

'Did we win?' he mumbled.

Silas counted the unconscious bodies in uniform, sprawling throughout the bar and nodded with satisfaction. 'And they'll pay.'

Ben stood up shakily and stepped to the bar. He reached for a cloth, wiped blood from his mouth and asked for a beer. The Chinese barman, still timorous, poured out a glass and handed it over, still clutching the bottle. Deliberately Ben crossed to a prone body and emptied the beer slowly into the face of the large man from steamship *Otranto*, whose eyes flickered then again closed. Hughie and Billy began to go about checking their respective crews.

Dr Murphy approached the two captains and grinned. 'Well, boys,' he began in his lilting accent, 'you've not lost your touch.'

Silas nodded wryly at the balding plump Irishman he'd known since the old days. 'And neither, I'll warrant, have you – you old fox.'

'Business, Captain Hayes,' smiled the doctor, 'should always begin with a little tipple, don't you think?'

'Have you got your bag?'

'Always ready for any emergency,' said Murphy, indicating his table in the corner and the doctor's bag beneath it.

'The barber's shop?' suggested Silas.

'It'll be cleaner,' replied the doctor. Whisky was poured, added to "the damage" and drunk quickly as the cut and injured assembled themselves slowly in the hope that the good doctor, who now pulled out and donned glasses to examine his patients, would stay sober enough to administer at least a semblance of first aid.

Repairs were conducted next door, where Whampoo's élite team of barbers supplied hot water, bandages, lint and even several splints, as the doctor practised efficiently but with little sympathy towards the hardy seamen who, in the main, gritted teeth rather than screamed at the unfortunate but necessary pain. Murphy was also an excellent book-keeper, and after an hour he had totted up a princely sum, which he added and presented to the two captains whilst taking a moment to sip, as he put it, and wash his hands. 'Did you know that Black Plague has broken out up north?' asked Silas.

Eli stared at him. 'Has it?'

Silas nodded a reply and continued, 'That would provide you with work enough here, would it not?'

Dr Murphy's eyes narrowed. 'I hear that it is only a rumour.'

'It's a fact,' stated Silas. 'If it's on paper – official, if posted in public.'

'I've been signing Port Authority paper for years and never had cause to represent an epidemic of the Black here – yet.'

'If you could be convinced' – Silas used the word carefully – 'that there was a danger, how would it affect commerce?'

The doctor settled himself in a barber's chair, appraised himself in the mirror and rolled up his shirt-sleeves a second time to conceal the bloodstains on his cuffs.

'Impounded ships – examined cargo – quarantine. It would be a problem and cause some panic. Is that what you wish to hear, Captain Hayes?'

Silas smiled. 'Unpleasant,' he said.

'And impractical, unless *proved* true,' stated the wily doctor. 'I would never be so unethical as to commit my name to paper, whatever the reward – so don't ask me, Silas.' Murphy was ahead of Eli, who remained mystified. The doctor stood up, seeing several of the bloody sailors moving impatiently on the long benches against the wall. 'I've work to do and you've a bill to pay.'

'I'll double it,' said Silas softly.

'Silas!' snapped the doctor. 'I may drink but I've still a reputation to keep here.'

'Not,' said Silas slowly, 'here.'

'I don't understand you,' said the doctor.

'Have you ever been to Singapore?'

'Once,' answered the doctor, and beckoned for the next man, 'but I've no intention of going on your behalf.'

'Are you in telegraphic communication with the port authority there?'

'Occasionally,' murmured the doctor, and began to examine his patient, who winced. 'But at the moment, things are bad here so I've no way of knowing if – '

'Leave that to me,' Silas interrupted, clasping his friend Eli about the shoulders and making to turn for the door. 'I'll explain when I pay you later – over a big drink.'

The doctor shook his head but moistened his lips at the thought.

It was late afternoon, gloomy and still pouring with rain as Silas and Eli stepped out of Whampoa's best barber's into the mêlée of the harbour. Activity, despite the rain, continued with ever more bustle, it seemed to the two men as, with collars up, they pressed through the crowds. It was hot and humid; even the rain was warm. The stench of people, cargoes, horse dung and a nearby brewery intermingled, causing Eli to retch and pray for the open sea that with some luck would soon be his.

'Damn this city,' he spat. 'What in the hell have you got planned now, Silas Hayes?'

'A surprise,' answered Silas, 'for more than you Eli. And our gain shall cost us no more than a handful of Shanghai currency, worthless when we've gone, and two bottles of whisky.'

'And what's our gain?' asked Eli.

Silas stopped and pointed through the rain to the quayside where their two charges waited. '*Vesper* and *Chantril*,' he said.

Both men trudged on, unaware of the tall black man with massive shoulders ill-concealed in a dark, severely cut suit, who smiled a mouthful of white teeth, in the shadows of a narrow alley. He readjusted his Homburg and, ignoring the teeming rain, stepped out on to the cobbled quayside.

Eli Lubbock needed little persuading to enter the Port Authority telegraph office. Several Government officials and Customs officers recognised Silas Hayes and his companion, and regarded them with suspicion as they shook the rain from their clothes on to the marble floor. Crossing between pillars supporting the ornate roof, Silas led Eli to a section of the long polished counter where he saw the clerk he wanted. They had once served together, until the man lost his feeling for the sea, persuaded by an ankle effectively crushed between two spars.

'Hello, George.'

The man's narrow, sorrowful face lightened as he saw his old Scottish fellow shipmate. 'Well, well,' he began, then softened his voice, seeing the officials and officers at the counter peering curiously towards him. 'To what do I owe the honour?'

'Business, Macintosh,' Silas replied with a grin.

George Macintosh coughed and lowered his head,

eyes fixed through rimless glasses at his former mate. 'And the nature of that would be . . . ?'

'Telegraphic communication,' said Silas quietly.

The clerk noted bruises and cuts about the faces of both men before him. He shook his head. 'Fighting at your age, Silas?'

Eli leaned on the counter, water dripping from his peaked cap. 'A dispute,' he said. 'The nature of which was the distance to the Frenchy's canal in Egypt.'

'I know the time it takes to send wires to Port Said but not the distance – so I can't help you.'

'Oh but you can,' said Eli, smiling. 'You see I've a brother serving out there.'

'When do you close up today?' Silas asked.

'Eight,' Macintosh answered.

Silas began to move. 'We'll be back.' he said.

The two men crossed the marble hall and, having gleaned the information Silas had come for, stepped out into the fading day, the pouring rain – and the awesome presence of a huge black man who barred their way.

'Mr Hayes, Mr Lubbock?' he asked in a deep resonant voice.

'Captains both,' replied Eli genially.

'Who might you be?' snapped Silas, already anticipating trouble.

'Egerton,' stated the man simply. 'My master sent me.'

'Master what?' asked Eli, detecting an accent. 'Seaman?'

Egerton ignored the question, his face impassive. 'Come with me please.'

'Where?' Eli questioned, glancing at Silas.

'This way,' answered the black man, and indicated the long quayside where, at the end of the wharf, a warehouse glowed.

Apprehensively, the two men followed the massive

black man through the guarded entrance and, thankful to be out of the rain, stood looking at stacked crates sealed and Customs stamped.

'What do they contain?' asked Silas.

The black man's teeth shone. 'My master will explain. Will you wait, gentlemen?'

'I'll be damned if I will,' snapped Silas. 'If you or your master want these shipped I'll have no mysteries.' He reached out, beckoning Eli to take one side of the nearest crate. Egerton hesitated as the two captains lifted their load awkwardly. They replaced it gingerly. Eli grinned as Silas shook his head. 'Too heavy.'

Egerton merely said, 'We are early for my master.'

Silas was already striding towards the entrance. 'Too late for me.'

'*We* are fully loaded,' emphasised Silas, and we sail tomorrow.'

'This cargo must be shipped,' Egerton rumbled.

'Where?' asked Eli.

Egerton hesitated, then smiled. 'Africa.'

Silas observed the man anew, staring at him for several seconds as the pieces fell together in his mind. He now recognised the accent as Dutch, something he had thought unusual, but now realised, perhaps not. . . .

'We sail south of the Cape, big man. Try Mr Jackson. He has space and steam.'

Egerton remained still as the two men pushed past him. 'My master will pay in gold.'

Silas nodded to himself; if he had had any doubts at all, they were dispelled. He turned for a moment. 'In – gold,' he repeated. 'As he paid for the Customs seal and clearance?' The black man said nothing. 'Goodbye, Mr Egerton.' '*Otranto*,' Eli reminded him, and pointed through the gloom and rain.

The two captains stepped back out into the late afternoon downpour.

'What was all that?' asked Eli.

'Best kept out of,' growled Silas. 'We've a bill to pay Murphy and I ain't got gold, only an idea.'

'Another one?' grunted Eli sourly. Silas held up two fingers and walked away. Eli followed a pace behind, cursing the rain, the heat, the city, even the prospect of sailing half the world in command of a real ship as he had always dreamed because at the end, as both he and Silas had foolishly gambled, they would lose – all of it.

'I ain't gonna be washed up in Limehouse,' he spat.

Silas glanced at him as he caught up. 'You won't be, with some luck.'

'Luck ain't enough,' grunted Eli.

'You're right,' grinned Silas wryly. He wiped rain from his face, looking ahead where already lanterns glowed outside the barber's. It was undoubtedly the gloomiest autumn he'd ever experienced in China.

'Eli, we've got to be sure we got at least half a chance.'

'How?'

'Bunker ports,' murmured Silas, and opened the door into the crowded barber's shop.

A semblance of order had been created by Dr Murphy's commanding Irish voice – fuelled and strengthened by whisky – together with the men's increased respect at his efficient administration of medicine. The two crews had lined up obediently against the wall to allow the Chinese barbers space to clean up.

Silas and Eli surveyed the victims of the brawl.

'What a way to start,' grumbled Eli.

'So far, so good,' stated Silas.

Dr Murphy, washing his hands in the sink, beamed at the two captains. He had relaxed at their arrival, knowing his bill would now be paid.

'Come along lads,' he shouted, 'back to your ships.

You're off on tomorrow's tide.' The men filed out. 'Providence is an awkward customer.' The Irishman's voice trailed off as he began to dry his hands.

Eli stepped forward. 'What do you know of a big black man called Egerton?'

The doctor nodded and bent his head as if musing to himself. 'Egerton,' he repeated slowly, 'and black too . . . well now. . . .' His eyes peered from beneath thick brows and he ran fingers through his thinning hair as he glanced at the two men. 'I know the man,' he stated brusquely, 'and it's a dubious reputation he'll be having. But then that's horses for courses around these parts, wouldn't you say?'

'Lucrative business?' suggested Eli.

'Dangerous,' snapped the doctor at the veiled inference. 'And if you think I've anything to do with him, you'll be wrong.'

Silas smiled at the wily old man. 'Gossip, eh, Murphy?'

'I hear things, of course,' replied the doctor.

'Gentlemen, what say you we repair ourselves above?' He indicated the Navigator Bar. 'No doubt they'll have it habitable already so as not to lose trade.'

An hour later, a mutual understanding was arrived at, hands were shaken and money exchanged. Silas paid for the two bottles of whisky they had consumed, largely emptied at a prodigious rate by the Doctor. Satisfied that he had both kept his head and improved their chances in the race to come, Silas stood up, made his farewells and, followed by Eli, went down the steps.

Eli grinned. 'Black Plague, eh?'

'A pestilence sent by God,' stated Silas with a straight face.

'It's no guarantee,' said Eli.

'It's a chance,' answered Silas grimly. 'It's all we've got.'

'What about this Egerton and his master?'

163

'Leave that to me,' replied Silas. 'I've to see Macintosh now – he'll be sure the wires are sent.'

Eli pulled up his collar, realising it would be inadequate protection for the teeming rain once they stepped from beneath the shelter of the overhanging eaves. 'We're making a mess of trouble for Jackson.'

'I hope so,' grunted Silas.

'I've my charts to check over,' muttered Eli, gazing across the crowded quay where *Chantril* moved on the tide, straining at her ropes, seemingly as anxious as her captain to leave her mooring.

'At dinner, then,' said Silas. The two friends shook hands and stepped out into the rain, bound for different destinations.

Silas Hayes spent several minutes with Macintosh at the long counter in the marble hall of the Port Authority telegraph office. The man's eyes were wide by the end of the whispered conversation, but a bargain was struck and sealed, and an envelope passed between the two men. The roll in Silas' wallet was fast diminishing but it would, he hoped, be justified. Ironic, he thought, as he strode between the pillars back to the entrance, that Jackson's money might well, in the end, buy them what he had declared already lost.

Outside, the continuing rain and oppressive humidity depressed Silas Hayes. Suddenly what would begin on the morrow no longer appeared as challenge, excitement and adventure, but merely the unyielding strain and responsibility of leadership. He looked down at the rainwater sluicing over the cobbles.

The sound of the port, of the city, of China itself, faded – and for a moment Silas was alone in a silent world of his own. It was here he had learned patience, been given solace, made decisions when all about him were confused. No one had ever been invited or gained access to this part of himself, or understood the strength he absorbed from his inner peace. If he was resilient, tenacious and durable it was because he had learned to listen to the voice of reason and wisdom within.

The last night ashore, then a hundred more at sea. It had been a long time, as Silas well knew, since he had endured the sustained hardships of a long voyage. He hoped his knowledge and instincts would not fail him. Just at this moment his confidence had been shaken. Why, he did not know.

'If you're there,' he mumbled, conceding at least the possibility of a Creator, 'be with us.'

Cursing the fact he'd let his carriage go, he pushed on through the harbour bustle, determined to be back at the American Consulate and in the sanctum of his rooms quicker than it took a knot line to gauge the speed of a clipper with all canvas up. The thought gave him pleasure; instinct hadn't failed him, he was already thinking nautical even as he thrust into the milling Chinese all about him.

9

Hot water gushed from a tap topping up the filled bath as Silas Hayes gingerly stepped into foam made by scented crystals. Emily spun the tap shut, sat on the edge of the large enamel bath and gazed down into the face of the father of her child with a pleading expression Silas could seldom resist. He grunted, closed his eyes and settled back comfortably in the soothing water.

'Silas,' Emily began, then hesitated. 'Silas, I can't remain here. Please, I want to be with you when you – *we* arrive in England. Please?'

'Too dangerous. It's a long voyage.'

'I've sailed before. . . .'

'Not the way I'll sail her, you haven't.' He opened one eye and stared at his woman. 'You're nearly five months pregnant. . . .'

'Does it show?' Emily interrupted.

Silas saw the blush and reached out a foam-laden hand to grasp her delicate fingers. He smiled. 'Only in your face,' he said softly. She leaned forward and they kissed long and sensuously.

Emily's lips parted reluctantly.

'I want to come with you,' she whispered urgently.

Silas fixed her with a look of authority and command but spoke gently. 'You'll go to your family in Sydney. I'll return to Australia from England on a wool trader or, if luck, fate, chance, even God will have it, I'll be sailing into port at the helm of *Vesper*.' Emily's eyes were moist as she spoke with lips quivering. 'How can you be so cruel? I'll be alone when the child is born . . . Silas, please!'

'You'll be safe with your family. *He*'ll not be three months old before I set eyes on him.'

'I want to see the New Year in with you, Silas Hayes. . . . It'll be the dawning of a new century and the beginning of everything I ever dreamed.'

'Me?' asked Silas, admiring his woman's emotional courage.

'Yes, dammit, Silas Hayes – you,' replied Emily, smiling through her tears.

He opened his eyes and grinned. 'You shouldn't swear.'

'As a lady I shouldn't do many things I'm told by an old sea dog.'

'All women are not ladies,' responded Silas.

'They could be, if influence and encouragement were to come from a gentleman.'

'By God, I do believe you're getting smarter by the minute.'

'It has become an issue no doubt to be resolved in the future, the world over . . . by women.'

'Women resolve nothing. Men do that.'

'A lady, Silas Hayes, must resolve many things when confronted with a man she desires.'

Silas felt himself on the verge of checkmate, so he reached out and seized Emily's face, his large hands framing delicate features. 'You'll not charm me, lassie.'

'Captain Hayes,' said Emily huskily, a steady gaze from her beautiful eyes conveying all the love of which a man dreams, 'how could I?'

Silas kissed her hungrily. For a moment she responded, then gently but firmly pulled away. He sank back into the foam, looking at her as she stood up. She brushed down her dress then stared him in the eye, silent and already secretly resolved.

'What are you about, young lady?'

'Business, Silas.' She touched her slightly swollen belly. 'Remember *we* too are to be travelling – soon.'

167

She stepped to the door and, before closing it, turned with a smile. 'Dinner is at eight-thirty. If you sleep, I'll wake you in good time. Enjoy your bath.'

Silas heard rustling in the other room for a few minutes, then silence. Only the rain continued outside, gurgling from the roof, pouring from the lowering sky to interrupt his thoughts.

'Women.' He yawned.

Guards at the entrance of the open warehouse saw the approaching figures bent beneath large umbrellas and admitted them, once identified. Jackson and his captain stamped their boots and cursed the weather as a large, well-built, balding European, accompanied by the towering frame of a black man, crossed between cases from a rear, poorly lit office to greet them. The white man shook with genial laughter as he extended a hand.

'Kimmen!' he said.

'The Dutchman,' whispered the Captain to Jackson, who nodded, then shook hands.

'Well, well, Mr Jackson,' began Kimmen, the words sounding more like 'whol, whol' in his Dutch accent. 'You come, you see' – he indicated the stacked cargo – 'let us hope we conquer!' He roared with even louder laughter as Jackson appraised the consignment. 'At least we must agree – transport for a price is the way the world turns, is it not?'

Hollis Jackson turned his full attention to the well-cut tailoring enveloping large shoulders and an ample girth. The man looked powerful; his full but well-boned face – the jaw firm, the eyes small but bright and the nose long but broken – revealed clues to an interesting past. 'Not an average businessman,' thought Jackson but asked, indicating the cargo, 'Sewing machines?'

'Duty paid and Customs sealed,' smiled Kimmen.

The Captain took off his cap, shook it and coughed to attract attention. 'Mr Lubbock and Mr Hayes have made the introduction, Mr Jackson; in view of the weight here, as you see, it's all too obvious – ' 'I do,' interrupted Jackson quietly. Silence held for a moment; only the incessant rain poured on outside.

Unruffled by Jackson's lack of enthusiasm, Kimmen stepped to a wide table surrounded by chairs, and the men seated themselves.

'Genever, gentlemen? Egerton, pour before the rain dampens our – prospects.' The tall black man in his severe suit seized the bottle of Dutch gin and filled glasses placed on a silver tray. 'Shanghai in the wet, Mr Jackson.' He shook his head disapprovingly. 'It's good to be going, isn't it?'

Jackson accepted a glass. 'The weather's much the same every year,' he stated, watching the Dutchman wipe perspiration from his face with a white silk handkerchief, 'if you know the China coast.'

'I do, Mr Jackson. I know it well.' Kimmen's eyes gleamed.

'From business?' Jackson asked, sipping the drink.

'From business,' repeated the Dutchman, seizing a glass, 'Prost! My heart, *Mr* Jackson, lies in. . . . business.'

'For seamstresses?'

The Dutchman became wary, sipping his genever cautiously, watching every move Jackson made. The Englishman remained still. 'Africa has vast resources and needs machinery of every kind to exploit its full potential. What is your saying, "clothes maketh the man"?'

'We have many sayings in England, *Mr* Kimmen. What do you want from me?' he asked bluntly.

'A hold – for freight,' answered Kimmen, no longer smiling. 'Do you have space?'

Jackson looked again at the stacked cargo. 'Perhaps. Destination?'

'Zanzibar.'

Hollis Jackson shook his head. 'That's out of our way.'

Kimmen pursued his lips and glanced at the impassive face of Egerton, who reached down and lifted a small leather case on to the table, with, curiously, a single handcuff and chain attached to its handle. It seemed unusually heavy. Kimmen unlocked the case and opened it. Gold gleamed dully. Jackson swallowed as his captain coughed.

'A matter of days, Mr Jackson. This is international currency. Please. . . .' Kimmen took up a thin bar of the payment to be made and handed it to the Englishman. Jackson examined it, seeing the hallmark and stamp unmistakably revealing its origin.

'South African?'

'Twenty-two carat,' stated Kimmen. 'The best.' Jackson said nothing. 'Do you have any doubts?'

'The gold is genuine, Mr Kimmen – is the cargo?'

'What you are saying to me, Mr Jackson?'

'What are you asking of me, mynheer?'

'Transport,' snapped Kimmen. 'I have made it clear you will be well paid. This case and its contents are yours.'

Jackson smiled. 'Open a crate,' he asked quietly. The captain coughed nervously. The rain teeming outside seemed to intensify. A rumble of distant thunder filled the silence between the men. Kimmen hesitated a moment longer, then snapped fingers at Egerton, who crossed to the stack, lifted one of the long crates and placed it on the floor of the warehouse, nearer the men. They stood and watched the giant black man lift the lid, expertly using a crowbar. Amongst packing wads stood three sewing machines side by side.

'Singer,' grinned Kimmen. Jackson nodded slowly, the gold already sufficient inducement to waive moral considerations. After all, business was business – and

170

here was a damn good price, and here were indeed sewing machines. He turned to his captain.

'A matter of days only?'

The Captain nodded slowly. 'A week, maybe a day or so more.'

Jackson stared at Kimmen, considering the extra journey, knowing they had ample time even with the race at hand. *Otranto* would still be in with twenty days' lead.

'Deal with my captain for bills of lading.'

'You are satisfied?'

'It is acceptable.'

'Excellent, Mr Jackson.' Kimmen paused. 'Will you dine with me this evening – I am sure we have many things in common and could perhaps explore other possibilities?'

'Maybe,' said Jackson. 'We have an entire voyage to explore them – almost. *Now* I have a lady waiting.'

Kimmen bowed deferentially. 'Of course.'

Jackson snapped open his umbrella. 'Load early, we leave tomorrow – at midday.'

Followed by his captain, Hollis Jackson walked out of the warehouse into the evening rain.

Eli Lubbock stepped into his charthouse aboard *Chantril*, cursing the weather as he knew any man in his right mind would. No surprises in Shanghai, always a thick humid summer and early autumn storms leading to the heavy monsoons. God help them all, he thought if the rebellion and insurrection in China continued unchecked. After the great battles around the legations of Peking, anything was possible.

He found a cloth laid by one of the boys on his bunk bed, wiped rain from his face and hair cursorily and began to unroll the last of the China Seas charts obtained by Jackson. Inaccuracies, and there were many, had been corrected after recent British naval assessments, and discoveries inserted. He shook his head; so much to absorb in so little time. He had pored over the old charts but the new ones demanded even more concentration. He knew that if he could get the north-east monsoon winds behind him early on and make Anjer in under thirty days, prevailing winds would, with all canvas up, take him across the southern Indian Ocean in almost the same time. Perhaps, he fondly hoped, they'd make three hundred knots a day.

He had a mate of great ability in Billy, whose number one and two had been chosen with some care from friends ashore too long in Shanghai, but about the rest of the crew he was dubious. An inherited list of Portugee boatmen, working a way back to Europe; others who could not find a steamship passage and numerous Chinamen whose declared abilities could only be corroborated by the hard facts of ocean weather. Weather, he mused. It all came down to that. Steam kettles could ride it out with or without a blow but he and Silas would need every shred of knowledge they retained of the four winds as they shifted between the tropics, across the equator and back.

For a moment his brow furrowed, his eyes closed and he pressed the bridge of his nose with thumb and forefinger. In his youth he would have had no qualms at such a voyage – in such times clippers had been the élite, as were their crews and captains. Now boilers and coal dominated the seven seas and only bravado and a last lust for adventure had given him a command of a real ship in what would be perhaps the last true race of square riggers in history out of one of the great China treaty ports.

'*Chantril*,' he said aloud to himself. For a moment he felt as if the spirit of the ship responded to him. Every captain he'd ever sailed with swore each ship had its own character full of 'good luck' or 'bad omens'. If anything, he'd always thought, it was their wish to be attendant to the desires of a partner rather than burden their minds with full responsibility against such mighty forces of extreme elements. But now, standing in the chart area he had designated within his cabin, he understood that desire to be wedded for a duration. The ship was like a wife to turn to in dire straits and see it all out for better or for worse. He smiled at the thought. He'd always avoided such commitment. Perhaps the time had come. At least Silas had a son and indeed a new wife-to-be. Youth had escaped him, age was yet to come, but the joints were stiffening and his resolve softening. Maybe, he speculated, they would end up just two old sea dogs, as he and Silas had termed each other so often, in charge of some bar on a Thames reach, yarning embellished stories of distant times in almost forgotten places. He gritted his teeth and muttered to himself, 'Not yet – by God, not yet, my boy.'

A voice spoke back to Eli Lubbock as feet sounded on the steps down from the poop deck. 'It must be encouraging, Captain Lubbock, for a prospective traveller to hear the captain of a ship appealing to God, although I would hope him to be more than a boy.' Emily closed her umbrella and smiled at Eli beneath a large hat and veil before looking about the cramped cabin lit only from two lamps.

Eli shook his head, 'Why are you here this evening when we are to dine all together in' – he checked his pocket watch – 'less than ninety minutes?'

'It is,' she hesitated to find the words, 'a private matter.'

'Indeed. Then I grant you privacy.'

Emily bit her lips, stepped forward, lifted her veil and looking into Eli's eyes beseechingly, spoke softly. 'Take me aboard as a passenger.'

Eli Lubbock grunted, turned away, crossed to a box, opened it, took out a cigar, lit it and leaned against the cabin wall to appraise Emily and her motives. The two lamps moved with the returning tide, etching the features of the undoubtedly beautiful young woman who had seated herself on Eli's bunk.

'I have a full complement,' he said.

'Add one – please.'

'Sail with your husband to be.'

'I cannot.'

'Why?'

Emily paused. Honesty failed her as she knew it would fail to gain her a passage. So she lied – convincingly; all the time praying to God to forgive her the sin.

'We have argued. He wishes no more to do with me, I believe. He of course has to put on a brave public face, but I fear that if he is to travel to England, and sends me to Australia, as he wishes, we will never again meet.'

'Do you love him?' Eli asked.

The flush on her cheeks and neck answered the question before she spoke. 'I am fond of the gentleman, as you well know.'

'He's no gentleman, Emily, but he is the greatest friend I've known, and if it is your wish to be with him, it is mine that you should be – together.' Eli paused and drew on his cigar. 'I will take you to England.' Emily stood up and ran to Eli, enfolding him in her arms. He felt the warmth of her body and in that momentary embrace realised her worth to Silas and exactly what he in turn was missing.

'It must be a surprise to him,' she said. 'Please, Captain Lubbock.'

'I am sure it will be,' he replied. 'And to you.'

'Why?' asked Emily, drawing away.

'It will not be easy – a fast voyage under all sail can never be comfortable.'

'I shall endure what is necessary.'

174

'Then let me show you,' said Eli, and pointed to the cabin steps down into the bowels of the ship. Emily approached and grasped a rail leading below. To one side Eli opened a door into a wood-panelled room with a long wide table filling most of it. Two oil lamps swung slowly above the polished mahogany. 'Where we eat.' Eli looked at Emily for a reaction.

'Really' – she began, and coughed politely – 'pleasant.'

'Two meals a day,' said Eli.

'And shall there be milk aboard, because. . . .' She stopped herself. Truth she would save for the open ocean.

Eli smiled, thinking only that good breeding had led Emily to expect such luxuries. Silas should have already blunted some of those niceties, he thought ruefully.

'Well, Miss Emily, we have limes and lemons to prevent scurvy, pigs and chickens to give us fresh meat for greater energy, and we also have goats to drink from. . . .'

'Goat's milk!' she exclaimed.

Eli nodded. 'The only cattle inhabit the crew's quarters. We have condensed milk also.' Eli paused. 'I take it you've not travelled – extensively?'

'I was educated in Australia and lived with my family. I came to Shanghai from Sydney by steamer.'

'A different experience, no doubt,' said Eli ironically.

'But sails are so . . . romantic,' suggested Emily, trying to please Eli.

He burst into laughter. 'Tell me after a week in heavy squalls.' He closed the door and led the way ahead to the stairway. 'Come on down.' The two figures descended into the gloom, ill-lit by well-dispersed lamps hanging above the long walkway. Shadows moved menacingly about them, it seemed to Emily, as she followed Eli.

'Cargo, storage,' he was saying as she tried to absorb the realities of what had been, in the carriage to the harbour, an adventure in a comfortable dream. 'Crew's quarters below, others above. . . .' Eli stopped and opened several doors opposite each other in a panelled area beyond midships. Here the lamps burned from turned-down wicks and it was barely possible to make out the contents of the small rooms.

'Where you sleep,' grunted Eli. Emily peered into the cramped cabin. She swallowed at the bare essentials but, putting on a brave face, she turned to Eli. 'It is not luxury,' said Eli, and puffed his cigar.

'It is not,' Emily agreed quietly. Eli closed the doors and began to lead the way back. As Emily moved, to her consternation, the ship seemed to move faster, suddenly heeling over. She reached out to steady herself and took a deep breath.

'The ship, it appears, has a mind of its own, Captain Lubbock.' Even as she spoke the words, she saw that the lamps were still barely moving and realised what had happened.

'Are you not well?' asked Eli, seizing her arm firmly.

She smiled and straightened up. 'Perfectly, thank you. I missed my footing.'

'Keep it up top on deck, or you must remain below.' Eli led on, up to the poop. 'The world's oceans, Miss Emily, are to be used, but also to be wary of. As respect grants us order in society, respect preserves lives at sea. Should that sea take you from the deck of a speeding clipper, believe me, it might as well prove to be a vat of acid.' Emily paused at the bottom of the steps, absorbing the harsh words of warning, watching Eli mount before her. 'We would never find you, even if we could stop – which would take us more sea miles than you would care to know.'

'I know enough, Captain Lubbock, to regard myself as privileged.'

Eli put out a hand, helping Emily first into his cabin then on up to the poop deck. He snapped open the umbrella she proffered, noting the Marines guarding the gangway and the carriage and driver waiting.

'We sail at noon.'

'I shall be aboard, Captain Lubbock. I have sufficient money to adequately reimburse you for passage. Silas must know nothing until we are arrived. Then he will see me.'

Eli nodded. 'We'll be waiting for him, having off-loaded before he even reaches the English Channel's "downs".'

Emily made to go, then took his hand. 'I don't know how to thank you, Captain,' she murmured.

He glanced the length of the deck where he could make out the watch, huddled beneath oilskins. Beyond, lights glowed from *Vesper* but no activity showed aboard. 'Where's Silas?' he asked.

Emily's face paled, as if expecting a sudden inquisition. 'Asleep, most like, if he has stepped from the bath I ran him.'

'You ran him?' grimaced Eli and shook his head. 'He's a lucky old dog to have a woman like you.'

'He's twice lucky then – to have a friend such as you are to him.'

Eli acknowledged the pleasantry with a grunt. 'We'll see who's friends when we're racing. I mean to win. I doubt this'll ever happen again . . . them old tea days made a boy feel a man, slipping out of Pagoda Anchorage at Foochow or tugged into the channel here. When we're beyond the silt of the Yangtse and those sails crack in open sea, by God, lady, you'll see some paces. . . .' Eli caught himself reminiscing and wiped rain from his mouth. 'The word'll be out by telegraph to London. Believe me, there'll be some wagers laid and money to be made, and I mean to take my share.'

He escorted Emily to the gangway ashore.

'How will you stake your bet?'

'I've done so,' said Eli. 'My entire salary.'

Emily gasped. 'But Captain Lubbock . . . so big a risk . . .'

'No risk. I'll win – I feel it. A gambler's blood is thick and my instincts, this time, are sure. Besides,' he grinned, 'I stand to lose all if I don't lee up to the white cliffs first so. . . .' He shrugged.

Impatient horses whinnied and stamped on the wet cobbles below. Emily acknowledged her waiting driver. 'Can I take you?' she asked. In answer Eli, throwing away his cigar, grasped the umbrella and held it above them both, and they descended the gangway together. The US Marines saluted. Eli winked and both he and Emily settled into the carriage. With a crack of the whip, the driver began to steer the horses through the throng on the quayside.

'Perhaps you've brought me luck,' murmured Eli.

Emily only smiled, content.

Cornelia Morgan strode ahead of Hollis Jackson through the first-class section of *Otranto*. Luxury abounded, even to plush crimson pile on floors the length of panelled corridors. A spacious dining room, ample chesterfields in the smoking room, awnings to cover deck areas for clement weather in the tropics; finally the bedrooms and en suite bathrooms.

Cornelia, with practised skill, concealed her total approval and murmured reluctantly that it was all ' . . . not de luxe but will suffice, I hope.' She gazed at Jackson, who contentedly puffed at an imported cigar as she pulled on her gloves. 'Must you smoke that foul cheroot?'

'Madam, it is the best.'

'But one of the worst habits,' she snapped.

'Do you know others?' responded Jackson.

'Mr Jackson,' smiled Cornelia coolly, adjusting –

despite the heat – a mink stole around her shoulders, 'we have weeks afloat together. To date, our . . . friendship has prospered. Do not jeopardise the possible pleasant consequences of proximity at sea with vulgar wit.'

'Cornelia, my affections for you have become . . . could we not . . . ?'

'Easily,' she interrupted quickly. 'I will admit, here, privately, that we might indeed have – prospects.' She paused, her face now near his. 'Are you ready . . .' she began.

'Oh yes,' Hollis said quickly.

' . . . for dinner?' Cornelia finished.

Hollis Jackson, surprised yet again by this intriguing woman, nodded slowly.

Two stewards bowed as they left the saloon, where lights were again turned low. Uniformed crew, holding large umbrellas, aided Cornelia and Jackson down the wide walkway to the quay and the waiting carriage. Jackson checked his pocket watch as the carriage moved off. In the confined space, despite the rain outside and the humidity within, the smell of leather, polished brass and varnished wood, combined with the fragrance Cornelia favoured, made him heady and excited – as she did not fail to appreciate. Cornelia had never rushed anything or allowed instant emotion to colour decisions. Detachment, she had decided early, should be fostered and enthusiasm disciplined. Real pleasure and true happiness demanded work, and she never shirked any toil which led to self-gratification.

She travelled in silence as Jackson continued to smoke his cigar. Only as they passed through the entrance of the American Consulate, when her companion threw the cigar butt out of the window, did Cornelia glance at him with obvious disapproval. Closer relations with this man, who had so far lived up

179

to her expectations, at least in wealth, she knew would need more thought.

She alighted on the gravel beneath a large umbrella held by a Marine, then ascended the steps graciously, followed by Hollis Jackson, who took her arm. From the Chinese quarter the sound of explosions came clearly, alerting the Marines between the columns guarding the great doors. Jackson and Cornelia halted beneath the protecting portico. The Marine saluted, folded the umbrella and left them.

'I thought the rain might have dampened their spirits,' murmured Jackson staring into the distance.

Cornelia smiled, 'Real spirit, Hollis, is never dampened. Even the worst occasion should present a challenge.'

'Have you ever known "a worse occasion"?' asked Jackson wryly.

Cornelia's eyes hardened and she examined the man's face for a moment with pursed lips in a frozen expression.

'Mr Jackson, my character, should you ever come to know it, may well present you with a challenge and, if you should care to cope with it, what you may discover might come as a distinct surprise. You have dragged yourself resourcefully from the depths to reach the plateau in life from which I have always had a clear view. Please learn to appreciate your new-found privilege – if you have need I will help you. . . .'

Jackson shook his head in both disbelief and admiration.

Then Cornelia applied her devastatingly warm smile. 'Shall we?' she suggested softly, and led him into her father's consulate, which represented the power of America in Shanghai.

180

10

Naked, but for a lit cigar in his mouth, Eli Lubbock gazed at himself in the long mirror, reflecting the truth of time's ravages to his body. He shook his head, begging for a moment that fact was a lie and his swelling girth a removable object.

For many years, age had been a benevolent friend, work a necessity to survive, love an occasional gift, exercise an endurance to provide, gambling his flaw, the authorities an increasing problem, Silas a perennial friend and ambition a receding dream. Now one chance presented everything that ultimately might save him from a workhouse on the Thames, a slow end in a Chinese opium den, premature death on a foreign shore or the lingering nightmare of official incarceration for life. A last great race. A ship to command – a moment in time, a place in history. Eli blew smoke at his reflection and smiled. He'd win. He knew it. There was too much at stake to think of unacceptable alternatives.

'Am I interrupting?' asked a voice softly. Eli turned and saw Adèle closing the door behind her quietly. She stared at him, eyes wide, then cocked her head, smiling wickedly.

Eli blushed unmoving. 'You have the advantage of me, Miss Morgan.'

She nodded. 'And I intend to keep it.'

'Have you,' began Eli hesitantly, 'a robe of sorts?' Adèle walked to a cupboard, opened doors and took out an ornate dressing gown. She presented it to Eli. Eye to eye they made an exchange; he took the gown, she took the cigar from his mouth. He belted the thick velvet robe, embroidered with dragons, then coughed politely.

'You are a surprising woman, I do believe. . . .' Feeling water on his body and running from his hair, Eli brushed drips from his forehead. 'I'm wet still,' he murmured.

Adèle stepped closer, put her arms around his neck then, raising herself up on her toes, pressed against him.

'Indeed you are, Mr Lubbock,' she said, and kissed him. As their lips tasted each other's desire, the gown's belt loosened and the robe fell open. Adèle's eyes widened and as Eli reached down to fumble for the belt, she stopped him. With their gaze locked upon each other, expressing both humour and passion. Adèle replaced the cigar then slowly pulled the robe together, gently touching the protrusion and placing it to one side as she wrapped the velvet against Eli's body before firmly belting one embroidered dragon upon the other. 'Such a large cigar, Mr Lubbock, must often get in the way of so many *things.*'

Eli puffed. 'It's gone out.'

'Pity,' murmured Adèle, 'I like the aroma of a good cigar.'

'Then you are not offended?'

Adèle began to laugh and shook her head. 'As a modern woman, Eli, I have ceased to be offended by so many things. Instead I find I enjoy them.'

'You mean you too would smoke . . . ?'

Adèle's eyes danced. 'If you offered me one,' she murmured. Only then did Eli catch the inference and marvelled at the young woman's courage and wit. 'You are indeed a surprise, Miss Morgan.'

'Indeed,' responded Adèle. '*I* am surprised you should find me so.'

For a moment, Eli was nonplussed. He put the cigar in an ashtray then gently held the young woman by her shoulders. Looking down into her eyes he said tenderly, 'I think I am lucky to find you at all.'

Adèle's eyes instantly misted with happiness. 'Now you have taken advantage of me, Mr Lubbock,' she said huskily.

Eli leaned down to kiss her once more but she broke from him and turned away abruptly. She paused at the door before leaving.

'Dinner is in ten minutes.'

'I look forward to it,' said Eli.

Adèle opened the door and, for a moment, looked back longingly at the sea captain. 'Oh, Eli Lubbock . . . so do I. With all my heart, so do I.' She went quickly, leaving Eli puzzled at the welling emotion he could feel inside.

'Not at my age, surely?' he muttered, then, 'Not at *her* age . . . ? He shook his head and strode quickly to the built-in wardrobe, sliding it open to reveal pressed and laundered clothes hanging neatly on a long rack. 'Come hell or high water,' he said to himself, 'we'll get there.' In his mind, the words were describing *Chantril*'s destination, but his heart knew he meant something altogether different.

Jamie Morgan, dressed for dinner in green velvet with white ruffs, lingered in shadow on the upper hallway and watched Adèle glide down the long stairway singing to herself. He could already hear the crowd gathering below, most of whom knew it was their last night ashore. He glanced about him and, ensuring he could not be seen from the entrance hall, crept along the wall of the wide corridor, treading softly on the thick red pile carpet until he reached a closed door which led into a spacious suite of rooms. He heard voices raised inside, so he put his ear to the panelling and listened.

Silas Hayes paced the lounge, securing the polished

buttons of his dark jacket. 'I want a child I can be proud of . . . not some weak softie in velvet and lace. Australia is a rugged country and Sydney will be a fine city for us,' he told Emily. 'We'll be together after all this. . . . You'll have an old sea captain to look after who'll make your life a misery – is that what you want?'

Emily bit her lip. 'Silas, you know what I want.'

He nodded. 'I think I do – I also know that I don't want no sophisticated nonsense for this one. . . .' He leant down and touched her barely rounded belly. 'A fancy education's a good thing for "soirées" – he emphasised the word with dislike – 'and parties, but it don't do much for real living.' He straightened his lapels and began to tie a bow from the black silk strands hanging from the crisp white collar. Emily stood up and tied it for him. He grunted his thanks and went on, 'When the boy's born and I've returned, we'll tell the world of our secret. I'll teach him – with experience.'

Emily kissed him lightly. 'Women can see already, Silas. What if it's a girl?'

Silas held her soft face gently and kissed her forehead. 'I want a son.'

He opened the door and stepped out into the corridor. Immediately he saw Jamie walking away. Recognising his son in the dim lamplight, he called, 'Jamie?' The boy walked on quicker, so Silas lengthened his stride and caught up. They took several paces together as Silas felt his chin and grinned at his son, whose pale face contained burning eyes fixed only on a door at the end of the corridor. 'I've shaved,' said Silas and laid a hand on the boy's shoulder. Jamie turned away and fell against the wall beneath a gas lamp. He began to sob. Confused, Silas knelt quickly beside him and looked him in the face as tears flooded from the boy.

'You have . . . a son – me!' The pain in the boy's

voice was like a dagger in Silas' heart. 'I may not be the son you wanted . . . but how could I be? I never saw you – you were never there. . . . Oh, Father, I only ever wanted you home!'

Silas, desperately trying to control his own anguish, moved to enfold his son, but the boy pulled away and ran on down the corridor and burst through a door at the end. Silas stood up and followed, stepping through the door to see his son lying on his bed sobbing.

Jamie's room was a sanctuary, a private place, already full of many personal mementoes for one so young. Two lamps on the wall and another on the dresser revealed everything. Silas felt his throat tightening. How could he have known? Everywhere were pictures of windjammers, artifacts from ships, wall charts, keel plans, constellation maps and several models painstakingly crafted. In the centre of the dresser top, beautifully framed in tortoiseshell, was a photogravure of a younger Silas Hayes gazing out into the future with brutal confidence.

He walked across the room slowly and sat down on the bed beside his son. He waited. Slowly the sobbing lessened and the boy turned round, looked at his father, sat up and the two of them embraced. Years of responsibility bore down on Silas and brought tears to his eyes also.

'Were you listening, boy?'

'Yes,' Jamie answered softly and hung his head, sobbing still – but lightly.

Silas waited until his son lifted his head again. 'You're quite a collector.'

Jamie returned the smile, proud for a moment he was in his father's arms after so long, and now recognised. He said nothing.

'How's San Francisco?'

'It's school,' shrugged the boy.

'Do you still go to your mother's home in Chicago?'

'Sometimes. When were you last there?'

Silas remembered the vast mansion and its assumed elegance, concocted history, mannered sophistication, uniformed servants, regular hours, enforced pleasures and a whole watershed of sycophantic neighbours only too willing to jump at any invitation to associate with great wealth.

'A long time ago,' he heard himself say, 'You were just . . . a babe.'

'Why did you go?'

'Too far from the sea, boy.'

'But the Great Lakes are just – ' began Jamie.

'Lakes ain't sea, boy.'

'Looking out at the water, I used to imagine you. . . .' The boy stopped himself and wiped his tears. 'You weren't in San Francisco, at school, when you were as old as me – where were you?' The question was fair and the boy's longings justified.

'Times are changing, Jamie, that was another era. . . .' Silas heard his voice weaken, the words unconvincing to the boy whose eyes were now desperately seeking truth from his father. 'A man's life is like a compass, Jamie. He may go in many directions but he is lucky to find it. . .' Silas paused and looked kindly at his son. 'There is only one true north for each of us.' The boy's eyes still pleaded for an answer. 'I was already at sea at your age.' Silas hesitated. 'Now I'm older and wiser and – different. . . .' he finished lamely.

Silas glanced again at the mementoes around the room, lingering on a small, delicate, lovingly made model of a clipper, before looking back into his son's bright, defiant expression.

'And I'm your son.' Jamie spoke the words firmly, with proud confidence.

Silas enfolded the boy and hugged him tightly. 'By God you are, laddie,' he said, and had never felt himself more honest or vulnerable.

Footsteps sounded outside. Framed in the doorway, Cornelia could have been posing for a portrait. Light behind her silhouetted the perfect figure, perfectly dressed, perfectly groomed. Lamps in the room illuminated the beauty of her face and caught the triumphant hardness in her eyes, as Silas could see quite well. She smiled slowly as a gong sounded loudly from below, announcing dinner. She put out a hand for Jamie, who looked at her without emotion as Silas released him from his embrace.

'He can write to you,' she said.

The gong sounded louder.

'Come, Jamie.'

'I want to go with Father,' he blurted out.

'Jamie.' Cornelia spoke ominously. 'Come now.'

'I don't want to go back to San Francisco . . . back to school. . . .' His resolve failed him, seeing the anger in his mother's eyes.

'Go with your mother,' said Silas quietly.

Cornelia glanced with hatred at her former lover, erstwhile husband and father of her child. 'He is quite capable of obeying a voice of real authority which comes from a concern for his discipline and well-being; he needs no intrusion from a man whose influence he is well without.'

Silas heard the venom and saw the hate, and although it was distasteful, at the same time it reassured him that their final parting could only be for the good. He stood up slowly. 'You, madam, are a woman. Is that to be his influence?'

Cornelia's beautiful lips became ugly as she answered. 'If you had ever proved to be a real man you would have shouldered your responsibilities and become – '

Silas interrupted harshly. ' . . . your plaything and the Morgan family's pawn? A rough diamond to be cut in the city? You married a captain of the sea not industry . . . remember, the sea is bigger than any manufactured ambition.'

'You left me,' Cornelia snapped. 'For that I will never forgive you.'

Silas stared at the woman whose pride had always exceeded her proffered love and nodded. 'I never left the boy. You took him.'

'For his own good.'

'Look around you,' said Silas. 'Ask him.'

'He will grow out of it. Jamie, come.'

'Please, Mother. . . .' The boy shuffled forward.

Silas leaned over the dresser and blew out the lamp, then lowered the wicks of those on the wall and turned to see Jamie reluctantly holding his mother's hand. 'I'm also dining tonight, as I'm sure you hadn't forgotten.'

Cornelia pursed her lips. 'The lawyers are waiting below.'

Silas took the boy's other hand. 'Then if it's to be a last supper – shall we?'

The three of them, son proudly between his parents, descended the wide stairway together.

Dinner that night in the vast banqueting room of the American Consulate, although lit from both candelabra and wall lamps, was a dismal affair. Fine fare, served without ostentation but presented exquisitely despite the crisis in the city, was consumed without gusto and with little appetite by nervous guests, some perspiring in the humidity, others forlorn that they were destined to remain and face the uncertain and probably dangerous future.

After initial exchanges and pleasantries, silence became accepted by all but the few who continued to prattle without an audience. Cutlery, china, coughs and polite refusals to further courses punctuated the meal, as did explosions and the sounds of violent rioting from the Chinese quarter – even, at one stage, the distant exhortations of what appeared to be a huge and fast-moving running horde. Warm rain fell heavily and unceasingly.

Some of the refugees brightened at the prospect of departure; albeit into the unknown, it was at least away from the mounting chaos. Even the idea of being at the mercy of the elements while crossing half the world was no longer a nightmare. Shouts, cries and rifle fire came from the night, together with further explosions, and unsettled several of the women, who began to cry.

Coffee was presented. The Consul stood up, gesturing that the gentlemen should follow him into his private study. While they selected generously poured digestifs, the Consul accepted papers from two lawyers who had been waiting in some agitation for dinner to be finished so they could do their business and be gone. Signatures were witnessed, then the Consul beckoned Eli over. 'Mr Lubbock, if you would be so good . . . ?' he said. Eli signed beneath Silas. The two lawyers smiled, their fees now assured. One said with a cough to Silas Hayes, 'You are now divorced – sir.' Then they were ushered out and the steward closed the door.

Cigars were lit and the gentlemen sat about waiting for a lead. The Consul stood up and walked slowly to the tall window, where he leaned against the frame, staring out at the Chinese city glowing in the distance, from the results of insurrection.

'Horrifying,' he said to himself.

'Divorce?' suggested Silas softly.

The Consul turned to see his former son-in-law standing at his shoulder sipping port. 'China,' he said and looked hard at Silas. 'Are you sure you know what you have done?'

'Yes,' answered Silas.

'Help the boy,' urged the Consul quietly.

'How? He himself is about to leave for San Francisco. He is destined for another life in another world.'

'And you, Silas?' The Consul laid a hand gently on the shoulder of a man he had grown to like and was sorry to lose, appreciating that in all possibility they would never meet again.

'I am destined for' – Silas paused and grinned at the word – 'Gravesend.'

The Consul smiled. 'So are we all. . . . I would prefer you to say London.'

'England, then,' said Silas and raised his glass.

The two men drank port as the Consul glanced across the room to the others talking quietly amongst themselves. He went on brusquely, 'I shall personally bring Adèle to you in the morning.'

'Do you think it's a good idea?' Silas hesitated as Hollis Jackson stepped away from the group in the middle of the room and approached, followed by Eli Lubbock. 'A fast voyage in a clipper under all sail is, to say the least, far from comfortable.'

'One hundred days at sea,' stated the Consul, 'requires a measure of discipline – something from which I believe she will benefit.'

'She could travel with me, sir,' suggested Jackson, arriving with the decanter of port.

The Consul shook his head. 'She was once family for Silas, Mr Jackson, and he more than most knows that the two girls in one house were at best a trial. Since their mother's death. . . .' He paused and coughed, unwanted memories stimulated. Turning directly to Jackson he went on quickly, 'I do not wish to give you a further handicap; I am quite confident Cornelia will provide you with sufficient, ahem, diversion.'

'But I'm sure, sir – ' began Jackson.

Silas cut in. 'Take advice, Hollis, there's more rungs to her ladder of society than there are steps on the stairway to Heaven.'

Jackson glared as Eli joined them. 'Is that a compliment to Cornelia?'

'Judge for yourself,' smiled Silas. 'If you get there.'

'Get where?' Jackson spoke the words angrily.

'Why, Heaven, Hollis – surely?'

Jackson now caught the dubious inference and stepped towards Silas. 'Are you being deliberately ill-mannered? Because if you are I might remind you that the lady is no longer your wife.'

'I had already forgotten,' said Silas, standing his ground.

'Port?' asked Eli Lubbock diplomatically. Jackson shifted his attention slowly and poured absently from the decanter. The Consul accepted a further tot.

'So, with Adèle aboard *Vesper* and Cornelia ensconced in undoubted luxury with Mr Jackson, only Eli is without a lady aboard,' he said.

Eli, attention focused upon him, merely shrugged and glanced quickly at Silas. Nervously he raised his glass. 'To the ladies,' he said.

When Silas woke, dawn was an hour away. He lay silent and unmoving for some time, feeling the warmth from Emily beside him, analysing the decisions he had made and must make for one of the must crucial days he would experience since first he had arrived on the China coast so many years before. He turned his head slowly to make out the finely etched profile of the young woman breathing so softly she did not even disturb the night candle guttering on the table next to the bed.

Outside, the noises of the night in Shanghai had subsided. He knew if he ever returned to the city it would never again be the same. The coming twentieth century seemed to bode greater changes than the slower pace of the previous years. Stability was almost at an end and, Silas reflected, Britain might well be shaken from its perch throughout the world by Victoria's death after half a century on the throne of England. The colonial victories which had established an empire were long behind them; now power would be wrested from the ageing lion, as was the nature of things. Emily turned in her dreams and faced him, still slumbering with a smile on her lips. Silas kissed her lightly and slid carefully from beneath the covers. 'September 22 nineteen hundred,' he whispered to himself – it was a date he was sure he would never forget.

In the dressing room, Silas clothed himself carefully, knowing that in all probability he would be unable to change for several days, certainly not until they were well out to sea and far down the China coast. His trunk was already in the hallway, where he could detect the first sounds of activity. For almost a minute he stared down at Emily, undisturbed and sleeping still; her relaxed face seemed to Silas, in the faint light of the night candle, like a child's. They had made their good-byes during the night, with kisses and tears from Emily, who had clung to Silas until merciful sleep proved more persuasive. He blessed her silently then went out. He smiled. The rain had stopped and he could hear a wind.

Silas slowed as he reached the top of the stairs. Below, in the half-light, porters and Marines were moving out cases and trunks through open doors. Silas turned to grasp the brass knob gently; opening Jamie's door, he walked in quietly. The boy was in an untroubled sleep, on his face the innocence of the young. The lamp on the dresser flickered dimly, the wick turned almost to the brass. Silas took from his pocket a small gift and placed it beside the framed photogravure his son so cherished. He wished the boy well and felt in his breast unfamiliar longings that things might have been different, but accepted life's lesson of the way things were; the Greeks had created a word for it even before Jason penetrated the Hellespont – Moira. Fate and Destiny both. The father looked back at his son. Soon they would be half a world apart. He fought the grief that seized his throat, accepted the inevitable separation and slipped back into the corridor, closing the door softly.

Jamie's eyes snapped open. He waited until he heard his father descending the stairway then leapt from beneath the sheets to kneel at the bottom of his bed. Turning up the lamp, he examined the gift with curiosity. It was a small brass compass. He grinned to himself.

'True north,' he whispered, and slid over the eiderdown to put on his shoes. He was already fully dressed and his resolve had never been stronger. He tied his laces and stood up. As he stepped forward he realised with pride, pleasure and excitement that he had taken his first pace into a world of his own choosing. Come what may, he had become his own master.

11

Silas Hayes waited several minutes in the hallway for his friend Eli Lubbock to arrive at a time and rendezvous clearly agreed the night before. He checked his pocket watch on several occasions, grumbling to himself and nodding reassuringly towards numerous apprehensive faces amongst the assembling groups.

'Good morning,' came Eli's voice brightly.

'You're late,' grunted Silas. 'The carriage has been waiting for four minutes.' He began to stride towards the tall open doors, where light already showed. Placing his peaked cap on his head he descended the steps quickly and leapt into the open carriage. Lying back in the landau, he ignored Eli as he stepped in and closed the door. Immediately the driver cracked a whip and the horses drew away from the consulate's columned portico, threading amongst other waiting carriages, US Marines, porters and stewards loading heavy trunks.

'Rain's stopped,' grinned Eli. Silas merely looked at him as if he were a fool. 'And we've a wind,' continued Eli genially.

'I hope you've not forgotten how to use it,' Silas growled.

Eli's eyes narrowed. 'Out of sorts, are we?'

'Out of Shanghai,' Silas muttered, almost to himself, and nodded absently to the Marine guard as they passed through the entrance into the streets.

'Why are you not travelling with Emily?' asked Eli gently, guessing at his friend's ill humour.

'Why are you not travelling with Adèle?' snapped Silas in retort, staring hard at Eli.

'It was her father's wish she should be with *you*,' replied Eli. 'It was certainly not mine.'

'Lovesick, are you?' asked Silas with a wry expression.

'And you are not?' smiled Eli.

'At your age. . . .' Silas shook his head.

'Then there is little between us,' suggested Eli, and settled deeper into the leather, reaching for a cheroot from the case in his inside pocket.

Silas began to laugh. 'Only half the world,' he stated, and accepted a proffered cheroot from his friend. The two men lit up as the horses broke into a trot on the wide, cobbled and tree-lined boulevard. Avoiding the first trams of the morning and the already numerous rickshaws, their landau joined several others at the intersection that would take them down to the port. For a moment they rode parallel to a very elegant polished landau containing, as both men recognised, an exceptionally well turned-out gentleman.

'Good morning, Hollis!' shouted Eli.

Silas touched his cap and a grin spread across his face. 'I hear gold is taking you out of your way?'

'Rumour abounds in Shanghai, Silas Hayes.' The two pairs of horses, strangers to each other, bucked in their shafts and whinnied loudly.

'Heavy cargo, Hollis?' asked Eli loudly.

Hollis Jackson merely attempted a withering look towards Eli, who, in turn, merely smiled knowingly and touched his nose.

'Dutch gold?' asked Silas irreverently.

'It is . . . South African, as I am sure you are aware.' Jackson muttered at his driver to urge on the horses, but with other carriages in front he could only shrug helplessly.

Silas shook his head and leaned towards Jackson's landau. 'Greed before speed, Hollis, has many times slowed a ship's passage and lost her the way in first. . . .'

'Steam before sail, *Mr* Hayes; the one is without competition from the other. There is no question as to first – even should I linger as I please.' Jackson smiled at the thought, pulling at his soft grey leather gloves, which complemented his suit, cut from cloth of a darker hue. He glanced at Silas, a look of pity in his eyes. 'The only contention is how far behind your two canvas and caulk hulks will be.' He began to laugh at the thought.

Silas nodded, ignoring the probable accuracy of the statement. 'The rumour you refer to; indeed, the good port doctor – Murphy – confirms to me that Black Plague has broken out up north. . . .'

Jackson raised his brows. 'Why should that concern me?'

'Have you no compassion for the afflicted?' asked Eli, and coughed to control his laughter, knowing Silas was sailing near the mark and had already given Hollis clues.

'I'll save my compassion for both your long faces – when you arrive,' he said, then grinned as his landau jolted forward, the driver having found a way ahead. 'I'll be waiting for you two windbags – in London,' he shouted over his shoulder.

Jackson's departure seemed to take with it the humour of the two friends. Silas slumped into his seat and growled at Eli, 'The damn truth of it is – he might well.' Their carriage began to force a passage through many rickshaws backed up amongst roadworks, where tramlines were being re-laid amidst piles of torn-up cobbles. First sunlight penetrated trees to one side of the boulevard and a soft wind rustled the falling leaves, lifting Eli's spirits.

'We've a chance, Silas – there's always a chance.'

'A chance,' agreed Silas, 'but no advantage.'

'We have experience,' Eli reminded him and smiled, feeling the morning air on his face. 'And a wind.'

'The sea has no favourites,' murmured Silas. 'I said that to Jamie. It is a teacher of men and always the master.'

Eli shivered unaccountably at the sudden seriousness in his friend's expression; the words were familar but had been given feeling by Silas' mood. 'Every voyage can be a last passage,' Eli said. 'But we have accepted responsibilities for souls at sea; let us trust to God . . . and also luck,' he suggested.

Silas stared at his friend, serious still. 'We have both gambled, Eli, but these are the highest stakes we've taken; let us trust in only two other things. . . .'

Eli frowned, 'What?'

Silas smiled, now hearing the noise of the dockside they were approaching. 'Macintosh,' he said, 'and telegraphic communications.'

Eli extended a hand. 'We'll beat Jackson,' he said. Silas shook it firmly. Eli pulled him closer and stared into his friend's eyes wickedly. 'You have yet another problem but half the world's water and Hollis Jackson.'

Silas' dark brows lowered. 'And what is that?' he growled.

'I intend to be first!' stated Eli.

'Damn you, Eli Lubbock,' grinned Silas.

'And be damned, Silas Hayes,' replied Eli.

'First,' they both stated, and shook again, by which time their carriage was already entering the open gates of the bund, where the great port of Shanghai roared with the activity of dense crowds, giving off not only the stench of animals and unwashed humanity sweating already in the morning's intense humidity, but also the distinct and detectable odour that anticipation, excitement and apprehension combined put into an atmosphere charged with the unavoidable fears of an immediately unknown future.

*

Silas was the first to alight from the carriage. Instantly US Marines surrounded him for protection from gathering creditors all holding aloft voluminous bills and shouting attempts at English in a combination of accents. He smiled gamely, waved farewell to Eli and watched his trunks being loaded aboard as the carriage moved off. Acknowledging the creditors pleasantly, he marched aboard *Vesper* between guards who pressed a way through the Chinamen. Arriving on the poop deck he shook hands with Ben Hardy then Hughie Sutherland. 'They seems capable, Captain,' said Hughie referring to the crew. Ben's dog, Polly, poked a nose from inside his loose jacket and barked agreement.

Silas stroked the small terrier. 'Ben?'

'Ship-shape *and* Bristol fashion, sir. We'll be having any malingerers on short rations, denied completely if they prove stubborn.'

Silas nodded and stepped to the poop rail, watching the crew at task, rolling his cheroot between his fingers. 'Assemble them,' he said.

'Aye aye, sir,' Ben snapped and took the stairs down to the main deck two at a time.

'What do you think, Hughie?' asked Silas quietly.

'Well, sir. . . .' Hughie hesitated. 'Nothing like the old days.'

Silas nodded agreement and looked at his mate. 'Nothing ever will be, Hughie. Your father would be the first to attest to that. . . .'

Hughie grinned. 'He was the best pilot on the Yangtse Channel, sir, and could advise a captain how to back up a clipper into Whampoa under sail.'

'I'd heard talk,' said Silas, 'but never believed it –

Hughie interrupted vehemently, 'It's true, sir – know, I was aboard the old *Flying Spur* when she – '

Silas grinned and puffed on the end of his cheroot, cutting in, 'Went aground?'

'No one ever said he didn't drink, sir. . . .'

'No one ever would have done, Hughie,' said Silas, blowing smoke. 'Rum aboard here's to be only once a week or in heavy weather.'

'Yes sir.'

'All of us.' Silas fixed Hughie with a stare.

'Yes, sir.' The mate wiped his mouth and unshaven chin.

'Where's your flask?'

'Back pocket, sir.'

'Put it in the chart room,' commanded Silas.

Hughie hesitated, 'Your cabin, sir?'

'In the drawer beside the reference maps – it'll be there if you want it. Just let me know. In a hard blow I want all your senses.'

Hughie nodded, remembering knowledge of his recent exploits had travelled in the city. 'It was only 'cause I was shorebound, sir.'

'I'm banking on it, Hughie – you're soon to be at sea.'

'An' lookin' forward to it, sir.'

'So am I, Mr Sutherland,' said Silas softly. 'God damn it, so am I!'

The crew assembled and Silas appraised them one by one as they lined up on the deck before the poop. Ben's dog growled as the Second Mate joined Hughie and Silas.

'Are they all here?'

'Some had shore leave, Captain.'

Silas checked his pocket watch. 'We're early.'

'Yes, sir,' answered Ben. 'But they're good lads.'

'Then we'll wait,' said Silas. 'They have six minutes to board.' He looked impassively at the group before the mast, sullen and in the main weathered, although some of the wet-behind-the-ears greenhorns shuffled uncomfortably under his appraising eyes. 'Is this all there was?' he asked Hughie Sutherland.

'All who would sign.' answered the Mate.

199

'Does Eli have an edge?'

Hughie grinned in reply, 'Only with dry canvas, sir.'

Shadow concealed the tall figure in a long plain robe but his eyes glittered as if lit from within. Looking beyond the balcony on the first floor of a harbour building, Kin Sang spoke softly, as if to himself.

'Remember that the journey is long and revenge is sweetest at a man's own door.' He turned slowly to see several of his Triad followers kneeling on the floor of the gloomy room, where only red and gold lacquered panels on the walls reflected first sunlight appearing from morning cloud hanging low over the distant river to the east. Kin Sang smiled viciously, seeing two of the men press their foreheads to their Malayan daggers, the honed blades made in the shape of a moving serpent, designed to decapitate with a sweep of the arm. He bowed, acknowledging the courage of the two Triads who had accepted the difficult task that now lay ahead.

'You, as his crew, must learn patience and await the perfect opportunity.' Kin Sang paused. 'If you survive, our brothers in London's Limehouse will give you sanctuary.' He turned slowly, seeing the halted carriage below and Eli stepping down. Immediately the US Marines surrounded him, keeping the crowd of creditors at bay. Eli waved cheerily before running up the gangway to the ship's rail, where he stopped a moment to ensure his trunk was being allowed through the press of Chinamen at the quayside. Kin Sang frowned as he saw Eli check the pistol thrust into his belt, but knew his men would not fail. Their dedication was a sworn oath.

'Goodbye, Mr Lubbock,' he said, and made a small gesture which amongst the brotherhood was both curse and sure sentence of death.

*

Captain Silas Hayes stepped forward to the poop deck's teak rail and leant upon the brass acorn caps, arms spread, surveying his crew all the while. For a moment longer he said nothing, silence commanding attention. He could feel with his feet the brass-hooped, rope-handled fire buckets in the rack built around the stanchions and hoped they would never be necessary.

'I am your captain,' he began, his voice projected powerfully without need to strain. 'You obey my orders.' He paused to allow the import of the words to be completely understood. 'Many of you have never been out of Chinese waters, so remember that we are indeed "all in the same boat" and your total contribution to the running of this ship is expected at all times. Mark your step always, the sea's a living thing and only too eager to swallow up those who make even one mistake.' Some of the younger, inexperienced seamen shuffled again, uncomfortable at the thought. 'It will be too late, should you find yourself in an ocean one thousand miles from anywhere,' Silas emphasised. 'This was once a crack ship and I want you to live up to that reputation.' He stood erect and tall, squaring his shoulders, back straight. He raised his voice:

'At sea, I am the only thing that stands between you and the God in which you believe. Do not forget it!' His eyes ranged over the group, all of whom to one degree or other were impressed. 'Go about your duties – execute them well, and you need have no fear of me.' A murmur of respect came from the men. Silas glanced at Hughie Sutherland and nodded.

The Mate stepped up to the rail and bellowed. 'Dismissed!'

Silas checked his pocket watch. 'Soon,' he murmured to himself, and looked far up to the top mast, where a pendant fluttered in the increasing breeze.

Eli's eyes narrowed as he saw two Chinamen run up the

gangway on to *Chantril* and quickly join the assembled group before him, between the deck house and the mizzenmast. He checked his watch, as did Billy.

'Time,' he muttered.

'Just,' grunted Billy.

Eli stood, arms akimbo and began his address with the firm confidence of experience.

'I began helming ships like this when I was barely more than a boy. Heavy weather and strong winds over half the world under more than thirty thousand square feet of canvas will teach you all who are deep-sea sailors amongst us!' He stopped and made a grimace. What more was there to say, he thought. He could see out of the corner of his eye that Captain Van had arrived at the quay with a contingent of British Marines. No doubt, mused Eli, they would wait patiently in the hope he had not cast off by noon, after which, if still in port, Eli would once again be in the hands of the British authorities – as the Consul had declared. He coughed to cover the pause and checked his watch – time was racing, as he knew he should be. Replacing the pocket piece, he pulled out his .32 rimfire Remington pistol and held it high above his head, pointed to the sky.

Below, his creditors, arguing loudly with the US Marines, had begun to distract some of the crew. Eli pulled the trigger and the sharp crack from the gun stilled everyone.

'Let's get this ship underway!' he commanded.

12

The Oberheimer grandfather clock chimed eleven, pealing out into the grand hallway of the US Consulate in Shanghai a sense of urgency, communicating to the many elegantly dressed refugees who were to travel at noon that they had now less than sixty minutes remaining on Chinese soil. Chaos reigned unchecked, it seemed, as servants, porters, US Marines, coachmen and personal staff moved as quickly as the trunks, cases and portmanteaux they were shifting allowed. All at the same time were shouting orders, repeating instructions and arguing at ill-advised commands, creating a din which almost deafened young Jamie Morgan, who stood above it all on the stairs, peering down, searching for his mother and her sister to appear. His grandfather, the Consul, had occasionally during the last few hours walked amongst the agitated would-be passengers, reassuring them and attempting to create calm where there was rising panic. As loaded carriages crunched away on the gravel outside, the sobbing throng of well-wishers were reluctant to cease their cheers, hurrahs, and cries of farewell until each of the landaus, broughams, coaches and even traps had long since travelled down the drive and turned out of the guarded entrance between the high outer walls, into the streets of Shanghai.

Jamie was nervous but determined. He had already charted his course and smiled to himself at his private thought – if he reached the Cape of Good Hope in safety, when his father's clipper turned into the Atlantic, it would certainly be true north. But that was still half a world away; time was running out and the ladies were leaving it until the last moment. He swore a schoolboy oath under his breath and immediately apologised to the Creator that he had ever cursed his mother.

'Where are they?' he hissed, and crouched lower behind the balustrade. He would be called to say goodbye, he knew, but he wanted no one to see the small knapsack he had prepared. He was due to leave in three days on the American Line steamer for San Francisco, but the letter to his grandfather, if he was successful in boarding *Vesper*, would, he hoped, alleviate fear at his disappearance and explain his decision to travel to an altogether different destination.

Cornelia bustled into the great hall, nodding greetings to numerous faces she recognised and pulling on her pale blue gloves, which perfectly matched her dress and her large hat with a sweeping brim and raised veil. She called clearly across the crowd, 'Jamie!'

The boy emerged at the top of the stairs, where Adèle was indicating her trunks to several porters. They paused in amazement as she counted out five of them, and numerous cases, together with a single beautifully crafted but undoubtedly heavy portmanteau. As Jamie descended to the marble hall, he heard the consternation of the porters, who knew Adèle's brougham was not big enough for so much baggage and so many passengers. A second carriage specifically for the excess luggage was declared the solution, and as Jamie heard this he decided immediately that it would also provide him with the answer to his problem of transport to the harbour. He arrived beside Cornelia.

'Yes, Mother?' he asked, smiling pleasantly.

'We must make our goodbyes. You will be off yourself shortly. Your grandfather will escort you to the steamer for San Francisco, where you must promise to do well. . . . Yes?' Jamie nodded. 'I am bound for England, and from there it is my intention to travel on

New York City. We will meet in the spring at the house on the lakes . . . you like the lakes, don't you, dearest?' Jamie nodded again. 'Chicago is pleasant in the spring,' she said. 'In California you will miss the real winter and I have instructed your grandfather, who will join you for Christmas, to escort you to the house during the spring recess. . . .' Cornelia fluffed the white ruff at her neck, felt the gold-framed cameo at her throat and smiled at her son. 'It will be very pleasant for us all to meet up in such a way after time apart, don't you think?' Jamie nodded. 'Kiss me,' she said, and bent fractionally towards him. Jamie kissed both her cheeks dutifully. 'There now,' she said, 'school must be a great success which I will reward with a surprise.' Jamie nodded once more.

'Well, have you nothing to say?' asked his mother. Jamie shook his head. He was already fighting to control trembling from sheer excitement. She turned away brusquely and was about to stride through the great doors and out to the pillared portico, when she stopped and turned, tears in her eyes. She knelt quickly and kissed her son, hugging him close until his cheeks were wet with her tears. 'Be good,' she whispered, 'and take care of yourself.' As Jamie reached out to her, she broke away, stood up and brushed down her dress.

Reassuming her public manner, she touched Adèle's cheeks with her lips, sniffing still and forcing a smile. 'In England then,' she said. 'I'm sure we will be waiting for you.'

'Silas intends to beat Hollis, Cornelia,' grinned Adèle.

Her elder sister nodded and said ironically, 'Silas has always had intentions: seldom fulfilled.' She dropped the veil over her face. 'Au revoir,' she finished, and strode out to the steps and waiting carriage. Jamie kissed Adèle quickly, shook hands with his grandfather, who had promised him a lunch in private so they could be together, then removed himself to a corner and was almost lost amongst the continuing chaos.

He had no eyes for the lady in black with a thin lace veil who waited, equally nervous, for her chance to board the landau she had arranged once the dignitaries had departed. She checked a small timepiece pinned to her bosom and gasped; loading the huge array of luggage both sisters were travelling with had taken up many minutes. They would be late leaving, Emily realised, and the fact increased her consternation; she whimpered and unconsciously touched her belly. Beside her hovered Awan, the loyal maid determined to accompany her mistress, shivering in apprehension despite the heat.

Jamie glanced quickly through the crowd, saw his mother boarding with her maid, and the Consul and Adèle waiting their turn for their carriage to arrive in tandem with the now loaded luggage bearer, a fat-bodied brougham drawn by two patient well-groomed drays. He walked back to the stairs, withdrew the knapsack concealed between the balustrade, then turned and stepped through a swing door into a waiters' room just outside the kitchen. A second swing door gave him access to all the glistening brass, copper, iron and steel cooking paraphernalia, where gas hobs were already lit in early preparation for lunch. Surprised chefs watched the familiar figure, some even calling his name, when he began to run. As he passed a huge platter of newly made sandwiches, he reached out and grabbed a handful, stuffing them in his pocket. A cry went up from the sous chef, but Jamie was nearly at the back door and freedom.

'Goodbye!' he shouted, and with a kick opened the swing door into the kitchen yard and was gone.

Jamie passed the stable area briskly, appreciating the smells of horses and tackle. Only for a moment did he hesitate, then, seeing the rear of the old fat brougham groaning with Adèle's luggage, he grinned, crouched low beside the thick hedgerow and reached the duckboard. He hoisted himself up exactly as the driver bellowed at the drays, cracked his whip and pulled forward with a jerk to take his place in line with the moving carriages ahead, which were already receiving a tumultuous farewell from the well-wishers crowding down the steps from beneath the columned portico.

Jamie almost lost his grip and fell back on to the gravel drive, but clung on, climbed over the folded hood and lowered his slim body between the heavy trunks. He settled on the floor, amidst the stacked cases, pushing several aside in an attempt at some form of comfort. He found none, but even in his suffering he grinned with satisfaction.

'So far so good,' he muttered, and closed his eyes.

Most of the way he was jostled unmercifully, the suspension on the old carriage long gone so that, crushed between the trunks and cases, Jamie could feel every cobble and tramline. Shouts from stevedores and Chinese porters and first hoots from tugs plying Whampoa's Channel indicated that he was arriving at the quayside. Inching his way painfully between the still moving luggage, he was able to find a grip on the rear edge of the carriage's folded hood. He peered out between two trunks to see another carriage directly behind him, containing a lady in black and what seemed to be her maid, already turning off to the mooring of *Chantril*. Jamie held on tightly as the old brougham stopped, throwing him against the luggage. He suppressed a cry of pain and climbed quickly over the hood and down on to the duckboard, then jumped on to the still muddy cobbles.

The stench of the harbour filled his nostrils and he could feel the heat of the sun on his back as he ran through gangs of coolies to hide in the shadows of a warehouse. He surveyed the moorings and assessed his situation. He could see his grandfather and Adèle making their way across to *Vesper*, where US Marines had created a path through the mêlée. The noise was deafening as all around Jamie horses, carriages and wagons laden with goods negotiated passages into the crowds. The humidity was intense and even young Jamie could feel the sweat running down his back. He glanced through a barber's shop window, and saw from a clock on the wall that it had gone eleven-thirty. He looked nervously across at the set of tackle and yards on his father's ship and saw that the running gear had been reeved, the sails bent and everything appeared set for a fast departure once *Vesper* had been pulled up channel and found a wind. 'Stamp and go' choruses indicated to a practised ear an imminent voyage as all hands on deck or those aloft running up the last sails to shouts of 'mount a reevo!' gave out,

> Running down with a press of sail,
> Slinging the water over the rail,
> Running down to Cuba,

sung loud and lusty. Jamie bit his lips and his eyes misted at the fearful thought that he might be left ashore as the ship dropped moorings and drew away from the quay. Resolution flooded him as blood rushed through his veins. In that moment, he knew he would not fail; he was his father's son and today, 22 September 1900, was outward bound for strange adventures across wild oceans to a distant destination where the landfall that would come with a cry of 'land ho' would be – England. Pressing the small knapsack beneath his arm, Jamie stepped into the hurly-burly to fight his way across the dockside towards *Vesper*.

Adèle and her father, the American Consul in

Shanghai, were ushered aboard Silas Hayes' clipper command with salutes not only from a bodyguard of US Marines but also from sailors who had once served in the forces of Her Majesty Queen Victoria and were now crew signed on to *Vesper*. The Consul acknowledged the men with a nod and led his daughter to the poop deck, where Silas waited at the rail.

'Welcome,' smiled the Captain.

Adèle curtseyed, which raised Silas' brows. 'Captain Hayes, my father told me I am to respect the commander of my ship, come hell or high water.'

'Did he indeed?'

'Not quite in those terms,' coughed the Consul.

'She has the gist,' said Silas.

'Will you show me to my quarters, Captain?' asked Adèle formally, but there was a glint of mischief in her eye. 'I am sure they must be much the same as Eli has aboard his vessel,' she finished, turning to her father.

He coughed again, not wishing to be drawn by her longing and obvious preference for Eli. 'Let's go below.'

'Then we'll be quick,' said Silas, checking his pocket watch, 'we're bent and reeved to catch the tide.' He indicated the steps down into his cabin. Adèle hesitated, as did her father, who was checking the luggage being boarded. Adèle only had eyes for *Chantril*, desperately seeking the figure of Eli Lubbock.

'You didn't say anything about a maid,' stated the Captain of *Chantril*.

Emily lifted her veil now she was safely below decks on *Chantril* and smiled winsomely at Eli. 'Her name is Awan. I begged her to stay but she refused.'

'I've seen her before,' mused Eli.

'She has been with me since I arrived in Shanghai, and was always a friend of Silas. Please, Eli, we can share the cabin.'

Eli Lubbock listened to sounds from up top of the

ship in preparation for departure, last loading, braces set, winches turned, the windlass spoked. . . . His eyes were on the two women in the gloom of the cramped cabin, their pleading faces lit only by shafting sunlight from the small porthole. He nodded to himself, which the women took as acceptance of their passage.

Emily rushed forward and embraced him. 'Oh, thank you, Eli,' she cried.

He continued to look at Awan. 'I remember you,' he said. The Chinese woman's eyes fluttered, uncertain of his meaning. 'You have a child.'

Emily pushed away from him immediately, then saw with relief that he was addressing Awan. The woman nodded as Eli went on, 'A son, who sells paper candle boats at the Festival of Lost Souls.' The woman nodded again. Eli smiled. 'Then you can sail.'

Emily spun round to the woman. 'Think again, Awan. You cannot leave a son. . . .'

'She won't,' said Eli, stepping to the door. 'She's going with him.' Awan's eyes widened. Emily frowned, not understanding. 'It was a promise,' said Eli, 'and was also to be a secret.'

'Cha-ze?' whispered Awan.

Eli nodded. 'He's aboard, signed to sail.'

Awan smiled broadly and hugged her mistress with joy as Eli pulled the door shut. In the small communal living area outside the cabins, other passengers moved to and fro, staking claims to what space they could for their possessions. Their babble irritated Eli, whose thoughts were already concentrating on the immediate problems of getting underway.

'Lewis Ellory,' grinned a young man, dropping a bulky suitcase and extending a hand.

Eli shook it and duly grunted, recognising the young man not only from the bowler and loud checked shirt but by the large box camera tucked beneath his arm. His over-enthusiasm had rankled with Eli when he sought passage but he had paid adequately and been recommended by the Consul.

Eli walked the length of the ship and took the steps two at a time to be up on the poop. The brilliant sunlight caused him to squint at his pocket watch. Twelve minutes remained until noon. Eli could see Captain Van and his British Marines waiting below. And now, there beside them in a carriage, sat the British Consul staring up at the ship. Only the US Marine detachment, with some difficulty, held back the suddenly screaming creditors, who, seeing Eli appear, surged forward, knowing that *Chantril*'s departure was imminent.

Eli replaced his pocket watch and quickly surveyed the yards and braces. 'Are we set, Billy?'

'Aye sir – almost.'

'All aboard?'

'Every mark taken, sir.'

Eli nodded. 'Pilot with us?'

Billy pointed to the Chinaman standing beside the wheel and looking towards the Channel, where a small steam tug was fast approaching. Eli bit his lip and stepped to the rail, followed by his mate.

'Cast off,' said Eli quietly.

'Aye sir,' Billy answered, then shouted, 'Gangway and lines fore and aft!' A great wail came from the Chinamen at the quayside, and suddenly as one they all moved forward, breaking the cordon of the US Marines, surging on to the gangway and running up to *Chantril*'s deck.

Eli swore loudly. 'Get that tugline, Billy, fast! I'll be below.' He ducked down into his cabin as the creditors fought past sailors on deck to reach the poop and their last opportunity of payment from Eli Lubbock this side of paradise.

13

'My creditors,' grunted Silas, and indicated the waiting group angrily shouting up at him from the quay. They were incensed now, having seen their colleagues penetrate the Marine guard to *Chantril*, but were forcibly held by the stronger contingent at the gangway of *Vesper*, reinforced by the Consul's personal bodyguard.

The Consul nodded. 'They'll no longer be a concern of yours after the noon-day gun.' He smiled warmly at Silas. 'You're an old rogue, Silas, but I've always liked you. . . .'

'I know that, sir. It's a feeling that's always been reciprocated.' The two men shook hands firmly.

Suppressing emotion, the Consul stared into Silas' eyes. 'If only. . . .' He paused. 'I'd have liked it to be different, you know.' He glanced at his daughter Adèle, who, again on deck, was gazing with curiosity at the commotion aboard Eli's *Chantril*. She accompanied both men to the gangway.

'She's not a bad girl,' the Consul went on, referring to his older daughter. 'Cornelia was spoilt from the beginning . . . my fault, I suppose, but her heart is warm, you know – there's kindness in her, affection.'

'She's a selfish bitch,' stated Silas. 'And I loved her.'

'I know you did,' the Consul answered quietly.

'As I do the boy,' continued Silas. 'Take care of him.'

'I will,' replied the Consul.

'Teach him,' said Silas, 'that money is not the only freedom in life – wealth traps the spirit and *there* is freedom you cannot buy.'

The Consul shook his head and smiled sadly. 'By God, Silas Hayes, I shall miss you.'

Silas smiled. 'Goodbye, sir.'

'Will we meet again, do you think?' asked the Consul.

'Of course,' said Silas, glancing below at the waiting Marines.

'As God guides us,' added the Consul.

Silas' face hardened. 'I believe in the constellations; they guide me.'

'Have faith,' urged the Consul, holding Silas' arm.

'I need no comforter,' replied Silas. 'I present myself to life as it shows itself to me. There is no other way. The sea teaches that from the beginning.'

The Consul narrowed his eyes suddenly. 'It's been a time, Captain Hayes, since you saw blue water.'

Silas recognised his ex-wife's mind and tongue in her father and nodded. 'Then I'll have much to learn,' he replied.

'Indeed,' said the Consul.

'Again,' smiled Silas.

The Consul actually grinned, beaten by the riposte. 'She was never a match for you, Silas,' he said ruefully, thinking of his older daughter.

'We were once – she shouldn't have fought me,' responded Silas, 'Then we might never have parted. Now it's over for all of us.'

'Goodbye,' said the Consul. The two men clasped hands again.

Adèle kissed her father, who nodded to the First Mate, Hughie Sutherland, then turned to leave.

'Look after the boy,' said Silas.

The Consul held up a hand to shade his eyes from the sun and see his ex-son-in-law. 'Why must we always speak the truth when it is too late?' He paused. 'As you are everything I could have ever wished in a son, so you are all Jamie has ever wanted in a father.' He pursed his lips, lowered his head and raised it again, remembering his place, his station and his men waiting below. 'God speed,' he said.

'Make way!' shouted a Marine sergeant, and even as the Consul walked down to the quay, bolt ropes securing the gangway were let go by crewmen, who waited until the United States representative in Shanghai was ashore with both feet on the ground before loosening the stays, unlocking the clips and pulling in the single access to the shore of China; only the lines remained. . . .

Jamie ran as if his life depended upon it; and, had he known – it did. He leapt from the quayside for the poop mooring as all eyes on the dock turned towards *Chantril*, where loud commotion had focused all attention. Young but strong, Jamie climbed hand over hand, feet crossed on the rope until he was at the pipe. Here, unable to climb through the sheath, he reached up, precariously releasing one hand, and grasped the first stanchion his fingers could find. Reluctantly he let go of the rope and seized the teak with both hands. In the next moment, he had pulled himself up and over the taffrail on to the empty poop deck. Glancing below to the harbourside at several Chinese porters agape at the boy's swiftness, he grinned, waved, then plunged below into his father's cabin.

Jamie looked around him at the charts and artifacts, personal possessions and necessary instruments of a clipper captain. Already the small mahogany panelled room seemed lived in; to have a spirit. Jamie stepped forward, hearing urgent voices outside snapping orders. He could feel the Whampoa beneath him for the first time as the ship rode the tide. With a deep breath he entered the communal dining room. It was deserted. Lamps hung above a long polished wooden table which filled most of the space. Again, rosewood panelling gave a warmth to the room, only the raised lip around the table with insets in the wood, to contain sliding plates and protect moving glasses, gave rise to speculation of heavy weather at sea. Voices above alerted Jamie and he moved on, opening a door cautiously to see stairs leading to darkness below. Feet sounded on the stairs of his father's cabin, and he went deeper into the hold of *Vesper*.

The long walkway ahead of him, lit by lamps, was empty. Above, a cacophany of noise indicated the completion of the imminent sailing procedures he had seen ashore. Loud hooting from a tug to port reversing its engines with a sound like thunder confirmed that *Vesper* was within minutes of departure. Ahead of him, sailors appeared, with several passengers anxious to be on deck for last farewells. Jamie pressed himself against the wall but only felt stacked chests of tea. Opposite, he saw bales of silk and realised he was in the upper hold; even if the stability of China was threatened, sailing ships provided opportunity for commerce which his father had not ignored. As the passengers took steps to port and starboard amidships to go up on deck, the crew continued along the open corridor towards the stairway behind Jamie, which led back up to the poop deck.

Jamie reached out, grasped a handle and opened a door. He stepped into darkness and fell into oblivion. For a moment he was stunned, then his hand found small dry grains of rice. He had split sacking in his fall. Despite his circumstances, he giggled with relief – but it was short-lived. The light from lamps outside, penetrating the rice hold, widened to reveal faces. The crew stared down, wondering why a door they had just secured was again open. Grumbling, they stepped back, and one of the men slammed the door shut and, worse, slid a bolt.

To Jamie, listening to their feet continuing to the poop, it was, even in darkness, the beginning of the

215

dream for which he had longed. No obstacle or challenge was too much for him; his imagination had ranged abroad so often in the past that now it was reality, all he had to do, he was sure was to 'think it out', as his grandfather always said. After all, he was about to go to sea, and within him was his father's spirit.

'God bless this ship,' he whispered, 'and all who sail in her.'

Entertainer extraordinaire Stanley Grace, in a loud checked suit and bowler hat, stepped on to the gangway of *Otranto* with a grin. His China tour cut short by nationwide insurrection, several successful stints in Shanghai music-halls completed, a contract for pantomime promised by his agent upon his return to Great Britain and a ticket to London nestling against the 'telegraphic guarantee', he felt, after the several gins he had allowed to pass his lips during a late breakfast, that he had cause to be pleased with himself. Thumbs in the pockets of his matching waistcoat, he paused half-way to shipboard and half-way from China. Turning, he took a last glance at the city he had much to thank for. Shanghai had wiped the memories of his disasters in England, where his honed acts had not been improved with white spirit from a green bottle. Shanghai had given him back the greatest asset a performer with talent could wish for – confidence. Stanley Grace waved goodbye to the immediate past, as his coolie porters bent beneath the weight of his trunks.

'All aboard, boys,' he grinned.

Hollis Jackson hastily pocketed his watch and smiled a welcome as Cornelia appeared on deck, opened her parasol and spun it on her shoulder, looking for a moment at the porters with her maid San, who were being ushered to the allotted cabins by smartly dressed stewards.

'We're ready to leave,' stated Jackson, 'and you are here at last.'

'I saw no reason to linger aboard for hours while you loaded,' she said, 'but now I confess if not excitement, then at least anticipation.'

Jackson took her hand. She willingly moved towards him. For a moment for the two of them, the sounds of the harbour were lost. The noise of hatch-covers closing, steerage ports being secured, arguing passengers and crew, whinnying horses and shrieking tug horns all faded as Cornelia's eyes, shaded by the parasol, met Jackson's, and as he stared down into what he had begun sincerely to hope would be his future. It was then that his past intruded – loudly.

'Lawd luv a duck!' came the voice of Stanley Grace. Jackson looked up to see a figure fast approaching. 'Allo, me old China!' bellowed Grace. 'I ain't seen you in years!' He appraised Hollis Jackson. 'My, my, my, we 'ave done well! It said on me ticket, "Jackson Lines", but I didn't think for a minute. . . .' He shook his head. 'Who'd 'a thought it? Old Lucifer Jackson himself!' Grace glanced at Cornelia, nodded to the lady then noted Jackson's consternation. 'Don't you recognise an old China plate?' he asked. 'Pennyfields?' he prompted. 'Limehouse!' he added. 'Cor blimey, we used to do the docks together! That's where it all began, innit? You jumped ship and I joined the Army.' Cornelia smiled and looked at Hollis with growing amusement. Grace took the hint and the initiative; seizing her hand, he kissed the glove lightly, doffing his hat. 'Miss Morgan, in'it?'

'I do not recall . . .' began Cornelia.

'Who'd forget an 'Elen of Troy like you. . . . Remember Mr Stanley Grace, Entertainer Extraordinaire! The Consulate, your father's place . . . ? My first contract on the China coast, an' pleased to 'ave it.'

'You have a better memory than I Mr . . . Grace,' said Cornelia.

'Got to 'ave in my business,' said Grace, talking ten to the dozen. 'Look at 'im.' He clapped Jackson about the shoulders. 'The match king o' Limehouse he was! An' smart!' He tapped his nose. 'We grew up together more 'an forty year ago dahn London's East – on the docks! I stole coconuts an' he sold matches – wot d'ya think 'a that?' He grinned as another thought came to him. 'An' we've met along the way since! What is it now? Twenty year ago?' He moved closer to Cornelia, assuming a confidential manner. 'I 'elped him hout of a spot of bother in this very Shanghai when I was a sergeant-at-arms in 'Er Majesty's Forces.' He paused for effect and nudged Jackson, winking again. 'But that's another story, ain't it, Lucifer?'

Jackson was unable to conceal his obvious embarrassment. 'Are you in steerage?' he asked.

Grace roared with laughter, pulling a ticket from his pocket. 'I'm POSH!' he stated, pointing to the sheaf of papers. 'Port Out, Starboard Home. Star treatment! First-class all the way!' He spun on his heel, distracted for a moment by his porters shouting for payment.

Cornelia smiled sweetly. 'Ten whole weeks at sea,' she murmured to Jackson. 'How amusing – Lucifer.'

Jackson gritted his teeth as she nodded to 'Mr Grace' and took his arm. They walked the length of the deck to the rail at the rear overlooking the steerage section, where the deck below was packed with the cheap passengers barely able to pay for the minimal cost of their tickets. Many of them were arguing, others even fought as the crew attempted some control.

'And you would have consigned your friend to this, Hollis?' asked Cornelia, disapproval in her voice.

Jackson nodded, remembering. 'It's the way I first came to China.' he answered.

'How intriguing,' she whispered, and seeing several young women below staring above at the rail where she stood with Jackson, recognising it as the hurdle to another life, she felt compassion for a moment. 'Poor creatures,' she whispered.

Cornelia turned away from the rail to see several tugs churning water to starboard, hearing the loud exchange of directions as the two captains settled upon their places for towing *Otranto* out into the Channel, down the Whampoa to the Yangtse river, where the China seas lay beyond.

Impatiently Cornelia sighed heavily. 'Then let us set sail, Hollis, with no further delay.'

'An unfortunate word for a modern steamer,' he replied, 'but if you will observe to port, we have already loaded, boarded and dropped our moorings.'

Cornelia saw that *Otranto* was indeed moving slowly away from the quayside. 'At last,' she said, smiling, 'we're off.'

Hollis Jackson nodded absently, looking ahead, where he could see *Chantril* and *Vesper* being towed out to the deeper water of the flowing Whampoa.

'Yes we are.' he murmured.

'Good luck,' she said softly and kissed Jackson on the cheek.

He looked at her, seeing in the steady blue eyes strength, humour and perhaps affection. 'Do you think I'll need it?'

Cornelia smiled. 'You now have only a ship.' She pointed to shore. 'You're leaving everything else you own behind you, Hollis.'

'I know,' he muttered.

'Wave,' she said brightly.

Arms aloft, standing in their respective carriages, the

American and British Consuls to Shanghai waved farewell to those aboard the three ships moving slowly down river. Despite his self-control, Morgan stifled a sob at seeing his two daughters going from him, knowing that a departing ship is a sobering sight, taking with it warm hearts, cherished dreams and a hundred other futures that could have been. There were laughter and tears both ashore and aboard as many 'hurrahs' were shouted from people lining the quaysides and crowding the rails.

A loud explosion sounded, startling everyone who had forgotten the noonday gun. The American Consul checked his watch, then sat down on the carriage's soft leather, leaning against the folded hood and feeling the sun on his face. He wiped perspiration with a cotton handkerchief, still staring towards the moving ships, where several sky sails were already showing from the clippers' yards. He glanced over his shoulder and acknowledged the British Consul in conversation with Captain Van, who appeared disgruntled, knowing his quarry – Eli Lubbock and Silas Hayes – had escaped him. The Consul sighed. Small problems compared to his in Shanghai, or indeed Eli's and Silas' once they were in open water. He resettled himself and thought of a pleasant lunch with Jamie.

'Home,' he said to his driver.

14

The babble in Eli's cabin aboard *Chantril* was like a Chinese market and had begun to irritate him as he attempted to go about his duties, preparing charts for calculations at sea. He was head and shoulders above most of his creditors, and their waving arms contained not fond farewells but voluminous bills thrust at him with increasing aggression.

'Gentlemen!' he said loudly, creating some peace for a moment. 'Would you like a drink?'

From the shore battery on the bund he heard the boom of the noon-day gun and smiled to himself. With the Whampoa beneath him and Shanghai by the minute behind, he allowed himself an instant of pleasure. His good humour was noted immediately by the Mate, Billy, who entered the cabin and looked quizzically at Eli surrounded by the Chinese merchants.

'These gentlemen, Billy, were just informing me of some figures. Perhaps you would care to let me know the facts?' The sound of hooting came from the tugs outside, answered by the deeper note of *Otranto*'s horn. Eli nodded with satisfaction and actually grinned at Billy. 'Speak up, Mr Mate.'

'The pilot wants his "packet", sir.'

Eli understood and, reaching into an inside pocket of his dark jacket, took out a small bag containing several gold coins. The Chinamen's eyes fell on the money bag and they stared expectantly.

'I was just telling these gentlemen that it is inconvenient to pay them at this moment,' said Eli, and turned to address the creditors directly. 'When I return,' he began, and in the moment they were distracted he threw the coins across to Billy, over their heads. Their instant cries were cut short as the Mate crossed the cabin and ran up the steps to the poop, where, exactly as he disappeared, the pilot ordered the wheel over to bring *Chantril* into the centre of the channel, causing the ship to lurch against the current. Alarm amongst the Chinese was immediate. Eli's hand rested lightly on the revolver at his belt, exposed by his open jacket.

'Gentlemen, I shall be delighted if you would be my guests – although we shall be at sea for some time.' He smiled, his eyes following the creditors as they crowded to the steps and pushed their way up to the deck, money forgotten, their concern now only to escape.

Above, seeing their predicament, they sounded a great wail. Eli lit a cheroot and followed them up to the poop deck. Most of his creditors were peering over the rail at the murky brown water sluicing by, others babbled at the pilot, who deliberately ignored their protests.

Eli grinned at Billy, strong sunlight, a building wind and the prospect of open sea lifting his spirits. He leaned on the taffrail and stared back at the familiar skyline of Shanghai as it receded. A junk was being towed behind, seemingly for the creditors; more irate Chinese protests came from the sailors aboard, who were shouting for *Chantril* to let go their ropes.

Eli shook hands with the pilot, who had ordered the tug to let go its line for'ard, then watched the lithe figure scramble down a rope to his steam pinnace churning the water beside the clipper. Immediately, she pulled away, hooting shrilly. With a last wave, the pilot was on his way back to the great treaty port. Eli's creditors had all gathered together as their fears grew. He gestured to the closing junk now almost below the poop-rail.

'Gentlemen, your own lives will suit you better than a sailor's – I can promise.' He glanced at Billy and meaningfully regarded his pocket watch as the babbling creditors hesitated at the rail. 'I suggest you jump,' he said.

The first man, understanding, leapt up and poised himself on the rail set on to the teak stanchions. He timed it well and fell amongst ropes gathered at the prow of the junk. Screaming last obscenities in Chinese, the other creditors followed, each shaking their fists symbolically at Eli Lubbock before leaping down to tumble amongst others extricating themselves from the junk's prow. Only when the final creditor jumped, missing the junk and plunging into the swirling brown river with a shriek, did Eli order his crew to release the lines. The junk fell away at once. Shouts came from for'ard and Eli saw the tug-line being let go.

He looked up, hearing Billy bellowing instructions to his second and third mates, to see mizzen and main royals unfurled from the yards, and once clewed in they filled instantly on the following wind. He smiled with increased satisfaction and took a last look at distant Shanghai, which was partly masked by the rapidly approaching steamer *Otranto*. Ahead, the river widened into the Yangtse proper; further down, it would open out to the estuary and lighthouses at the mouth, where silt pouring into the China seas coloured the dull water almost to the horizon. It was familiar and for the first time in years would be a welcome sight to Eli. He looked over at Silas, barely one hundred yards to starboard, running parallel. He was waving across, gesturing towards the junk falling away from *Chantril* as the two tugs ahead of the clippers turned and, hooting noisily, passed perilously close between them to return to the river city.

'We've a good tide!' bellowed Silas.

'And the wind is with us!' replied Eli, cupping his

hands over his mouth. Sunlight glistened on the brown water and for a moment he was barely able to make out the tall figure of Silas Hayes beside Hughie Sutherland at the wheel.

'You've kept your head, after all!' came the cry, which caused Eli to grin.

'Keep yours and you'll give me a race!' he shouted back. Silas made a movement of his arm all too clear in its implications. Eli laughed and glanced above, always checking the luff of the sails billowing in the increasing wind. Billy thrust the 'letter to be opened on departure' at his captain, who read it quickly with an expression of dismay. Eli waved it at Silas, who waved a similar letter above his head.

'We're delivering corpses,' shouted Eli between cupped hands.

'What's that sir?' asked Billy.

'He wants them broken up when we reach Gravesend,' answered Eli angrily.

'Who?'

'Jackson,' answered Eli. 'But not if we win.'

'By God, sir,' responded Billy, sharing Eli's anger. 'Then let's give them a damn good last run.'

Eli nodded. 'We will,' he said, then bellowed across to *Vesper*, 'Good luck!'

As Silas' royals fell to their yards and braces were adjusted to take full advantage of the filling canvas he heard, almost lost on the wind, the retort from his friend of so many years. 'You'll need it!'

Ruefully and privately Eli admitted, as he guessed Silas himself was doing at that very moment, that he would indeed need all the luck he could get.

Otranto's tugs fouled their lines, which was only the beginning. As they turned to release the hawsers, the winches, tight on the wire, began to pull the ocean steamer out of the deep-water channel.

'Full ahead, mister!' Hollis Jackson ordered his captain.

'But we'll pull them across our bows, sir.'

'I'll drag them to England if they don't clip their lines,' answered Jackson, leaning on the compass housing in the wheelhouse. 'Look ahead of you, where two old hulks are eating the water of a mere river! What am I to expect at sea? Further incompetence?'

'Mr Jackson, sir, it is none of my doing. . . .'

'You are responsible, Captain . . . see to it!' Hollis Jackson strode to the door of the flying bridge and stepped out. He felt the strong breeze on his face relieving the heat and humidity, at first with pleasure then with resentment as he realised it was the fuel to his competition. Up ahead, lines from the reversing tugs finally parted and were winched back on decks. Jackson grunted then shouted through the open door into the wheelhouse as he shaded his eyes against the strong sunlight.

'The twentieth century belongs to *us*, mister! and the sooner those two caulked windbags know it the better!'

'Aye aye, sir!' replied the Captain, staring out at his owner with growing respect not only for his position but for the competitive instinct the man had honed almost to self-destructiveness.

'They've had their day!' growled Jackson, and looked back into the shaded cabin to see the anxious eyes of his captain, who had grasped the telegraph handles which communicated with the engine room. 'I said full ahead, mister!'

The Captain pulled the lever a half-circle, almost to the polished brass support, so that the metal arm rested on the words in the sectioned face: 'full speed ahead'. The binnacle set, bells rang throughout the ship and forward movement was noted even above deck at the prow, where sailors were raising sea flags. The packed steerage passengers in their cramped stern quarters heard the increased thunder of some of the most powerful steam-driven engines in the Far East.

Heavy buckets full of iron grits deep in the hold of *Vesper* were lugged for'ard, effectively shifting ballast, at the Captain's instructions to trim the ship as she set into the waves fully laden, with spray beginning to break over the rails. Hughie Sutherland emerged on to the poop deck, filthy but pleased, inclining a hand almost to horizontal at Silas, who nodded, knowing that his clipper now could sit on even the roughest sea with the confidence of an evenly balanced hull.

'She'll do,' he muttered.

'She will indeed, sir,' replied Hughie, white teeth appearing in grimy features.

Either side of the mouth of the Yangtse estuary, lighthouses flashed morse messages bidding farewell to *Vesper*, slightly ahead of *Chantril* as both captains spread canvas for the open sea. Strong winds in the late afternoon had brought them both on ahead of *Otranto*, and in sight was the seemingly limitless horizon.

'Half the world,' Silas reminded himself as Hughie washed his face in a bucket of sea water.

'We've done it before, sir,' spluttered the Mate.

'But each time, Hughie, is like the first,' stated Silas. 'Make no mistake.'

'We won't, sir,' replied Hughie, and wiped his face dry. Spray cascaded over the bowsprit as *Vesper* turned points to starboard towards the South China Sea.

'Say goodbye to China, Hughie,' murmured Silas, and watched the shoreline of that great country slowly begin to slip away as if it had only ever been a dream. 'Memories,' Silas added quietly.

'You can always take 'em with you, sir,' responded Hughie, rubbing the grey stubble on his chin.

'The best you must always leave behind,' replied Silas, leaning on the rail, and still looking back.

'Why, sir?'

'Because you've no future if you cling to the past, Hughie.'

'All some of us have, sir, is the past.'

'Not while we still live, Hughie.' Silas smiled and lifted his head, feeling the wind against his hair, which he had shaved close behind his ears where that sensitive area could detect even the faintest puff in still weather. He stared across at *Chantril*, half a mile distant, plunging into rising waves.

'Let's see her paces, Mr Mate!'

Hughie grinned and answered with the enthusiasm of an ensign on this first voyage, 'Yes, sir!'

15

Passengers emerged cautiously from below decks on both clippers as a steady wind cracked spread canvas securely clewed to fore, main and mizzen-mast yards, rushing the ships over a lightly breaking sea where foam-flecked waves chopped against the copper-clad water-lines, which glinted in the strong late afternoon sunlight.

Squinting southwards, many squeamish stomachs and faint hearts wondered at the very beginning what the voyage would bring before its end, so many days away.

High, scudding clouds in a clear sky were indications to both Silas and Eli that the lighter breezes below would be replaced before nightfall by stronger forces. Silas grunted, satisfied by the movement he could feel beneath him. 'She'll do,' he murmured.

'Indeed she will, sir,' replied Hughie at the helm.

Silas glanced across, where half a mile distant and still parallel, *Chantril* made the most of the prevailing conditions. Eli's competence was obvious to all expert eyes as he gave orders for the adjusting of braces to angle his sails for maximum advantage. Silas could make out Eli beside Billy on the poop, spread-legged and confident. So he waved hugely. A moment later Eli responded. Silas grinned. 'He'll give us a run, Hughie, have no fear of that.'

'I don't, sir,' smiled the Mate. 'Eli's good.'

'He better be,' growled Silas, then went on, his voice more commanding, 'If we hit rough weather, mister, be sure the oil bags are filled. They're to go over for'ard. It'll at least smooth the ride for the passengers.

And. . . .' He paused. Hughie looked at him quizzically, trying to read his captain's mind. 'I know we can out run any junk,' confirmed Silas, 'but. . . .' He paused again, then stared at his mate, not wanting to reveal very real fears for all travellers along the China coast.

'Check the for'ard guns, Hughie, and while you're at it, load the rifles. These yellow faces have grown cocky since they've got themselves a real war and they just might – ' Silas stopped himself, feeling the wind shifting points to port. 'Now, Hughie, let's see that foremast sky sail, inner and outer jibs do their work!'

Hughie nodded and beckoned to Ben, who ran up the steps to the poop followed by his little terrier close to heel. He took the wheel, allowing the First Mate to go down to the main deck and give orders to the waiting crew. Silas took out his pipe, which was already packed tight to smoke, lit the tobacco and puffed contentedly as he surveyed the set of his canvas.

'We've a race to win, Ben,' he murmured. Ben grinned as his dog answered with a bark. Silas knelt and fondled the terrier. 'We'll take 'em, won't we?' The little terrier seemed to smile, nod and agree, but could only second Silas' hopeful conviction with an affirmative whine.

Barely half a sea mile apart, *Vesper* and *Chantril* thrust confidently into waves of the running sea, accepting the fine spray that flew about their rails as first blood of the long battle ahead. Sunset clouds on the western horizon accumulated as if they too would slip away with the sun to leave a vast pale twilight and clear night sky.

Eli grunted his approval at the taut braces holding the yards at the angle of his command, their sails filled, bowed from the clews, canvas testing the freshening breeze. He watched the crew climbing the rat-tails with increasing confidence and nodded to his First Mate, Billy Williams.

'These top gallants must be clewed in tight, Billy . . . I want to make Java Head in thirty days.' Eli paused, distracted by the emerging Lewis Ellory who, once on deck with his large contraption and tripod, began setting up with desperate speed. Curious, Eli continued speaking to Billy whilst watching the earnest young man with his camera. 'We'll have been drunk a week before Silas sees our faces in Limehouse.'

Billy grinned in answer as his captain went on, 'We've plenty of time to find our sea legs.' Eli stopped as he saw Mr Ellory's tripod collapse on to the moving deck. He shook his head, seeing Ellory's obvious frustration in the distance beside the main mast and stepped around his mate to gaze ahead where twilight glowed brightly.

'This is a Steele Company boat, Billy, and they made the old *Ariel* and *Taeping*. She's as tight as a drum and I can already feel her spirit.' He took the wheel from his mate, who gratefully nodded his thanks and lit up a pipe.

'Aye, sir,' he said, puffing the tobacco hard between cupped hands. 'She's a Clyde ship and no mistake.' Green and red, port and starboard lights were lit. Eli could see Silas, still half a mile distant, had already done so.

'We'll take the Formosa Channel, Billy, but I'll guess we won't be out of trouble until we're long past the Amoy light and beyond the islands of Hong Kong.'

'Sir?' questioned Billy.

'Pirates,' Eli answered quietly. 'We used to have friends in these parts, remember. . . .'

Billy nodded, understanding the dangers.

'We've night runs along the China coast under a full moon,' Eli mused, and prayed privately that the threat would not materialise. He had seen for himself an

230

heard terrible stories of clippers caught by junks in a light blow or becalmed offshore.

Billy raised his head and turned to look east, where stars already shone. 'The wind's easing for us, sir.'

'Damn,' Eli muttered, and looked up at flapping canvas before glancing across at Silas. 'But not for him, Mr Mate!' Both sailors aboard *Chantril* saw *Vesper* forging ahead, bearing strongly in a following blow, south-west into the night. Young Lewis Ellory was equally angry, surrounded by passengers and crew with hurricane lamps. The Captain had merely lost the wind, whilst he had lost the light.

Food had been consumed and the raw smells lingered still in *Vesper*'s dining saloon as a coolie steward wiped down the mahogany table until it shone beneath the gently swinging lamps. He replaced numerous chairs and surveyed the empty room, then stepped below, whistling a badly remembered sea-shanty. Ghosts seemed to murmur lost conversations – but the noise was only the creak and groan of moving timber and copper, beams, pins and plates as *Vesper* settled in the dark waters of the China seas.

Silas, sprawled on his bunk in a light sleep, was disturbed first by the watch bells, then by Hughie Sutherland, who stepped into the Captain's cabin adjoining the dining saloon and turned up the lamp wick.

'First watch, sir. Calm sea and we've a north-east breeze, veering east.'

Silas grunted and sat up. 'Where's Eli?'

'We've outrun him, sir,' grinned Hughie. 'He lay too near the shore and lost the wind.'

Silas stretched and glanced at the chart, illuminated by the hanging lamp. 'Knot line?' he asked.

'We've eight knots holding regular and there's a light mist along the coast. The moon's up and there's fishermen dead ahead.'

Silas stood up slowly, now wide awake. 'Fishermen?' he growled.

'Yes, sir.'

'Then let's take a look at what they're out to catch.'

Silas was already moving when Hughie asked, perplexed at his captain's sudden suspicion, 'Sir?' He shook his head and followed Silas up to the poop; fishermen were fishermen, surely . . . ?

Ben, grasping the wheel, stared ahead with some concentration whilst his little terrier whined, spread-legged, on the saloon roof. Silas stood beside his second mate and surveyed the moonlit sea where, in the glittering water, numerous junks were dispersed and moving slowly.

'Haulin' nets, no doubt, sir,' muttered Ben.

'They're not a mile away,' murmured Hughie.

'I don't like it,' Silas stated and reached into the box before the wheel, took the telescope and walked quickly to the steps leading down to the main deck. He strode to the foredeck, lay against the bowsprit, where watch hands respectfully moved aside, and put the open telescope to his eye. He found the first junk, a black shadow against the sheen of moonlit water. The second and third straddled the path *Vesper* must take south-west. A silhouette appeared, then several others Silas could see were Chinamen with serious intent.

'Not nets,' Silas whispered to himself. He could see clearly what they were doing. Traversing his telescope fast, he saw the first junk's crew were armed to the teeth and pouring . . . 'Oil?' muttered Silas, then realised. 'Jesus Christ,' he swore under his breath. 'All hands!' he bellowed, pressing the telescope closed. He pushed himself off the bowsprit and began running back to the poop deck, shouting to his men all the while. 'All hands, reef and furl the jibs, foresail, mainsail, cross jack, now!'

He leapt up the steps to the helm. 'Clew in the top

232

gallants, mister!' he shouted at Ben. 'An' if you've time, strike out the royals and sky sail on the main! We've to keep our speed but lose our lower canvas or we'll lose the ship – in this wind at eight knots it's too damn late to go about.'

'Why, sir?' asked Hughie.

'We'd put ourselves broadside on so slow they'd board us in a minute.'

'Who, sir?' asked Ben, still at a loss.

'Pirates, Mr Mate!' snapped Silas, pointing for'ard. The full moon in a clear night sky illuminated the scene ahead, where junks lay to port and starboard of a wide space they had left for *Vesper*'s passage.

'What are they about, sir?' asked Hughie. 'We'll outrun 'em!' he stated with confidence.

Silas shook his head. 'Go to the for'ard guns and break out the rifles, Hughie. Give 'em to the best shots and get every spare hand, crew *and* passengers, to take on water – bucket it from the sea. Ben – take the wheel. I'll go for'ard to sight and shoot. Guide her straight as a die! We'll have to go through it head on.'

'Through what, sir?' asked Hughie.

Silas glanced at his first mate then stared for'ard as they were fast approaching the waiting junks; already he could hear chanting from the pirate hordes. A flicker of light showed distantly and he pointed as it arced on to the glittering water.

'That, Mr Mate,' he said grimly. From the pinpoint of light where the torch landed, a huge sheet of flame erupted then rapidly spread in a line, forming a wall of fire in front of *Vesper*.

'My God,' whispered Hughie.

'He won't help you,' snarled Silas. 'We're on our own. Move, man!'

Barely four hundred yards to *Vesper*'s lee and weather beams, the numerous junks – Silas made out at least eight – crowded with cut-throat Chinese pirates, manoeuvred in the steady breeze to encircle their victim once it had become engulfed in the flames.

Crude bombs, made of what seemed to Silas a form of Greek fire, were hurled in *Vesper*'s direction from primitive catapult devices, but they fell short – unlike the rifle fire. Head down against wild hits on the rail, wires and stanchions, Silas made his way to the fore-deck amidst screams and shouts from passengers and crew. Men at one of the fixed breech-loaders had removed the canvas and aimed the gun, glancing nervously at their captain.

'Fire!' bellowed Silas. The ring was pulled and a deafening report followed. A geyser of water aft of the nearest junk brought cries of fear from the pirates, who were now aware the fight would not be as one-sided as they had hoped.

Silas could see the armed brigands packed at the prow of the junk awaiting their chance to board their victim. He glanced ahead at the wall of flame they were fast approaching, then aft, where on both sides of the main deck crew had organised passengers to lower buckets time and again into the sea, scooping water in readiness for the fire. Anything that would hold it was filled with China Sea.

'What are your cartridges?' snapped Silas.

'Well, sir,' began one of the crew, looking down at the several large ammunition cases the men had broached, 'we've a mixture – '

Silas interrupted, ordering, 'Canister and grape only when we're on 'em to starboard. We'll pass them devils nearest.' He looked to port, where he could see, even through the flames, junks positioning themselves to best advantage for attack. He nodded to himself grimly and pushed aside the crew at the port gun. 'I'll fire the high explosive.'

The crew loaded the guns a second time. Silas locked the breech, sighted, and pulled the ring. A deafening report merged with cries of triumph as all on the ship saw the first shell landing squarely on the nearest junk with a great flash, blowing a hole in her side.

Vesper was now so close to the wall of fire that flames danced in Silas' eyes as he watched the gun being loaded again. Bullets smacked against wire and wood, forcing all on the foredeck to keep their heads below the well wall. Taking the chance, Silas stood quickly, aimed and fired again. A pillar of water rose up beside one of the junks to port, cascading down over the chanting pirates on board.

'Load,' Silas bellowed to some of his more reluctant crew. 'You should need no bidding! If they board us we're done for, boys!'

The fire wall was barely one hundred yards away as Silas shouted the length of the ship, 'Rat tails and halyards!'

Some of the crew nodded at the instructions to douse the vital ropes first.

Silas aimed again, glancing to starboard, where the nearest junks were barely a stone's throw away. Several fireballs catapulted from these vessels, soaring over *Vesper* ahead of the bowsprit. 'Canister and grape ready!' he commanded.

'Aye aye, sir,' replied the seaman at the starboard breech-loader.

'And all rifles bring to bear on the first junk!'

One of the sailors, an Irishman, was muttering Hail Marys as fast as his tongue would allow. Silas grunted. 'You'll find more comfort in a hot Winchester, Mr Malone,' he said disparagingly, and pulled the ring of the starboard gun. The shell hit the ramped stern of the leading junk, manoeuvring to pick up other pirates in the water. Screams sounded clearly across the water even above the steady roaring of the flames directly ahead of the clipper. Fire broke out aboard the stricken vessel, then a great flash lit the sky as the Greek fire ignited.

'Be Jesus Christ in Heaven!' exclaimed Malone, standing in awe. But in the next second he entered his own Hell. A fusillade of bullets from the junk to starboard ripped into *Vesper* and Malone's chest. He was thrown across the deck and fell from the bowsprit, through the martingales and into the water, exactly as the canister and grapeshot fired from the breech-loader raked the nearside junk's deck and *Vesper* entered the wall of flames.

Cries of 'Water here!' gun volleys, again the canister and grape, screams of 'The sail's caught!' as a firebomb burst on the half-furled mains'l, figures cowering from the intense heat, orders, commands, deafening reports from Silas' port gun, courageous crew at the rat lines bucketing the canvas, another roar of triumph and cheers for the captain as a direct hit blew apart one of the approaching junks – the battle raged. But as *Vesper* emerged from the flames, hot oil slicking her water-line, the fight turned in favour of the clipper.

Bodies in the sea were testament to that – and wreckage. The brave flags of several bands of pirates no longer fluttered, they lay limp in the oil and dark water as the few brigands who could swim thrashed about with pitiful cries. Some had been burn in the flames which now guttered behind *Vesper*. The remaining junks had turned towards land, their silhouettes clear on the moonlit water. Silas sighted and fired several parting shots in their direction, watching them re-brace their single-sectioned sails to zig-zag in the hope of avoiding the deadly accuracy of the clipper's guns.

Silas lay back against the bowsprit as Hughie approached.

'All right, sir?'

'Malone's gone,' said Silas. 'Anyone else?'

'A few wounded, sir. Hole in the mains'l – but it's part of the old set. . . .'

'Have you checked for damage?'

'Yes, sir.'

'Every brace, stay, rat tail and foot rope . . . ?'

'They're doing that now, sir.'

'Passengers?'

'Safe, sir.'

Silas looked at the moon shining in bright innocence of the scene below, obscuring the stars. Despite himself, the Captain of *Vesper* muttered, 'Thank God.'

Lewis Ellory's face glowed with enthusiasm. He ran his fingers through his tight curly brown hair then wiped his mouth with a napkin. Dinner was over on the clipper *Chantril*, but passengers lucky enough to be invited remained in the Captain's dining saloon, lingering over port and conversation.

'Captured!' Ellory declared, pausing dramatically. 'Imagine!' His hands swept the table, slowly securing his audience. Only Eli Lubbock showed obvious scepticism.

'Battles,' Ellory went on, 'great events, important people, moving clouds, shifting seas.' He surveyed the table, noting Emily's eyes wide in wonder. 'Everything!' he exclaimed. 'Anywhere.' Lamps swayed above the table, as did the twin circular wooden glass-holders hanging from long brass hooks.

'Here, Mr Ellory,' Emily asked, unconvinced. 'You could turn your camera handle, even here?'

Ellory nodded encouragingly, but immediately judged the panelled room too dark. 'Light,' he said. 'Here I would need more light. During the day' – he indicated the skylights – 'it might be reasonable to expect. . . but at night, well. . . .' He shook his head, then smiled winningly, speaking with distinct admiration. 'The moving picture camera is remarkably robust, but' – here he pointed an admonishing finger to anyone who might think otherwise – 'equally sensitive.' Ellory reached down and picked up his camera, the latest 16 mm American-made Johnson & Rickard hand-cranked special. He placed it on the mahogany dining table and, about to illustrate its mechanisms, clung to it fearfully as the clipper shuddered momentarily in the lifting sea.

Eli sipped port and smiled at both Emily and her maid Awan. 'Is it resistant to water?' he asked the young man.

Ellory hesitated and coughed, releasing his grip on the black box. 'Ahm, to light, yes . . . but, ahm, no – it is not waterproof.'

'So,' said Eli, 'you reveal the mystery of these modern inventions which are so practical, as is seen here.' He indicated the camera. 'You need light, but are proofed from it, yet water which you do *not* want may enter your device at will.' He stood up. 'Thank God the manufacturer does not build ships.' He nodded to the ladies, 'Excuse me,' he said.

'I should explain,' stammered Ellory, 'that the lens here lets in just sufficient . . . that is, if the photographer is aware of exactly . . . providing the conditions remain constant . . . if it has been established by a practised eye.' He stopped.

'Goodnight, Mr Ellory,' Eli said, then turned and stepped out of the dining saloon.

Up on the poop deck Eli stood next to his mate, Billy, who was allowing the wheel to play lightly in his hands whilst he referred constantly to the compass in the binnacle.

'Report,' Eli said, looking up at the full moon almost obscuring so many familiar constellations.

'The watch reported fire ahead, sir.'

'Indeed?' Eli took the telescope from the box and

238

examined the glittering sea for'ard. 'Wreckage,' he murmured.

'*Vesper*, sir?' Billy asked, genuinely concerned.

'Let's see,' Eli answered, and snapped the telescope closed.

At almost nine knots, *Chantril* cut through oil-slicked water, patches of it still burning. Cries for help in Chinese sounded from the dark sea but no attempt was made to rescue any of the swiftly passing bodies. Passengers and crew, summoned to the rails by natural curiosity at the news of a disaster, looked on, pointing at the waving arms and burnt faces of the drowning Chinese as they were revealed in the pathway of glittering water etched in the sea by the moon. Emily seized Eli's arm, her eyes pleading for compassion from the Captain.

'There's nothing to be done for 'em,' he said quietly. 'They're fish meat.'

Ellory stuttered, 'Couldn't we – put out a boat?'

Eli shook his head and laughed grimly. 'To find drowned rats in the dark?' He leaned on the rail and stared out at patches of flowing oil sliding by amongst wreckage from the stricken junks. He had already assessed the situation accurately and his admiration for his friend Silas Hayes was increased immeasurably. 'The lucky old dog,' he murmured.

'Who, Captain Lubbock?' asked Emily.

'Could be a friend of yours,' smiled Eli.

'Silas?' whispered Emily.

'He's ahead of us,' Eli answered, 'and Hollis is behind us both.'

Lewis Ellory coughed loudly. 'Humanity should dictate to you, Captain, that we heave to and at least attempt – '

Eli cut in harshly, 'Listen, boy, one thousand tons of ship under sail at night on nine knots ain't no toy. She sure as hell won't stop without a good mile o' sea room.' He turned to the young man, who paled beneath his gaze. 'If there was a way to turn up the moon on these *pirates*, boy' – Eli emphasised the word – 'you could use your camera to capture everything.'

Billy, standing beside Eli, burst into laughter at this but Emily's eyes clouded with tears at the ruthlessness of his words. Ellory, cresfallen, looked anew at the water and the passing indications of a sea battle, then, realising the import of the word with shock, stuttered, 'P – p – pirates!'

16

Black figures from a gang of half-naked workers seemed to dance before the white-hot flames of a huge furnace revealed by open doors. Resembling apparitions from Dante's *Inferno*, they tirelessly shovelled coal into the all-consuming maw, sustaining a heat to create intense steam, recycled by a condenser, driving the great pistons of *Otranto*'s engines harder, forcing her speed – at the Captain's command – to a maximum they had never before attained. The thick iron doors were slammed shut and the glimpse of Hell, familiar to the black gang, was closed off until the next time an indication of falling steam pressure would demand more sweat and effort.

The foreman of the gang lay back against an iron rib disappearing above him in the gloom of inadequate lighting. Bare torso and face black, only the whites of his eyes showed as he lit a small cheroot. Against the all-pervading coal dust mixed with the perpetual perspiration, he thankfully smelled the aroma of rough tobacco. He checked the steam gauge and rang up on the telegraph to the engine room. The vast, dark, hot cavern echoed with his shouted confirmations to the engineer, a harsh voice, deep-throated above the thunder of engines and roar of the furnaces. Slamming down the telegraph, he drew long and hard on his cheroot, blowing smoke towards sprawled colleagues taking a moment's rest.

'No money is worth this,' he mumbled, and thrust his shovel into a huge pile of coal brought in from the equally large storage hold.

'What's that?' shouted someone.

'I said,' he began, then stopped and grinned, gaps showing between yellowing teeth. He hit a bicep with his palm and raised a forearm topped with a fist taut against all he was learning to hate. A moment later he had seized his spade, tipped his cap – pulled tight to give some protection against the ever-present coal dust – and posturing like a music-hall act he had once seen, stepped around his upright tool.

Class! – Class is wot we got.
Class is wot we're not.
When you're in first, you're somethin' of a toff.
Second is 'ad – e – quate' your life's at a loss,
'Cos middle ain't anywhere – you ain't top or bottom.
Third tells you one thing, you know you ain't rotten,
'Cause even in steerage there's one rung below,
And that's for the black gang who've no hammocks to stow
Who sleeps amidst coal dust with no place to go.

The chorus of 'La-de-da' was sung loudly by the fore-man's men three times, then all the gang raised their arms topped with a fist and shouted, 'Come the revolution!'

A bell rang shrilly and the foreman grabbed the telegraph. 'Yes, sir!' he shouted respectfully. 'Yes, sir,' he answered, and replaced the receiver.

'The doors, men!' he ordered, and the furnace was again revealed as the gang queued with full shovels to bring the fires once more to white heat.

Plush red velvet glowed in the low light from orna-mental lamps perfectly offsetting the sheen on the rose-wood panelling of *Otranto*'s spacious first class dining saloon. The gentlemen were on their feet at the long Captain's table as they bid the ladies good evening, watching them retire to the ante-room, where some made their farewells and went on to their cabins to sleep. Stewards served brandy and cigars, ending a well-presented meal of acceptable quality. The atmosphere was convivial enough for the passengers to continue their attempts at getting acquainted. Stanley Grace had quickly established himself as the life and soul and, unwanted though he had been to some of the dinner guests, he had at least broken the ice. Conversation, slow at first, had become animated before the meal was over, increasing the prospects for their long voyage ahead. Two journalists – Meyer and Marsh – were travelling for their papers, to report, after months in Shanghai, on the improvements in modern sea transport.

Puffing his Havana, Hollis Jackson surveyed the Captain's table and smiled at Kimmen, the Dutchman, who preferred to light his own cigar, manufactured in Holland.

'Cuban quality, Mr Kimmen,' said Jackson, rolling the large cigar between his fingers. 'Surely you appreciate their superiority over all other smokes?'

'Nah nah gentlemen,' interrupted Stanley Grace. 'We ain't gonna argue taste for ten weeks at sea, are we? We've all our own preferences, and to tell it true, I likes the Virginia me'self.' Saying this, he lit a cigarette and inhaled deeply. 'They all send us to Heaven or Hell,' he said brightly.

'Frankly,' interceded Marsh, a short, stocky, balding man who was perspiring heavily in contrast to his tall, dark, cool companion. 'I've always hoped there's something in between; after all, harps and flowers or fire and coals – neither has attractions to draw a majority.'

'Death ain't an election,' said Grace.

'It is if the opposition has a gun,' smiled Kimmen. A moment's silence at the table produced only coughs, some embarrassment and a general wish to improve the conversation.

Jackson smiled at the two journalists, who were busily writing notes. 'Mahogany, brass and velvet, gentlemen. Mr Meyer, Mr Marsh as men of the press you must appreciate luxury after the deprivations of your no doubt harsh experiences.' He used the word so that it sounded almost delicious. 'Luxury,' he repeated, 'will become synonymous with ocean travel, mark my words.'

The two men nodded. Meyer, about to speak, was silenced at a gesture. Jackson, his audience assured, was determined to go on.

'You will also, I am sure, appreciate equally the now familiar sound of the future – the regular noise of the ship's engines ploughing into hostile waters, taking us all towards our desired landfall.'

'Very poetic, Mr Jackson,' Kimmen said softly.

'Thank you,' replied Jackson quietly. 'Brandy?'

Poverty at sea was best epitomised by the steerage class and all that went with the bleak, bare, cold communal holds where meagre rations and minimal facilities offered an altogether different experience of ocean travel for emigrants or refugees forced to flee from social failure, political unrest or starvation and unemployment. Surly cooks served soup to jostling queues supervised by numerous burly uniformed crew, who bullied the weaker travellers to their places at the long tables where third sitting for last service of dinner lasted merely long enough to consume the lukewarm liquid with black bread from tin plates. Bodies crowded together and voices babbled in languages representing a myriad countries. Men, women and children then repaired to bunk beds, which were stacked one atop the other, lining the sides of the deep hold of the steamship *Otranto*.

Here below, the regular noise of ship's engines was not muted by distance as above in the grand saloon; it reverberated with the noise of overhead thunder, forcing all communication to be loud – which naturally often led to heated tempers and conflict. Here was no mahogany, brass or velvet – merely bolted planks set before benches lit by poor light dimmed to near darkness at night. The crew only opened doors to the rear deck at appointed hours to allow a breath of air from the stifling conditions imposed on these already weary travellers, beaten even before the outset by their social-outcast status. All dreamed of a new life at landfall, but most knew it would in reality only be a continuation of the hell on earth they had been unfortunate to inherit. Poverty, the rich had always attested throughout Victoria's reign over a third of the world – despite the unforgivable conditions – carried its own rewards, which remained curiously unspecified. The fact was hypocrisy ruled, with a class-conscious lip-service to revolutionary changes, and whilst Great Britain was the richest nation in the world, half her population, without shoes, walked their narrow corner of it in bare feet.

'Enough,' murmured Cornelia Morgan, which was sufficient indication that the polished brass tap spewing hot water be turned off. San, her maid, sat on a small stool protectively beside her mistress, who was lying back in the long bath, exploring the newly added warmth with her toes. She smiled approval and sat up, inclining her neck, and allowed San to lather her back before taking the perfumed soap and gently contouring her own breasts until an adequate lather formed. She then lay back, sighing with pleasure as the hot water enveloped her torso. Helped to her feet, she turned for San to soap her buttocks and legs, then – again taking the perfumed cake – she lathered between her thighs. Slowly she sank into the water and lay for a moment in the delicious heat, feeling the cleanliness of her pampered body, until a disturbing thought made her turn to San with a suddenly sour expression.

245

'God!' she exclaimed. 'Ten more weeks of this!'

Her pale, perfectly proportioned figure emerged from the water as if Venus de Milo had been reborn. Coquettish Cornelia might be, but coy she was not; a delicately wielded razor had left her completely smooth from ankles to navel – after all, as she had confided only to San, if the days were to be increasingly laborious and no doubt boring in public, it would be as well to anticipate alternative behaviour in private at night. For months Mr Jackson had shown far more than passing interest, and it might well be, Cornelia decided, that the time had come, albeit forced by circumstances and her own physical needs, for that gentleman to be rewarded for his attentions.

Ensuring she was completely dry, she slid on the first of her garments: cool pink silk bloomers, cut short in the modern way. For a moment she appreciated the eroticism Hollis might well enjoy later, if he was lucky – sheer silk against the equally soft skin of her hips and legs. If anything, she had grown more beautiful over the years and had always believed in equal rights for men and women, provided the female retained her advantages – and she had lost none of those. The only disadvantage she had discovered was that her sexual appetites often exceeded her partner's abilities – at least, after Silas. She sighed away the unwanted memory.

She lightly kissed San gratefully on the cheek as she pulled up silk stockings, clipped on a garter belt and accepted the basque to mould her body from waist to breasts; yes, she decided, she was definitely in the mood and determined that during their arranged and clandestine assignation, Hollis would have to be very persuasive to have her in turn reveal her secrets. She would, of course, but slowly. After all, she thought with a smile as she belted the embroidered robe and stepped

246

into heeled slippers, they had half the world and all the future before them.

Hollis Jackson knew he had alternatives but, sure of his advantage, decided on a single course of action. He paused, wondering for a moment whether to light the cigar between his fingers as he stared at the interconnecting door to the next suite. He struck a match and muttered, 'Convenient', as he puffed on the tobacco then stepped to the door and knocked. Hearing no invitation, he knocked again and turned the handle. The door was unlocked, which was invitation enough, so he opened it and entered the suite he had personally assigned to Cornelia Morgan. Elegant in his long maroon velvet robe, cologned, bathed, shaved and suave, he smiled a greeting at the woman propped up against pillows, lying, ankles crossed, and reading on the large four-poster bed.

'Good evening,' he said.

Cornelia merely looked up, acknowledged him, then again regarded her book. Jackson closed the door, locked it and crossed the spacious cabin, which was decorated as if a room in a large country house. Luxurious drapes, carpets and furniture had been chosen tastefully and blended in a way pleasing to a discerning eye. He sat on the thick eiderdown, composed and self-assured. Only the rumbling engines, generator and lazily spinning fan in the ceiling intruded on the silence as Cornelia continued reading her book.

'*Great Expectations*,' Jackson said quietly.

'Dickens,' Cornelia added, without looking up.

'Interesting?'

'So far,' she murmured. Jackson blew smoke gently from his Havana away from the bed. It created moving forms, hanging above the yellow and grey Chinese thick pile carpet, dissolving images etched in light from the lamps either side of the wide padded headboard.

247

Cornelia looked up and pursed her lips, eyes admonishing.

'Surprised?' asked Jackson.

She turned to indicate the side table where a tray had been placed containing a bottle of champagne in an ice bucket with two long-stemmed fluted glasses. 'You seem to have thought of everything.'

'Imagination – has its rewards.'

'Does it?' she asked with raised brows.

'Aspiration and achievement are kissing cousins.'

Cornelia smiled, 'I would have said "distant".'

'Family at least,' suggested Jackson.

'Neighbours,' Cornelia said, and closed her book.

'What shall we talk about?' Jackson asked genially.

'Do we have a common subject?' replied Cornelia.

Jackson grinned. 'Money?'

Cornelia smiled slowly. 'Champagne,' she said. Jackson reached out for the bottle, took it from the ice and deftly began to take off the wire to extract the cork.

'You seem to be an expert.'

'Practice.' The cork popped.

Cornelia nodded approval. 'Perfect,' she added. Jackson poured the chilled wine and offered one of the fluted glasses to Cornelia. Touching rims lightly in an unspoken toast, they at first sipped, then drank thirstily.

'Pleasant,' she declared.

'I'm pleased you like it,' said Jackson, and he moved a little closer to her, noticing with mounting excitement the shadow of her cleavage, the loosely belted robe, partly exposed ample breasts. Cornelia deliberately put her half-empty glass between herself and Jackson before speaking with allure, practised to perfection whilst sipping champagne.

'You must remember that a woman at sea is a very vulnerable creature, Hollis.'

'Really?'

'Circumstances throw people together for a period of time neither can avoid.'

'Really?' Jackson said again.

'It can sometimes be very – difficult to resist . . . the idea of. . . .' She paused, hesitating to continue.

'An affair?' he suggested boldly but with tenderness in his voice.

' . . . of the heart,' she finished with a whisper. Both of them, eyes dancing in the flickering flames of the bedside lamps, finished their champagne.

'There is no sin in that,' Jackson stated softly.

'The only sin in life, Hollis,' she said quietly, 'is that of boredom.' She offered her empty glass, and their fingers touched, communicating equal desire. He leant to kiss her lips but Cornelia, indicating her glass and the cigar in his other hand murmured, 'Fill this up and put that out.'

Jackson smiled. 'At the same time?'

Cornelia's lips parted sensuously,

He took the empty glass and filled it whilst he dropped his long cigar into the ice bucket. Turning back to Cornelia, he tasted the bubbles then offered her the fluted rim. Her seductive face reflected the possibilities of the night ahead. She drank, then shook her head almost imperceptibly.

'Enough?' whispered Jackson. She pursed her wet lips in answer and slowly reached out to the further lamp above their heads.

'On or off?' she asked softly.

Jackson put down the glass and found the other lamp, his fingers already turning the wick. 'Off,' he said.

As both lamps faded, the two lovers-to-be leaned towards each other and, as only embers glowed, Cornelia, enfolded in the arms of Hollis Jackson, sank down into the yielding bed, her lips, trembling with anticipation, meeting others equally warm with passion and the promise of fulfilment.

Captain Tom Wallis, puffing on a cherished meer-schaum whose bowl glowed red against his cupped hands, stepped into the wheelhouse of *Otranto* and stood beside the sailor at the wheel, who immediately referred to the compass then again stared intently ahead. Instruments glimmered, indicating the generator was hard-pressed, causing the Captain to frown. The steam-ship's south-west course put her in a path of moonlight, which *Otranto* seemed to be riding to the horizon. Idyllic and romantic as it could have been described, the Captain was practical.

'Wind and sea?' he asked.

'Veering north, north-east on our weather beam – sea running south; any spray is off the wind, sir; nothing to worry about.' The young seaman looked at his captain confidently and received an amused but reproving glance.

'Really?' said the bearded Tom Wallis. Brought up in clippers, he had transferred to steam in the late seventies and, knowing the magnitude of revolutionary change twin screws and the Suez Canal combined would make to world trade, had capitalised success-fully. He had established valuable experience which had allowed him to tender for the job he now held, Captain not only of *Otranto*, but nominal commander of Jackson's entire fleet of more than twenty merchantmen. He was proud of his new charge. *Otranto* had completed trials and run out from England on her maiden voyage to be delivered in Shanghai to Jackson Lines, initially to run the China coast to Japan and on north to Russia. The situation had changed whilst she was at sea on her way to her first destination. Assuming command, Tom Wallis had received orders to fuel up and turn around. Now he was Blighty bound for the

250

first time in ten years and, if truth were told, as he had confessed only to himself, he was pleased to be going to the place of his birth. Like so many Scottish colonists and remittance men, he had travelled far and made mark and fortune, but increasing years created a nagging longing at least to see the old country again – where the faces that filled the streets would all be babbling with accents familiar from his childhood.

'Where do you think they are, sir?' The young seaman's voice intruded on his thoughts.

Captain Tom Wallis smiled and puffed smoke into the wheelhouse, where it curled against the windows.

'Riding it out side by side, I shouldn't wonder,' he said.

'You were in clippers once, sir, weren't you?'

'Once,' murmured the Captain.

'Which is better?' asked the young man respectfully.

'We're all at sea,' said the Captain. 'Given a good wind and a steady blow there's not a lot in it. Steam has its advantages' – he emphasised the word – 'but coal ain't canvas, boy.' Wallis paused for a moment, thinking of the past.

'Do you think they've got a chance, sir?' asked the animated seaman at the wheel.

Wallis nodded. '*Chantril* and *Vesper?* I wouldn't put it past them.'

'What would you say was the real difference, sir?' asked the young man earnestly.

'Between coal and canvas?' asked Wallis, puffing on his meerschaum and staring out through the glass into the moonlit night. The young sailor nodded. The Captain of *Otranto* smiled. 'Romance,' he said.

17

'Thar she blows!' bellowed the old Peterhead whaler, his voice resounding the length of *Chantril*'s decks from bowsprit to taffrail, causing Eli Lubbock to scramble from his charts in the Captain's cabin and take the steps up to be beside Billy at the wheel on the quarter deck of the poop.

'Old Moss, sir,' said Billy. 'He's spotted her ahead.'

Eli pulled the telescope from the box and focused. Finding *Vesper*, he grinned with triumph. 'She's there, all right. Give Moss some rum – he's better eyes than I have, even with a sighting.'

'Aye sir,' answered Billy. 'He was just as good with them leviathans – I did two winters with him in the late sixties. We caught enough blubber to give us a handsome profit.' He grinned at the memory. 'We called him "Bonus" Moss.'

Eli nodded. 'So now, Billy, let's catch Silas Hayes and not lose him again. It's taken us four days to find that old windbag.'

'Aye, sir,' the Mate answered and seized the wheel tighter as if his grip would promote *Chantril*'s forward passage.

Foam sprayed from the waves as a shallow running sea, wind blown from the prevailing north-east monsoon, allowed the two clippers, still miles apart beneath the cloudless sky, to forge ahead with all stuns'ls, royals to'gallants, topsails and mains, even the cro'jacks on their mizzens, billowing as both captains adjusted braces to catch the last breath of air. To several passing junks, nervously out of sight of land, the two ships appeared as great cumulus clouds passing low over an increasingly blue ocean flecked with white horses.

Passengers aboard both ships, relishing the fortifying elements, leaned over the rails to observe their competition, acknowledging the discernible speed with praise for their respective captains. Hands secured hats to heads, large fashionable chapeaux for the women, bowlers or Homburgs amongst the men. The heat remained, even at sea, although the humidity was relieved by the freshening wind, constant with the season. Eyes squinted against the strong sunlight, peering towards land, straining to identify any coastline or islands in the haze. Then, with a watch cry, attention turned to the horizon, afore *Chantril* and astern *Vesper* as the two clippers – the one sea miles ahead – scudded over the slight chop of the serried ranks of waves.

Bets were laid, favourites' odds improved upon and generally, in the ambience of a pleasant lunch period as wine and port settled stomachs growing accustomed to the now reassuring movement of the ships, tempers softened and uncertain attitudes were improved by increasing confidence in the abilities of both Eli Lubbock and Silas Hayes.

Vesper's captain strode the length of the main deck, legs straddled against the slight roll and buck of the groaning composite-built clipper. Iron-framed, timber-constructed and copper-clad below the water-line, her creaks and groans were music to the well-tuned ear of Silas Hayes as his sharp eyes examined the shrouds and halyards, rat-tails and sheets, checking taut braces and the strain of canvas clewed to their yards.

The tightly caulked deck would show wear by the time they reached Anjer, and Silas knew if there was time and a lull in the wind, he would order spare hands to rework the hemp and pitch filler between the tightly laid planks. Beyond the Sunda Straits, with a strong following monsoon blow, their consequent speed with its accompanying spray would make it almost impossible to indulge in any deck improvements – come the Cape of Good Hope, perhaps, but that would be after the long track across the Southern Indian Ocean, when they would all need a rest – if the Atlantic doldrums didn't immediately impose one.

Nodding to passengers up for air, he presented a stern image as his preoccupation with the days and weeks to come allowed him little outward geniality. Silas stopped a moment beside the open door to the crew's kitchen in the centre deckhouse and wrinkled his nose at the pungent smells. The tall thin Chinaman grinned at his boss again, bowing his thanks at the promise kept by 'Mister Captain Sir'. Min Ho always did his best, and indeed his cooking had improved since first he sailed with Captain Hayes. The crew of the relieved watch were about to eat and Silas checked the contents of several large bowls full of what looked like a foul version of bird's nest soup. He took a ladle and sipped the hot liquid. No denying it was, if not good, not without taste or vitamins. Large jugs of fresh lime juice and water awaited serving, set upon wooden trays. Silas merely nodded and received a deeper bow from the almost toothless and nearly bald Chinaman.

'Me no "run lick" no more,' he said, with obvious relief that his rickshaw days were quite literally behind him. He had actually begun to fill out his exceptional frame and resumed tasting his own food, chuckling to himself that he had indeed been able to trust the man who had offered what he had 'putee in book'. As a result, he was now master of his own small domain. Silas withheld further comment, concealing his affection for Min Ho with a grimace before continuing down the deck. Here behind scuppers and wire netting were cackling chickens. He peered into the run to see fluttering wings, flying feathers and, amongst the straw,

254

a single broken egg. He grunted annoyance and stepped on up to the poop. Hughie Sutherland at the wheel scratched his thickening grey beard and smiled a welcome.

'No eggs again,' growled Silas.

'They ain't layin',' stated the Mate.

'They're layin',' Silas contradicted, '*and somebody's* eating a fresh breakfast.' Ben's terrier barked and leapt up the steps to rub himself against the Captain's legs. Hughie coughed, embarrassed at what Silas might think.

'It ain't us, sir,' he said. 'Or the terrier; he can't get in, an' would eat the chickens afore the eggs. The watch ain't reported a thing and they've their own French oeufs up for'ard.

'Well then, we've a little mystery, Hughie,' Silas declared emphatically, stroking the now whining dog. 'Which'll be solved . . . I'm determined o' that, so keep your weather eyes open.'

'Aye sir, I know 'ow you likes to have your – ' Silas silenced him with a hard stare. Eggs were a single indulgence, at breakfast – fresh, and in bars – pickled. It ran in the family; his father had been the same. Maybe it was Scottish blood, he mused, surveying the filled canvas with pride, and remembering also that Scottish blood in the Steele yard had built up this 'greyhound of the seas' which could still show her paces. Many a heart in far away Greenock would have swelled to see her now.

'She's doin' us proud, Hughie,' he said, and glanced behind, disgruntled to see *Chantril* approaching with stuns'ls set even on the to'gallants. 'Hold the course tight and keep our distance,' he said, analysing Lubbock's sail plan. The Mate pointed over his shoulder with a thumb. 'Old Eli ain't doin' so bad himself, sir.'

'You don't have to tell me, Mr Mate – just make

way and we'll see what the afternoon brings. We've time aplenty and enough sea ahead of us to lose an entire fleet.'

All the same, he took out the telescope and focused on *Chantril*. He muttered words known only to himself as he watched Eli's clipper coursing towards *Vesper*, hardly more than a mile abaft her weather beam

'Damn him,' he hissed, as Hughie looked above, where a few clouds had appeared to give small indications of wind strength but wheeling sea birds offered more clues. Those above Eli's ship floated on thermals taking them up and fo'ard, where they began to plunge the full distance towards *Vesper*'s stern, flattening out to see any refuse thrown overboard. Silas shook his head angrily.

'He's found a lee shore wind, sir, and at points to out starboard has several knots' advantage.'

'How far?' asked Silas.

'A sea mile abaft and half again – we're soon to be lying on his port bow.'

'How long?' snapped Silas.

Hughie held a silence before. 'Half an hour,' he said. 'At most, then we'll be running with him.'

Silas smiled to himself. 'Then stay close and we'll teach him a lesson.'

Hughie grinned, knowing. 'By takin' his wind, sir?'

Silas folded the telescope and nodded. 'It's been done before,' he said calmly.

Hughie nodded, emphasising, 'Indeed *we* have, sir!'

'First blood, *Mr* Sutherland,' Silas ordered, 'Hold hard and let him seem to find us lacking.'

Hughie grinned at the psychological ploy Silas planned; no captain bent on passing competition ahead liked to find the wind, in every term of the meaning, taken out of his sails. He knew Eli almost as well as Silas, and if ever 'Captain' Lubbock erred it was in over-zealous application of what must be generally

256

acknowledged as brilliant seamanship. Here was his Achilles' heel; Silas knew it and intended to rap him hard by showing all passengers, officers and crew on both clippers quite clearly.

'Let him come,' murmured Captain Hayes quietly.

'Aye sir,' muttered Hughie, and quickly glanced behind before counting the seconds. Fifteen minutes later *Chantril* was within loud-hailing distance as Adèle Morgan appeared upon the poop, parasol casually over her shoulder, eyes fixed abaft to starboard. Silas had lit a pipe and lounged in his canvas chair, seemingly unconcerned with anything but filled canvas and fixed braces. She smiled a greeting at the Captain, who nodded, then leaning against the taffrail, Adèle turned and said with mischief in her voice, 'Will it be dangerous if he comes closer?'

Silas glanced up and puffed smoke, which was whipped away by the following wind. 'If you both know what you're about, it ain't so bad.'

'But if the conditions were to – perhaps – suddenly change . . . what would Captain Lubbock do?'

Silas ventured a smile. 'Well, I'd say. . . .' He paused. 'Anything you asked him.'

Adèle pressed her lips together before retorting, but hearing Hughie cough, she stifled a reply. Silas sat up in the chair and gave her his full attention.

'You were a nasty little nipper when I married your sister, and now look at you – a beautiful young woman, mooning after an old man!'

Adèle immediately folded her parasol and in a fit of uncontrolled temper began to sweep it towards Silas, who ignored her and deliberately bent to re-pack his pipe. She stopped herself, applying practised decorum, sighed deeply and stared at the fast-approaching clipper.

'He is not old!' she declared.

Silas looked up again, shaking his head and

reminded her, 'Your sister fell in love with a seaman –
and regretted it, young lady.'

Adèle's eyes narrowed in an expression of superiority. '*I* am a *modern* woman, *Captain*. I am also very
rich now that I am become twenty-one.'

Silas nodded. '*That* is honest enough.'

'*That*,' stated Adèle, 'I intend shall also make an
honest man of Captain Lubbock!'

'Well, now,' began Silas, and whistled softly to
himself. 'What am I to say to *that?*'

'I would suggest, Silas Hayes, that you *do* something
if you wish to *win* this race.' She pointed her parasol
towards *Chantril*, where passengers could be made out
quite clearly, waving towards *Vesper*. 'If he gains on
you now, my guess is you will not see him again until
we dock in England.'

'Your guess, is it?' said Silas, and stood up slowly,
making as if to see Eli's clipper for the first time. 'Why,
Miss Morgan – here is a sailor indeed.'

'*Indeed* a sailor, Captain Hayes,' Adèle pronounced
imperiously. 'Good afternoon.' She turned and,
ignoring Ben's barking terrier, stepped over it and took
the steps from the poop one at a time.

Silas shook his head, leaning over Hughie's shoulder
to see the compass against the strong sunlight. 'Love
always obscures more than it reveals,' he said quietly.

'What's that, sir?' asked Hughie, who was staring
above at the changing patterns in the building light
cloud.

Silas laughed to himself. 'Give me a steady wind for
a week rather than a tempest for the night, Hughie,
any time.'

'I'm sorry, sir . . . ?'

'I'll be below,' Silas told him, and glanced up at the
moving clouds. 'The wind'll veer in twenty minutes;
tell me the points and I'll adjust accordingly.'

'Aye sir.'

Silas went below to his cabin. Nothing was unfamiliar and yet everything was again new to Silas Hayes as he pored over his charts, measuring distances and calculating alternative times with variations of speed, understanding the potential differences made by the variable wind strengths and the constantly inconsistent cross-currents between the myriad islands and ever distant mainland. Shoals and reefs were marked, but the always present dangers of miscalculations troubled him; he had already ordered each watch to inform either himself or the mates of anything untoward – from foam sighted on a calm sea to still water amongst breaking waves.

Slide-rules and measured distances on any chart were accurate to the degree of the master mariner's abilities, but the charts themselves were not like the star patterns, eternally placed. The shifting oceans, as opposed to the fixed heavens, had often beguiled past navigators, impairing their accurate knowledge. A single island put down out of true alignment with others in a straggle offshore of a foreign coastline could mean the end of a ship, its crew, passengers, officers and cargo. A solitary light mistakenly identified at night as a port or point, where in fact dangers lurked – and they were all undone.

He praised the navigational aids at hand but trusted also in his instincts, as he believed solely in the constellations above. His faith rested entirely in his own abilities to evaluate not what seemed, but what was; it was he who must be prepared to command and stand by his decisions, not only for that moment, but in any court of law, should it be necessary. Such accepted responsibility dictated his course of action and direction for the future of the ship and all who sailed in her.

A cough interrupted his concentration. Continuing to lean over the charts of the Cochin coast all the way out to the Paracels island group, he turned briefly to see the priest, James Collins, smiling at the doorway.

'Sorry to intrude,' said the man of the cloth, 'but I felt it my duty to represent myself to you. May I come in?'

'You are already,' snapped Silas.

'Captain,' began the priest, 'as we are now well at sea, I thought it prudent, in the name of the Cross, to present a petition which will, I am sure, benefit us all.'

The priest suddenly clung on as the ship bucked. Shouts were heard from above, causing both men to look towards the open doorway and up to the poop deck. Collins was wearing a black suit with a stained white collar, complementing his teeth; the bland expression he assumed was meant to importune pleasantly. Limpid eyes in a generously fleshed face told Silas of years spent in a protected indulgent society.

'What do you want?' Silas asked bluntly.

'Captain – I appreciate formalities are a luxury aboard such a ship as this, but we should, I believe, foster a certain sense of – '

'What?' Silas rounded on the man and stared silently. The priest stepped forward uncertainly. 'I have suggested to the passengers and crew, Captain, that I conduct a regular service and I wanted to secure your. . . .' He paused.

'Permission?' asked Silas.

The priest coughed again and placed his hands together, covering his groin. His smile was trained to be as beatific as is humanly possible. 'You, I would imagine were brought up in the Scottish church. Am I wrong?'

Silas straightened up and leaned back against the fixed table, securing himself as the ship rose and fell in what felt like a rising sea. He looked long at the man before him, whilst registering calls and orders shouted from above.

'I was *brought up* in poverty. Born into a Glasgow

260

slum, I had no choice or advantages in life in any other way than I learned how – the hard road, which only the wealthy describe as the "real way". I knew nothing and I was given less than a fighting chance to survive – '

Collins interrupted with conciliation and conviction, 'But the Church, Captain, at such times surely it offered. . . .'

Silas narrowed his eyes and the gaze was enough to stop the priest in mid-flight. 'Men like you,' stated Silas, 'sold salvation in the hereafter for the last farthing those poor devils around me had to their name. And, like fools, they gave it to avoid the damnation you preached from every pulpit you were allowed to enter with your bigotry and self-gratification, where you pontificated with the same invented ideas and disgusting sense of superiority.'

'Christ is no invention, Captain,' said Collins smoothly, 'he is the truth, the *only* way and the light of mankind.'

Silas Hayes began to laugh; finally he managed to speak and when he did it was an explosion.

'You glib parasite!'

James Collins' florid features went white and he swayed either with anger, shock or the movement of the ship.

'Captain!' he retorted, 'I have been in China for a number of years and I have, contrary to your *opinion*, if it is one – which I vehemently contest – I have,' he repeated, 'every confidence that the Church has done everything. . . .'

Silas stepped forward, causing Collins to flinch and lean back as if to escape, but he was trapped by the narrow cabin and his own tongue.

'In China!' bellowed Silas, 'The *Church* has condoned the open policies of every Western government responsible for slaughter, slavery, opium and starvation! I know! I worked for them and I willingly took their money.' He stared into the dilating pupils of Collins' eyes. 'You may have confidence in that – priest!'

Collins closed his eyes in an attempt at composure. 'The Lord said, Captain Hayes, that "thou shalt not – " '

'Always what *not* to do,' shouted Silas. 'I *do* what is necessary *when* the occasion arises!'

'Captain,' stuttered Collins, 'God is everywhere!'

'How convenient,' responded Silas. 'Then he has no need of you, and neither, I hope, have my passengers or crew!' He paused, now face to face with the man.

'God will forgive you,' whispered the priest.

'For what?' snapped Silas.

The priest smiled, a monkey hoping to calm the tiger, inching toward the door and steps back up to the poop. 'Only you may answer that,' he said quietly. 'Good day.'

The priest slid from the edge of the table, turned quickly and suddenly was swallowed by the late afternoon light.

Silas sighed deeply, knowing he had been drawn. 'Be damned,' he muttered under his breath.

'They're comin' 'a beam!' bellowed Hughie from the quarter deck. In an instant, Silas had donned his dark jacket and was on the poop deck beside the wheel. What he saw was an impressive sight: an almost full set of sails on a square-rigged ship passing very close on his lee at a healthy lick. Silas nodded to his mate, his mood soured by the priest, and his determination to show Eli a trick or two doubled.

'Let him go a pace, Hughie, I'll tell you when. . . . Are the men at the braces?'

'Aye sir.'

'Stand by to put over the helm and haul away.'

'Aye aye sir,' repeated Hughie, now licking his lips

nervously, knowing the manoeuvre was only possible at some speed but was also 'a bit tricky', as Silas always said about precision seamanship.

Ben stepped on to the quarter deck and Hughie hissed, 'His dander is up.' Immediately Ben winked and whistled silently, reaching out for his terrier, who was panting, seemingly with equal excitement, on the low roof of the rear deckhouse.

'He's going through her lee,' whispered Hughie as Silas strode to the rail to calculate the exact moment.

Ben's eyes widened. 'He's goin' to sail round her?' Hughie nodded. 'I've never seen it done,' Ben said in awe.

Hughie smiled. 'He's a master; Eli and you'll be seein' things today, all right – watch!'

The two clippers, barely one hundred and fifty yards apart, slid through the following sea side by side as if favourites bent on a final spurt before the finishing post of a steeplechase. Sails filled, clewed canvas strained at the yards, taxing every breath of air sucked from the land, but, on the lee side of *Vesper*, *Chantril* had taken the initial advantage and began to forge ahead to the sound of repeated cheers from all on board Eli Lubbock's command.

Silas Hayes grunted, watching Eli wave from his poop deck; beside him a woman had appeared, with a pink parasol matching a flowing dress, seemingly attractive even from a distance, so Silas shaded his eyes to make her out.

'By God, Hughie,' Silas murmured, 'he's taken himself some beauty aboard. *She* should help him pass the time!'

Chantril's stern rail began to run the length of *Vesper*, fore-reaching with every minute.

'Mizzen and main stuns'ls, sir?' Hughie asked anxiously.

'Unnecessary, Mr Mate,' Silas answered calmly.

'But, sir. . . .' Hughie began.

'The wind to remain constant is all we require, Mr Mate.'

'Yes, sir.'

'Trust me, Hughie,' Silas smiled.

'How could I not, sir?'

'You are an able seaman and a mate of the first order. Your responsibility must lie in confidence drawn always from experience and never from the bottle.'

Hughie gripped the wheel tighter and glanced at the fast disappearing poop and taffrail of *Chantril*.

'At sea, the bottle and I are never –'

'Flask?' interrupted Silas, fixing his mate with a stare of pure insight. Involuntarily Hughie touched his back pocket. Ruddy as he was, his colour intensified. 'I want this ship docked not wrecked,' stated the Captain of *Vesper* harshly. 'And you can test your abilities now.'

'How sir?' asked Hughie.

Silas smiled like a tiger then ordered quietly, 'Hard over on the helm.'

Hughie hesitated only a moment then, looking at his captain, began to spin the wheel hard over. Immediately, *Vesper*'s bows turned against the following sea, spray cascading along her starboard rail. Unsuspecting passengers shrieked as the China Sea erupted, pouring through the scuppers and across the polished brass, finely misting the air with brine as elegant suits crumpled in the humidity and contoured dresses and lingerie sank heavily against moist flesh. Passengers leapt for the deck-houses as the crew jumped for the rat-tails; then, realising what their captain was about, gave a great ovation of encouragement.

'Braces!' bellowed Silas, astride the quarter deck. As one, his men on the lines securing the positions of his yards pulled hard and swung them around so that the sails remained filled from the now quartering wind. *Vesper* turned behind *Chantril*, her full canvas billowed taut, swallowing the air from the north-east, and in that moment depriving Eli of his forward momentum. Seeing the suddenly loosing sails flapping at their yards, broadside on to the failing competitor's stern, *Vesper*'s captain saluted laconically. Poop passed poop hardly fifty yards apart and, with a full set above him, Silas knew he had taken his friend, losing him, in those seconds, the knots he had gained, slowing him instantly with a cloud of sail and shutting him out.

'By the devil's curse Billy!' cried Eli Lubbock. 'That mother's foundling's done us proper!'

'Bear away, sir,' shouted the Mate, already spinning the wheel to port.

'Hold the course!' commanded Eli. 'Or we'll lose the damn wind.'

'But, Eli,' began Billy Williams, his gnarled face propped upon a turtle neck of tanned creases which, stretched to straining, supported an expression of disbelief, 'he can't – '

'He's doin' it, Mr Mate,' snapped Eli, 'but by God he ain't goin' to get away with the lee turn.'

'Captain Lubbock,' came the quiet voice of Emily, dismayed and obviously disturbed at the sudden anxiety she felt. 'Is the wind . . .' she hesitated, finding the word she had learnt, ' . . . veering?'

'Aye,' answered Eli, 'and so is your blasted husband-to-be.'

'But he is behind us, is he not?' She turned to see *Vesper* and gasped.

'Silas will have a glass on us this close and he'll recognise you without a doubt. Retire for the moment until we outrun him,' Eli urged.

'I am obliged for your consideration,' said Emily with a smile. But she was unable to tear her eyes from the swiftly moving clipper passing impressively across the stern of *Chantril*. Eli's hand slipped from Emily's waist to her hips as he guided her to the steps leading to his cabin and beyond, the saloon and the corridor giving access to passengers quarters.

Emily nodded her thanks and took the stairway below gingerly.

Eli whistled, stilled by his discovery.

'What is it, sir?' asked Billy.

'The bitch is pregnant,' he muttered, shaking his head at the possible implications. He spun round. 'Damn you, Silas Hayes!' he shouted, and shook a fist vehemently towards *Vesper*. His reply, as he saw, was merely a relaxed salute. Silas, having no need of a glass so close, could detect every crease of anger in Eli's face and took all of it to be directed at his manoeuvre. After all, in Silas' mind, Emily was already on her way to Australia.

'Hard on the braces, Mr Sutherland,' ordered Silas.

'Aye, sir – haul boys!' Hughie bellowed, stepping forward to the poop break as his captain took the wheel.

Athwart *Chantril*'s wake, *Vesper*'s momentum carried her into the hard turn to port on the lee side of Eli, who could only watch helplessly as his sails, windforce sucked from them, began to flap. Immediately, *Chantril* began to slow, even as *Vesper* came about.

Silas pulled with Ben, using all his muscle to spin the many-handled wheel, straightening up the rudder. Foam churned in their wake and spray filled the air, not only at the fo'c'sle but whipping the length of *Vesper* as she righted herself, feeling the surge of power the wind off the distant shore gave the straining canvas.

'Haul, hard, boys!' Hughie sang out, grinning as he watched the crew sweating at the starboard braces to bring round the yards and their full sails.

Astride the wheel, Silas nodded to Ben. 'Check out the to' gallants, Mr Mate. They'll feel the force of it; no wonder Eli was scudding. This is a lee shore freak we was just outside of. . . . Double clew 'em if you must.'

'Aye, sir,' Ben said, and ran to the steps, followed closely by his terrier, who barked excitedly.

Silas glanced across at Eli's starboard rail, a mere hundred yards off and slowing perceptibly against the smooth line *Vesper*'s shining brass knight heads made, speed seeming to merge them as one – into a bright streak for all eyes aboard *Chantril* to see, cutting through the blue grey sea where white horses leaped between flying fish and breaching dolphins. Above, Silas could see the thin cloud, lower than the high cumulus appearing rapidly in the hitherto clear sky, moving across the prevailing wind.

'It's veering, all right,' he snapped.

'Aye, sir,' agreed Hughie, and nodded to himself. 'An' in our favour.'

Silas grunted and crouched a moment to look to the bowsprit, seeing it now beyond *Chantril*'s figurehead. Running so close and parallel, he knew he had the advantage only for several minutes.

'Right, Mr Mate,' he growled. 'Let's take him.'

'Braces?' asked Hughie.

'Braces,' confirmed Silas.

'Full hard haul!' bellowed Hughie. 'Wait for it!' Leading seamen shouted back affirmatives and seized the brace ropes and wire, attention focused on the poop, waiting for the Captain's 'wear ship!' and proud of it for the morale of the entire crew.

Fractions of a league passed as *Vesper*'s two hundred and more feet slid the length of *Chantril*'s two hundred and more feet carrying slackening sails flapping in an attempt to carry on again in the wind, now points to starboard of *Chantril*.

'God damn you, Silas Hayes!' Eli roared so loudly that the words floated across the churning water and caused Silas to turn and wave farewell.

Two hundred yards ahead on a closing tack Silas commanded, in a stentorian voice, 'Now!' and immediately began to spin the heavy wheel to bring the rudder hard over.

'Haul hard!' cried Hughie, and watched the seamen pull at the braces until the yards were forming only a shallow degree across the decks but holding their sails full to the wind.

'When we're standing across her bows, Mr Mate,' shouted Silas above the orders, wind, cries and some screams from the apprehensive female passengers aboard, 'I want a full three cheers for *Chantril*.'

'Yes, sir,' grinned Hughie.

Vesper's port side bent into the chopping waves as her prow began to cut over the path of *Chantril* at more than eleven knots. Passengers and crew who were not at the braces rushed to the rail in awe, ignoring sea spray thrown into the air on the strong breeze. Astonishment prompted laughter and applause as one clipper bearded the other.

Silas caught Adèle's anxious face gazing towards the filling sails above *Chantril*'s plunging bows.

'The sea's picking up,' grumbled *Vesper*'s captain with an expression not unlike a cat's with the cream.

'By all the powers,' began Hughie as Ben jumped up on to the quarter deck of the poop, grinning hugely.

'I'll be damn well jiggered before I forget this day, Silas,' Ben blurted, seizing his terrier, who, sensing the atmosphere, was barking uncontrollably.

'Put it in the log, Mr Mate,' said Silas quietly.

'I'll put it in history!' retorted Hughie loudly. *Vesper*'s taffrail passed barely fifty yards from *Chantril*'s rising bowsprit as her chain martingales sluiced sea water.

'Haul away, Mr Mate,' commanded the Captain, and he immediately began to spin the wheel, joined by Ben, who grasped alternate handles of the twin adjoining 'sister'. With the rudder straightening, only

268

the starboard braces needed hauling fast to keep the sails filled. Secured, the yards held the clewed canvas tight, full luffed, billowed clouds above the wet decks of the square-rigged clipper.

'Three cheers for *Chantril*!' sounded out and was repeated.

'Sky sails, Ben,' muttered Silas.

'Sir!' snapped the Mate with respect.

Vesper came about and fore-reached on *Chantril*'s port weather beam, as the crew stormed the rat-tails, shouting to each other, attempting several sea-shanties to aid their efforts, knowing they now had something to tell their grandchildren about the voyage.

Ben saluted, seeing the crew already ahead of their orders. 'I ain't never seen the like sir,' he spluttered.

'Neither will you again, Ben,' Silas stated grimly. 'It's just that conditions were right.'

'It takes more than that, sir,' interjected Hughie. 'You 'ave to be able . . . want to. . . .'

'Ben!' snapped Silas. The Captain's second mate nodded and ran off to supervise the upper sails from the main cap.

'Sir,' Hughie began.

'Resume course, Mr Mate.'

'Thank you, sir.'

'Thank the crew, Mr Sutherland – rum to all.'

Hughie grinned proudly, as Silas stepped to the taff-rail, looking back at *Chantril* wallowing in the box waves of the China seas, birds circling above her extensive canvas, which was again slowly filling in the lee shore breeze no longer denied.

'She looks like a pregnant sow, sir,' said Hughie, grasping the wheel, as the foam-flecked figurehead of *Chantril* rose from the lifting waves.

'She's still beautiful,' murmured Silas, and taking his pipe from a side pocket began to pack tobacco. 'And there's plenty of life in her yet,' he muttered. All the same, *Vesper* had the edge and began to draw away as the afternoon waned and building storm clouds threatened evening thunder with the possibility of precipitation and heavy seas.

18

Night rain poured from the monsoon winds in the early hours of the last day of September 1900 which was as black as the few swinging lanterns atop *Vesper* allowed. Watch crew, hunched in oilskins, checked the knot-line, logged the speed and reported below as bells rang for the change, when shouts of relief sounded louder than the ringing brass. God must have been listening, for within minutes the rain stopped, clouds cleared and the already waning moon showed brightly.

Rubbing his eyes, Silas stumbled on to the quarter deck and took both the wheel and a steaming mug of hot tea from Ben, who tapped the crewman, indicating his duty was over and he was entitled to a sleep of eight hours' duration, below and fo'ard in the fo'c's'le berths. Checking the compass reading, Silas nodded, remaining silent as both he and Ben searched the clouded heavens for constellations they might find and recognise. The movement of water was a reassuring background.

'We're going east of the Paracels, Ben, and we'll stay well out from the Cochin coast. When we sight the shore land of Borneo, I've calculated the best way through the Api Passage, then we'll go south by the Gaspar Strait directly to Anjer.'

'By Macclesfield, sir?' Ben asked apprehensively. 'It ain't the easiest route, even if it is the most eastern channel.'

'It's the fastest,' answered Silas. 'I'm makin' the most of the monsoon winds.'

'Them small islands is . . . hazardous,' stated Ben.

'I'm not unaware of the dangers,' replied Silas, 'but

Banca Island could be worse, becalmed off Sumatra; we've already had a taste of pirates and I don't want more – and it would be Malay this time. Pirate proas gathering around, pickin' at, and pluckin' a chicken, and that would be us if'n we lost the lee shore winds – I prefer inconstant nature to predictable inhumanity. Ben, trust me.'

'I do, sir.'

Silas smiled. 'You're for the dog watch tomorrow.' Ben's terrier nosed out of the seaman's jacket and whined, curious at the cackling of chickens for'ard of the poop. 'Go below, Ben, and get some sleep.'

'Aye, aye sir.'

Ben left the quarter deck and Silas, alone beneath the clearing sky and heaven's familiar firmament, sighed – content for the first time in many years. Here at the wheel of his own ship, striding oceans beneath the stars, there was no longer even the contest of another trader, merchantman or clipper. All he surveyed was the worlds' sea, which he had once before mastered; with luck, he reasoned, if there were gods, it would be his again to conquer.

Then the chickens cackled loudly. Silas stared towards the shimmering moonlit water ahead of *Vesper*; the clipper's decks were empty. Only a crewman on watch moved at the fo'c's'le, ghostlike beneath the pale canvas bowed by the saving wind from the north-east. Windlass, capstans, rigging, deck-houses, oakum and planks glistened in the lunar light, creating a magic even for the seasoned seaman, so that Silas, for a moment, believed in all the concepts, ideas and precepts, beliefs or religions proffered as truths or mysteries. Then reality intruded.

'No will-o'-the-wisp makes chickens wake,' he growled. It took only seconds for him to take the belt from his waist and lash it between the spokes of the wheel and the upright support. Pulled tight with the buckle secured, the course would hold, he knew, for the seconds he needed to satisfy his curiosity. He glanced quickly at the large compass set in the binnacle, its glass reflecting the shining moon and the light of the hurricane lamp. Checking his bearing, affirming it to be accurate, he then quickly stepped down from the poop to the main deck. A fruitless search amidships, even to the fo'c's'le, where he grunted a brief greeting to the forward watch, revealed not even a clue to any poacher, but the chickens continued to cackle, obviously disturbed.

Silas strode back to the poop and took the steps up to his quarter deck, where he unlashed the wheel and re-belted his trousers. Above, the night sky, now clear, revealed its wealth of stars, new constellations showing as *Vesper* moved ever more south-west towards the equator. Peace, in the knowledge of filled sails, ample sea room as yet from the dangerous waters – strewn with islands, shoals and reefs – they were approaching and the sound of a steady purling wake, lulled Silas' spirit and filled his mind with strange imaginings. He looked down at the binnacle containing the ship's large compass indicating, beneath the glowing hurricane lamp, points south and a true course set and held. Silas smiled a smile of professional pride, pleased at his accurate navigation; only the hens cackling with the crowing cock irritated him. Then he suddenly stared. There, at the very centre of the glass on the main compass, lay another very small brass compass – the gift to his son. He reached out, dumbfounded, and only as he felt the metal in his fingers did he understand.

'Jamie,' he whispered. The chickens cackled more contentedly, then for no apparent reason stopped. Silas frowned, surveying the length of the ship.

'Jamie!' he bellowed.

Only the steady wind and foaming wake answered him. He felt the brass gift in his hand for reassurance that he was not hallucinating, and repeated the name quietly.

'Jamie?'

First a shadow, then a pale face appeared in a pool of light cast from the hurricane lamp. Uncertainly, Jamie smiled. For a moment Silas was astonished, as if the boy was an apparition. Then, accepting reality, the boy's father bent forward, seized his son and lifted him high. The two stared long at each other as watch bells rang in the distance.

'I can feel your ribs, laddie,' he murmured, controlling a welter of emotions. 'Where did you stow yourself?'

'Amongst the rice, sir,' whispered the boy.

Silas frowned. 'The door's bolted; how did you get out?'

'With a penknife, sir . . .'

' . . . and patience,' finished Silas.

'Each night,' began Jamie.

'To steal food?' asked Silas sternly.

Jamie lowered his head. 'Eggs,' he mumbled.

Silas shook his head in some wonder and began to laugh. From the corner of his eye he saw movement on the poop. 'Ben!' he shouted, and lowered the boy to the deck. 'By God, laddie, I'll make you work, if it's a seaman you want to be!'

'Sir,' Ben interrupted, 'watch reports all quiet and all well. What's this?' he asked, seeing Jamie.

'Feed him,' Silas ordered, 'then bring him back here. He can start this morning.'

'Aye, sir. Who are you, lad?' he demanded, grasping the boy roughly. His small terrier poked its head from the lapels of Ben's coat and barked loudly. Jamie stared, wide-eyed and frightened.

'He's my son, Ben,' said Silas quietly. The Mate looked at his captain in disbelief.

'That baby o' yor'n? But 'ere's a grown boy!'

Silas smiled. 'Growing, Ben.'

'Come on, lad,' Ben said, more kindly, 'I'll take you below.'

'Thank you, sir,' said Jamie.

Ben smiled. ''Ee's bin taught 'is manners, then.'

'We'll teach him somethin' altogether different,' growled the Captain. He watched boy and Second Mate go below, then grasped the wheel firmly, checked the compass and gazed up at the vast heavens. The full peace and beauty of the night struck Silas at that moment as unlike any other night in the past, and only then did he admit to himself, feeling his swelled heart bursting, the pride of a father whose son had given him something beyond price. Silas could offer only skills and adventure; Jamie had presented his trust and love.

Vesper 'ghosted' on south towards the charted but dangerous waters off Borneo and on into the Malay archipelago, but with *Chantril* behind and *Otranto* outward bound to her first bunker port, Silas Hayes allowed himself a smile of contentment.

'The wonderful thing about life,' he mused, 'is that it is full of surprises.' Then a rumble of thunder came from far away and the following flash of lightning illuminating the horizon confirmed his immediate suspicions.

'Here it comes,' he growled.

19

Otranto's bow wave disturbed the almost perfect reflection the steamship made in the Malay waters within sight of land. Passengers crowding the rails looked towards the approaching port as if it were their ultimate landfall instead of merely a stop on the way to their final destination, still so far off.

'Singapore, ladies and gentlemen,' Hollis Jackson announced from beneath the awning on the first-class sun-deck.

'And how long do we anticipate our stay to be?' began the journalist, Mr Meyer, who was already taking notes.

'Not more than a day or so,' Jackson answered confidently. 'We have a schedule to keep.' He glanced at the Dutchman, Kimmen, who merely smiled in return and blew smoke from a cheroot into the strong sunlight. Even in shadow beneath the stretched canvas awning, everyone, including the ladies, was perspiring. The heat and humidity in the straits seldom dipped below eighty Fahrenheit, and only cold drinks, more often than not alcoholic, offered some temporary respite from the discomfort of a permanently ferocious sun almost directly overhead, or rain, of course. When clouds gathered from the day's heat, building high above Singapore island, the cosmopolitan population, a generous mix of races, knew the resulting downpour especially in the monsoon season, would steam amidst the lush vegetation, forcing most of them to remain in houses or hotels where lazily spinning fans cooled and newly installed electric lighting illuminated the hours spent at imposed leisure.

Cornelia Morgan appeared on deck, twirling her parasol; a symphony in pink with a large-brimmed matching hat shading her features. She smiled at Jackson as she approached. She had pleaded the vapours for several days when *Otranto* was in some 'China chop' – a following sea which produced what was for some a disconcerting sensation as the ship rolled and pitched at the same time. The doctor aboard did a roaring trade in sickness antidotes.

'Feeling better?' asked Jackson, genuinely concerned.

Cornelia nodded. 'Better,' she murmured. 'What is that?' she asked, and pointed, her lace-gloved fingers pink in the sunlight. She withdrew her hand immediately back into the shadow. 'The heat, Mr Jackson, is quite . . .'

'Intense,' he finished for her. 'And *that*' – he indicated the fast-approaching port – 'is our first landfall before we take the Straits of Malacca and the old spice route to India.'

'Should I be impressed?' she asked.

He nodded. 'You would be if you met a tiger.'

'A what?' said Cornelia, astonished. 'You mean there is a circus?'

'No, my dear,' smiled Jackson, 'they swim across, I am told, from the mainland and prowl the streets at night.'

'Why on earth . . . ?'

'Man has cut back the jungle and reduced their natural prey, so they have little choice but to partake of man himself.'

'Do you know the island?'

'Since some years,' replied Jackson.

'Is there any genteel accommodation?'

'There is indeed, and renowned.'

'The establishment's name?'

'Raffles,' grinned Jackson.

'Really?' she said.

'It has,' he quoted from memory, 'an unrivalled panoramic view of the harbour and the adjacent islands and is conveniently situated within easy reach of the chief business centres.'

'How . . . convenient,' she smiled.

'I hope you like it.'

'How could I not, if it is your recommendation.'

'The proprietors are Armenian, Tigram and Arshak Sarkies – they are both of my, acquaintance.'

'So far from home,' she said.

'As we all are,' said Jackson, narrowing his eyes as he saw a cutter fast approaching, flying a yellow flag, closely followed by the pilot and a Customs launch which began to flash morse code. Sensing trouble, Jackson excused himself and walked up to the flying bridge, where the Captain was deciphering the message.

'Well?' he asked, arriving on the exposed bridge and feeling the uncomfortable heat without pleasure.

'Plague,' stated the Captain simply.

'What?'

'Quarantine,' said the Captain. 'They're requesting us to moor opposite the medical station.'

'I don't understand.'

'Neither do I,' murmured the Captain. 'Yet.'

Bells rang in the wheelhouse and *Otranto* slowly came about as asked, dropping anchor a short way from the quayside. The gangway was winched down as the cutter and launch slowed alongside. Doctors, police and port officials ran up or slowly negotiated the steep incline to the deck of the steamer. Hooting from other moored ships was answered from *Otranto*'s wheelhouse with the deep noise of a thunderous response as steam blasted from her tall central stack. The out islands returned no answers to the mystery, as the echoes faded across Singapore island itself beyond the narrow causeway and on into the forest jungle of the southern

Malayan peninsula. In the past, prowling tigers had often replied to the given challenge with full-throated roars from thick, tropical undergrowth.

Several of the officials winced at the noise before arriving to present their case to Jackson and the Captain in the wheelhouse. Bells rang from the telegraph as it was pulled to 'stop', and anchor chains rattled out of their housings fore and aft to secure the ship offshore of the P & O wharf.

'Well, gentlemen,' Jackson began between gritted teeth, having listened with mounting anger to the tale of suspicion cast upon his steamer. The plump, florid-faced English official representing the port authority made little impression on Hollis Jackson, who did not conceal his exasperation. Limp white suits and solar topees reflected in the thick glass of the wheelhouse windows as within, the relative cool emphasised the odour of perspiration from the new arrivals. Jackson's nostrils twitched as he stared out towards the crowded harbour of what had now become the seventh busiest port in the world. Gin was dispensed by a steward from a silver platter, together with tonic waters and quinine. A soft-featured, English-educated Malay-Chinese babbled on pompously about the need to prevent any form of epidemic, and constantly referred to a tall, thin doctor in a grubby suit who said nothing.

' . . . statutory law still holds, however – as it must. *SS Otranto* will remain impounded whilst it is searched and fumigated. If it has rats' – the man shrugged – 'we must rid you of them.'

'Impounded?' muttered Jackson.

'How long?' asked Captain Wallis.

'Perhaps,' suggested the English official, sipping gin, 'what with bacteria tests and laboratory reports . . . two weeks.'

'Impossible!' Jackson exploded. 'On whose – '

'The port authority!' the official interrupted loudly,

with an ill-concealed nasal accent Jackson recognised as coming from somewhere near the London suburb of Dartford.

'Your passengers and crew will be allowed ashore once they have been examined – as you also can be quickly cleared. The ship will take more time. It is normal procedure in such cases.'

The pompous voice of the Malay-Chinese took over as he presented a cable to the Captain. 'This came from the Port Doctor in Shanghai, should you require further proof . . . allegations of plague aboard your ship. Apparently "the black" has broken out all along the Cochin coast, having come down from the hinterland and –'

'What's the doctor's name?' snapped Jackson.

'Murphy,' stated the Captain, having found it at the bottom of a document.

'Damn him!' cried Jackson.

'Sir,' the Captain began, 'the good doctor is known to me and –'

'*And* is a friend of Silas Hayes, Tom!' cut in Jackson. 'There is no Black Plague aboard this ship or in Shanghai. It's a ruse, can't you see?'

'Mr Jackson,' said the English port official officiously, 'all *I* see is a wire which clearly states a need for thorough examination of certain vessels that are to call here. I have my orders. It is the law.'

'Wire them back,' said Jackson, an idea forming to examine not his ship but the port doctor in Shanghai.

The official raised a hand and waved a finger. 'All communications to the China coast have been cut. I am sure you know the situation better than we do – things are obviously bad there.' He grinned, revealing yellow, uneven teeth. 'I hope, rather than *suffer* your time here, you will *enjoy* our island paradise in the East.' He chuckled to himself at the half-truth. 'To England, the Empire and her colonies,' he toasted.

'You're a long way from Dartford, sir,' growled Jackson.

'As you are from home, Mr Jackson,' answered the official superciliously. 'At least you will have sufficient time to bunker. You may not know it, but supplies here are short – demand, you know. We have become quite active and, indeed, important.' Jackson looked the man up and down, unable to hide his distaste for this jumped-up clerk.

'God help us then,' he muttered.

The clerk lifted his half-empty glass again, joined by others. 'I am sure you will find it most agreeable in Singapore. Welcome.'

20

Immediate examination of the wheelhouse crew and watch stations of *Otranto* showed no symptoms of plague, ague or even gout, and the doctor in the grubby suit was cursory enough to allow both the Captain and Jackson signed clearance to disembark before the tedious process of individual analysis of all on board began in earnest.

A launch took Hollis and Captain Wallis the short distance to the wharf, where they found themselves besieged on the quayside by would-be travellers, traders, coolies, touts, sailors and rickshaw drivers. They climbed into separate rickshaws and in tandem were run through the crowds to an even filthier part of the docks half a mile away.

Captain Tom Wallis knew his way about the bustling port and, despite the heat and humidity, remained fully buttoned in his uniform when he and Silas arrived at the bunkering wharf, where they were allowed passage through an archway into a huge courtyard piled with heaps of coke, coal and lignite of varying hues, from grey to black, and even dirty brown.

'I don't like it,' murmured Captain Wallis.

'Let's see what they have,' countered Jackson, and the two men descended to the cobbles and walked over to a Malay foreman who was ambling to meet them. Above, thunder rumbled in the heavy sky as clouds began to build rapidly, crossing from the mainland to accumulate high above the settlement.

'Storm,' predicted Jackson.

'Rain,' said the Captain.

'Gentlemen, sirs,' began the Malay, almost swalowing his words in a guttural accent, 'you are vishing?'

'To be long gone from here,' said Jackson, and ointed to a pile of coal stacked almost fifty feet high.

'It is all sold. Good business here. Much trade.'

Captain Wallis had bent to examine the dirty lignite.

'That too,' said the Malay foreman, wiping grime rom his sweating face with a greasy black sleeve.

'Will it burn?' Jackson questioned sceptically.

'Anywhere,' the foreman grinned, 'anytime.'

'I don't like it,' grumbled the Captain, straightening up.

'Load it,' Jackson grunted. The Captain shook his ead, and pointed. In the distance a similar vast pile f lignite was being hosed down, having ignited from elf-combustion.

The two men looked up as first drops of rain began o fall.

'It is all sold, gentlemen, sirs,' said the dark face vith an accommodating grin. 'We will have more in a nonth.'

Jackson reached into his pocket for money. 'Today.'

The foreman watched Jackson counting English ster-ing notes.

'Three weeks,' he suggested.

Jackson frowned. 'Two,' he said.

The foreman hesitated, then accepted the money, a andsome deposit against the tons of fuel required to ake *Otranto* on to Ceylon.

Jackson and the Captain returned to their waiting ickshaws; the coolies had already raised the hoods gainst the increasing rain.

'Master-tuan,' said one of the 'boys', 'where we go?'

The two men stepped in to their respective transports nd Jackson slumped heavily, hearing the rain on the anvas hood. 'Raffles,' he said, as rolling thunder eralded the afternoon storm.

*

By the time the Captain had been returned to the P & O wharf and a waiting launch to be ferried out to his ship, Hollis Jackson had reached the Sarkies brothers' hotel in a gloomy mood and beneath what had become a deluge.

Reconstruction, extensions and refurbishment had made Raffles an hotel of some splendour, enhancing a reputation which had already been established. Remittance men and rubber planters in outstations made their way south along the Malay peninusla to indulge their appetites, after the hard work of supervising others actually labouring. Singapore, across the narrow causeway, offered the increasing delights of a civilisation they were long denied in their up-country primitive conditions. From jungle outposts, these colonials arrived to mix with regular locals in the famous Long Bar or Tiffin Room, to do business with traders from the docks who were men of growing prosperity, or to dine and dance with passing strangers only 'days over' in port.

Cornelia Morgan arrived at her accommodation in time for late afternoon tea. She came with her maid and two large portmanteaux, under a huge umbrella and in a furious mood. The spacious public rooms and immediate attention of the staff cooled her temper as she shook spots of rain from the hem of her dress. Electric fans, together with punkah-wallahs, moved the heavy air as she instructed her maid, issued orders to the receptionists, verified her suite was of the finest available and crossed to sit in the palm court. Above an elaborately ornamental skylight, the daylight faded, whilst it drummed with the sound of incessant rain. A trio of musicians played discreetly in one corner as tea was ordered and served, as Hollis Jackson arrived for the rendezvous.

'Well, well, Mr Jackson, what a surprise!'

'I thought we had . . .' he began.

'Singapore!' she exclaimed, and slowly removed her lace gloves.

Jackson smiled, beginning to relax. 'It is modern,' he said, 'which I appreciate.'

'I gather we have some time here?' she said, pouring tea. Jackson's face soured as he stared about him at groups of elegantly dressed patrons, some of whom he recognised from *Otranto*.

'Time lost,' he muttered. Stanley Grace waved to him from a distance; Jackson merely acknowledged him with an almost imperceptible nod. More lights were switched on as the day rapidly waned towards imminent twilight. Tea and light conversation ended. The ladies retired to bath before an early dinner, the men, having looked 'longingly at the Long Bar' – a crack Stanley Grace could not resist – ordered Singapore slings or stengahs and ambled into the billiard room, which was well served with four full-size tables.

Coloured balls potted across green baize lit from low lamps, along with further cocktails, promoted a convivial atmosphere; Hollis Jackson and Stanley Grace, coats off, both smoking cigars, even began to reminisce.

Dinner was a more conservative affair, and few amongst the elegant assembly, as fine wines were broached and beef carved from the famous silver trolley, spared a thought for those less fortunate; unable to afford shore accommodation, the other classes aboard *Otranto* rode out the evening sickeningly at anchor in the shifting harbour waters. The two-storey dining room, with its grand proportions, Carrara marble floor, and galleries supported by ornate columns and arches, emptied slowly as the sounds of a full dance orchestra lured diners through to the ballroom. By this time, for most, the rain was forgotten, anything could be forgiven and everything was possible.

'Can you believe,' smiled Cornelia breathlessly as she swirled to a fast waltz in Hollis Jackson's arms, 'I am to be sleeping in a suite overlooking Beach Road which was once occupied by the old American Consulate, I am told?'

Jackson nodded, knowing of the acquisition. 'Armenian enterprise, dear Cornelia, knows no bounds.'

'My father would be . . . shocked.'

Jackson smiled as the music came to an end. 'I believe he may actually have arranged the deal. Most lucrative, *I* am told.' Applause drowned her response.

Half the 'glowing' ladies decided to sit out the following quickstep. Hollis Jackson excused himself and walked out on to the covered verandah to light a cigar. Unabated, the deluge continued, but now it seemed to Jackson to create a cocoon for his thoughts. Arc lights illuminated lush vegetation and lawns almost masked by the sheeting rain. Despite the conditions, Malay boys and Chinese coolies continued their tasks, picked out, ghost-like as they passed to and fro into the night. Roars of laughter came from within as several groups sitting it out became raucous.

Cornelia sashayed from the ballroom on to the verandah, then sidled up beside Jackson, waving her fan. For a moment she respected the man's introspection until he allowed her to intrude into his thoughts with a brief smile of welcome.

'So comforting to be again part of the civilised world, don't you think, Hollis?' He glanced at her, then again stared out into the night, where the wretched state of the poor was obvious as they huddled against the downpour.

'Others have to endure discomfort to provide the likes of us with a pleasant existence.'

Affronted, she stepped away and waved her fan faster.

'The likes of *us* Hollis?' She stared at him, '*We* are *poles* apart!'

Jackson didn't even look at her, knowing the haughty expression which went with the calculated hardness in her voice, and wondered yet again what he found so fascinating in Cornelia Morgan.

'Slumming it, are you?' he asked.

'With you, Mr Jackson, what other choice would there be?' she snapped. 'We are people from different parts of society, which is an important consideration.'

'For *real* people,' he said quietly, 'it is not important where you come from, the *consideration* is where you are going!'

'Mr Jackson, I said *society!*'

'And I, Miss Morgan,' he snapped, rounding on her, 'say *real* life. That is a "*pole apart*" from your *society!*'

She smiled wickedly, appreciating her ability to rouse the man. 'Only those denied entrance to *proper* society denigrate it, Mr Jackson – in my experience.'

'Your *experience*, Cornelia, is as limited as I have ever witnessed. Bigotry is no substitute for compassion.'

Cornelia's jaw tightened and she actually flushed. '*I* was brought up and educated with understanding *and manners*. I know *my* place. What is yours?'

'I have no idea,' said Jackson softly, and looked her in the eye steadily before finishing, 'yet.'

Disconcerted at the man's sudden strength, she turned her head away. Here, after all, she thought, beneath a surface she had grown to appreciate, was merely another Silas Hayes. She shivered and, knowing immediately that she had given herself away, she determined to take herself off.

'Goodbye, Mr Jackson,' she said.

He touched her arm, causing her to turn back into his gaze.

'Cornelia,' he said, 'be a woman. You are no longer a girl.'

She slapped his face hard but he did not flinch. 'The truth should never hurt, if you have courage,' he said slowly, tasting blood.

'What do you know of either quality, sir?'

'I'm learning,' he answered quietly. He threw away his cigar into the rain, seized the woman with both hands and drew her to him. Ignoring her blazing eyes, he kissed her lips forcefully. Cornelia's mind fought, but her body melted against him. They parted with some reluctance, leaving Cornelia blushing and confused.

'Goodnight,' she whispered quickly, spun round and strode back into the ballroom, passing Captain Wallis, who looked over his shoulder and almost spilled two glasses of champagne he was carrying carefully out on to the verandah. He handed one to Jackson.

'You have blood on your mouth,' he said, curious.

Jackson licked his lips then sipped champagne. 'Thank you, Tom.'

The Captain grinned hesitantly, sparkling eyes in a tanned, lined face, white teeth framed by his full dark beard.

'This is the life, Mr Jackson, isn't it?' he said, as the orchestra struck up a slow, romantic waltz. Jackson nodded before staring grimly out into the night and privately into his past.

'Make the most of it,' he growled.

A tiger was shot beneath the billiard tables at the Hotel Raffles, which caused concern for future safety of the inhabitants and gossip for a week as speculation became rife as to Charlie Phillips' companion when he was roused to deal with the beast. Some said he was alone, others that he had retired late from the Government House ball with an 'amour de la nuit'. But he

288

shot the creature all the same, utilising his renowned marksmanship, a cool nerve and a Lee Enfield .303 to blow out the brains of the wretched tiger which had been cowering in the gloom between foundation stilts of the building. Sad, it was eventually agreed by all when the poor animal was discovered not to have been wild but escaped from a travelling circus.

Only Cornelia was totally pleased at the revelation, as it confirmed her initial reaction to the ludicrous statement Hollis had made about prowling man-eaters throughout the island.

After eighteen days in port, tempers flared, a cook was hacked to death with a Malay kris, a coolie shot in the belly and the famous Long Bar was drunk dry on several occasions. Eventually everyone had had enough and it was with some relief that the ordered lignite arrived, the ship having long since been cleared of the plague which Jackson had rightly surmised to be a successful ploy to detain his steamship. A final lunch was convened aboard beneath the awning on the first-class deck. Elegantly presented, it served as a farewell gesture for some of the local dignitaries and personalities who had proved to be something more than passing acquaintances. The heat was also companion, if unwelcome, at the gathering, together with the other uninvited guests – humidity and mosquitos.

Laughter at the table and thunder in the hold disturbed the early afternoon as thin wit and coarse lignite competed for dominance of the last recorded hours *Otranto* was to spend in Singapore. Final bunkering was certainly underway, but coal dust rising through the open hatch as the derrick withdrew to swing back to the wallowing tug and barge, indicated to curious eyes straying from the table that it was not yet completed. A black film of coal particles had settled not merely upon the canvas awning, but also beneath it and especially on anything white, presssed and cut for the tropics. The fine cuisine and appropriate table-ware of silver and china suffered equally, and most people who were not already oblivious or tipsy inspected their crystal glasses before sipping the chilled white Hocheimer Jackson had insisted accompany the poached fish freshly caught up-country.

Hearing the derrick winching up another load, he checked his watch, grumbling with obvious irritation in the direction of Stanley Grace, 'Eighteen days and we're still in port.'

The 'entertainer extraordinaire' put down his glass, accepting more wine from the steward, and wagged a finger at his readopted friend humorously. 'Think o' small mercies, Lucifer. We ain't no longer plague-ridden as we was when we come. . . .'

Laughter fluttered about the table, immediately obliterated as more lignite roared down into the hold. Captain Wallis leaned towards Jackson.

'I don't like the colour of it, sir.'

'If it'll get us to Ceylon, mister, it'll do.'

The Captain remained unconvinced but hesitated to say more, seeing the owner's soured expression gazing toward the rising coal dust above the hatch.

Jackson surveyed the table, seeing the affected society created, promoted and maintained by the laides come out to Singapore, elevated in their minds alone by distance from what might have been called real society in Great Britain. The largely boorish collection of gentlemen with these women were obviously self-indulgent in several or all of the vices which gave sensual pleasure or immediate self-gratification. Jackson smiled, a malicious glint in his eye.

'Ladies and gentlemen,' he said, 'as we shall be leaving this afternoon, I feel it my duty to thank you for your hospitality. I hope,' he continued, 'that in the future, should you yourselves travel east or west from your undoubted paradise here, you will use steamships like *SS Otranto*.'

Murmurs of agreement came from the guests. Then the sound of gears shifting prompted him. 'A toast,' he suggested loudly above the noise of the derrick, which was moving again. Glasses were raised. 'To the future,' he said. Crystal sparkled in the sunlight and the musical notes of fine glass met, corroborated the owner's toast. At that moment the turning derrick, its long arm half-way between the barge and the ship, jammed its gears, causing the lignite load to swing from its pannier and plummet into the harbour waters. All heads turned as shouts of alarm and confusion exploded from the crew aboard and the coolies in the barge. Coal dust hung in the air and began to drift towards the luncheon deck. Cornelia glanced at Jackson, who regarded her in exasperation. She dabbed perspiration from her forehead with a silk handkerchief.

'This, Hollis, is the future?'

He made a grimace. 'It's the best we have,' he said, and meant it.

'Then we must make the most of it,' she murmured, and for the first time outside locked doors, feeling spontaneous compassion and affection, she kissed him lightly on the cheek.

'Well,' he whispered, 'I have something now to remember in Singapore.'

Cornelia blushed.

At five o'clock precisely, after farewells and thanks had been exchanged, lorchas, sampans and cutters assembled to take off the perspiring and largely intoxicated guests. *Otranto*, with a full hold and a complement of more than willing passengers, blasted her horn three times to indicate her departure. Making steam, with smoke trailing from her funnel, she cruised slowly

between the out islands of the great colonial settlement toward the Straits of Malacca. Beyond lay
the Andaman Sea and all the mysteries of open
ocean.

21

Squall rain and feathered foam lashed at Eli Lubbock's oilskins as he swore for the hundredth time that early morning in October stepping down from his 'trick' at the wheel into his damp but warm cabin to 'peel off' and rest awhile. Wiping himself down with a moist towel, he scowled at the chart stretched on the board. Pinpointing his position, he traced a finger south-south-west, hesitating at Banca Island, which lay off Sumatra, only several degrees south of the equator.

Billy Williams put his head around the door, then his hand, offering a mug of fresh tea. His florid, plump features lit up as Eli sipped the hot liquid greedily.

'Thank you, Mr Mate,' said Eli, staring still at the chart.

''S what the doctor ordered, sir,' grinned Billy. 'Several of them young 'prentices is in need o' somethin' themselves,' he laughed, 'still washin' off the paint from our line-crossin' party!'

'Indeed,' grunted Eli, 'then I hope they find it in time to negotiate the channels ahead. I'll need every hand and all their nimble fingers to play our canvas now we've crossed the tropics.'

'Which route have you decided, sir?' Billy asked, knowing the choices.

'Well,' muttered Eli, 'I've had friends run aground on Pulo Leat in the Gaspar Straits . . . the deep water is not as safe as we're told – remember the *Lammermuir* in '62? She went on to the Amhurst reef and stayed a wreck there for years. Discovery reef's as bad. As for pirates. . . .' He stopped and sipped more tea, shaking his head. 'Borneo, Sumatra, Java, Banca, Billiton,

Lombok and the rest are all havens for proas with bad intentions. They'll sneak up on us if they see us in difficulties, believe me!'

'So it's the Banca?' asked Billy.

'We're well over on a 2.20 degree latitutde 105.50 degree long, so my guess is to make a run of it.'

'Aye aye, sir.'

'We'll stay on the Banca lee and well out from them Sumatra swamps. I want all watch hands with rifles day and night.'

'Aye, sir; let's pray for a steady blow.'

Eli, feeling the rise and pitch of *Chantril*, glanced through the hatch where dawn light showed more brightly. He knew the hazards of these perilous waters, the intricate navigation required and the arduous seamanship demanded of his crew, who at all times needed to remain alert. He put down his mug of tea and bent his head, giving in for a moment to exhaustion.

'Damn it, Billy, it'll be God-given when we get the trades of the southern ocean, then we can show our paces. These north-east monsoon winds just ain't constant. If there's not a squall sweepin' out of nowhere we get baffling airs blowin' half a gale. We're blinded by rain tryin' to negotiate a badly charted reef; rocks have blocked the fairway of every narrow channel we've chanced and there's not a current that 'asn't behaved contrary to any sailing instructions I've read.' He sighed deeply, 'Billy, I'm convinced if our lives depended on a steady blow, we'd be becalmed!'

Eli's mate smiled encouragement, knowing the trials ahead. 'Take heart, sir,' he said. 'We ain't been out much more'n twenty an' four days; we've a deal to do yet.'

Eli sipped his hot tea and nodded agreement. 'Eyes peeled Billy,' he murmured to the older seaman, 'and I'll chart our course for the turn.'

'Aye, sir, I'll warn the crew.' He buttoned his oilskins and went above.

Captain Lubbock's fears were justified within twenty-four hours. The wind died as they entered the channel and with little headway possible, *Chantril* began merely to glide between dangerous shoals seen only from aloft in the shallow waters or from foam churning in the strong currents. Brilliant sun made a sheen of light on the water, confusing all aboard but the man in the chains heaving the lead which was passed back by the watch hands to the leadsman aft, who for hours on end counted the fathoms as the set course continued slowly along the deepest path Eli had found in the charts.

'Where do you think old Silas has got himself?' asked Billy, playing the wheel lightly, judging *Chantril*'s, pace to be barely six knots.

Eli grunted. 'Gaspar more'n likely. If he tries the Macclesfield at night I doubt we'll see him again.'

''As it been done?' asked Billy.

'Not often,' Eli answered with irony. 'It ain't prudent. There's no leading lights and with submerged rocks and growin' coral constantly changing the reefs, without a wind he'll have to anchor, and run for it in the day if he finds one. Not for me,' he finished. 'We'll gain days on him if'n he's forced to care and wear ship.'

The heat became oppressive; humidity intensified on the second day when *Chantril* was forced nearer land on the Banca side. As evening fell, all above on deck seeking the mere whispers of moving air could hear distinctly the chattering of monkeys in the trees and the exotic screams of tropical birds above the sustained singing of others, causing many a shiver amongst the passengers. The crew's eyes remained always on the creeks, coves and small bays, jungle-clad to their narrow shores, harbouring the substance of nightmares and terrible dreams. At after-glow and throughout the night, eyes strained for the hint of a fire amidst the dark forests or the soft disturbance of water when a flock of swift Malay pirate proas with their long sweeps, packed with bloodthirsty ruffians, might emerge and surprise the anxious vessel as it coasted along under an encrusted eternity.

Lewis Ellory filmed each day, documenting life aboard ship and, with the strong light he had declared he so needed, creating moving picture history with his numerous shots of the strange and largely unknown land before him. One night at dinner he created even more – a mild panic amongst the more timorous diners – by swearing he had heard, quite regularly, the roar of tigers. This was hestitantly confirmed by several other passengers; but when he stated that it was a fact they could swim, terror became quite apparent in the eyes of all, especially the ladies whose fanciful imaginations saw them being eaten alive in their bunks or, after *Chantril*'s fateful grounding ashore, awaiting their horrible fate beneath palm fronds. Days passed and the worst was proven to be, as is often the case, only in the minds of those who created their own phantoms in the dark.

At dawn on the twenty-fifth day out of Shanghai, *Chantril* emerged from the Selat Banca into the wide expanse ahead of the Java Sea, to shouts and hurrahs of relief from both crew and passengers. An easterly wind was found almost immediately and cracked the limp canvas. Within the hour the desperate shores of Banca Island were rapidly receding and all around *Chantril* a blue sea danced, throwing flecks of foam from shallow waves and allowing the clipper a speedy passage south to the narrows where Sumatra almost touched the island of Java. Landfall would be between the great volcano of Krakatoa and Anjer, where they might take on fresh fruit and report their safe arrival through dangerous waters. Eli leaned on the taffrail, feeling the hot sun on his face cooled by the swirling air of the freshening breeze, watching Billy confidently adjusting the great wheel to the compass points set south.

'Anjer it is,' he murmured.

'Aye, sir,' grinned Billy. 'Then we'll see some sailin'!'

'We will indeed, Mr Mate,' said Eli. 'We will indeed.'

Absently Eli withdrew his revolver from his belt and began to spin the chamber slowly, checking the safety and each cartridge in place. To his left, on the port side at the rail, two Chinamen were pressing oakum into the deck, re-sealing the planks where the sea had done its damage. As Eli pulled back the trigger and pointed playfully above their heads, they froze. Eli registered their faces perspiring beneath headbands.

'Get to it!' he commanded, and waved the revolver. They bent to their task with a will, although each kept an eye open for Eli's next move.

'You'll frighten 'em to death, sir,' grinned Billy.

Eli nodded, replacing the secured revolver in his belt, and stepped to take the wheel, squinting the length of the deck to see Emily and Awan each clutching their hats to their heads against the building north-easterly.

'We'll take on the royals, Mr Mate, and lower and top stays'ls. Make the sheets fast and we might even anchor off Java Head tonight with a view that'll shake 'em all.'

'What's that, sir?' asked Billy, noting the two Chinamen listening to every word.

'We'll be in sight of a volcano that's blown its stack an'll still throw lava into the night. Perhaps Mr Ellory should be informed so he can capture it?'

Billy laughed. 'Like them pirates Silas tackled?'

Eli shrugged humorously. 'Well, we're nigh on a full moon!'

'I'll let him know, sir,' said the Mate, and left the poop deck. Eli glanced down at the two crew pressing oakum and for a brief moment caught a disconcerting expression in their eyes.

'What are you two yella' faces starin' at? Work!' Both men, as one, bowed their heads with acknowledged respect and continued as ordered. Eli looked on, aware he felt uneasy but at a loss to explain why. For no apparent reason he glanced over his shoulder, where far to the north-east, now several thousand miles away, lay his past of many years. Despite the heat he shivered but was content to know that with distance he had successfully buried all his fears for the future.

At dusk land was sighted and by nightfall they were anchored off Anjer, to which they reported with morse light. Krakatoa was true to its reputation and after early supper kept most of the passengers entranced and in awe as a red glow on the horizon to the south-west was suffused with more brilliant shafts of orange light, indicating molten lava shifting in its bed upon the earth's core. The night passed. As it does in the tropics, the dawn did not linger; the sun rose swiftly and within minutes the familiar heat was added to the continuing humidity and the virulent mosquitoes which had plagued all aboard *Chantril* throughout the night.

Shouting on deck from the crew on watch brought most passengers to the rail, thankful to leave their cramped quarters below. Here they saw that the ship was surrounded with proas and sampans. Initial alarm turned to amusement when they realised the small vessels were laden with fruit and yams, even eggs. Pandemonium reigned as bartering was conducted loudly in a variety of tongues – all captured in black and white by an excited Lewis Ellory. Baskets were lowered over *Chantril*'s side to the smooth water where traders jockeyed for position to take the money in exchange for generously given supplies. Ellory's single frustration was the knowledge that the myriad colours of the still morning would be lost to posterity, and even perhaps fade in the memories of all present on such a perfect, windless day.

Eli Lubbock, at the helm, watched with mild curiosity but was more concerned that his towering canvas remained slack, and he couldn't have given a damn what intense shade of clear blue the sky appeared above; all he was praying for was a wind.

'Not a cloud in sight,' he muttered, as Billy Williams joined him on the quarter deck. The Mate stepped to the binnacle, opened the clips to the weathered but waterproof mahogany box and took out the telescope. Elbows on the rail, Billy focused and found, clearly framed, what he had hoped to see.

'A cloud, sir,' he called triumphantly.

'How is it moving?' Eli asked eagerly.

'South-south-west, sir,' Billy answered. Noise from the bellowed trade almost drowned his voice.

'What?' Eli frowned. 'What kind of cloud – cumulus?'

Billy shook his head and stood up. Gritting his teeth he said, 'Canvas.'

Eli snatched the telescope and grasping it tightly saw for himself.

'God damn him!' he exploded. 'We've got the view and he's taken the wind!' Hearing the loud exclamation with some apprehension, Emily, having stepped up to the poop to wish the Captain good morning, faltered in her stride.

'What is it, Mr Lubbock?'

He spun round, snapping the brass telescope shut.

'*Vesper!*' he roared.

'But. . . .' She hesitated, seeking the ship on the horizon. 'I thought we'd lost him!'

'*He's* found *us!*' snarled Eli, and he turned on his

mate, gesturing to the traders still bartering. 'Clear them off! We're moving out now!' He began pacing as Billy shook his head.

'But how, sir? We ain't got no. . . .' He stopped. Looking up he saw the mizzen top-gallants had begun to swell in the very whisper of a breeze. He grinned hugely and clapped Eli on the back. 'Aye aye, sir!'

'I want those trades, Billy! Up anchors!' He turned to stare towards the horizon. *Vesper* had already approached at some speed. He could make her out clearly, most sails set – stuns, stays, even moonsails. Grunting to himself, Eli seized the taffrail and began to rock back and forth.

'Mr Lubbock,' Emily asked, astonished, 'what are you doing?'

'Praying, madam, that either he sinks or that we swim!'

'Is that not harsh judgement on a friend?' she suggested.

Eli turned on his heel and strode to the cabin door, where he paused to offer some explanation.

'At sea, madam, all must be done to ensure the outcome of a race – and I mean to win.' This last he said with such aggressive conviction Emily was shocked and stepped back. She began to mouth society's accepted words of consolation to possible losers, but Eli was already gone below, taking his anger with him. The real consolation was that he still had almost half the world before him.

Silas Hayes opened his eyes to shouts of 'hurrah' from above at the helm, on the quarter deck. After thirty-six hours on the poop he had retired to his cabin, leaving the door open. Fine spray filled the air as it cascaded the length of *Vesper* and swirled about the Mate at the wheel. Silas swung his legs from the bunk,

300

feeling more heavy than refreshed, and hung his head, to collect his thoughts.

'Java Head!' he heard shouted with wild excitement by his old shipmate, Hughie Sutherland. He looked up as his son burst into the cabin and saluted. Tousle-haired, now bronzed from the sun, wet and with a wide grin across his face, Jamie was only distracted for a moment as he heard Ben's terrier barking loudly.

'The Sunda Straits, Father!' Silas looked long at his offspring then stood up, feeling the age in his bones. 'It's *sir*, boy! And we ain't through 'em yet!'

'Ben says that we've outrun *Chantril* – sir – an' they've spotted him on the lee off Anjer and we're to go past Krakatoa where the volcano – '

Silas held up a hand interrupting the rush of words. '*Chantril?*' he asked.

The boy pointed through the wall of the cabin. 'He's becalmed offshore, *sir*, and we're running a full league away from . . . Eli, Ben says.'

Silas stepped to the chart spread upon his navigation board. 'And you listen to what Ben says, laddie.' The terrier jumped down into the cabin and immediately nuzzled into the young friend he had made. Silas leaned on the chart and began to trace his finger through the narrow straits of Sumatra and Java, beyond which lay the vast tracts of the southern Indian Ocean.

'Ben's been telling me – sir,' Jamie stammered, 'well. . . .' He paused. 'Just about everything. I've gone over our whole route; I know all the winds, where the islands lie from Christmas to Mauritius. Ben says it's at most ten days if we make more than three hundred sea miles a day so. . . .' Silas glanced at the boy. 'Sea miles eh?'

Jamie became serious for a moment. 'Six thousand and eighty feet, sir, eight hundred more than a land mile, so we travel faster.'

'We travel as fast as the sea and wind allow, boy,' said Silas abruptly.

'But Ben says, Father, that you are the very best sea captain that ever sailed a square-rigged clipper.'

Silas nodded with a wry smile. 'I pay Ben, so what else would he say?'

Jamie's face fell and he frowned indignantly. 'Ben would never say what he does not mean – sir!' The terrier barked, seemingly in agreement. Silas ruffled the boy's head, then the terrier's.

'Can you swim?' he asked.

Jamie became proud. 'I was first at the end of every year at school, sir, and one day I want to be a champion.' Silas saw in the pale innocent eyes of his son not only the truth but a confidence imbued in him by Cornelia. The boy's voice contained no false boasting, only a fact, even if it was improper to say it.

'Good,' said Silas, appraising him. 'You look fit enough, you've been nigh on thirty days aboard – can you climb?'

'Climb, sir!' exploded Jamie, 'why I could – '

'Go aloft?' asked Silas.

Jamie's mouth fell open. Silas put an arm around the boy and drew him to the charts. The terrier jumped up on the board, straddling the China seas. Silas pushed him away and showed his son the route beyond the narrow straits.

'When we get out into open ocean and feel the trades, you'll need to learn to hold on tight,' he said. 'The Sunda Straits are the end of one world. Here we leave the mysteries of the Far East behind.' More shouts sounded above and spray filled the air about the cabin door. Silas pointed at the chart, Jamie splayed across it, chin in hands, eyes wide. 'When we get out into open ocean,' Silas repeated, 'under the Southern Cross,' he whispered, 'you'll see glistening bonito, shining skipjack, leaping dolphins, flying fish and huge whales breeching and plunging into the depths.'

'Flying fish!' exclaimed the boy.

Silas nodded, creating the scene with a father's relish. 'And high above the waves, gliding on the swirling air, great wide-winged albatross, and storm petrels and navigator birds, turning on the wind. We're going to cut through the foam like a whale boat in tow of a strike.' Silas' voice was raised in an excitement he had not felt for years. Gazing into his son's trusting eyes, forgetting his authority in that moment, he began to eulogise about time past, expertise, wisdom and respect for knowledge gained the hard way. 'I'll put up every inch of sail and you'll feel in every shudder, every roll, every pitch of this gallant clipper, the way we used to bring back tea to England, in the old days. . . .' He hesitated, remembering, but seeing his boy's eyes wide, continued rapidly. 'We did it so quick, them leaves were still damp from the morning dew of a Chinese field.'

The air in the cabin filled with more sea salt from the spray. The terrier panted as if equally impressed and Jamie remained open-mouthed, clenched fists supporting his awe-struck face.

Silas said gruffly, 'Now then, laddie! Work!'

Jamie jumped from the table, followed by Ben's terrier, who barked again, already a seasoned seaman.

'Yes, sir!' snapped the boy, and he ran up the steps to the helm.

Silas Hayes smiled to himself, proud of his knowledge, proud of his command and proud to be a father. He suppressed his emotion in a cough, buttoned his coat and went up to the bracing air of the quarter deck above.

Straddling the caulked teak, Silas' sea legs took his weight as the ship, increasing speed as she emerged from the Straits of Sunda, began to feel her way into the larger waves of the Indian Ocean. The pitch of *Vesper*'s boom indicated to Silas how he should shorten or pile on canvas. Estimating the constant south-east trade wind as a long-term companion, he surveyed his spread of sail as he supported himself by grasping the burnished brass on the wheel which Hughie held firmly.

Ben Hardy arrived at the double on the poop, seeing his captain at the helm. His terrier, having run up from the cabin, barked in anticipation of Silas' orders, which were rapped out loudly.

'Mr Mate! I want ringtails outside the spanker, a watersail beneath the boom, mizzen stay sails and lower stuns . . . the spare flying jib on the fore royal and all sky sails.'

Ben grinned. 'We've moons'ls up like ol' Coulson's *Maitland* out of Sunderland, sir – them's from ol' Jackson's store, I wouldn't bet.'

'Some would say they're just "fluff" Ben,' Silas retorted, smiling, 'but look at 'em when they billow, feel the wind and tell me they ain't workin' like a main course!'

'They'll do the trick, sir,' Ben agreed.

'An' you can take mine,' grunted Hughie.

'Yes sir, Mr Mate,' Ben answered, and stepped to take the wheel. Silas stayed him and beckoned to Jamie, who approached his father cautiously.

'Hold the wheel, Hughie,' he said with authority. 'I've a few plans to make a seaman today.' He winked at his first mate. The terrier cocked its head at Jamie's feet and whined.

'Aye, sir,' smiled Hughie. The ship juddered a moment but the Mate seized the wheel with powerful hands and steadied *Vesper* as she righted herself.

'We're goin' to do the fastest run possible to Mauritius and the Cape, Hughie. I want three hundred a day from her. She'll do it too, by heaven – I feel it in my bones. And those ain't Yankee miles of longitude below the fiftieth degree, those'll be sea miles!'

'I don't understand, Father,' said Jamie, perplexed.

'The old Blackballers – emigrant ships around the Cape o' storms, the Horn to you, travelled a narrow world where degrees is less than sixty and more'n like forty, so they'd quote degree miles of longitude to keep their passengers happy and not the real distance covered. Even *Thermopyle* never bested three forty, so how could *Lightning*, *James Baines* and *Red Jacket* do four hundred and thirty and more?'

'Them was tricky boys, Fenright an' the like,' muttered Hughie.

Ben ruffled Jamie's tousled hair.

'They was romancers,' he said.

'Strangers to the truth, more like,' grunted Hughie.

Silas looked at Ben. 'Take the boy only as high as the main cap, then let him help set the bowsprit's Jamie Green – personally.'

'Oh, sir!' exclaimed Jamie excitedly.

'Take him off, Ben,' Silas commanded gruffly.

Ben, his terrier and Jamie left the poop, but not before Jamie saluted with a suddenly applied, serious face. Silas watched them go, feeling the increasing wind on the exposed skin behind his ears where he could detect even a vesper.

'It's his namesake, Hughie,' he murmured.

'Sir?' asked the Mate.

'I christened the boy years ago to watch him lay it out . . . I've waited for this day, which I'd never thought to come,' Silas said quietly.

'You must be proud, sir.'

'I am.'

'He's a good lad.'

'He is,' Silas agreed, and coughed. As Ben and Jamie reached the rat-tails and began to climb, Silas winced.

'I'll go below and check the . . . charted course, Mr Mate.'

'Aye, sir,' said Hughie.

Silas paused at his cabin door. 'Ah. . . .' He hesitated. 'Keep a weather eye on him.'

'Be assured, sir.'

'I hope to be, Hughie,' murmured the Captain, but he stepped below with the justified fears of a father.

Smart, steady breezes south by east drove *Vesper* away from Java and all her adventures in the East. On the fifth day they were past the Cocos Islands and at 12°.15 latitude, 94.53° longitude, fast approaching the ninety east ridge running more than a thousand miles north, and south from the equator, below the 30° line. The wind freshened, veering easterly during the course of each day, causing jubilation from the crew as the ship maintained a constant speed, despite their back-breaking work at the stays and braces. Several yards were relieved of their strain and one, when a jackstay parted on the main top gallant and it was discovered to be rotten at the cap, was removed. The carpenter worked night and day and the new yard was winched aloft, secured to the truss, fastened to the buntlines and allowed to play on the braces until the crew swarmed on to the footropes and wove the rope yarn rovings through the eyes of the sail, which immediately billowed then cracked open, with the others quickly being pulled in tight. The crew checked the clewlines and clew iron and heaved at the main sheet until it was taut, before descending to the deck of the racing clipper.

Throughout, Jamie had contributed from the cap platforms, having been allowed higher, passing rope and tackle, even aiding with the swing of the yard – a dangerous procedure under sail – as it was placed on to the gooseneck. With the main mast standing sixteen storeys high, it took nerve to be even half-way to the top, but to work in a moving ship as she pitched and rolled took more even than courage. The seasoned crew developed a trust in each other amongst the shrouds nd canvas that they did not always maintain over chow or in their cramped quarters. Familiarity established a confidence based on nimble fingers, a complete lack of vertigo and a sense of urgency communicated to all at a captain's order, when lost time in either furling or spreading canvas could well mean a damaged or, worse, a lost ship. Those who did not pull together were soon persuaded by the others, and time taught the best lesson of all – it was not merely a question of the voyage to be run but, often, a question of survival – for which each must be able to depend upon the other. Thus a seaman learnt that differences were superfluous to skills to be utilised, developed and respected for the good of the ship, and indeed for all their lives.

Jamie's confidence grew in proportion to his abilities, which were prodigious enough to astonish Ben on more than one occasion and to make the boy popular with the crew, in his own right and not merely because he was the son of the Captain. What had sounded like pontificating at the outset in the cabins or at mealtimes became of interest to the sailors aboard, unaware of much of the history Jamie had consigned to his memory. Practically, he had much to learn, but of the theory and tradition of the sailing fraternity he appeared to know enough to draw admiration even from the oldest salt.

Initial reluctance to climb above the main cap became a challenge which Jamie seized and, looking down from the to' gallants, he smiled to himself, knowing, as he rove in a new sail with others of the crew on the swaying footrope high above the deck, that he had conquered his last fears, having been more frightened to fail than fall.

Two hundred and eighty sea miles became three hundred in the log directly above the great ninety east ridge fathoms beneath *Vesper* as she scudded on a south-west course, scything through a running sea under an azure sky where ochre-tinted titanium-white cumulus travelled in consort with the racing composite and canvas below. In open ocean the leadsman was unnecessary, but the knot line and sand timer were in regular use as the count gave a constant fourteen or fifteen knots for the Mate to report to Silas. He wrote it down in meticulous handwriting, concealing from all but Hughie that he had capitulated to the indignity of reading glasses for close work. The morale amongst the crew was high, all knowing they had bearded, beaten and gone ahead of *Chantril*, who, it was generally agreed, wallowed behind, way beyond the horizon. Even at the main moonsail yard, the sharpest eye with a telescope focused to the north-east could find nothing.

On the seventh day out from Anjer, although the conditions prevailed, the sea picked up and a strong blow from the south-east brought *Vesper*'s yards close to her starboard shroud. The figurehead, bowsprit and martingale tasted the ocean as spray fountained the length of the deck, soaking but refreshing all passengers who ventured above to see rather than feel the long waves they were riding out at a fair lick.

Min Ho in the crew's kitchen on deck grinned at Jamie as he stirred vegetables into a swill stew heating in a tureen on a burner.

'Me no run lick no more, young number one – your number one he takes us lick, lick.'

Jamie nodded at the reference to his father and sneaked a morsel of corned beef from beside the cleaver, agreeing with an innocent expression as the cook turned back to him, showing more gaps than teeth. 'We go quick, quick England side, no wait me China, stay me Britannia cook man.'

Jamie smiled and took another morsel under the very eyes of Min Ho, who merely shook his head and giggled. 'You little man, big man come.'

'Thank you, sir,' mumbled Jamie, glad of the respite from swabbing the decks and tredding the yards. Min Ho opened another large tin of beef and again cut it with the cleaver as if it was a large raw joint. He pointed at a bucket of garbage on the floor of the cramped kitchen-house on deck, indicating it was full and should be dumped overboard.

Jamie took the handle and lugged the bucket to the bulwark, nearly slipping through a flapping scupper as sea water sluiced back into the ocean. He upended the contents of the bucket: kitchen residue, tins, stumps, skins, boxes, paper, packing, grease, oil, lard, grime and even feathers from deceased chickens of the previous lunch, into the sea. Immediately it was all carried away into *Vesper*'s wake. A moment's fascination caused Jamie to linger, peering over the side and staring at the flotsam and jetsam which, a moment before, had been secure aboard and was now lost and gone upon God's vast ocean. Only fingers at his ear pressing hard and the barking of a snapping terrier at his heels disturbed his morbid thoughts.

'Is this work?' growled Ben.

'I was just – '

'In the kitchen?' Ben's voice was sharp.

'I was . . . hungry,' stated the boy, eyes pleading that his ear, now painful, be released.

'You'll eat with the rest,' snapped Ben. 'Jump to it!'

'Yes, sir,' answered Jamie, grateful for his release and rubbing his ear.

'At the bowsprit, at the double!' The boy ran off as Min Ho put his head out of the door, and Ben handed

309

back the empty bucket with a wink to the grinning Chinese face.

'He plucky boy.'

'He better be,' Ben grunted and, bracing his legs against the pitch and spray, made his way forward.

The fresh breeze stiffened and foaming spray suffusing the air seemed like curdling milk as it enveloped the deck from the fo'c's'le along the for'ard bulwarks and out of the scuppers amidships, which lifted sharply as the stern of *Vesper* was thrust up and into the head sea by following waves. Astride the end of the bowsprit, Ben and Jamie, clinging to the stays, laughed as spray exploded behind them whilst they, above the sea, merely brushed their feet into the waves, as the Mate had shown the boy, whilst they cleared snagged lines.

Below them, schools of dolphin raced beside the figurehead as it cut into the clear water forming the bow wave curling back either side of *Vesper* then, almost as one, the dolphins curved into the air with cries of salute before plunging again into the ocean.

Jamie was entranced then amazed as Ben pointed out a lone albatross, great wings spread, circling majestically on the thermals. Storm petrels and navigator birds dived from on high before the foremast, so close it seemed they would collide with the stretched jibs, skimming over the sea surface, avoiding the heaving water with practised ease even though they seemed at any moment about to be swallowed by the cresting waves. Ben indicated the knot he was tying and Jamie leaned in close, his hair curled, his face salt streaked but eyes bright and inquisitive. *Vesper*'s second mate formed the figure eight then pulled the rope strands tight to create a Cumberland.

'The way a ship turns back on itself!' he shouted above the roar of water and motioned with his hand, tracing the full figure as a clipper with all speed might bend its course describing two full circles over numerous sea miles and find itself back on the same course. Jamie frowned, then, eventually understanding, nodded enthusiastically. Ben laughed loudly, his voice whipped away by the wind and sea, unaware that with pride and in some awe, the knot line at the poop had been pulled by the crewman, showing *Vesper*'s thousand tons and a million-pounds-weight cargo to be travelling at an almost unheard of seventeen knots. Astride the bowsprit Ben pulled *his* knot and shook the Cumberland free so that the rope hung as straight as *Vesper*'s charted course.

Man and boy laughed from sheer exhilaration as once more the clipper plunged and spray, from their position high above the sea surface, seemed to obliterate the ship in a flurry of foam. Each indicated to the other that all was well: Jamie's small pressed fingers extended to Ben's clenched fist and their thumbs touched.

22

Sunlight glinted on dull tin to starboard of *Chantril*, catching the eye of Billy Williams, who nudged Eli Lubbock. The Captain squinted and made out the floating remains of garbage thrown from *Vesper* by Jamie. He grinned and slapped his mate on the back.

'So – we're right behind him! The old dog!'

'He'll not better fifteen knots, even in this blow,' muttered Billy, surveying his set of straining sails and feeling the wind direction on his cheek. 'We'll catch him, sir,' he said, and took a mug of fresh lime juice and water from the Chinese boy Cha-ze. Eli also accepted his juice and touched the boy's pigtail for luck as he bowed respectfully then smiled mischievously before scuttling away. Eli watched him and sipped the juice, feeling the sharpness in his mouth of the scurvy preventer.

'He's proved to be a good lad, sir,' said Billy.

Eli nodded, 'His mother's loyal, strong-willed and hard-working – Emily's lucky to have her. He has some of her qualities.'

Billy, feeling the buck of the ship, steadied the wheel with both hands, slopping juice from his mug.

Seeing the boy now on the main deck and making back for the cook-house amidships, Eli saw Cha-ze stride the pitch and roll of the clipper as if he were a veteran. Ignoring the flying spray he ducked into the distant kitchen out of sight.

'Maybe he'll bring us luck,' suggested Bill Williams.

Eli shook his head, 'We don't need more, Mr Mate. This is a lucky ship. I feel it.'

Billy's expression was dubious. 'Only for some,

maybe. You can never get too much if chance ain't on your side.'

'Are you really superstitious?' asked Eli, genuinely surprised.

Billy wetted his lips. 'Careful,' he said quietly.

Eli looked long at his mate and sipped more juice. 'Do we have all sky sails aloft?' he asked.

'We're pressing sail now, sir. In this blow – '

'I'll decide that,' snapped Eli. '*He'll* have 'em up, and by God if it takes a water-sail beneath the for'ard stuns or a moons'l to take the edge off his royals, then we'll place 'em and keep 'em there!'

'Aye, sir,' Billy said reluctantly, and relinquished the helm to Eli, who checked the compass bearing and stood astride the big wheel, feeling the power of the sea against his firm grip as he applied pressure to bring the rudder exactly in alignment to his charted course. Billy was about to go, instructions for the crew assembling in his mind, when he thought he heard Eli growl with determination.

'You'll not lose *me* Silas!'

'What, sir?' he asked. But the words were obscured; taken by the roar of the wind and the surge of the ocean

'The sea's pickin' up, sir,' said Hughie, seeing Silas emerge from his cabin on to the quarter deck. *Vesper*'s captain saw with satisfaction all his sails full blown and grunted as he acknowledged the white-capped waves appearing around them, more shallow than the long-reaching water earlier in the day.

'It'll do.'

'Sir,' began Hughie, 'the wind – '

'Is ours to use, Mr Mate,' cut in Silas. 'Knots?'

'Fifteen, sixteen, sir . . . been seventeen.'

Silas nodded. 'Then we'll go with it, Mr Sutherland; we'll not break records with reticence.'

'We're sailin' fast, sir,' Hughie said, as if they should not. Silas rounded on him. 'Then maintain it, Mr Mate, and we need go no faster.' *Vesper*'s jib boom plunged again, but her bow picked up immediately, driven strongly from abaft the beam, and onward she thrust, south-west into a building sea.

Watch bells rang at the hour of tea, as the ladies would have it. Above, crew changed, as below crockery in the ill-lit, claustrophobic passengers' quarters fell from tables and clattered from trays upset as cups and saucers spilled hot liquid upon trousered thighs moving quickly to protect voluminous dresses. Eyes attempted to penetrate the cabin's ceilings as if they could see the waves jarring against the fast clipper. Heavy luggage slewed from port to starboard between the compartments as *Vesper* rushed forward with the noise of sustained thunder. James Collins had conducted and concluded a service and retired with the others for tea.

'So difficult to create, maintain, even a semblance of proper behaviour,' said the priest to the young daughter of Consul Morgan. Adèle merely smiled and tried a second time to put cup to lips before hot tea flooded her mouth, so she was forced to spit out on to the floorboards. Eyebrows were raised until others were forced to follow suit. 'Mr Hayes appears to be pressing hard,' stated the priest, coughing to conceal his embarrassment as he wiped tea from his jacket.

'And you, it seems, Reverend, are a victim,' giggled Adèle.

Collins' face composed itself. 'Not I, Miss Morgan.' His smile was almost supercilious, definitely unattractive. 'But others will suffer his . . . ambitions, I am sure.'

'Is that the word of God?' asked Adèle, to gasps from others around the makeshift table of the passenger quarters.

'No,' answered Collins slowly, 'I say it as I know him.'

'Do you?'

'Well enough, I believe,' the priest replied. *Vesper* juddered, crockery fell, someone caught the large silver tray.

'Do you?' asked Adèle again.

'What?' snapped the priest.

'Believe,' murmured Adèle, sipping tea.

'God's will is unassailable,' the priest answered and swallowed the hot liquid.

Adèle's wry smile contained wickedness. 'Listen to the roar of the sea and the blast of the wind, Mr Collins; you are in a vessel guided at the helm by master seamen; in what do you trust? *Their* experience, culled from tested knowledge, or the ephemeral concept of God guiding us all to heavenly grace before landfall.' She paused effectively. 'Ships sink, you know, in full sight of God, *Mr* Collins.' The priest coughed.

'More tea?' asked Adèle and attempted to pour.

White water waves appearing throughout the afternoon prompted caution at *Vesper*'s helm as Hughie evaluated the conditions but his orders were to maintain course and speed, as Silas slept below in his cabin, allowing him little leeway other than furling sky sails which had begun to strain at their clew irons.

Ben brought Jamie to the poop, where the boy was able to appreciate the speed of *Vesper* as, in awe, he watched more than two hundred feet of ship travelling ahead of him – groaning, sighing, shrieking and moaning as if she were a live animal driven to the limits of endurance. Above him the sails were taut and the deck glistened in the sun. Spray lashed along the rails but the sky was deep blue, the sea azure and only the white water matched the cumulus which built up and dissolved in the sharp and constant wind, veering only points abaft. Now Jamie realised the true power of sail, seeing the sheets tight, canvas stretched and bowed, seemingly about to be torn from the yards.

'She's goin' quite a lick,' he stated, remembering Min Ho's words.

'Indeed she is, boy,' Hughie grunted, holding the wheel firm and steady.

'Water sails, Ben?' he asked.

'Aye, Mr Sutherland, but they'll all tear if we pick up even another knot. . . .'

'I'll decide that, Mr Mate,' snapped Hughie, and he glanced at his number two in warning.

'Aye, sir,' nodded Ben, accepting the reproach, 'but they'll go all the same.'

Silas Hayes stepped up on to the poop, interrupting further contradiction between his mates.

'Report,' he commanded, tugging for a moment at Jamie's tousled hair. 'You'll need it cut laddie.'

'Who'll do it?' asked the boy, pulling away.

'I will,' growled Silas, and winked at his first mate.

'We've the luck of the gods, sir,' Hughie grinned. 'Wind's strong and ain't varyin' more'n a point or two. We've almost all canvas up and she's just cruisin',' he finished.

'Almost?' replied Silas, picking up the word.

'Sky sails are down,' Hughie admitted.

'With water sails below the lower stuns! Why?'

'Two of 'em blew their clews, sir.'

'Then double 'em up!' ordered the Captain.

'We're at sixteen, seventeen knots now, sir,' Hughie told him. Silas surveyed the sails, his eyes absorbing the luff and roach of each one he could see. Appreciating the lick o' speed, he smiled wryly.

'Then we'll save 'em, boys,' he said, relaxing against the taffrail, feeling with pleasure and pride the movement of his ship. 'Jamie Green stretched, Ben?' he asked.

316

'Aye, sir. The boy done it well.'

'Good lad,' said the father to his son. 'Go for'ard and check the jibs, let 'em out, Ben, if they're tight. We'll suck every breath from this blow and take ourselves a good league more from our Eli.'

'Aye, sir; come boy,' said Ben. Jamie glanced at his father and smiled.

'Thank you sir.'

'Did you eat, laddie?'

'Min Ho gave us all a stew I think it was, sir.'

'He ate with the crew, sir,' nodded Ben.

'You gettin' on, son?' asked Silas.

'I wouldn't be anywhere else, sir,' Jamie answered.

'Come on, lad,' Ben commanded him gruffly. The Second Mate and the boy went for'ard. Water sprayed over the rails and sluiced through the scuppers as the two of them made their way past the cook-house. Jamie waved at Min Ho, who bowed respectfully before giggling at the urchin look the son of his captain had now assumed. Ben assessed the situation at the jib and decided to loosen sheets to spread the luff and curl the roach of each sail, reaching far out to the end of the boom. Ordering crew to his side, he quickly indicated what was necessary and they immediately began to loosen the starboard ropes, hauling to port. Swirling water at their feet made the job difficult but braced legs allowed them initial success. The strong east wind kept the canvas bowed even as it was released and spume filled the air about them so they all breathed salt.

Jamie went to it with a will, helping where he could, watching when it was prudent. Accepted by the crew, the boy, no longer bombastic and pretentious but merely a fledgling 'prentice humbled by the might of the sea about him, took turns at the ropes and pulled with the best of them. Several of the Chinese slipped as spray lashed *Vesper*'s decks and some of them showed

317

alarm. Ben shouted above the roar of the sea and his commanding voice calmed most, reassuring Jamie, who, blinking sea water, smiled confidently and signalled 'thumbs up' to his new-found friend. It was then that the first big wave inundated the fo'c's'le and obliterated everything. As the water rushed down the decks, Jamie saw Ben staring over the bulwarks, leaning on the rail, still grasping the ropes.

'Man overboard!' bellowed the Mate.

Immediately at the poop, Silas and Ben reacted to the single horror of every deep-water sailor. Leaning far out over the rail, staring the length of *Vesper*'s ebony side, Silas saw, clinging to a rope trailing at the water-line, one of the Chinese crew screaming with terror. Frantically the man tried to climb up, but slipped further into the foaming bow wave almost directly beneath the anchor. Above him several other Chinese crew, Ben and even Jamie had seized the parted shroud and were hauling away, ignoring more water as it broke over the bow and surged about them.

'Pull hard, boys!' bellowed Silas. The rope began to slip in their hands, despite their efforts, until Ben shouted something in Chinese and Jamie watched the men slip the rope around their wrists, securing their grip. With a face of determination Jamie managed to do likewise, and almost at once felt the weight of the man over the side. Spitting salt, the men and the boy pulled with all their might, and to their relief the rope responded, as the Chinaman's shrieks of fear gave them renewed strength. A moment later they saw a terrified face appear and a single hand grasp for the rail, fingers seizing the brass as if they would leave impressions.

'Lift him in, boys!' shouted Ben, and he braced his back, taking the extra weight with Jamie as the Chinamen ran to help their fellow crewman. Ben glanced the length of the rushing ship, noticing the increased pitch and roll, and nodded vigorously towards the poop deck, where he could see Silas transfixed and pointing for'ard.

Puzzled for a moment, Ben licked his lips and turned, but Jamie saw it first. A huge white water wave had risen out of the breaking sea and bore down on the bowsprit with a great roar. Jamie's mouth fell open in awe, Ben's eyes widened in fear and apprehension. The Chinese at the rail saw it all too well too, but their screams were drowned as the great comber hit the ship so hard she juddered. It exploded into the air as high as the royals and fell on the men like some great predator come to feed. Everything was obscured as Jamie's world became all sea; he had opened his mouth to shout, but a solid wall of water seemed to mould his face, filling his throat and thrusting him back. Helplessly he was carried down the deck, but suddenly jerked still as his wrist, caught in the rope which pressed against a knighthead, held him fast. For a moment the boy felt Ben's hand grasping for him, then it was gone. The Mate had slithered across the deck and was dragged off the fo'c's'le then slammed down on to the for'ard winch. Groaning in agony, Ben stood up in the salt-filled air as the great wave bore away down the deck, breaking up against the masts and shrouds. He pulled himself up the starboard steps to see the fo'c's'le cleared of crew, and the Chinamen gone, but Jamie writhing in pain as he lay sprawled at the edge of the deck, his wrist trapped beneath the trailing rope.

'Jamie!' cried Ben, and he began to run forward, realising that the Chinaman at the water-line, by some miracle, had managed in sheer terror to hang on. Without thinking, knowing in his heart there was no choice, Ben reached for his clasp knife – one life for another. . . . If a second great wave came now. . . .

'Ben,' whimpered Jamie, his young face screwed up against the obvious suffering.

319

'I'm comin', boy,' replied the Mate, and he knelt to begin cutting the shroud. Below, in the curling spray of the bow wave, the flash of steel above caused the Chinaman, inching his way up the rope to be back aboard, to shriek in horror as he realised what Ben was doing. He began weeping and pleading, riding the blue-water waves, knowing as he dragged himself up with his last strength that he was lost if his hands slipped or Ben severed the rope before he could grasp the brass rail. *Vesper* plunged again and foam roared over the fo'c's'le, dislodging Ben as he was swept away from the boy, and reached out for anything he could now grip to save his own skin.

Silas saw the plight of his son, and was just able to make out that the lad still held on. He was unable to see what Ben was about. He knew three crew had gone over, and now, seeing his mate again being swept from the fo'c's'le, leaving the boy exposed and alone, he began to run the length of the ship.

'Jamie!' he roared, and saw his small son's face turn to his, mouth open and sucking for air. 'Hold, boy!' Silas was past the aft deckhouse and running flat out. Jamie tried to pull himself up, saw a hand grasp the brass rail, then found he was looking into the terrified eyes of the Chinaman. The boy began pulling to release his wrist but the man's weight held him trapped.

'Father!' he shouted, and turned again to see Silas fast approaching, now beside the fore deckhouse, nearing Ben, who was standing groggily, dazed and holding his head where blood showed between his fingers.

'Hold hard, laddie!' bellowed Silas. 'I'm with you!' He leapt for the steps just as *Vesper*'s bows plunged, throwing her captain against the bulwarks then, as she rose in a mountain of sea, rolling to port. Silas fell across the deck and hit the winch, seizing the chains to support himself against the might of a sea determined to tear him away. Head down, he locked himself against the rushing water until he felt its power lessen as the ship righted herself. 'Freak waves,' he swore beneath his breath, knowing they were probably tsunami: waves formed from volcanic activity on the seabed. Since Krakatoa had exploded in '83 the whole run from Sunda to the ridge carried with it more than usual apprehension for sea captains familiar with the waters. Silas looked up, squinting against the fine spray lashing his face. In a moment he was up the steps and braced on the fo'c's'le, where the rope, now slack, trailed in the sea. The Chinaman was gone – and so was his son.

Like a wounded animal, Silas spun round, staring towards *Vesper*'s wake, and his shout might have woken the dead.

'Jamie!!!' he cried, then suddenly began to move. He jumped down on to the main deck, brushed Ben's arms away and ran with bursting lungs back to the poop, bellowing all the while. 'Run out ropes – furl all sails. Lower the gig on a line. Now!' Confused crew on deck were puzzled, seeing their captain charging and ranting like a madman. Leaping up to the quarter deck, Silas seized the wheel from Hughie Sutherland.

'Silas!' the Mate exclaimed, and fought against his captain as he tried to spin the great spokes hard over.

'We'll do a Cumberland knot!'

The Mate cried out, 'We can't do no figure eight in this wind, sir. You'll put her over, Silas!!'

Hughie held the wheel firmly against Silas' ebbing strength as the anguished father recognised the truth. Ben stepped up and shook his head towards Hughie, who bit his lip. Silas walked to the taffrail, feeling the ship steadier now and rushing on obediently towards her set course, south-west in the Indian Ocean, ignorant of the tragedy aboard.

'They're gone, sir – you know that,' Ben stated

321

gently. 'Even if we could turn or get a gig into the water' – he joined Silas at the stern rail – 'it would take too long to come about, at nigh on seventeen knots. You know it, sir. We'd be almost two leagues distant before we'd furled sails. . . .' Seeing Silas' eyes glistening, he glanced at Hughie with gritted teeth. Silas' head fell forward on to his chest, his shoulders hunched, arms locked, fingers clutching the brass. Below, the wake churned and boiled. Sea birds dived, calling their haunting cries with unknown intentions. 'The sea has him, sir,' whispered Ben, hesitant even to touch his captain when he wanted to enfold him in his grief. 'The boy's gone. At his feet the terrier whined, knowing something was wrong. Silas said nothing, feeling the wind on his face, hearing his ship's timbers and shrouds, canvas, brass and copper exchanging information with indecipherable creaks and groans.

Silas raised his head, on his face an expression as if carved in granite; his gaze fixed as he stared intently to the north-east into the distant wake, so quickly swallowed by the white-flecked waves.

'He wanted to know so much but understood so little,' he murmured.

'He never lacked courage,' Ben responded quietly.

Unwanted tears filled Silas' eyes as the image of a tousle-haired, suntanned urchin with bright blue eyes and a generous smile burnt itself on his memory.

'My son,' he said hoarsely, 'my dear son – God bless you.'

23

High above *Chantril*'s deck on the footrope of the skysail yard, Cha'ze, now further from his home on the Shanghai waterfront than he had ever dreamed existed, rove in the new sail, having released the old battered canvas to Billy Williams directly below. The First Mate watched the boy with growing respect as his light weight, proven competence and complete lack of vertigo, even one hundred and fifty feet above deck, enabled young, nimble fingers to secure rope and canvas where older hands might have deemed it hazardous. Other crew below applauded the Chinese boy's efforts as the new sail unfurled, was clewed in, filled, billowed and cracked, tight-luffed as all the others abreast the yards to drive the ship on at break-neck speed, south-west into the foam-flecked waves of the vast Indian Ocean. The boy grinned with pride; showing not even a vestige of fear, he scrambled back to the upper cap as the clew irons were pulled hard until the sail was taut.

'Well, boy, you're earnin' your keep,' Billy told him with studied reluctance.

The boy smiled and looked above. 'Me go high climb – no fear.'

The ship bucked and both he and Billy clung to the ropes, as did the descending crew. The Mate squinted ahead, shading his eyes from the strong sunlight. Diving sea birds had caught his attention. 'Whales, maybe,' he murmured to himself; dangerous at night, they could prove difficult during the day in a churning sea, their solid tons an obstacle to even the best-constructed clipper.

Cha'ze looked south-west. 'No whale me see from book picture – no blow water-fountain.'

Billy marvelled at the boy's pidgin English but corrected him. 'Spout, boy. You'll see 'em if they're there.'

Cha'ze concentrated for a full ten seconds, his gaze fixed, his eyes sharp – then reported, 'No whale – bodies.'

Billy turned to the boy, astounded. 'This is the Indian Ocean, laddie.' He began to laugh. 'That's impossible.'

'You bet dollar or pound, fi'?'

'Five dollars,' grinned Billy.

'Bodies,' stated Cha'ze emphatically, and only then did Billy begin to descend to the deck, glancing for'ard uncertainly, as if the boy could be right. On firm, caulked teak, travelling fast, he realised the boy had given away a large part of his agreed pay, and by the time the First Mate was again on the poop deck beside Eli Lubbock, he was chuckling at the Chinese malaise – gambling fever – in one so young. Even so, he took the telescope from the box and focused ahead, where approaching waves broke in foam, making it difficult to see anything. Then, 'Bodies sir, in the water,' he shouted.

Eli braced at the wheel, stared at his mate and peered ahead as spray filled the air from the sudden fickle wind and cross-breezes laced foam across the deck. 'If they're floatin' they'll only be coolies fallen off *Vesper*. She's ten leagues in front, and you know those yellow faces can't swim, unless it's face down.'

'Shall we shorten sail, sir,' Billy began.

Eli glowered at his mate. 'There's no time, and you know it! We'll be on 'em and past in the next minutes. They don't have a – '

'There's *always* a chance, sir,' Billy interrupted with compassion. 'If it was you or I, Eli. . . .'

324

'White men is different,' Eli stated dogmatically.

Billy shook his head. 'You ain't changed, Eli. If you still believe that's a fact, then tell *them* up there' – he pointed into the shrouds above – 'what's carryin' you across this ocean.'

Eli gazed aloft. Made aware of his callousness, he gripped the wheel spokes until his knuckles showed white. 'Yellow faces,' he grunted then examined the rugged features of his first mate. 'Well goddammit – move! Put the gig over the side on a line, an' if there's one alive he'll be the lucky man. We ain't stoppin', so you've the one chance – go to it!'

'Aye, sir!' Billy ran to the poop steps.

Cruel metal glinted in the sunlight as Billy seized two long boathooks, throwing one to a crewman, who gripped it with equal dexterity. In the two sailors' hands they looked like gladiators' weapons waiting to do battle. Billy snapped out his instructions to his companion as he watched the little cutter being lowered over the side into the swiftly passing ocean, then gingerly led the way over the brass rail and down into the bucketing gig. Each man lashed a body-and-soul line to his waist, securing him in the boat, then peered grimly ahead through the foam-laced air to seek and discover the fast approaching bodies in the water.

Blue-green waves, purple troughs and foaming crests constantly moved beneath diving sea birds curious to see, so far out from their distant island shelters, exposed flesh and clothes in the surging sea. Their cries sounded full of pity as with graceful triumph they floated for a moment to inspect the bodies, then, with the barest flick of slicked feathers and sinew, soared away up into the sky, calling out to other gulls, high above descriptions of what the ocean had claimed for itself.

The Chinaman was no fit companion for the young boy whose gentle features and pale skin showed as plainly in the troughs as they were lost amongst the foam. His clear grey eyes stared heavenward. Unanswered prayers had left his body at the mercy of the waves as it floated in the running sea, shrouded in wind-whipped spray which swirled and sparkled now like millions of diamonds, now like amber sparks from a fire of exploding logs, particles caught in the light of a setting sun.

Several hours had passed since Jamie had gone over from his father's ship, and although now he knew all hope had gone, he was still alive. Tears of self-pity had been replaced by sheer exhaustion as his young limbs slowly capitulated to fact, despite the will Jamie had desperately summoned in the hope of a miracle. Memories of life had fuelled his resolve as he remembered his best days, moments recollected in such detail he had been astonished. His father's face, his mother's smile, Ben's advice, Shanghai, his grandfather, San Francisco, school and the boys he would never see again, Min Ho, the kitchen galley of *Vesper*, food – just a morsel, as he would soon be for some great predator of the deep, perhaps at that very moment rising from the depths towards its helpless victim. Then above the now familiar roar of the sea and rush of the wind he heard another, new sound – like the combined groan and shriek of a great behemoth finally come for him. Fearful at first even to look, courage allowed him to turn to meet his fate. Spray lashed his face, obscuring everything for a moment, then, squinting, Jamie saw, bearing down fast, almost upon him, the huge bow of *Chantril*.

Billy saw the Chinaman's body first – wallowing in a trough, head down, inert and bloated – obviously drowned. He relaxed his grip on the boathook. 'So, Eli was right,' he grunted to himself.

A shout from the crewman alerted him again, and he followed the pointing boat hook, grasping his own again firmly. The crewman had seen the tousled hair of a young boy. The gig was secured half-way down the length of *Chantril*'s almost two-hundred-foot water-line, where it bounced high and low on the sluicing water purling back from the bow. Billy glanced quickly over his shoulder; Eli was leaning over the poop rail with the telescope focused ahead. He bellowed something which carried on the following wind, and sounded to the first mate like, 'It's the boy!'

Then everything happened so fast Billy hardly had time to think. He saw a hand raised from the sea, small fingers clutching at air . . . a face emerged from a wave, cresting with the foam, and Billy saw the white features clearly as his crewman reached out unsteadily at the prow of the gig with the boat hook. The boy was forty feet away and being thrust apart from the ship . . . thirty feet and a wave bore him back against the side. Billy stood up and roared, 'You've the one chance, boy!'

Above him, at the rail, passengers and crew holding on tight were aghast at the scene before them. Only Lewis Ellory, holding his camera, jammed between the rat-lines, cranked the handle as if his life depended on it.

Jamie's fingers touched the metal of the boat hook – extended as far as was possible by the crewman, who was now kneeling and shouting encouragement. The boy gripped the metal and immediately all but his hand was lost in foam as the almost seventeen-knot forward speed of *Chantril* dragged Jamie's fingers from the hook. Twenty-four feet long, the gig rose and plunged in the sluicing sea at the water-line of the clipper, forcing Billy to bring all his experience to bear as, spread-legged at the stern of the Captain's small vessel, he thrust the long boat hook into the water, seeing the boy slip from the for'ard crewman and disappear amidst the waves and spray. In less than a second the boy had hit the single obstacle that now lay between Earth and sea

327

or Heaven and Hell. Billy saw first an arm then the two hands frantically seize the wooden shaft of the boat hook. The boy's head formed a cone of water all about his face as he sucked for air.

'Hold, boy!' bellowed the First Mate, and he tugged once against the sea and Jamie's weight, then a second time. The boy was now only two feet from the gig as the for'ard crewman scrambled over the plank seats to aid the rescue attempt. Jamie tried to change his grip to be more secure on the shaft, but his strength failed him and the sheer force of water against his body proved too much. The fingers of the first hand were dragged into the foam, then, as Billy exerted all his strength to lift and pull the boy over the gunwhale, the pleading eyes of Silas' son vanished with his other hand into the ocean.

Instantly Billy struck out, plunging the boat hook to find its mark, then he twisted and pulled in one movement as if he were gaffing a huge fish. The curved metal dug straight into Jamie's shoulder – blood in the foam showed that – but in a second the boy was pressed to the gunwhale and dragged over into the gig by the crewman and Billy, and he fell to the wooden grating at the mate's feet.

Carefully Billy turned the hook and withdrew the metal. Pain flooded the young boy's face, his eyes screwed tight and his mouth open in a soundless scream of agony. Billy knelt and held the boy gently in his arms, tears on his cheeks, compassion in his heart. He took off his woollen cap and ineffectually pressed it to the torn flesh in an attempt to stem the profuse bleeding.

'I'm sorry, boy – but you're saved,' Billy whispered hoarsely.

Jamie's eyes opened and his pale lips moved in his white face. 'Thank you, sir,' he murmured, then fainted.

24

Trout and carp, bred in Singapore and bought by the head chef of *Otranto*, swam lazily in a tank normally placed against the end wall of the first-class wood-panelled dining room, but now they were wheeled to a table by two waiters, who stood in attendance patiently.

Cornelia Morgan pointed to fish eyes which had made the mistake of pausing to gaze at her through the glass. 'That one,' she said, and watched as it was caught and scooped from the tank with a net. Then the fish were again trundled back to their place beneath low lights, and Cornelia turned to the table and smiled.

'How cruel,' she said. The ship lurched and rolled a few degrees to starboard. Hands touched silver and held glasses.

'I'm sure you will enjoy it, all the same,' suggested Hollis Jackson, dressed, as were all the others, in correct evening clothes.

'I enjoy anything well presented.'

Kimmen sat against the back of his chair, already anticipating his main course, having consumed soup, appetisers and smoked salmon. 'You speak well, madam, if I may say so. You are by far the best presented object in this dining room.'

Cornelia smiled and broke open a bread roll, looking at the Captain across the table, wondering in the back of her mind why his expression was both serious and anxious. Her attention returned to the Dutchman.

'I am sure you are attempting to be gallant, Mijnheer Kimmen, but I am neither an inanimate nor edible object of any kind, therefore I hardly think I brook comparison with anything in a dining room.'

'As you wish, madam,' Kimmen said lazily, wafting a hand as if words meant nothing to him.

'No, Mr Kimmen, it is as *you* wish.'

A door opened, allowing the noise of an increasing wind, whistling eerily outside, into the plush and comfortable room. A young officer made his way quickly to the Captain, who excused himself and listened to urgent information. The officer saluted as the Captain reseated himself, obviously agitated and checking his pocket watch as the wine was served by a steward. Cornelia saw the growing concern on the Captain's face.

'Is something amiss, Captain?'

He shook his head and glanced at Jackson, whose eyes had narrowed, knowing his captain of old.

'Nothing to concern yourself with, madam. A slight problem has arisen but it will be dealt with. Mr Jackson, might I have a word with you?'

Jackson nodded. The two men stood up, excused themselves and, buttoning their jackets, crossed the room, nodding to other guests, and went out quickly through the same door as the officer. Again for a moment the wind erupted into the room. Heads rose, voices softened and eyes met others instinctively seeking some reassurance for a deep and common fear that had unaccountably arisen. The ship lurched now more heavily. Some glasses smashed, a laden plate careered across a white tablecloth, upsetting itself in a woman's lap. Her dinner companion placated her, a joke was made, nervous laughter followed, then a steward closed the door, securing the handle properly, and the dining room became once more the epitome of evening elegance, a warm cocoon safe against the world. Man-made spinning fans gently stirred the air and nature's rougher intrusion was, if not forgotten, at least relegated, replaced by thoughts of greater immediate import giving rise to words of wit and wisdom about food and wine and society's misdemeanours. Cornelia remained frozen, her nostrils flared. She surveyed the table of genial faces where only Kimmen looked on sullenly.

'Is someone already smoking?' she asked pointedly. Heads shook but the Dutchman deliberately inhaled loudly and, identifying the smell, began to laugh at the woman's proven stupidity.

'Sulphur!' he roared.

The wind invisibly tearing at his clothes on the exposed upper deck alerted Jackson first, then he saw the sea's surface. A disrupted calm were the first words which came into his mind. Spray whipped from shallow waves, then only at the last moment he saw, coming out of the night, lit from the ship's lights, a real comber. It hit squarely, the boom against the plating resounding with the ocean's power. Jackson stopped their brisk walk, clinging to the rail as did the Captain, watching the wave break down the length of the ship before rolling back into the night. Captain Wallis stared after the comber, ignoring the wind plucking at him as if to lift him off and away into the darkness.

Raising his voice, Jackson shouted. 'What is it, Tom?'

The Captain of *Otranto* turned to his owner and shook his head. 'I've seen a few things in my time, sir, but I have the feeling we're goin' to learn from the old man himself tonight.'

'I don't understand,' Jackson cried above the wind. The Captain moved closer, his face only inches from Jackson's, his grim expression evident. Jackson bit his lip and suddenly shivered.

'Hollis, you've known me long enough. I have respect for you, and the responsibility of this ship is something that makes me proud. But we're all goin' to earn our money tonight.' He made to turn away. Jackson stopped him.

'Tell me everything!' he said, holding the man firmly. The Captain glanced into the night for the merest of seconds then decided to reveal what he would normally have shouldered entirely alone.

'Hollis, we are in open ocean, half-way between Sumatra and Ceylon. We have no chance to run and within ten minutes are to be hit by a huge cyclone that we've managed to avoid all afternoon. We tracked it to the horizon but it's veered towards us.'

'My God,' mouthed Jackson.

'It's bigger than anything I've seen before,' said Captain Wallis. 'The barometer's been falling all day and I've just had it reported that the compass needle's vacillating.'

From the corner of his eye Jackson saw the great wave before it hit. He grasped the rail as the ship heeled with the blow. Water poured over both men.

'What can you do?' shouted Jackson. The two men began to make their way unsteadily, as the ship righted itself, to the bridge.

'If we can stay outside it or at least on the periphery, we'll just be knocked about – it'll shake the passengers but she'll do it fine, but. . . .' The Captain paused as he opened a metal door and stepped into a corridor leading to the bridge. Gratefully the two men shook their clothes and wiped salt spray from their faces once the door was again fastened tight.

'But what, Tom?' asked Jackson, appreciating the comforting sound of the generators and regular throb of the ship's powerful engines. The lights flickered for a moment as the Captain resolved to tell the truth.

'If it swallows us, if we're sucked into the vortex, if we can ride it out we'll have a bigger problem.' Jackson listened patiently, watching the Captain acknowledge two sailors running at the double, following an officer to the bridge. 'We may know what's up and down at the centre of a cyclone but it's difficult to know which way is out. We'll have no compass, no stars, and the wind'll hit us from every which way.'

'How would we get out?'

'Let's hope we don't get in,' the Captain answered, and began to walk quickly. Jackson followed and the two men stepped into the wheelhouse. Jackson put a hand on his captain's shoulder as the man reached for a pipe.

'How, Tom?'

'When you're in a whale's belly and can still think, you can only be grateful that you're still alive.' He began packing the pipe.

'How, Tom?' repeated Jackson.

'Wind force rising, sir,' reported the strained voice of a sailor on watch, 'force seven to eight, fluctuating.'

'Tom!' Jackson dropped his hand.

'What do you want me to tell you? That it's all right, everything will be fine in the end? The answer is, I don't know – and how we avoid all this will depend on two things.' He lowered his eyes, seeing the apprehension of the young seaman at the wheel. 'My instinct,' he stated, 'and *our* luck.'

Jackson surveyed the modern equipment all about them in the wheelhouse and shook his head, staring out into the worsening night. 'We have all this and you say, "luck and instinct".'

'You asked for the truth.'

'Sir!' a voice interrupted. Captain Wallis saluted a young officer, who began talking fast, his voice lowered. Immediately the Captain took him aside. Jackson followed.

'They've a problem in the for'ard hold,' stated the Captain simply, 'I hope it's not what they think . . . I'll have to see for myself.'

'I'll go,' snapped Jackson. 'You've enough to do here. Lead the way!'

The young officer saluted and Jackson followed him out. The noise of the wind had become shrill, contesting the steady thunder of engines as the sailors in the wheelhouse checked their equipment with mounting disquiet; all had been in storms but this was 'unusual', as the Captain had pointed out. The *SS Otranto* had begun to pitch and roll as the sea picked up. White-water waves appeared from nowhere – out of the night – lit split seconds before pounding across the decks and sluicing from the scuppers back into the dark ocean, there to reassemble for an even greater assault on the increasingly helpless ship.

'Batten down, everybody.' The Captain turned to his second officer. 'Prepare hurricane stations throughout the ship: all hatches watertight; secure doors, moveables and passengers. Where there are double bolts, throw them, or you'll see those hatch covers sucked off by winds that will take the hair out of your head.'

'Yes, sir,' the officer answered crisply.

'Pressure and compass reading!' barked Captain Wallis.

'The needle's spinning, sir,' came the quiet reply. 'The barometer's fallen to – ' The man bent to examine the figure he had previously deemed impossible.

'We ain't bound for Davy Jones' locker, are we, sir?' blurted the young sailor at the wheel.

Captain Wallis smiled. 'You have family in England?' The sailor nodded. The Captain took his time lighting his pipe, which glowed brightly as the lights were turned to half as ordered. 'Then, boy,' – the Captain contrived confidence in his voice – 'we're bound for home.'

'Yes, sir,' said the sailor, to a degree reassured.

'You ever seen a sixty-foot wave, boy?'

'No, sir.'

The Captain sucked his pipe. 'You will,' he murmured. 'They'll come at us like express trains, roaring down on this hull of ours; hundreds of tons of sea salt the length of the ship. . . . Time?' he asked.

'Almost twenty hours, sir,' came the reply.

The Captain nodded. 'Five minutes, and we should know what we're up against.'

'Sir . . . I . . . !' The young sailor blanched.

'Don't worry, lad. You elected to be a sailor, here's where you learn what no one can teach but Mother Nature herself. Like any woman, she's a right to be temperamental, and tonight I'll wager she'll give you something to remember.'

Watch bells rang and a sailor arrived promptly to take over from his young shipmate. The lad hesitated at the door, but, anxious to be fed and in his berth below, he turned quickly before stepping into the corridor and saluted his captain. 'Thank you sir.'

The Captain nodded acknowledgement. 'Before you close your eyes tonight, put in your prayers to our Maker.' He winked at the older sailor at the wheel. 'Ask him to keep one eye open for us.'

'Yes, sir,' said the lad.

'And be prompt for the forenoon watch.'

'Sir!' The boy snapped to attention then went quickly.

Captain Tom Wallis puffed tobacco, riding the pitch and roll of the ship expertly, and hoped prayer would comfort at least half of the ship who might truly believe: when they felt the imminent assault it would be enough, he knew, to shake any man's belief in a beneficent God.

'Wind force nine rising to ten . . . and beyond, sir,' came the report, the sailor's voice broken in disbelief.

'Time?' snapped the Captain.

'Two minutes, as you estimated it, sir.'

A huge comber rose above the bows as *Otranto*

335

plunged, rolled over the foredeck and hit the bridge, obliterating even navigation, port, starboard and hurricane lights.

'Let's be having you,' the Captain muttered to himself grimly, and bit hard on his pipe as smoke curled from its bowl against the thick glass of the wheelhouse.

Descending into the bowels of the ship became increasingly difficult for Jackson and the young officer leading the way as the storm mounted in fury outside, causing *Otranto* to heel and pitch alarmingly. At least in the centre of the ship beyond the engines and boilers, where the stokers shovelled their lives away amidst the furnace heat and coal dust, there was some stability as the Captain turned the ship into the heavy sea. The Chief Engineer, Mr Reinhardt, tall, gaunt and animated only about his pistons and power, followed Jackson and the officer past the stokers to the first bulkhead door leading to the first fuel store.

'They wanted more supply, sir,' explained the officer, referring to the stokers. 'The steam pressure was dropping, as reported by Mr Reinhardt, and he's asked permission to open up before time, but the Captain says we're short and must conserve it.'

'I know,' Jackson cut in, stepping to the door. 'I bought it myself – and it's all we could get.' The engineer and mate waiting at the door saluted Jackson. 'Well?' he asked, knowing the smell and fearing the worst.

'I don't know how bad it is, sir. We haven't opened the door.'

'Sulphur,' stated Jackson, and he began coughing.

'Clamp the door and turn the wheel; we'll have to see.'

'Aye, sir.' The officer immediately organised the stokers. Clamps were placed quickly on the burning metal and the wheel spun slowly.

Jackson looked back. Open furnace doors in the distance beyond half-consumed piles of cheap coal showed roaring flames, which threw great shadows as the stokers worked the hold. Nothing could be worse, mused Jackson, than conditions like these; perhaps Cornelia was right – was this really to be the future? The door was released and the stokers pulled it open. Instantly sulphur fumes poured out, engulfing the men inside the hold; flames leapt from a white-hot centre. Immediately, even as the stokers choked and fell to their knees, Jackson and the engineer rushed forward, slammed the door shut and spun the wheel.

'God in heaven,' murmured the chief engineer, 'the lignite's combusted!'

'We'll have to fight it from above,' began the officer, wiping sweat from his brow and coughing into his hands. 'We'll lift the hatches and descend from the gantry – '

'Lift the hatches,' Jackson countered abruptly, 'and we'll be feeding fish before midnight.' He turned to the earnest young sailor. 'Mister,' he began, 'the first hundred tons of sea water that finds its way down here will take us all to Hell! The hatches stay bolted!'

'But, sir, how – '

'We'll go down on foot ropes, ladders – whatever you can attach to the gallery rail. There's two doors in from the second-level corridor. We'll need masks and hoses. Man the electric pumps and run out the canvas from the nearest attachments. The Mate and Chief Engineer nodded, saluted limply, but went off at the run to do as ordered.

'Sir,' began the officer, hesitant now.

'What?!' bellowed Jackson, tearing off his coat and pulling at his tie.

'There's cargo for'ard of the lignite.'

'Then move it from the bulkhead wall, mister. It'll already be red-hot, and anything placed against it will itself ignite — move it!' he repeated. The officer saluted. 'Lead me back!' ordered Jackson, and began following the officer through the labyrinth back to the upper decks. Grim determination had replaced fear and frustration. 'This is my ship,' Jackson shouted above the noise of the thundering engines, 'and nothing is taking it from me!'

With a wind force above the register behind it, the first giant came from the darkness and hit *Otranto* so hard her very frame seemed to shriek with fear. Her bow was submerged in the night sea until, plates groaning, it forced itself up, streaming foam. One anchor was torn from its housing and thrown on deck; slithering with the water, trailing heavy link chain, it smashed against the for'ard winch. Orders were immediately issued for the watch, now in oilskins and wearing lifelines, to secure the three tons of iron before it came free and broke through the ship's side to plunge overboard and act as a drag on *Otranto*'s future manoeuvring. Captain Wallis was informed of the situation below decks, which he accepted without a murmur and kept from others in the wheelhouse, having already entered his own private hell of certain liability and full responsibility for so many lives aboard his command.

Reports from the steerage section revealed chaos. The lights had failed and, with no back-up generator, the crowds were huddled together, some beneath the bolted tables and benches, others wedged into their bunks as sailors picked their way amongst the prostrate bodies, distributing emergency hurricane lamps. The meagre meal had just been served before the main force of the storm hit and would have to last them until they were free of the enveloping cyclone, no matter how long, the mate in charge decided. He was glad to get out and count his men; so many together in such conditions, with fear he could actually smell, was dangerous. In second and third, the small cabins, crowded generally with four or six sleeping together, allowed little opportunity for panic to spread. Lights remained on and several preachers, a minister and a priest were going about distributing, if not calm, at least God's word and belief in salvation through prayer, although it became clear that few amongst these instant congregations were prepared to journey to the here-after, now they were faced with the distinct possibility. Rum, dispensed at a reasonable price, solved the problem for many of the men and numerous willing women who, as *Otranto* was thrust deeper into the roaring cyclone, slid into another world of hazy night-mares and fanciful dreams.

In the first-class dining room, everything moveable had been thrown sideways when the great wave hit. Confusion reigned and the shrill whine of the tempest was punctuated by screams of terror from both men and women. Sailors, stewards and waiters persuaded, cajoled, bullied and threatened – and quickly brought about a semblance of order. The lights had gone immediately but the generator recovered and, with buckets of sand dousing the numerous fires, most hazards within the spacious room at least, were elimin-ated. Passengers needed little instruction to discover that the safest place to be was on the floor next to any firm or fixed object.

Cornelia was now quite willing to be compared to the furniture, as Mijnheer Kimmen pointed out, assuming a confident air of mocking humour. Knowing only half the story, he declared himself to have been in storms before, and assured all who would listen that the condition was temporary and the wind and sea would quickly blow themselves out. Most remained unconvinced, as the howling outside made conversation below shouting almost impossible. Egerton, Kimmen's black manservant, made his way from the cabin area to join his master and give him fresh confidence.

'Champagne for everyone,' the Dutchman bellowed in the direction of a nervous steward, who attempted to comply, falling behind the bar several times as the ship pitched then slowly righted herself.

Outside, sailors – all with life-lines – managed to close the metal shutters, screwing them tight to protect the windows. That at least muffled some of the sound, which had become a high-pitched shriek penetrating the ear until it filled the head as it stirred the mind to terrible imaginings. One of the crew burst in, pressing hard on the door, helped by a steward who bolted it. After a brief exchange, the man was led across to the Dutchman. He saluted respectfully.

'Sir,' he shouted close to Kimmen's ear. 'The for'ard cargo must be shifted. I must have your permission. The crates are against the bulkhead, which is already so hot that even when we hose it down steam. . . .' The sailor saw alarm in the passengers' faces and glanced around, aware of curious eyes and straining ears. He moved closer and whispered, 'There is a fire in the hold.'

Kimmen's eyes widened and he pulled himself to his feet, beckoning Egerton. They followed the sailor to the door. Cornelia called the steward over and reminded him of Kimmen's offer of champagne, insisting it be brought, then turned her attention to the two journalists, Marsh and Meyer, who were both scribbling furiously. She moved closer and pointed to one of their writing pads, mouthing the words: 'His cargo is sewing machines.' She had already guessed at the Dutchman's fears, if not why they were founded.

In the wheelhouse, Jackson saw for himself the awesome power of the sea as wave after wave towered towards *Otranto* out of the black night, thundering over her sides as she was lifted by others and thrust in any direction the ocean chose. Only her size and recent sturdy construction was consolation.

'My God,' said Jackson, 'I've never seen anything like it.'

'Neither have I,' muttered Captain Wallis, 'and we're being drawn into the storm centre.'

'We're north of the equator; where is it moving?'

'It's of no consequence to us yet,' said the Captain. 'We're moving with it wherever, at the moment. I'd guess it's circling slowly. If it's more than fifty miles across, well, we'll suffer badly anyway, but *if* we reach the vortex it should be relatively calm although it won't be comfortable. It's then our problem really begins. If we come out the wrong side of the eye we'll not be thrown out of this circling wind and water, we'll be sucked back in for more of the same or worse.'

'But we could be days trying to. . . .'

The Captain shook his head as a great wave hit over the entire wheelhouse and the whole ship shuddered. 'She's a strong vessel, Hollis, but we can't take too much of this. The plates will go, then the frame and so will we.' He paused and puffed his pipe, a professional accepting the facts. 'I can't leave the wheelhouse now. You just put the fire out, Mr Jackson,' he stated formally, 'or you'll have no ship to worry about.'

Jackson smiled grimly, shook hands with Tom Wallis, wished him luck and was gone.

Two doors either side of the for'ard bulwark wall at the second level led out to narrow platforms linking them. At the middle, a gantry crossed the entire hold, essentially for a foreman to supervise loading in dock, now the rails had been tied with ropes and several adders. Metal stairways set into the wall, sheer from each door, led down into the hold, where it was now impossible, even with the many hurricane lamps and the diffused light from lamps inset behind thick glass, to make out anything below through thick smoke and noxious fumes except the white and red hot coals. As the ship pitched and rolled, the load shifted and the movement allowed more air deep into the huge pile, adding further oxygen, and the conflagration gained strength. Already the metal bulkheads were too hot to touch. Jackson stood at one of the doorways, over-looking the inferno, swiftly calculating what must be done. The shrieking wind and thundering waves outside only disturbed his concentration as the ship seemed to flounder for a moment until a following comber broke against her stern, thrusting her up and forward. Water hosed on the coals had temporarily doused the flames, but hot steam now added to the vapours emerging from below and Jackson guessed it would not be long before the pile ignited again. He turned to the young officer and Mr Reinhardt, whose fear for his engines had brought him as an observer, and rapped out orders.

'We must go down – take the hoses, find the bed and hose the brightest coals before it has a chance of spreading further beneath the pile. Is the cargo on the bulkhead wall shifted?'

'Now, sir,' answered the young officer.

Jackson nodded. 'Then make ready – we'll go down together. Masks and gloves and mind your feet – it'll be bad enough standing, if you slip as she's pitching no prayers will save any of you from incineration. Prepare the hoses and check the rope ladders; man the pumps.'

'Sir!' snapped the young officer as Jackson turned back along the corridor, found the door and stairway then descended into the for'ard cargo hold.

Sailors were already at the large crates, having loosened the cables holding them fast. Jackson stepped through the open watertight door and, seeing the sailor at task, took one of the many fire buckets lined against the bulkhead wall and threw the water against the hot metal. Immediately, with a hiss, steam formed. No words were necessary to describe the obvious danger to the sailors as they moved the released crates across the hold, aided by Egerton and Kimmen, who emerged out of the dim light and nodded curtly to Jackson. Several crates began to slide as the ship listed sickeningly to port, causing most in the hold to hang on, but Kimmen and his servant leapt after the crates. Egerton, placing himself in front of them both and bracing hard against the ship's iron ribs, caught the full weight of each crate, halting them before they split asunder on the ship's plates. Lifting first one, then the other, he carried them to be placed by sailors on the restacked pile at the back of the hold.

Jackson watched, curious at Kimmen's zeal – ordering Egerton, organising sailors, checking the tautness of the restrung cables – but in admiration of the huge black servant's strength. He had seen for himself sewing machines but . . . so many crates? Were there enough women settlers in East Africa to afford such a quantity of machines? Shouts from above disturbed his thoughts, and he made his way to the metal stairway out of the hold.

Confident that the cargo could be shifted out of danger, he shouted an incentive, all the same: 'Move it, Kimmen, or it'll go up in smoke!' The Dutchman glanced at the wall where a sailor threw buckets of water. Vapourised into steam instantly, the point was made clearly. 'Thank God they're only sewing machines!' shouted Jackson, and climbed quickly up the ladder.

Kimmen wiped his brow as sweat coursed down his face and watched Jackson until he had re-entered the corridor, wondering if he had guessed the truth. Behind, a crash sounded loudly, causing him to spin round and, despite the plunging deck as *Otranto*'s bows dropped into a vast trough, he scrambled across to Egerton, who was already pressing closed a fallen crate whose lid had broken open. For a moment, the ammunition boxes, so carefully packed, showed in the half-light – then Kimmen's black servant shut the lid. Kimmen looked about him; assured no one had seen the contents, he shouted at sailors to wrap cables and secure the loose crates quickly, thankful that the boxes had not spilled their contents, and gun muzzles from other crates had not burst through the wooden sides from their oil-cloth wrapping. Sailors were again throwing water on to the hot metal wall against which many crates remained stacked. Steam filled the hold as Kimmen bellowed urgently to the exhausted crew. He knew the increasing danger and silently began to pray for Jackson's success amidst the conflagration on the other side of the bulkhead, even as he ran to save the stacked contraband.

Hollis Jackson strapped a makeshift mask of cotton canvas around his head with a leather thong, accepted gloves and stepped out on to the narrow platform. Head down, he ran the width of the hold on the metal gantry through billowing smoke and steam. Grasping the attached rope ladder, he descended into what had become a fire-pit. Below, crewmen with shovels were attempting to attack the great mound of lignite as increasing water swirled about their feet. Jackson looked up, eyes squinting, his breath rasping against the fumes. He knew they could not remain here much longer. Fountains of water from hoses directed at the renewed flames were only having superficial effect on the outer coals. The hotbed beneath had built up to such a temperature that, given respite, the entire consignment would ignite as one, and within minutes could create a partial vacuum. Then an explosion would be unavoidable. It would tear the ship apart.

Otranto rolled heavily to starboard, causing men to fall into the water, which rushed to one side of the hold, taking the unfortunate crew with it. For a moment, they could barely stand and floated helplessly towards the outer temporary bulwark of timbers containing the lignite. Only as the ship righted itself before pitching forward could they grasp stanchions and ribs, and regain their footing.

Jackson, holding tight to rungs of the metal ladder leading directly to the gantry above, felt the heat even through his gloves and knew he would have to find a solution quickly. Above, the doors were open, aiding the natural ventilation through valveless deck funnels which were allowing sea water, as waves rode over the ship, into the piping, along shafts, around the upper hold then out through inset grilles, which sprayed sea salt into the atmosphere. Jackson cleared his head, wiped tears from his eyes and moved close to Reinhardt, who was resting against the ship's inner plating. Breathing was becoming increasingly difficult and talk almost impossible.

Outside, *Otranto* was suffering the effects of huge cross-seas and her bows rose up as she rolled to port. The Captain tried to correct his ship by throwing the wheel hard over. Reinhardt heard his engines straining and shook his head, pulling off his mask. 'We're goin' to go,' he shouted helplessly, and began coughing badly.

'It's my ship!' bellowed Jackson angrily through the cotton and canvas, clinging to a stanchion as the water surged in his direction and sluiced against the plating almost as high as his head. He gasped for breath and found himself staring at one of four wooden piles placed vertically at the corners of the large half-box, built on and secured to the floor of almost the entire hold, cross-timbers linking them waist-high to contain the lignite.

This was holding the pile together, keeping most of the water and recondensed steam out of the bed of the fire. In a moment, he realised the solution.

'Axes!' he ordered, his voice muffled through the mask. Reinhardt blinked. 'Axes!' Jackson shouted again. Above, the men heard him as he removed the cotton and canvas. He waved his arms until they understood and complied. Flames appeared, leaping up at the centre of the lignite, and the fumes with noxious odours intensified. Jackson began coughing and gagged as water again sluiced across the hold. A sailor climbed down the rope-ladder and unslung two axes, one of which Jackson gave to Reinhardt. He pointed at the tall wooden pile. 'I'll save your engines, if you save my ship!' he yelled, loosening the thong holding his mask.

The Chief Engineer nodded and stepped with Jackson towards the upright support. Wielding axes, the two men set to with a will. Jackson had realised that if the wooden support surrounding the lignite could be broken, then the water now flooding half the hold would inundate the inferno and extinguish the fire. Chopping into the solid wood of the upright became increasingly difficult, not only with the movement of the ship but, denied oxygen, the two men began to suck for air, energy spent. Fumes, obvious and invisible, had now so filled the hold that many of the crew were retching and staggering, reaching for ropes and rungs without strength, their one thought to get out of the increasing hell. Yellowish sulphur trioxide, nitrogen oxide, carbon dioxide and monoxide curled with the polluting smoke rising from the lignite, which burnt like peat. Eyes pouring with tears, lungs raw, Jackson paused to gather his resolve and assess the damage he and Reinhardt had done to the stubborn pile support. The Chief Engineer pointed to the wooden bulkheads built up either side of the lignite, where sparks were glittering.

'It's goin' to go up!' he shouted hoarsely.

Jackson nodded grimly. 'So are we when this falls.' He indicated the sagging corner support. The ship lurched heavily to port so that the filthy water swirled about their waists as it crossed the hold in a rush. Crew above continued to pour water down on to the hot coals in an attempt to contain the spreading fire, but the instant steam gave the lie to their efforts, as Jackson could see clearly. He knew also that the more difficult breathing became, the quicker the growing vacuum would blow the ship to kingdom come. Sea-spray hissed out of the grilled vents, adding salt to the already thick atmosphere.

Redoubling their efforts, Reinhardt and Jackson swung their axes, sinking them deep into the slivered wood. Glancing over his shoulder, Jackson could see that most of the crew had cleared the floor, having scrambled above to relative safety. Plunging, then rolling to starboard, *Otranto* forced all aboard to cling tight to whatever would hold them from falling.

Reinhardt slipped and actually disappeared beneath the surface of sluicing slime for a moment, before emerging, still clasping the axe, screaming with pure anger. He attacked the wooden support with the power of controlled rage, bellowing, 'My engines!' over and over. Encouraged, Jackson joined him, and both men saw cross-timbers loosen either side of the now almost severed vertical pile. Suddenly racked with coughing, Reinhardt bent double. Jackson pushed him away, taking his axe and throwing it against the ship's plating.

'Jump for it,' he shouted. 'Go, Reinhardt, go!'

The Chief Engineer hesitated for only a moment, then waded to the nearest rope-ladder and wearily reached for the rungs, pulling himself from the water, which was swirling yet again towards Jackson as the ship shuddered, hit head-on by another giant wave.

Ignoring the slime pressing at his waist, Jackson swung again, shouting between gritted teeth, 'My ship!'

The axe bit deep, the bulkhead creaked, cries from above warned him and, turning, he began to wade to swaying ropes hanging from the gantry. *Otranto* rose up, cresting on a wave and throwing Jackson back. He lost his footing and disappeared into the dark, filthy slime, rushing with it against the rear bulkhead wall then, as *Otranto* plunged into space and darkness above a huge trough, the water in the hold swirled back towards the collapsing temporary sodden timbers, carrying Jackson towards the conflagration.

Shouts of alarm from above caused Reinhardt, half-way up the rope-ladder, to look below, where Jackson was nowhere to be seen but the broken support was no longer holding the braces and timbers against the flood pouring towards the burning lignite.

'Mr Jackson!' Reinhardt yelled helplessly, and as if called from the deep, Jackson's hand reached from the surface and grasped for the rope-ladder. Seizing it, he pulled himself from the rushing wet slime as it broke through the timbers and inundated the lignite, flooding over the coals, submerging the hotbed, drowning the fire and causing an explosion of steam, smoke and fumes as Jackson climbed to safety. Willing hands helped him up on to the gantry, where, feet spread against the ship's roll and pitch, triumphantly he surveyed the water below spreading back and forth over the lignite. Steam obscured the view but the situation was clear.

He smiled grimly and nodded to Reinhardt. 'Down and out, mister,' he said, taking off his mask.

The Chief Engineer wiped sweat and filth from his face. 'Now my engines, Mr Jackson. . . .'

Jackson dropped the canvas, cotton and leather below. 'Make main steam available at all times, Mr Reinhardt, and with some luck Tom's instinct will get us out of this' – he paused as the ship shuddered; hit from port and starboard simultaneously by mountainous seas – 'predicament,' he finished, forcing a smile.

Reinhardt pointed below. 'But we'll be short of – '

Jackson cut in, stepping to the door. 'Just let's save the ship, mister; we'll have plenty of time to think about personal inconveniences.'

Climbing towards the upper decks, Hollis Jackson noticed immediately that the ship had somehow regained stability and that all sound had strangely disappeared. Hazarding his chances, he pulled himself from rung to rung then spun the wheel to open a watertight door out on to the funnel deck behind the wheelhouse. The sight that greeted him was astonishing. Sheet and forked lightning lit the night sky, making of it a flickering dawn. A greenish fire danced above the taut shrouds, derricks and masts, swirling around the top of the funnel and on the lines and braces. Spray blown from every direction filled the air, each particle refracting diamond light, diffusing the dark sea of cresting waves. The roaring silence pitched above the wind's distant shriek, so that for a moment he panicked – only as a sailor emerged in oilskins, bent against the wind force, bellowing soundlessly at Jackson, did he realise he was deafened. Safety valves in his head had shut down his hearing so the shrill, ear-drum-shattering decibels of rushing air could no longer damage him. The wind now was unlike before, when it had come at *Otranto* from beyond unseen horizons with greater might and speed than any invention conceived by mankind. It seemed to be gusting around the ship strongly, yes, but merely as a lion might taunt its prey before inflicting death. Then Jackson noticed there were, fluttering on the moving air, clinging to anything where they might perch, lining braces, yards and rails, sea birds – and even parrots, insects and large multi-coloured butterflies – exhausted, having been caught up in the cyclone hours, perhaps even days, before, and hoping, as indeed did Jackson and all aboard *Otranto*, merely to survive the awesome power of nature.

'Poor devils,' Jackson mouthed to himself, and now knew the awful truth – they were in the very eye of the storm.

In the dining saloon, taking advantage of the relative calm – although *Otranto* continued to pitch and roll – Stanley Grace sat on a stool bolted to the floor, facing a piano strapped to stanchions on the wall, which belted out notes sounding almost as loudly as his straining voice.

> Not for all the tea in China,
> Would I ever leave the sea,
> For I know of no life finer,
> Than on tall ships sailing free.
> So blow you stormy weather,
> To bear us o'er the sea . . .'

At this, as the ship lurched in a particularly strong gust, several passengers were sick into the buckets which had become their remaining lifeline to a semblance of elegance. Empty and broken bottles of champagne and wine were evident in abundance as Hollis Jackson stepped from the corridor to acknowledge greetings from curious and anxious passengers.

Cornelia was immediately on her feet. She crossed to Jackson amidst sustained applause from a gathering of others either still prone or just standing. As Marsh, close behind Cornelia, extended a hand of congratulation, his colleague, Meyer, took a photograph with a flash precariously balanced on a tripod. Jackson blinked, then saw that Kimmen and Egerton, in a condition hardly worse than his, sprawled on one side of what had recently been a plush bar.

'Is it over?' Cornelia asked. Jackson touched her shoulders for a moment, meaning to convey affection, but she drew away, seeing a very different man than the one to whom she had become accustomed. Jackson shook his head, glancing around at the suppressed fear in his passengers' expressions. As his captain, Tom Wallis, had said, what should he say? Facts might be difficult to accept – but at least they would go to their Maker in some knowledge. He smiled grimly.

'We're in the storm centre!' he stated loudly.

Kimmen stood up unsteadily and bellowed angrily, 'So our lives reamin threatened, *Mr* Jackson!'

'That's enough, Kimmen!'

'This ship could take us all to Hell!'

Jackson interrupted. 'We *will* reach Colombo – if we've sufficient fuel remaining.' He looked at Cornelia, who was still trying to comprehend the situation.

'Storm centre?' she asked.

Jackson nodded, and tried to explain. 'A moment of calm . . . we must now find the perimeter of the cyclone.'

'And if we do not?' she asked.

Jackson hesitated but Kimmen bellowed for all to hear, 'We shall sink!'

Jackson, exhausted, wet and unkempt, no longer the epitome of successful elegance, merely stared at Kimmen as the man approached him.

'And it will be on your head!' screamed the Dutchman, his face puce with affected rage, then as he finished with, 'entirely due to your incompetence as a – a . . . so called shipowner!' Then he made the mistake of raising a fist.

Jackson hit Kimmen hard in the centre of his face, splitting his nose and causing blood to flow immediately. The Dutchman was unconscious even before he staggered backwards and slumped into the arms of his black servant, whose eyes blazed at his master's assailant – but he did nothing. Cornelia, concealing momentary admiration, affected distaste at the action even as the ship rolled to port, flinging numerous passengers to the floor. 'Spare a thought for gentility, Hollis!' Jackson, bracing himself against *Otranto*'s movement by seizing the piano, glanced around the room at the frayed and fraught, most attempting to hang on to the last vestiges of society's veneer despite the obvious circumstances, then looked back at the inebriated Stanley Grace, for the first time acknowledging him as a potential equal.

'Go on,' he said, 'give us a reprise.' But even as the two men began to laugh, a familiar roar of the elements exploded outside as nature, the hunter, bounded towards what it now intended to devour.

In *Otranto*'s wheelhouse respite had merely brought anxiety for the Captain. He concealed it as he saw jubilation amongst his crew at the conviction they had ridden out the tempest. He was the first to see the dark wall, illuminated by lightning and fast approaching, and shouted a warning: 'Here it comes again!'

He reached out for the wheel. 'Hard over and face it as it hits!' The young seaman spun the wheel hard, as the telegraph bells struck and were lost to the whine of wind ripping into *Otranto*'s superstructure. Even the roar of engines, as the ship turned into the bastion of water towering over her bows, dissolved into a fantastic deafening silence. On decks everything moveable was whipped away, the whistling air taking the bird and insect assemblage in a fraction of a second. Captain Tom Wallis closed his eyes and prayed that his immediate action, which was mere instinct, would be accompanied with the luck they so needed. Fact was, they would be sucked back in or thrown out of the cyclone – and only God had already decided. . . . For the fearful eyes that stared at him in the half-light as the vast waves pounded over the merchantman, mere pinpoints of light in a huge, dark ocean, Captain Wallis conjured a smile and mouthed for all to decipher, 'We'll be all right, boys – we'll be – fine. . . .'

25

Windstorms north and south of the equator move in clockwise or anti-clockwise directions. The girth of the world at the line being greater, following winds dictate the movement. Time influences the speed, which can build up to tempest, hurricane, cyclone or typhoon proportions when, like a spinning top, force creates a vacuum which sucks in more air to maintain a natural dynamo destroying or absorbing all in its path – until warmth or cold is encountered, lessening the power of the vortex and eventually dispersing the mighty combination of elements. Avoiding them is often referred to, by seamen who are successful, as 'the secret' distancing them from the majority. Instinct, it is generally agreed, has much to do with it, and a good eye, sensitive ears, a smell for the unexpected – senses grouped in alliance to prevent possible tragedy. But, since sail carries souls into the unknown events of a voyage, luck has never been discounted by any man of the sea. It is no collateral to be drawn against, but it exists as solidly as metal and steam or timber and canvas. Captains and crew believe in a 'lucky' ship and bars on any waterfront the world over attest to the infinite mysteries of sea and sky against the probabilities of knowledge and experience. Talk is as cheap as opinions are varied. Stories abound as drink and convivial atmospheres relax the tellers; on solid ground, causing them to embellish the simple plot – that fear carried them through as fate gave them an arrival at their destination.

One thousand miles south-south-east of the island of

Mauritius, the clipper ship *Vesper*, forty days out of the port of Shanghai, on the last night of October encountered an electrical storm that enveloped the very imagination of every person aboard. Passengers trembled as the crew sought refuge in the work forced upon them by orders they knew must be obeyed unless they were all to flounder and perish.

Spread-legged on the quarter deck, braced against the compass binnacle, lashed by rain and beyond exhaustion after forty-eight hours without sleep, Silas Hayes was at least comforted that the following wind, a gale force and gusting between eight and nine on the scale, remained constant, having veered only several points during a period of three days. Ben returned from for'ard, a body-and-soul line clipped to a long rope which, like others, ran the length of the ship, secured at intervals to allow crew access along the decks without being washed through the scuppers. For days, great waves had tumbled over the bows and foamed their way to the poop-break, exploding in the fine spray now salting the night rain which poured from the dog watch's oilskins.

The Second Mate reported to his captain, shouting above the noise of seemingly constant thunder. Silas grunted acknowledgement and indicated to Hughie Sutherland at the wheel that he would go below. He looked up, and in the faint light of hurricane lamps, obscured immediately by each great flash of lightning, checked his light-sail plan, feeling the pitch and roll of his ship, knowing that more than to'gallants were unnecessary. In the strong wind it would be dangerous if the gale force veered quickly; not only would the canvas be torn to shreds, the ship could well keel over even further than her rails – one of which at any time seemed always to be in the dark turbulent sea.

'Eyes on the leechropes, boys!' Silas ordered. 'I don't

want 'em giving tonight – split sails'll have us wallowing and helpless!' He watched Hughie nod then point above. Silas smiled grimly, but others of his crew – especially the fearful Chinese – did not, seeing the dancing green light all about the shrouds, mastheads and rat-tails. Like tinsel, it seemed to caress and entwine itself around even the most delicate line, thinnest hawser or tautest wire. St Elmo's fire had been expected by both himself and Hughie, to whom it was no stranger but always a wondrous experience. Each man had seen it first as 'prentices in the old days, knowing it would come from the cirrus cloud and electrical activity they'd logged for days.

Silas shook rain from his face and for a moment the unwanted thought of his lost son forced its way into his mind. Despite himself, he felt his throat tighten with uncontrolled grief and he stepped through his cabin entrance and down, quickly closing the door in an attempt to keep out the briny rain.

Below deck in the Captain's cabin, Silas Hayes took off his oilskins for the first time in days and, drying his face and hands with a damp towel, feeling still the humidity of the tropics, he grasped the edge of his navigation table and bent to examine their course on a large clipped chart laid out beneath several swinging lamps. Shadows played over the southern Indian Ocean as he tried to concentrate his thoughts. Latitude and longitude he had estimated correctly, speed was gauged at regular intervals. Constellations, when they showed through thick cloud, gave him a precise position. *Vesper*'s progress had been excellent, due to the steady powerful following winds which had allowed Silas to put up everything until even water sails and ringtails had added to moon and stuns'ls, making of the fast clipper with more than an acre of canvas on the yards, man's image of billowing cumulus passing over the sea.

'Why are there clouds?' The question came clearly to Silas's mind. 'Where does the wind come from? Why is the sky blue? What is rain?' Silas felt the ship surge for a moment, as if it were a living thing wanting to race ahead, to command elements that dared play dangerously. *Vesper*'s captain stared into the flames of one of the swinging hurricane lamps. 'How far are the stars?' Jamie had asked. 'Where is heaven? Who is God?' A torrent of questions Silas had sometimes patiently although often not, attempted to answer.

'God is around you everywhere,' Silas had heard himself say, 'in all things. . . .'

'But can I see *him*, somewhere?' Jamie had countered.

'Perhaps,' Silas had answered, and ruffled the boy's mop of tousled hair. 'Perhaps you will one day,' he had finished more seriously, and stared into the open, innocent face, seeing wide, curious, trusting eyes.

'Where?' the boy had asked, and Silas had taken a pause before answering.

'No man ever knows that, laddie – until the time. . . .'

The boy's father looked into the lamp's flickering flames and thought for a moment of his lost son, whose grave was unmarked in a great tract of ocean beneath gentle waters or booming waves. Outside his small cabin aboard *Vesper*, Silas heard the roaring night, lashing rain and cracks of thunder. He could see the great sky-filling flashes of lightning even below deck, and felt the power of the sea's angry mood.

Contemplation was unusual for Silas Hayes, but his heart was filled with sorrow as his eyes were moist with grief; and he wondered in that moment what final fears the boy had suffered, what last terrors he had known before his death. The father bent his head, and for the first time in his life, unbidden, knelt upon the swaying

357

cabin floor of *Vesper*, clasped his hands and began to pray for his child's soul.

When he looked up, eventually disturbed, it was not into the face of Christ but at the dishevelled figure of the priest, James Collins, spread-eagled for support in the doorway. The expression on his face was one of triumph.

'So you are a man of God at last, Captain?' the priest said thickly.

The smell of vomit came to Silas' nostrils and he stared at the man desperately trying to remain upright as the clipper shuddered against the power of a mighty wave.

'State your business, priest,' growled Vesper's captain. A great crack of thunder drowned the priest's words, which were stopped, mid-sentence, as he vomited and fell out of sight, back into the dark narrow corridor.

Silas crossed himself, cleared his mind and stood up to face the more immediate and practical business of survival at sea – but first he knew he needed sleep. Gratefully he fell on to his bunk and into oblivion.

Eyes ashore in Trincomalee could see the battered condition of Steamship *Otranto* as she glided into the harbour, barely ruffling the calm waters. Unmistakable damage showed on her plating and superstructure, and only waving children ashore prompted any response from the crowded rails of the ship, where the faces were predominantly sullen, ashen and exhausted. Reverse engines thundered for a moment and rattling their chains, anchors were dropped into the sea, bringing a weak cheer from many aboard who only now realised that perhaps their terrible ordeal at sea was over.

'I want to be out of Ceylon as soon as . . .' Jackson began, but Tom Wallis in the wheelhouse pointed through cracked glass at an approaching naval cutter and interrupted.

'Navy,' he said simply.

'Well?' Jackson asked, not understanding why it should be a threat.

The Captain smiled. 'Ceylon is one of the British Empire's biggest naval bases out East. . . .'

'Then they can help us.'

'War,' stated Captain Wallis patiently, 'in South Africa.' He shrugged. 'I think it safe to assume the Navy will have priority over . . . everything.'

'Coal?' asked Jackson.

'Everything,' the Captain emphasised, and stepped out into the hot sun. The flying bridge gave him a clear view of the cutter coming alongside. His crew helped several officers on to the bottom steps of the lowered gangway. Smartly dressed in their tropical whites, they reached the main deck and immediately doffed their caps to numerous ladies who had quickly recovered from their trial at sea and, with the prospect of meeting young naval officers and time to come ashore, had presented themselves with little decorum and great anticipation. Ostentatious chivalry elicited obvious appreciation, and gusts of laughter floated on the still, warm, morning air as Hollis Jackson, also disporting himself in whites but of civilian cut, joined the Captain outside in the hot sun and grunted at the sight below. Cornelia Morgan had already gained the attention of two of the four officers.

'I see what you mean, Tom.'

'Well,' the Captain replied, 'it is a fact that we're behind schedule. We've lost days in the storm, and in my opinion – privately – are damn lucky to have got out. Then, with almost three weeks gone in Singapore, and we'll need a week here to rebuild the bulkhead – at least. Other damage . . . repairs. . . . we'll have to assess it. I don't really know yet how long.'

Jackson took off his white panama and began to fan his face. Only a light breeze controlled the heat and humidity, and although the view across the water was attractive – beyond coastal building, lush vegetation showed promise for excursions – his impatience at the prospect of further delay denied him any pleasure at the thought of a lengthy sojourn ashore.

'I'll tell you true, Tom. If fate's taking time from us all, well and good. But if there's a cable from Shanghai sent by any "friend" to cause us more trouble, we'll up anchor and turn right around for open sea . . . now.'

'How do you mean?' asked the Captain.

Jackson glanced at him, realising that perhaps his suspicions were becoming fanciful. Surely it couldn't be possible that . . . ? He stopped his thoughts. Perhaps they could all do with a rest, provided the time was spent usefully on refitting the ship. He nodded to himself all the same, perplexing Captain Wallis, who thought he heard his owner mutter, 'Silas Hayes.'

And, of course, there was no cable – in Trincomalee. *Otranto* had been charted to bunker in the capital – Colombo.

Blue water and long swells beneath a clear sky and before a crisp south-easterly wind brought *Vesper*, sailing fast on the 'Cape Doctor', her first glimpse of the Cape of Good Hope. Passengers aboard, with the fresh wind in their hair, braced themselves on deck and stared towards the tablecloth of cloud over Table Mountain, seemingly supported between Devil's Peak and Signal Hill. To some it was a familiar sight, others recognised with awe that they were looking for the first time at the tip of southern Africa.

Bells rangs for the noon watch as Silas Hayes emerged from his cabin on to the quarter deck. Morosely he surveyed the sail plan, checked the compass and estimated the speed of his clipper. He could feel the power of the Agulhas current thrusting the ship forward with the wind.

Hughie nodded to his captain. 'We've had a sighting of full canvas astern, sir . . . but lost it.'

'Identified?'

'No, sir, we're sailin' free afore a beauty and these troughs is like slippin' into the bowels o' the earth awhile.' He grinned as *Vesper* sank again into the great swell where distances between wave crests were more than a mile.

Silas turned to the poop rail, waiting for his ship to rise up. He reached for the telescope and pressed it to his eye. To the north was the great plateau mountain, meaning they had passed the political prison on Robben Island; but to the east . . . ? He focused and thought for a moment he detected spread canvas. Again he waited for *Vesper* to ride up the long swell, then clearly he saw the shape, unmistakable to him, of *Chantril*.

'Damn him!' he exclaimed and shut the glass.

'Well, he ain't no know-nothin' sailor, sir, if I may be so bold.'

'Is he closing?'

Hughie turned at this and, squinting quickly, found the distant smudge on the eastern horizon. 'We're holdin',' he stated confidently.

'Water sails?' suggested Silas.

Hughie shook his head. 'You know it ain't possible in troughs and peaks like these. It's mountains and valleys, and in a current like this they'd be more 'n like sea anchors.'

'I want to lose him, Hughie!'

'He'll be gone by nightfall, mark my words.'

'I hope so!' Silas snapped, and replaced the glass in the box.

A returning British naval frigate, bound for the base at Simonstown, flashed morse at *Vesper* for a description of crew, contents, passengers and destination, and received a reply promptly. The Boer War had made everyone in the area of the Cape nervous but, satisfied, the heavily armoured ship boomed out a farewell and, pouring smoke, made full steam and churned off to the north-east. Only as it began to turn towards False Bay did the watch alert the bridge that a second clipper was fast approaching from the east. Bells rang loudly, warning the sailors below of an imminent turn to starboard. The telegraph sounded in the bridge, confirming full speed, and the British frigate leaned hard into the long swell, throwing up a spray and foam as she pointed her bows directly at the oncoming vessel with all up.

'Tell them who we are,' ordered Eli Lubbock, and Billy nodded to a sailor holding a morse light and flashing the information sought by the British ship o' the line. Head on, glasses identified the flags and bare superstructure of a clipper out of a Far East port with almost full sail, satisfying the curious Navy, alert to any infringement of territorial waters in time of conflict.

Chantril continued to speed westerly as the frigate closed and came about, riding the long swell as easily as the clipper took it at a good lick. For a moment, the two ships were side by side only several hundred yards apart then, to the admiration of the British sailors, *Chantril* forged ahead, her grace in the water belying a considerable pace. Again the ship's horn boomed out 'God speed', and as commands were given leisurely to return to base in time for tiffin, many eyes remained glued to their glasses as watch officers refocused to keep the magnificent sight of a departing age in view until, as swell after swell came between the two ships, reluctantly they replaced dreams of their childhood in their memory.

Young Jamie leant against the aft hatch cover, grasping a brass rail firmly with one hand, and explored the sensations of his other – fingers, palm, then wrist, forearm, bicep and shoulder, where pain still throbbed at night. Activity during the day seemed to ease irritation, help circulation and aid the process of healing, quicker at his age than for an older man, as the attentive Emily had said to him. She had tended him for the weeks he had been aboard, together with the Chinese boy, Cha-ze, who had become a friend, teaching Jamie pidgin English 'China way'.

Now they were all on deck with Mr Ellory, who was already cranking his camera in the direction of the horizon. The first shout below of '*Vesper* sighted!' had brought so much excitement to Jamie's throat, he thought he would choke with joy. He had raced the length of the ship and, almost forgetting his damaged shoulder, had pulled himself up top.

'He there one way go on!' shouted Cha-ze excitedly, pointing and laughing. For a moment, Jamie couldn't see, his eyes not as sharp as the smaller Chinese boy's, and with the high swells off the South African coast rising and falling, taking *Chantril* at their will, he became impatient. 'Where!'

'There he go down!' laughed Cha-ze as the distant *Vesper* vanished again, sails obscured by the deep blue waters.

Emily brushed Jamie's hair from his forehead, feeling the fresh wind on her face and love in her heart. She smiled and said, 'Your father's there, Jamie.'

And the boy saw him. '*Vesper*,' he whispered. For a moment he saw the ship clearly, then the swell sank *Chantril* into a long trough and *Vesper* was lost. 'Where is he gone?' he asked, desperately seeking to find her again.

'He's there,' Emily reassured him, feeling the seed of Silas Hayes growing inside her and knowing the confidence it gave her to face the world. 'Just knowing that, Jamie,' she said, smoothing his brow, 'is enough.'

Billy came to stand beside the boy and, hoisting him up on to the hatch cover for a better view, began to point out the sights in the distance as *Chantril* rounded the Cape at speed. He told him of the post office tree in Mossel Bay where ships left letters in an old stump to be collected by other vessels with Cape business or just passing through. Jamie laughed when Billy told him the old tale of Jan van Riebeck, who, legend had it amongst the bushmen, had sat down on the slopes of the great plateau and smoked his pipe so long in contemplation that clouds formed and spread like a tablecloth over the mountain. The boy shaded his eyes from the sun to peer at Signal Hill, where a 'lion's head' emerged. The day was so clear and the colours so vivid, the freshness of the air and warmth of the sun so complementary that Jamie, his body invigorated, his mind stimulated and the pain of past weeks given a balm by the excitement of prospects new and now the possibility of catching up with *Vesper*, swore to himself to come back one day. Then *Chantril* left the Cape astern, as afternoon moved towards twilight.

Billy, returning to the poop from the galley, saw the boy still braced with one hand grasping the brass rail, dreaming away the hours. 'You all right, boy?'

'Yes, sir. Thank you.'

'It's the old "Cape Doctor" that's blown away your cobwebs,' Billy said, referring to the cleansing wind from the south-east. He saw Jamie glance the length of the ship, squinting towards the horizon ahead and knew what was in the boy's mind. 'We'll catch ol' Silas, don't you worry none about that!' he emphasised with seaman's pride, then realised the hint of disrespect and touched his cap. 'If'n you don't mind my sayin'?'

'No, sir,' smiled Jamie.

Billy nodded approval at the boy's confidence and sea legs as the ship rose and fell on the long waves. 'You be sure an' keep your feet this time, laddie.' He indicated the water overboard. 'You'll not be likin' a second duckin' afore you sees your father, or we'll have no story to tell him 'cause the proof'll be gone!'

'Yes, sir,' said Jamie, and grasped the rail tightly. Billy walked off and, as he did so, slipped and slid against a scupper, seizing a rat-line quickly. Jamie grinned, and Billy forced a smile as he recovered and walked away – but he knew, as seamen do, that overboard was 'all over'; the boy had been one in a million. As the Mate stepped up on to the quarter deck and saw the night and dark sea to the east, he shivered. The Indian Ocean was behind them now; ahead lay the Atlantic. He turned to take the wheel and felt the last warm rays from a spectacular sunset.

Both *Vesper* and *Chantril*, the one ahead of the other, lay in to the coast for several days before each captain decided to make a course change to pass St Helena Island. So it was that *Vesper* first, then *Chantril* – which, close-hauled, had made the most of the wind and more of her sea knots – lost all but the faintest breeze one morning off the German settlement of Luderitz. Fog shrouded both ships and each used a hand-cranked fog horn to sound warnings to fishing vessels, whalers out from German South-west African townships.

At 26° 40' south, 12° 40' east – as Silas reported it in his log – *Chantril* came gliding slowly alongside *Vesper*, ghost-like a hundred yards away. Crew exchanged shouts, mates bellowed at each other and passengers 'hello'ed' across the still, quiet water. Silas, in his cabin, when informed of the occasion grunted at Ben, troubled that they were not further from his rival but grateful in his heart that Eli had survived the rigours of the journey – so far.

Ben coughed. 'Well what is it?' asked the Captain, disgruntled after trying to catch up on some hard-won sleep.

'It's Miss Adèle, sir.'

'Well?'

'She is a determined little – '

'What?'

'She's packed and ready, sir. From the moment the watch picked up *Chantril*'s horn she's bin' whirlin' about the quarters puttin' all 'er things into 'er trunks an – '

'What!' Silas exclaimed and, shaking his head, stood up from the bunk. 'Where the devil does she think she's goin'?'

'I am transferring ships, Captain,' came a quiet, confident voice. Both men looked to the doorway of the cabin, where Adèle, demure and composed, smiled sweetly, dressed severely in dark but well-cut clothes which accentuated her remarkable figure.

'Are you, indeed?' growled Silas.

'I am,' stated Adèle, as Silas Hayes stepped to within inches of the young woman, towering over the upturned face and wide eyes. 'I need a skiff, or dory or . . . something.'

'Do you?' muttered Silas. 'Listen here, young girl. I promised your father you would remain in my custody till we – '

Adèle cut in, her full lips spreading over perfect teeth to maximum, devastating effect. 'Custody, Mr Hayes? I am not your prisoner, and neither am I "a girl" – I am a woman. I thank you for the voyage and merely wish to continue upon another ship.'

Silas pursed his lips and looked at Ben, who coughed, bowed his head and said nothing.

'You seem to have the crew under control already, *Miss* Morgan.' Then the thought hit him and he turned on Ben. 'Is there a gig in the water?'

Shamefaced, the Second Mate nodded. 'Mr Sutherland said 'as 'ow she 'ad to come and ask you first, sir.'

'Ask me!' bellowed Silas. 'Why, I hardly think it necessary!' He spun round on the young woman and, seizing her gently, bent to look into her eyes. It was a mistake – as she mentioned the man's name, tears appeared.

'I must see Eli, Silas – please.' She hugged him, and with that the battle was won.

'Ben,' he murmured, smelling perfume in her hair and feeling the longing in her body, 'take her – and have a care or she'll be a damaged surprise for our friend.'

'Aye, aye, sir,' smiled the Second Mate.

'Oh, Silas,' whispered Adèle, and kissed him hesitantly, then stood before his large frame, uncertain how to leave.

'What is it?' asked the Captain.

'I'm nervous,' she said.

Silas shook his head and pulled Ben towards the door. 'Heaven may have many wonders, as nature proves every day, but of them all I think a woman goes before and after every one!' He pointed. 'Out – and go.'

Adèle kissed him again, then ran ahead of Ben, who took her up top. Silas sat down at his charts and checked the time, which was almost midday. He opened the log to make the entry of exit at sea, feeling as he did so not the heaviness of the fog which diffused and darkened the sun, but a sense of loss. Adèle's obvious enthusiasm had stirred in him longings of his own – for quiet nights and easy days, affection and perhaps even some years of stability. What was gone was youth and enthusiastic expectations, most unfounded and many unproven, to be replaced by less ambitious possibilities. Emily was half a world away, and his son already gone to the next. He held his chin in the palm of his hand, elbow propped on the chart table, and wiped a tear from his eye before it could be seen or smudge words he was writing in the log. At least Adèle was going overboard in altogether different circumstances.

Eli Lubbock heard oars in the barely moving swell as he came on deck. He was surprised, as the orders he was about to issue would have put a boat into the sea.

'What is it, Billy?'

'We've a visitor, sir,' answered the Mate.

'What?'

Shouts came from the water-line of *Chantril* as *Vesper*'s gig came alongside. A gangway was lowered, winched down slowly as voices exchanged information. Eli watched Jamie escorted to the poop by Emily.

'Are you ready, boy?'

Jamie nodded.

'It seems your father's beaten us to it.'

The boy looked across at the ghostly shape of *Vesper*, barely discernible in the fog, then put out a hand to first the Mate, then Eli.

'One day, sir,' he said, 'I hope to be able to repay you for. . . .' He faltered. 'Everything.'

''Ere's a real little man.' Billy ruffled the boy's hair for the last time, suppressing a show of affection.

'Indeed you are, Jamie, and there's nothing to repay. Your courage is the talk of this ship, as it will be of London when we arrive – first!' Eli winked at the Mate, shaking the boy's hand.

'Take care of Silas for me,' murmured Emily, then she put a finger to her lips. 'But say nothing. Promise?'

Jamie nodded, then hugged her as she kissed him. 'Thank you, thank you,' he repeated, and fought the tears he angrily tried to conceal. By the time he reached the rail where the gangway had been lowered, his resolve was firm and he bade farewell to Cha-ze and the others aboard he had spoken to and made of them friends.

As Adèle stepped on board she was astonished to see the little urchin she at first hardly recognised. 'Jamie!' she exclaimed, and turned to follow him as he waved gaily and negotiated the steps down to the gig, waiting for instructions from the crew. They slipped moorings and pulled away, with the boy grinning at the two Chinese who had recognised his 'apparition', accepting his real presence after a moment as a miracle, so that their rowing was accompanied by constant mumbled prayer to distant gods.

Adèle was ushered on to the quarter deck of *Chantril* by two crew members. She shook hands with Emily, who immediately went to organise the storage of her trunks in the for'ard passenger area, where she assured Adèle she would find room and privacy.

Eli Lubbock watched Adèle Morgan curtsy before him, essentially for the eyes of the curious crew, and took her hand as she stood up to face the Captain of the ship she had been so determined to board.

'Well, young lady, to what does an old rogue like me owe the pleasure of a beautiful woman like yourself gracing our presence?'

She smiled, nodding to Billy the Mate, who took off his cap and attempted a bow in her direction.

'That your pleasure shall be mine, as mine shall be yours,' she replied.

Billy made a strangled noise in his throat and turned away as Eli felt blood flow to his neck. He coughed. 'You are very – forthright – Miss Morgan.'

She began to take off her gloves and readjust her hat, a small dark velvet cap pinned to her hair, which was piled expertly upon her head and drawn back from her brow, framing features Eli already conceded as familiarly attractive.

'I know what I want, *Mr* Lubbock. To be standing on this deck, I have travelled across much of the world, and I intend to travel the rest of it with you.'

Eli appreciated her words but would have preferred them spoken when they were alone in his cabin.

'Then,' he said quietly, 'it looks as though we're to go ashore together.'

The two of them looked long at each other; gone was the fog, the trials of the Indian Ocean, the heavy weather and the perils of the deep. They had found something to replace fear. Eli stepped closer.

'I am not young, Miss Morgan,' he said softly.

'No, Mr Lubbock,' she murmured. 'You are the Captain of this ship . . . and you are mine,' she whispered and, standing on her toes, she put her arms around his neck and kissed him. A breeze ruffled the hair on Eli's head as he lingered in Adèle's embrace, knowing something in that moment of which he had only ever before allowed himself to dream.

Billy broke the spell. 'We've found a wind, sir!'

Sails above, no longer limp, billowed in the morning air as fog began to swirl away across the now rippling sea. Eli looked up and smiled. 'By God, we have, Mr Mate.'

Ben's terrier began barking before the gig came alongside *Vesper*. Shouting had already started on deck as the canvas on the yards stirred and flapped. The Mate leaned over the rail as lines were let down for the gig, and men stood at the gangway winch to make ready to lift and secure. A look of disbelief remained on Ben's face even as he scrambled down the steps.

'Jamie!'

'Ben!' shouted the boy, and reached out when Ben leaned towards the gunwhale to pull in the little vessel as crew shipped oars. The stern came around fast as the Mate's hand missed the rollock and fell between the gunwhale and the bottom step of the gangway. The gig pressed against the timber and metal, trapping Ben's hand, and he let out a shout of agony – which

Jamie mistook for joy. He jumped towards his friend as the gig moved and released the Mate. The two of them, man and boy, fell into each other's arms, Ben fighting the pain quickly replaced by sheer wonder to see the boy alive. Jamie began babbling immediately as Ben led him up to *Vesper*'s deck, where the little terrier was leaping up and down in a frenzy of barking.

Silas heard instantly the crew's cries and Ben's barking dog, which disturbed his thoughts, alone in the Captain's cabin.

Hughie Sutherland rapped on the door and entered. 'A wind, sir! I've ordered sky sails and clewed in the royals. It's south-south-east and building.'

'Good,' said Silas quietly. 'Give me a compass reading and have chips at the knot line ready.'

'Aye aye, sir.'

'I'll be up directly.'

'Sir!' said Hughie, and left at the double.

Silas closed the log book and examined his chart. He unrolled another and clipped it into place at the edges of his navigation table. This showed St Helena, which they would now pass close to the east side before heading out west into the main Atlantic.

He stood up and buttoned his waistcoat. It was still too hot for a top coat, he decided, and opened the door to go up to the poop. The fog, which had a foul smell to it, was lifting quickly and sunlight sparkled on to the waves. Silas took a deep breath and glanced at the compass in front of Hughie Sutherland, who, grasping the wheel, was already adjusting the course. In the very centre of the binnacle's glass was a small brass piece, a miniature compass like the present he had given – 'Jamie,' whispered Silas. The Mate said nothing, having been told by Ben moments before. Silas shook his head then picked up the brass piece and snapped it open.

371

'Jamie!' he bellowed. The boy stepped from behind the First Mate.

'Oh, Father,' he said. Silas stared a full ten seconds, oblivious of all the activity on deck and above in the shrouds. Ben arrived on the poop, barely able to control his terrier, which was whining and barking at the same time with wild pleasure.

'Shut that dog,' growled Silas, still staring at his son. Ben muffled his terrier, which continued to whine and yap. Jamie approached his father, uncertain at his expression.

'How, laddie?' asked Silas, barely audibly. The boy's lips quivered and Silas reached out, seizing his son as laughter burst from his lungs, and pulled him into his arms. Jamie winced for a moment and a torrent of words came out of his mouth, but Silas heard nothing. He held the boy away from him, absorbing his face as if seeing it for the first time. Jamie stopped speaking and smiled through tears flowing unashamedly.

'North?' he asked, remembering his father's words of a man's destiny.

Silas could hardly speak, but nodded and chokingly answered, 'True north.'

26

Hollis Jackson traversed his double-barrelled shotgun, closed his eyes and pulled both triggers. The deafening blasts echoed away across the flat calm sea, which rippled only with *Otranto*'s wake.

Cornelia Morgan, amongst the group assembled on the first-class terrace deck, applauded lightly as she watched the unscathed clay pigeon fall into the Indian Ocean, then loosened the wide, beribboned hat protecting her perfect features.

'A week ashore in Ceylon seems to have dulled your edge, Hollis. We are again at sea, where you have declared yourself capable of anything.' She smiled. 'Try again. Do.'

Jackson scowled, reloading the shotgun. He raised it and made ready. 'Pull!' he commanded. The clay pigeon soared. Jackson fired twice. The single splash in the untroubled sea answered any unasked question. He lowered the gun.

Cornelia leaned towards him and whispered, '*You* load.' Jackson complied and Cornelia, with total confidence, acknowledging the expectation of the group around her, ordered. 'Pull!' She fired – once. The clay pigeon shattered. 'Pull!' she said again. She fired the second barrel. The target disintegrated. Applause broke out immediately and Stanley Grace actually clapped her about the shoulders as she handed the shotgun back to Jackson.

'You must learn to judge the distance correctly, between yourself and the . . . object.' She saw grudging admiration in Jackson's eyes. 'My father taught me well.'

'I am impressed,' he said.

'No, Hollis,' she countered, 'you are merely surprised. Men usually are.' She opened her parasol, placed it gently on her shoulder and spun it slowly. In a white dress with pink trimmings, which accentuated her slight tan, she was using her attributes and appeal to maximum advantage. 'I have always imagined that you men, having constantly to prove yourselves at all times in so many things, must, on occasions, find life quite tiresome. Is it?'

Jackson appraised the woman's composure. 'I accept your sympathy.'

She touched him lightly and murmured, only for his ears, 'If you have need of it, Hollis. . . . it is yours.'

The Dutchman, Kimmen, had appeared at the back of the group as they began to argue as to who would shoot next.

'Pull!' he commanded. Cornelia spun round, holding her hat quickly against a slight breeze which had sprung up. She saw the clay pigeon arc in the blistering sky. A terrific crack sounded from Kimmen's weapon and the target burst into fragments.

'Again!'

Applause denoted success. Cornelia raised her brows at Jackson.

'Again!' he shouted.

Once more the target shattered, splashing lightly into the ocean. Kimmen's beaming face turned to his appreciative audience as he held up the rifle for all to see.

'The new Mauser,' he said. 'Accurate.' He threw it towards his huge black manservant, Egerton. Immediately, Jackson reached out and intercepted it. As he examined the rifle, Cornelia coughed politely in the silence created by the Dutchman's disapproval.

'Hardly a sporting rifle, Mr Kimmen. No doubt by

the time we reach Zanzibar, you will be using an elephant gun?'

A gong sounded in the distance, declaring the midday meal was about to be served. Jackson threw the rifle to Egerton and turned to Cornelia. 'Shall we lunch?' he asked pleasantly.

'Delighted,' she responded, and held out a hand as the group began to move off, smelling the alluring aromas of excellent cuisine. It was then the increasing breeze lifted the hat from Cornelia's head and whirled it gently across the deck, trailing ribbons. It hovered over the rail for a moment, then spun away to fall into the sea, where, brim down, it floated into the wake of the steamship.

At the rail, Cornelia slumped, her vain attempts to catch the hat without success.

'It was my favourite,' she sighed.

Jackson took her arm, 'Do you really want it?'

'Of course,' she murmured. She looked at him; her wish became a challenge.

Otranto's horn sounded out loud and long and her for'ard speed showed. Jackson had instructed the Captain, and sailors were already winching down the gangway on the starboard side. In the wheelhouse, bells rang from 'dead slow' to 'stop'. 'Slow astern' was ordered and, churning foam, *Otranto*'s stern began to back into her own wake. Jackson, with the Captain on the flying bridge, wiped sweat from his brow then waved below at Cornelia, who waited at the rail on the terrace deck.

'Thank you, Tom.'

'It'll take a while to get back up to sixteen knots.'

Jackson shrugged. 'At least it indicates one advantage steam will always have over sail.'

'Perhaps,' said the Captain, unconvinced.

Fishing lines thrown from the base of the gangway dropped short of the hat now bobbing in the rippling waves from the last of the wake. The two sailors threw again, as if they were fly fishing, aware that numerous passengers who had been drawn to the rail above, sufficiently curious that *Otranto* was hove to in the centre of the Indian Ocean to have left their lunch, were a critical audience.

'I hope they do it no damage,' Cornelia murmured as Jackson joined her, seeing a third cast successfully catch the brim. He indicated to Tom Wallis on the flying bridge it was one minute before he could start up again.

The successful 'fisherman' began to reel in, to much applause from the rail, suddenly replaced by stifled cries. Jackson turned to see the hat being circled by several sharks lazily examining the object in the water from below. The passengers on the terrace deck held their breath; several of the women shivered with fear, as if the hat were not merely material but flesh and blood in peril, and they clung to their men, who murmured to each other apprehensively. The water parted, almost from respect for the great snout that appeared and turned to reveal a wide-open mouth of jagged teeth which gulped down the hat from brim to brim. The shark sank again into the ocean, which closed over with barely a swirl of foam.

Cornelia fell against Jackson, a gloved hand to her mouth. The passengers dispersed, most returning to their elegant lunch. The gangway was winched up and whistles blew to indicate it was fast and secured. As if awakened for the first time, Cornelia looked at Jackson with disturbed eyes. The ocean had become something more in her imagination than merely an inconvenience to be endured. Jackson took her hand to lead the way for lunch.

'The sea, my dear Cornelia, has an altogether different society of its own.'

Otranto's engines started up with a noise of thunder,

and her horn blasted out with a brash confidence. Soon, plying westward towards the African coast, her widening, foaming wake indicated a good cruising speed; steam guaranteed that Zanzibar was only days away.

' . . . then when all hope was gone, he dug it into my shoulder,' said Jamie, acting out with a face of agony the story he was already honing before an attentive Ben at the wheel of *Vesper*.

'Put down that boat hook afore you do more damage than your talkin' of,' he said, as Jamie wielded the metal in a scything movement over the quarter deck. Ben winced as he adjusted the wheel, which made Jamie grin, thinking it a response to his story.

'It hurt – badly, Ben,' said the boy, 'but look.' He moved his arm freely, concealing the stabbing pain for a moment as he lifted his hand horizontal. 'See – it's better. Miss. . . .' He stopped himself quickly, almost saying 'Emily', but continued, 'They said it was a muscular wound only, on *Chantril*, and Eli examined it. He said I was lucky to have been wearing velvet, which was wet and helped support the hook and that with no infection.'

Ben's terrier began barking, as if commenting on the details Jamie was revealing. The boy fondled the dog.

'Why is she called Polly?' he asked. Ben, wearing gloves, felt the swelling in his hand as he adjusted the wheel slightly.

'I wanted a parrot till I saw 'er,' he said.

Jamie laughed as the terrier licked his face, then the ship bucked and the wheel spun with Ben's hand between the spoke ends. With a crack, the brass top smacked against his weak hand. He grimaced at the sharp pain before stabilising the rudder. Jamie looked up, concerned at the Mate's expression.

'Are you all right, Ben?'

'It's nothing, little 'un. You're the brave little fellow.'

'Ben?'

The mate shook his head, smiling as Polly jumped up on to the hatch and whined, her head to one side. Silas Hayes and Hughie Sutherland emerged from the Captain's cabin, discussing the course set.

'We'll be off St Helena by noon tomorrow if the wind freshens,' said Silas, sipping tea from a mug. Hughie greeted Ben with a nod, checked the compass and looked down the length of the ship, examining wind-filled sails. Silas smiled at his son and joined Ben at the wheel.

'Main, fore, royals and top gallants, Mr Mate.'

Ben nodded. 'Aye aye, sir,' and relinquished the wheel to 'Mr' Sutherland.

Jamie looked up at his father, pleading silently. Silas understood. 'How's your shoulder, laddie?'

Jamie lifted his arm. 'Almost mended,' he replied, which was not a lie but it was far from the truth that he was fit enough to go up. But to a young man, forever staring above at the constant activity in the shrouds, on the yards, amongst the billowing sails, impatience and boredom found a charming way to modify the facts. Silas reached out and touched the healing wound beneath the white shirt and navy jacket Jamie wore. The boy winced but grinned bravely.

'See!' he said.

'Take him to the main top, Ben. No further.' The Second Mate nodded and led the excited boy, followed by the terrier, from the poop deck. Silas sipped tea and watched them go, feeling with pleasure the steady blow from abaft the beam. 'He's a game lad,' he stated with pride.

Hughie nodded. 'He's a willin' pupil – why, he knows more knots that I did at his time o' life.' His eyes followed the Mate and boy as they approached the rat-tails to go aloft. 'He's beginnin' to look like you,' he murmured.

'They used to say he took after his mother,' said Silas, staring after his son.

Hughie coughed and seized the wheel more firmly, remembering the old days and Silas' marriage. 'She wasn'ae cut out for the sea,' he said, hesitating as Silas turned his gaze warningly on his mate. 'If you don't mind my sayin' so . . . Silas . . . I always wondered how the two of you ever . . . ?'

'There was something – once, Hughie,' Silas interrupted, sighing for time past, 'but she asked – too much. *This* was all I ever wanted. To be standing at the wheel of my own ship. At sea I feel' – he paused, searching for a word to describe his fulfilment – 'alive.' He finished his tea. 'Land merely offers . . . other distractions.' He turned away from Hughie to face the wind, knowing it was shifting.

The Mate glanced at the steady sea, where steeper waves were cresting the blue, green and foam, sparkling beneath the open sky of swift-moving cumulus. 'We've a building sea and a veering wind, sir.'

Silas nodded affirmatively. 'Steer north by northeast; I'll go below and re-plot.' He paused and knelt as Polly, Ben's terrier, trotted back on to the poop and cocked a head, whining for his master. Silas stroked the dog, lost for a moment in time gone by and memories of other places, people, the woman he had once loved – when all things had seemed possible. His mate murmured to himself, distracting his thoughts.

'What?' he asked Hughie, looking up to see the man at the wheel staring fixedly at the rat-lines where Jamie and the Second Mate were already climbing aloft carefully.

'Just talkin' to myself, sir,' answered Hughie. Silas grunted, stood up and went below, leaving Polly on the hatch cover to look up and whine apprehensively. Hughie repeated his words softly.

'Ben *never* wears gloves!'

Fine spray in the air, then a bigger bow wave as *Vesper* began to plough deeper into the ocean so the feet of her figurehead dripped salt water, were the first indications to those on board who knew, that the favourable conditions were improving, provided that spread canvas could take advantage and the helm responded to cross-currents and prevailing winds somewhat at odds with what otherwise might have been deemed perfect sailing weather. Reefed sails were dropped from their gaskets, clewed in and set as sheets and halyards, adjusted to orders, pulled the canvas taut against the increasing wind.

High above the deck, Jamie felt the first unruly movement of the hitherto stable clipper. It bucked like a horse, rising and turning, at the same time causing the boy to cling tight, feeling the oiled rope pressing against his cheek.

Ben, already at the cap, shouted below, 'Come on laddie!' and smiled encouragement.

Grinning, Jamie waved back and, feeling the ship settle again in the blue water, glanced over his shoulder to see comforting sunlight dappling the sea through gliding clouds, glinting on a mere show of foam atop modest waves.

'I'm coming!' he shouted up, and, pulling harder with the one hand than the other, he continued towards the main cap. Ben reached down and grasped the boy, hoisting him to the platform to watch the crew further aloft release canvas and drop it to the yards, where others were waiting to clew it tight. Jamie looked all about him and saw what was ever a wonder, the back-stays, deadeyes, shrouds, lines, braces – rigging that delicately but with massive strength held the ship together. Her safety was based always on the fine judgement of her captain – his father.

Pride swelled in his breast and suggested that, as he was the son, he should travel further up. Ben was already rapping out orders to crew above, climbing higher and shouting to make himself heard over the wind. Jamie steadied himself against the mast on the main cap, the platform grill feeling less solid to the boy as the ship began its bucking pitch and roll. He turned and waved, able to see between the mizzen yards, knowing Hughie and his father might be watching, then he reached for the rat-tails and began to climb past the top sails towards the royals.

Aloft at the to' gallants, Ben was at the rat-lines leading to the sky sails, narrower at the cross-trees, and a steeper climb. He hesitated, seeing two of the crew having difficulty releasing a temporary reef, one of the knots proving stubborn. Impatiently he shouted to them to get it done, waving at them angrily. The ship rolled again and he clung tight to the oiled ropes leading out from a greased dead-eye. The men above seized the yard as their feet swung on the foot rope, halting their task for a moment longer. Ben Hardy shook his head and glanced below.

'No, boy!' he shouted, seeing Jamie, and indicated he should go back down, but the boy, climbing carefully, mouthed words lost on the wind and continued up. The ship steadied and Ben, hearing faint shouts above, looked to the high yards. Almost half a ton of canvas dropped to find the wind, just above his head, filling with a crack as men either side of him on the yards clewed it in securely. Taken unawares, Ben was shocked and stepped against the dead-eye exactly as Jamie shouted loud enough to hear, 'I'm coming, Ben!' Ben's foot caught against an eye-bolt on the fairlead plank, and he reached out for an iron bar in the futtock shrouds, missed it and fell on to a backstay, which he frantically sought to grasp.

'Ben!' shouted Jamie from below, in that instant seeing the fear in the Mate's eyes, then agony as his damaged hand would not take his weight. Ben's feet were on the cross-tree, body suspended and hands barely holding him aloft.

'Hold on!' screamed the boy, moving up quicker to come to his friend's aid. Ben's gloved hand opened despite all the will he could muster, and as the fingers parted from the wire, so with a single cry of terror did Ben's body from the rigging. He plummeted below, hands still seeking something, anything, to halt his fall. He hit the main-cap, bounced away, then, broken and limp, Ben's body smashed on to the ironwork wheels of the bilge pumps. Screams from below and shouts of alarm above from witnesses – both passengers and crew – were largely carried away on the wind, but Jamie seemed to hear them all as if merged into a terrible roar. He had fallen against the oiled ropes, clinging with fear, his eyes screwed tight, repeating to himself over and over, 'No! No! No!'

Hughie's bellowed warning had alerted Silas Hayes, who had just stepped below. He spun round and jumped back up to the poop deck. Hughie was pointing, grasping the wheel tight with his other hand. His face was ashen.

'It's . . . Ben, sir,' he choked. Silas ran fast, as if speed might alter events. It was too late; as he reached the aft deck-house he knew immediately. Ben lay inverted, head on the deck, feet over the bilge pump wheels. Silas knelt and gently touched Ben's face, which was white, drained of blood, eyes staring from the clear skin of what seemed no longer an old salt but the young man he had once been.

'Oh, Ben,' whispered Silas. The eyes flickered a moment and Silas thought he saw a faint smile, then the spark of life left Ben Hardy and the jaunty expression his eyes had always carried in a wickedly humorous glitter, died. Silas looked up, and blood on the iron jackstay, out and downhaul whips told him that the impact on the main-cap had finished him even before he hit the deck.

Curious crew parted as Jamie appeared between them. Silas glanced at his son. 'Go below, boy,' he said, 'this ain't for you.'

Tears sprang into Jamie's pleading eyes, begging all was as he knew it was not. He walked away slowly, hearing wailing from Ben's terrier Polly, speaking for all the hearts who had loved *Vesper*'s mate.

It was thirty minutes before Silas joined his son in the empty dining saloon. The glass racks swung over the table and the ship continued its course, the boy, head in his arms, leaned forward on the table and did not move as his father sat beside him. Silas said nothing until his son looked up at him, red-eyed and sobbing.

'Ben is my friend,' he whispered.

'Not now, Jamie – not now.'

'I don't want him to be dead,' he said vehemently.

Silas shook his head, his expression grim as floods of tears started again from his son. He put his arm around the boy, who fell against his father, clutching him tightly.

'You're growing up, laddie,' he murmured tenderly.

'I don't want to,' Jamie sobbed.

Silas nodded, understanding and remembering for himself the other times and other places of long ago. 'None of us ever do, Jamie. None of us ever do, laddie,' he said quietly, and only then did he too shed tears for the friend who had gone out of all their lives.

'I miss the boy, sir,' said Billy Williams in the Captain's cabin of *Chantril* as Eli rolled the charts and slipped them back into their place. Eli looked at his mate with a smile, for the old seaman who had spent so much time with Silas' son, telling him tales and teaching him the lore of the sea.

'We all miss someone, Billy.'

'But 'ee was a game little sprat, I thought.'

Eli nodded. 'Spunk the boy has, but then, with his parents, what else would you expect?' He indicated they should go up top. 'I just hope he learns without too much pain.'

Billy's expression became sceptical. 'At sea, Eli?'

Eli looked his old friend in the eye. 'We have our own problems, Mr Williams, and indeed an additional one in Miss Morgan – I suggest you put your mind to those.' The two men went up.

Below decks in the for'ard passenger area, Adèle was in conversation with Emily, with whom she had struck up a friendship. Both young and attractive, their ages within only a few years of each other, only the swelling womb of Silas' lady made a marked difference between the two amply bosomed but slim-figured women.

Crochet during idle hours had soon given way to stitching, of necessity – seams of not only their own clothes but those of even the male travellers where salt and sea had eaten way at even the toughest thread. When the weather was sufficiently clement, the ladies remained above in the company of others with whom they had established a nodding acquaintance. When it was advisable to remain below, the two young women occupied themselves and gossiped and giggled like two schoolgirls on a long outing from the rigour and discipline of schools they had each known. Grown accustomed to the sea after so many days of the voyage, both Emily and Adèle rode the movement of *Chantril* like the veterans they had become, pausing only as a needle came close to a thumb during a bucking wave. Some light filtered from thick glass in the small hatch covers above; other light was provided by the ever burning hurricane lamp always apparent from the smell of burning oil or, and more dangerous, paraffin. As Adèle quizzed Emily with some attempted subtlety about Silas, so curiosity about Eli was assuaged by the more garrulous Morgan girl, as *Chantril*'s captain had taken to referring to her in public.

'His gentleness is not always... obviously apparent,' said Emily hesitantly, 'and he is not consistently ... polite, but,' she added quickly, 'he is honest and loyal ... a true man I had always longed to find.'

'As I find Eli,' stated Adèle with a smile, happy to find a subject upon which they both totally agreed. Time had revealed the difference in their temperaments, and where the American was impulsive and passionate, Emily, born of both English and Australian parents, was content to analyse and evaluate before committing thought to words. 'Mr Lubbock,' continued Adèle, her grey brocade velvet dress unhooked from neck to waist, revealing her proportions only to the private quarters and friendly eyes of Emily, 'Mr Lubbock,' she repeated, 'has declared himself to me and I believe he loves me as I do him – very much.' She sighed and stitched another thread tightly into Mr Ellory's brown jacket's shoulder seam before putting it down in exasperation. 'God!' she exclaimed, 'how much longer must we endure this voyage to another world, as Mr Ellory calls it!'

'He is very poetic,' Emily smiled. The clipper rose up and fell heavily in a lively sea, causing the young woman to wince and clutch her stomach.

'Are you ... ?' began Adèle anxiously.

'Fine,' Emily replied quickly. 'Perhaps if we should take some sea air ... ?'

Adèle nodded. 'It would be very difficult to take any other, at present.'

Emily laughed and was helped up by her new-found

friend. Both women repaired themselves to go above, where they knew the scrutiny of men's eyes awaited them.

Plunging deep and rising, spewing foaming sea, *Chantril*'s figurehead led her charge north-west, passing easterly of St Helena without a sighting soon after eleven, sixty-three days out of Shanghai, as Eli recorded in his noon stint at the log. Chips indicated a steady eleven-twelve knot passage deciding, in the prevailing conditions, for Eli that more convas could be advantageous.

'We'll add sky sails and main stuns, Mr Williams.'

'But we've all up, Eli – that's safe, that is – with fore stuns and all fore s'ls, we've a good lick on now without chancing a week of carpentry with jury-rig forced on us. If we're to lose a top mast – '

Eli frowned and cut in: 'I'll be the judge o' that, mister! Upper stuns to boot, sir, and flying jib – sharp!'

Dubious, Billy saluted and began to leave the poop as Emily, with her maid Awan in company with Adèle, came up on deck. The women waved to Mr Ellory, who was setting up his camera. Eli Lubbock could only manage a scowl for him as he crossed to the crewman at the wheel, examining course and compass, and ignoring the imminent arrival of his passengers. In a bad mood, Eli was best left alone, as Billy Williams knew from many years. Each would have done anything for the other, but that friendship was cemented by a mutual respect common amongst seamen who were mates of long standing.

'Mr Williams,' said Adèle by way of greeting. Billy touched his cap and grinned, chancing his arm by putting out his hand to Emily's stomach, causing her to pull away.

'Just for luck,' he apologised, but Awan's protective expression caused him to leave in haste.

Eli nodded to the women who had struck up a

relationship which occupied Adèle's attention; for the most part Eli was thankful, as she had at first failed to understand the demanding hours for a ship's skipper at sea.

Pleased with his clipper's progress, Eli filled his lungs, appreciating the favourable weather and knowing more canvas would give him the extra knots to force *Chantril* on. Then he turned to the women, noticing Emily's increasingly rounded shape – her face, glowing with pregnancy and the sea air, a picture of beauty. He smiled.

'This would be a good life for a boy – don't you think?' he asked. The women's eyes widened, but it was Adèle who spoke.

'And if it is a girl, Mr Lubbock?'

Chantril seemed to hear and lifted to port, her bows plunging so fine spray flurried on the wind. The women hung on tight, grasping each other. Eli laughed good-humouredly.

'Women have their places, which are different from those of men, as they have indeed different attractions.'

'Can you name more than – the one?' challenged Adèle, regaining her sea legs.

Eli grinned and shook his head. 'How could I even begin – there are so many.'

'But, Captain,' said Adèle sweetly, 'we are at sea and time is plentiful.'

Eli pursed his lips, seeing Adèle's youth clearly obscuring her obvious intelligence.

'Sea and time, young lady, are for sailors to use and passengers to squander.' Awan scowled; her mistress blushed, before speaking politely. Emily coughed, almost by way of introduction. 'It is a hazardous business sailing a ship, Mr Lubbock. I cannot think I would ever be content to know that a son of mine was at sea – '

Eli interrupted, touching the curve of her belly

gently, as Billy had done. He spoke softly. 'You have obviously been content to think of Silas Hayes occasionally, Miss Emily. He is a sailor.'

Emily's colour deepened and she drew a hand to her lips as if to hide an expression or censor a reply. Adèle rose up with the quarter deck as a following wave lifted the stern and broke below the overhanging counter, and she seized the compass binnacle for support. Eli saw the fire in her eyes, recognising it as both alluring and dangerous.

'You have a sailor's tongue,' she snapped, 'with ladies, you should reserve it and speak with respect.'

'Respect,' countered Eli acidly, 'young lady, I reserve for the sea. All else follows.' He glanced about him quickly; spindrift from a mounting sea had alerted his instinct. 'The conditions are changing,' he said quickly. 'As it might become uncomfortable, I suggest you go below.'

Mr Ellory was already packing his camera awkwardly, finding it difficult to keep his feet against the building swell of the strong cross-current. Eli stepped to the wheel and took over, holding the brass spoke ends firmly. Squinting ahead, he could just make out Billy moving gingerly along the bowsprit. The Mate turned, shouting orders back to the foredeck, where the crew awaited commands to raise the flying jib, which they immediately began to haul way. Billy waved the length of the ship and Eli responded with a hand, but again swiftly grasped the wheel as *Chantril* plunged, throwing a spume of spray over the bow, lacing the air between Eli and his mate.

The women – joined by Mr Ellory, holding his hat to his head and camera and tripod with difficulty beneath his arm – could see Billy Williams now standing on the jib boom, confidently waving away the hoisted flying jib, his feet braced, fingers locked around, and forearm pressed hard against the jib stay. The sail snapped taut, held atop the mizzen mast and curled by the increasing blow.

Billy, satisfied, signalled to the crew a job well done and began gingerly to return to the foredeck, now grasping the rope rail leading out almost to the end of the long jib, where the martingales met a circular metal brace holding them tightly in place. He balanced for a second as *Chantril* crested a wave and sank suddenly into a trough. He bent double, knowing the breaking wave which might surge over him would inundate the bow, but, wet already, was determined to be back aboard deck before his ship again took water. Rushing sea swept over him with sustained force, so he dropped from his haunches, straddling the jib. No one saw the rope break; Billy was already part of the Atlantic Ocean, but he felt it give, then go completely and screamed soundlessly in the mighty sea as he was sucked between the chains, drawn beneath the starboard anchor and thrust against the ship's plating at the water-line as *Chantril* rose up into a wave closely following the first.

Eli saw the green wall topped with foam swallow Billy Williams and prayed in that second as *Chantril* heaved out of the exploding wave that his first mate had secured his grip. The unanswered prayer tore a cry of alarm from his throat. 'Ropes and lines,' he bellowed to the crew on the poop, bent to take the weight of water flushing down the main deck. 'Billy's in the water!'

Someone shouted the heart-stopping words, 'Man overboard!' then, as all experienced sailors knew, only seconds remained as life and death fought their constant mortal combat. A crewman took the wheel as Eli leapt to the starboard rail.

'Eli, what is it?' shouted Adèle.

Eli, leaning out, peering for'ard into the flying spray, roared, 'The fingers you have on two hands as you

389

count them are all he has left! Hard over!' he commanded. The helmsman, understanding instantly, spun the wheel, forcing *Chantril's* rail into the water as crew's arms extended over the wet brass, their own body-and-soul lines clipped securely, reached down in an attempt to find the panicking mate, who was sliding along the ship towards its wake. Coils of ropes were thrown over the bulwarks into the glistening water, trailing immediately before the approaching seaman, who, choking sea foam, vainly tried as each one appeared, to seize his only chance of life.

'The ropes, Billy!' bellowed Eli, as if it were an order. 'Take the ropes!'

The whole ship, creaking and groaning under the strain of the now ill-set sails to a contrary wind, joined the roar of the sea as if encouraging the struggling sailor. Like a man possessed, Eli spun round, seeing other crew at the stanchions over the stern counter lashing ropes fast.

'Can we not stop?' pleaded Adèle. Eli replied so quickly she only caught a few of his words.

'At twelve knots it would take as many minutes – or more – and we'd be miles away! How could we find him in this sea!' he exclaimed. 'If he misses the lines, he's a dead man – and he knows it!' he emphasised. Eyes wild, mind racing, he spun back to the rail. Below, Billy was taking mouthfuls of water; now he was almost below the first of the stanchions beside the mizzen poop break. The Mate's hand and wrist found a rope, and for a moment foam obscured him as he held on.

'Haul!' cried Eli as crew began to lean against the weight beneath them; immediately Billy emerged, suspended half in, half out of the fast-moving sea. Caution was thrown aside as several other sailors reached dangerously over the rail to seize their first mate. The weakened man slipped away as shouts of alarm came from every witness to the horror. Eli threw off his coat, dropped the gun from his waist, kicked his shoes across the deck and ran to the stern stanchion behind the wheel mechanism.

'No!' Adèle shouted, and made a move to stop him.

Eli had taken a secured rope and was knotting it about his waist. 'Hold the course steady now!' he ordered loudly and jumped up on to the stern rail, where he hovered over the counter, looking below at the churning wake.

'Eli! *no!*' screamed Adèle. Eli jumped. Sinking beneath the South Atlantic, Eli surfaced into foam already yards away from *Chantril*. He knew the rope coil was paying out fast and turned almost full circle, striving to find Billy. The Mate, coughing, hand flailing, was almost at his shoulder. Eli reached towards his friend, and hands met wrists a second time, exactly as the rope pulled taut, dragging Eli behind his ship, now with Billy locked in his grip. The initial pain became agony as Eli grimaced, screwing his eyes against the cone of water, hoping now that God and *Chantril*'s crew would save them both. As the rope snapped taut, Adèle exclaimed, 'Another rope now!' and her voice carried such authority crewmen immediately complied and another coil of thick hemp, weighted by a running bowline knot, was hurled overboard. It started to trail towards the two men, whose combined weight, increased by the sea pressure, was straining the rope at Eli's waist. He had managed to drag Billy towards him when the seaman almost drowned his captain; all aboard saw the two men go under as the Mate enveloped Eli's head with his long arms. Now the two, locked together, cut through the water like some great leaping knot line.

'Oh,' whispered Emily to herself, 'if the rope should part.' More crew had arrived to help, and all of them hauled hard on the life-line, oblivious of Mr Ellory, who, seizing his opportunity, had set up again and was cranking his camera furiously. Adèle saw Eli's free hand find the extended hemp, and his wrist slipped into the running bowline, which immediately pulled tight. With two ropes holding the men, Adèle, poised at the rail, turned and shouted: 'Pull – damn you all! Pull!' In her fear and excitement she even leaned over as if to take a hand, but her scream as the first rope frayed then snapped with a crack sounded even louder than her invective.

The men at the second rope, which was wrapped around the stanchion, felt the added weight instantly and others had to join them to take the strain. It was unnecessary to describe the pain all knew Eli was suffering as gradually the rope dragged the men foaming in the wake towards the rudder. Leaning over the counter, several 'prentices dropped a rope net as Adèle screamed again to the sweating seamen, 'Pull! Pull! Pull!'

Eli enmeshed himself first, then made sure Billy was caught like a spider's victim, legs and arms, before signalling above to raise them up.

The two men fell on deck and sprawled like landed fish. Emily appeared, at Adèle's instigation, with rum from the saloon. Both women administered the strong alcohol and watched as first Eli's then Billy's eyes opened. Tears from the women and shouts of joy from the crew were gratefully observed by the two seamen as they swallowed the liquor.

Eli looked at *Chantril*'s first mate and shook his head, humour replacing fear. 'Billy,' he began,' if you ever do that again. . . .'

The Mate's face still showed shock, and his seriousness was absorbed by all, who reverted to respectful silence as he stared about him and spoke quietly, 'I thank you, sir, as I thank the Lord above.' He choked with emotion, then said, 'I thought I was gone.' He closed his eyes gratefully and his head fell back on to the deck.

'God bless Ben Hardy's soul and consign him to the deep in peace,' intoned the priest, James Collins, at the port rail of the clipper ship *Vesper* in the first minutes of the afternoon, one hundred and eighty miles from the coast of Ascension Island.

Silas nodded and the waiting crew, wearing black ribbons, as did all aboard, lifted the carpenter's hastily made coffin covered in the white ensign, and let it slip overboard, where with a splash then a gurgling of bubbles it sank below the calm surface of the South Atlantic Ocean.

Vesper was ghosting along on a quiet sea under a clear sky; the silence from all on board out of respect for the burial was broken only by the soft purling of water passing along the hull into the wake and Polly, Ben's terrier, whining in anguish, so human that the women and even some of the crew began weeping at the pain and loss so obviously felt and displayed with such pathos. Jamie held the dog close, wiping his tears from the terrier's coat but giving comfort as Polly's wet tongue licked the boy's face.

Silas Hayes looked up at the few bent sails and felt the gentle wind on his face as he stared aft towards the helm. The assembly had become uncomfortable as the priest hesitated to continue and coughed uncertainly. Silas, angry, stepped forward; pushing Collins aside he began to speak with the voice of command and instantly gained attention and complete silence. For a moment grief was assuaged; even sobbing and the dog's whining ceased.

'When a shipmate you've worked beside, slept near, eaten with, slips beneath the waves it is always a sobering moment for us all. We are each reminded of our mortality. Our courage is challenged. It is a test sent' – he paused, and emphasised – 'by God, lest we forget who is master. Neither I nor the spirit of this ship, the winds, nor the seven seas – but *he* is in command of all our destinies.' A murmur came from the crowded rail and some of the group bent their heads in prayer. 'As the bounty of God,' Silas continued, lifting his face to the sky, 'we are given life, and at his whim it is taken away.' He surveyed passengers and crew, choosing words carefully. 'We are not here in this world to judge but merely to learn. *Trust* in that experience is our strength.' He paused again, now deliberately. 'God grant it to us all. Amen.'

The group as one murmured, 'Amen', then some stirred, some, reluctant to remain, slowly dispersed. The priest lingered, as did Jamie and the terrier, both crouching on the hatch cover. He coughed to gain attention. Silas leaned on the rail, staring below into the ocean, which was again almost without a ripple; only the gentle wake disturbed the water. His thoughts examined his friend's history. Ben was gone – all those years of striving and survival, now gone – as if he had never been.

'Excuse me, Captain.'

Silas did not move. Jamie sobbed once. Polly whined.

'Captain?'

Silas turned to face a man from whom he could not conceal his intense dislike not merely of the cloth he represented, but also the hypocrisy in the voice intended, practised, to conciliate and please whilst so obviously seeking to gain. 'Are you paid for the souls you buy, priest?'

'I beg your – ' began the man, astonished.

'Is your wage recompensed by numbers, or do you practise as you preach – badly – and it is of no consequence if you succeed or fail to convince anyone of this everlasting life of which you have no knowledge or experience?'

'God is –' started Collins, but Silas cut in.

'Say no more, priest – for you cannot. If you believe, it is your truth. If you do not, it is merely a child's fairy tale.' He indicated the sea behind him and smiled wickedly as his mate might have done. 'Ask Ben Hardy – *he knows*.'

The priest glanced uncomfortably at the boy, who was now curious, and the dog, who growled back, before assuming the taught role of superior without a single justification Silas would accept. 'I have seldom been to sea,' he murmured. 'I didn't know quite what to speak of . . . what might seem – appropriate.'

'The man is dead, and you of all people "did not know what to say"!' Silas' voice rose, making the man flinch.

He blinked and repeated, ' . . . appropriate, I said. I have no way of knowing what might be fitting. . . .'

'And neither, I'm sure, will I when I face my Maker – if he exists,' grunted Silas.

'If!' exclaimed Collins. '*That* is blasphemy, sir, along with your "*fairy tales*"!'

'Not if he doesn't,' Silas grinned angrily.

Collins breathed heavily, assembling forces learnt for just such an occasion. 'The scriptures clearly tell us . . .' he pontificated.

Silas would have none of it and wafted a hand, dismissing the cant for what it was – argument by rote.

'Your scriptures are real collateral, in this material world, for nothing. They tell me, as my charts tell me, of places I have never been, where other men I do not know have described the perils of dangerous coasts. But until I go to those places which I have not seen, they exist only on paper and in my imagination.'

'Are you saying, sir, that the Bible is not the one and the only reality?' shouted Collins.

'In life, priest, "the one and the only reality" is *death!*' snapped Silas.

Collins spluttered, 'I cannot accept that, sir!'

Silas nodded and glanced at his son, beckoning him. 'You should,' he replied. 'You'd be out of business without it!' He stepped away from the man and, followed by his son, walked towards the poop deck and the entrance below to his cabin.

James Collins knelt immediately and began to pray, partly for those passengers and crew who had witnessed the exchange from a distance, as he declared audibly for the Captain of the clipper ship *Vesper*, but, truth was, mostly for his own disturbed beliefs.

By evening a meal had been eaten, ordinary shipboard life had continued uneventfully and already to many on or between decks, time had absolved the fearful conclusion, made in the face of reality, that the idea of an afterlife might merely be fanciful. Such a notion had been dispelled by the soft tongue of the priest going about; on several occasions he had been forced to resort to harsh words, threats even, of the penalties of sin in thought or in deed. A lull persisted around the ship at twilight as aboard an uneasy peacefulness was reinforced by introspection or strained, failed humour. The sun set and took with it another soul.

Silas had remained in his cabin, hearing eight bells sound the length of his ghosting ship. Jamie entered and sat on the bunk beside his father. Polly sprawled on the cabin floor and sighed. Lamps had been lit and barely moved as the slight wind ushered *Vesper* forward quietly beneath a great firmament of stars above.

'I know almost all the constellations – Hughie told me,' Jamie announced quietly. Silas said nothing, merely gazed morosely at the lamp before him. 'Ben taught me from charts of the heavens,' the boy finished softly. The Mate's name stopped him and a tear appeared with unwanted grief. Silas looked up and tried to smile.

'All right, boy . . . I know,' he said. 'I know.' Jamie jumped down and fell into his father's arms as Polly crawled to the security under Silas's chair. Above, the watch changed and the flurry of movement became again only the purling wake through the open door up to the quarter deck, where Hughie Sutherland stood at the wheel, lost in his own personal thoughts.

'Will Ben go to Heaven, Father?' Jamie asked. Silas eventually nodded slowly. 'And will he be watching us down here?' Silas nodded again.

'And,' Jamie continued, but stopped as Silas sighed heavily and stood up. Man, boy and dog went on to the quarter deck to stand beside Mr Sutherland. Nothing was said as eyes absorbed the limp sails and the night stars, and sought answers within to demanding, unspoken questions.

'Father,' whispered Jamie. Silas looked down at his son. 'Can Ben help us now to win the race?'

Hughie began to chuckle.

'He might,' answered the father, eyes suddenly twinkling. He looked at Hughie, who had found in the innocent words a release from his pain and was laughing loudly. Polly barked as Silas joined his First Mate, both men roaring despite Jamie's continuing seriousness. Jamie looked up into infinity and closed his eyes to seek again the kindly expression of the friend he had grown to love.

'Please, Ben,' he whispered, 'please.'

27

Rowing in the South Atlantic was a new experience to many of the crew aboard the cutters out from the bow of *Chantril*. Becalmed, the clipper had suffered two days as 'a painted ship upon a painted ocean', when Eli ordered a pull party and, with few volunteers, had commanded several boatloads of 'willing men', promised extra rations, to go ahead on lines and lead the three-master into the semblance of a breeze. Irritation amongst all aboard was apparent in arguments, long faces and surly behaviour. Nothing new for Eli Lubbock, for some merely impatience, mainly from the complement of men he'd taken on, but for the passengers approaching the equator once more, it was a stifling time, when fears had become boredom and the daily experience of life in jeopardy had been substituted by inaction, creating a yearning to be moving on and sailing hard, even though the continuing voyage might well hold not only the uncomfortable but the unexpected.

'Nowhere can the delights of cruising be more fully enjoyed than aboard the steamship *Otranto*,' read Billy Williams. He held an informative pamphlet describing the attractions of 'tin kettle' voyaging which Eli had discovered amongst his papers. The Mate's voice became mocking and he shifted on his seat beneath the canvas awning stretched over the quarter deck. His audience was several crew and a number of passengers, including Adèle and Mr Lewis Ellory, who was setting up his camera to capture the afternoon. 'There is an unusual amount of deck space for games and recreation. There are two dining saloons, a remarkably cool Spanish smoking room, a card room, a writing room and two enclosed terrace lounges.' He turned to Eli, raising his brows and wafting a hand. 'Two!' he exclaimed. Eli, stripped to a shirt, sweating and with less than a perfect humour, took the paper and examined further paragraphs before continuing, 'The bedrooms are large and daintily furnished. Hot and cold water is provided and there are many private bathrooms. *Everywhere*,' he emphasised, 'a sense of spaciousness and comfort has been created to combine the atmosphere of a gracious home and a luxurious country club. . . .' Eli laughed with the others, stood up and took the telescope, feeling immediately the heaviness of the hot day.

'Spacious, gracious and dainty,' he muttered. 'It's a wonder they float.' He stepped to the stern rail; distantly, he could see *Vesper*, equally becalmed. He leaned on the dull brass and looked below at the barely purling wake. A flat sea and a blistering sky where nothing moved, not even a puff-ball cloud was showing, was no encouragement for a blue-water sailor.

'I see you, Silas,' he grunted, 'but where are you, Mr Jackson?'

An unruffled sea absorbed the thunder of ship's engines as *Otranto*'s bow cut into a glass ocean, throwing the barest shadow on her rippling water-line as she moved towards the great continent appearing on the horizon. Passengers ran to the rails as crew nodded with relief and the ship's horn sounded out deep and long. 'Zanzibar!' shouted an excited voice, and indeed it was; distant in the heat haze, the island was their first African landfall.

The engineer's telegraph was rung loudly in the wheelhouse, warning all below that new instructions might be imminent as the Captain examined his charts. He came back to the compass, checked the bearing,

399

then, unbuttoning his white jacket, walked out to the flying bridge and, ignoring the heat, sweat glistening on his forehead causing drops to course around his thick eyebrows, he focused his binoculars.

Hollis Jackson stepped out to join the Captain, smoking a cigar, his waistcoat undone. He took out a pocket watch, referred to it and frowned. Bells rang again from the wheelhouse to signal speed reduced on sighting reefs.

'No pilot cutter?' murmured Jackson.

The Captain shook his head. 'The main port is around to the north-west; Kimmen requested landfall further south.'

'The Dutchman wants . . . what?'

Tom Wallis lowered the binoculars, satisfied at identifying the headland south of the island.

'Off the cape 6°30, 39°30,' he smiled. 'I just promised to get him here.'

Laughter sounded from below and both men looked down to the terrace deck, where Kimmen was leading a group to the rail, obviously in an exuberant mood.

'I'll go down,' said Jackson soberly.

Captain Wallis nodded. 'I'll remain up here.'

Jackson opened the gate and took the stairway below as a shout went up and arms pointed towards the distant headland. A red smoke-flare was soaring into the blue haze above what seemed to be a large cutter making smoke and approaching fast. Disporting in elegant clothes, the passengers began to talk animatedly of the prospects on the tropical island across the water. Both journalists, Marsh and Meyer, attempted to buttonhole Jackson, but he fobbed them off with a forced smile, seeing Egerton, the big black servant of Kimmen's, arrive on deck with the first of his master's bags. Trunks followed, brought by sailors who placed them according to Egerton's instructions. Jackson, puffing at his cigar, watched – curious, and suddenly for no apparent reason but instinct, apprehensive. Stewards had begun to lay tea on a long table beneath a protective canvas awning. They hesitated, seeing the owner seemingly critical at their appearance, but when he snapped his fingers and turned his attention back to the sea they continued with practised efficiency.

'Zanzibar,' Marsh was saying loudly, 'is a protectorate of the British Empire, I believe, but' – he pointed westwards – 'that, I think – can it be so close – is German East Africa?' Faintly, along the far horizon, a dark line could be made out in the haze. 'Give me the binoculars, Meyer.' Marsh focused and, unable to make out anything clearly, traversed to find the cutter.

'What do you see, Marsh?' Meyer asked impatiently.

'Let me focus . . . it's big,' came the reply. Kimmen lit a cheroot, glanced at his manservant then smiled at Jackson as smoke curled into the humid air.

'No trouble,' he murmured, for the ears of Jackson alone. The ship owner nodded, beginning to understand as he squinted towards the cutter now making familiar thick black smoke.

'German coal?' he asked.

Kimmen shrugged. 'Dutch ship,' he replied.

'I say,' stuttered Marsh, 'the cutter has no . . . pilot flag!' He turned to the assembly generally, lowering binoculars before looking at Jackson. 'Do you think it's for us?'

Kimmen answered. 'Yes. For *us*.' He nodded to Egerton, who raised the Mauser rifle lazily, no longer held loosely with the bags.

Jackson's face hardened as exclamations of shock sounded from the passengers.

'No Customs. No Immigration,' he said. 'Now I understand.'

'Good,' smiled Kimmen, wickedly genial. 'You have been well paid.'

Marsh, having refocused the binoculars on the deck

of the closing cutter and seen the rough-looking, shabbily dressed, bearded crew, all armed to the teeth, spluttered for others to hear, 'Oh, my God!'

'Stop,' Kimmen commanded quietly. Jackson looked up to the flying bridge, where the Captain, who had already seen the potential danger, was considering outrunning the cutter.

'Gangway,' Kimmen ordered. Jackson hesitated. Egerton thrust a bullet into the breech of the Mauser and closed the bolt. Several of the women whimpered. Cornelia stepped forward from the group, her eyes blazing at the threat. Stanley Grace coughed. Jackson sighed heavily and nodded. Instantly the wheelhouse conveyed instructions, causing bells to ring loudly amongst the now silent, elegant group. They were stopping.

Kimmen bowed slightly, mocking Jackson. 'Comply with my requests and you will have no problems.'

'It is *my* ship, Kimmen,' Jackson said quietly.

'For the moment,' replied the Dutchman, 'it is mine.' The gangway fell into place and *Otranto* slowed to half ahead, then as the cutter came on course her engines went into thundering reverse, churning water to bring her dead slow before heaving to. Burly men, heavily armed, wearing a variety of dun-coloured clothes and floppy, wide-brimmed hats, all but a few bearded, ran up the gangway and, pushing aside all in their way, as if to precise planning, spread about the upper decks. Some others made their way to the for'ard hold. Obviously familiar with the derrick, some started the machinery as the others opened the hatch covers and descended into the hold. Cornelia appraised the most immediate ruffian and fanned her face to gain Kimmen's attention.

'Your men must be excited at the prospect of so much sewing. . . .'

The winch machinery for'ard burst into life and,

with chain and hook traversing the open hold, the operator made ready to lower away with shouts in a language strange for most. It merely confirmed Jackson's worst suspicions. His expression became grim as Kimmen extended a hand to his manservant, who flicked the safety catch and threw the Mauser to his master. Kimmen turned the catch, opened and pulled the bolt, then thrust it again, reloading the rifle.

'German,' he said loudly, '7.9mm, four kilos weight, 1.2 metres long, accurate to more than two thousand metres. Charge-loaded. A good weapon!'

Jackson gritted his teeth as gears changed for'ard and the hook and chain were released into the dark hold. 'But it won't make clothes, Kimmen.'

The Dutchman shook his head, grinning. 'No, Mr Jackson.' He held up the Mauser. 'These make countries.'

The stewards were allowed to continue laying tea, white tablecloths, lace covers, bone china, silver cutlery and cut-glass ornaments as the first-class assemblage watched the first load being lifted from the hold. The chain held others linked to it with a ring, from which smaller links supported four corners of a platform which had been stacked with Kimmen's 'sewing machines'. It swung on the traversing derrick and was halted, swaying, as men on deck checked the contents. Two broken cases showed in the one rifles, in the other ammunition.

'We will leave you the seamstresses' "weapons", Mr Jackson. The crates are marked and will be a present for your cooperation.'

Rifle shots echoed from the hold causing passengers to start. 'No trouble,' growled Jackson, and threw the end of his cigar over the rail. He stared at the Dutchman, hearing the shouts of triumph from the for'ard deck as the first load descended to the cutter at *Otranto*'s water-line. The group above him seemed to be waiting for a lead, uncertain how to behave, frightened to show outrage in the face of the lazily slouching, fearsome opposition about them but not wishing to reveal their lack of courage. They exchanged whispered comments, which were interrupted by Jackson's suddenly commanding voice.

'The British Army is fighting a war against tenacious opposition in South Africa's Transvaal. May I ask which side you have taken at the news of this conflict, Kimmen?'

'I like the word "tenacious", Englishman.' The Dutch accent did not conceal dislike for Jackson as the man approached, his words becoming ominous. 'I am from the border country of Holland and the great nation of Germany, whose sympathies are like my own.' He paused. '*Not* with your Empire, which is old and dying.' He held the muzzle of the Mauser beneath Jackson's chin.

A brave steward tentatively sounded a gong, declaring four o'clock and afternoon refreshments. Jackson, appreciating the gesture of civilisation even in the face of such barbaric behaviour, smiled with forced pleasantry. 'Tea, Mijnheer?' he asked.

Stanley Grace stifled a laugh, which was possibly what caused the whole subsequent incident at sea.

Kimmen's eyes narrowed, seeing the supercilious expression clearly in Jackson's eyes. 'It is tradition, amongst the English, Dutchman, to respect what has been handed down to us – an institution based merely upon dried leaves and hot water, from which our forefathers created a civilised attitude to the world and gave it – offered it – to those sensible enough to make it part of their own lives. What have you given for us to respect? Looking at you, I see nothing but a thin veneer without honour.' He paused, seeing the hate in Kimmen's eyes. 'It is not our Empire which is at an end but your cheap aspirations without substance, based merely upon destruction which will in turn destroy you.'

'Oh, well said,' murmured Marsh.

'Words, Englishman,' growled the Dutchman.

' . . . can kill faster than a bullet,' snapped Jackson.

Kimmen grinned, then with surprising speed for one so large, swung the rifle's butt hard, smashing into the side of Jackson's face, staggering him. Blood flowed and the passengers backed away from further violence. Cornelia stepped forward and spoke brusquely, taking a handkerchief to wipe Jackson's nose.

'I think we should leave Mr Kimmen to his business, Hollis. He quite obviously is a poor conversationalist.'

Kimmen smiled, nodding to Egerton, who stepped forward.

'The key, Mr Jackson, to the safe.'

'Robbery now?' asked Cornelia.

'Only the gold,' replied Kimmen.

Reluctantly Jackson felt in to his inside pocket and handed over the key to Egerton, who went below.

Jackson's anger was obvious to Cornelia and his helplessness was equally apparent. 'Not now,' she whispered, and smiled for Kimmen to see. The Dutchman had moved to the rail, watching the passengers retire to the tea table beneath the awning, into cool shadow out of the hot sunlight.

'It is *my* ship,' Jackson repeated determinedly.

'Then let us keep it, Hollis, and retire for tea.' She led him to the table, followed by the alert Egerton, who hovered behind, awaiting instructions from his master.

The winch and derrick sounded out noisily and Kimmen turned his attention to the more pressing matters of arming the enemies of England, waving once to Jackson, his thanks, as Egerton emerged on deck with the heavy case of gold firmly in his grip, and taking no chances, hand-cuffed to his wrist.

Tea was not an animated affair. Eyes searched the

faces of others at the table as cups clinked on saucers and liquid was spilt on the white linen. Apologies, excuses and low exchanges were substituted for what had normally become a lively party. In the background, reminiscent to some of the bunkering process, what all knew now to be guns and ammunition was lifted from the dark hold. Sweat showed on most brows as glances confirmed the continuing presence of numerous Afrikaners seemingly unconcerned at the heat, lounging, rifles slung over their shoulders, smoking cheap hand-rolled tobacco at the rail some yards distant across the newly caulked terrace deck. Blood stained Hollis Jackson's whites as, ignoring offered teapots, milk, cake and scones, he watched Kimmen and Egerton at the top of steps to the foredeck occasionally shouting instructions to the men below in their own language. Stewards arrived to clear, bring more boiling water and refresh the pastry stands. Jackson nodded to Stanley Grace and Cornelia, whispering, 'Be careful – and don't miss.'

'They now expect nothing, Hollis – we have men enough here – go.'

Jackson, appreciating the woman's courage, nodded, stood up and, with the stewards, walked from the table unnoticed into the dining saloon, where he began running.

'You know exactly where the guns are, Mr Grace?' hissed Cornelia.

The entertainer extraordinaire smiled and mouthed, 'I do, but when?'

'We wait for Mr Jackson's initiative,' she replied, and sipped freshly made tea from a delicately patterned bone china cup. Jackson had the sense to stop outside the door into the wheelhouse. Inside, he eventually made out through the reflecting glass, a broadly built Afrikaner standing patiently, rifle in hand, examining the machinery and instruments about him with innocent curiosity. Jackson caught the eye of the Captain, who understood his gestures and began to distract the guard. Jackson entered gingerly and leapt at the man, who proved immediately to be strong. He sagged as Jackson hit him with a succession of blows but threw aside the First Officer and Captain, swinging wildly with his rifle. Jackson, caught on the thigh, fell heavily but kicked up hard into the man's groin. His scream was drowned by the loud noise of the derrick for'ard as it winched up a last load from the dark hold. The Afrikaner began to stagger, bent in agony. Jackson wrestled for the weapon in the massive hands, which relinquished their grasp unwillingly. Immediately, Jackson smashed the butt into the man's snarling face, then swung hard, connecting with the jaw beneath the beard. The Afrikaner crumpled and lay still on the floor of the wheelhouse, half-conscious, groaning, blood spilling from the gashes in his head. Panting with exertion, Jackson held up the rifle to the sailors grouping around.

'British Army issue – stolen, no doubt, or taken from the bodies of our soldiers.'

One of the sailors managed to speak, 'They've killed two of our crew in the forward hold, sir.'

Jackson growled angrily. He turned to the Captain, ordering, 'Tom, when I shout, go to full ahead both!'

'Where is Mr Jackson!' bellowed Kimmen. Cornelia, offering him tea, appeared affronted for a moment. The Dutchman's patience was exhausted; he slammed the muzzle of the rifle firmly in his grip, against the full cup and saucer in the woman's hands. The china burst into slivers, the hot tea splashing on to the table. Cornelia backed away quickly – and deliberately – into Stanley Grace, seeing Kimmen traverse the rifle threateningly over the seated passengers' heads.

'I said, no trouble – and I wish none back.' He

paused, pleased that he had sufficiently cowed the table. 'I want Mr Jackson.'

'Kimmen!' came the voice of the man he sought. The Dutchman turned round and actually stepped out into the sunlight to see the figure of Hollis Jackson standing on the flying bridge. The Englishman bolt-loaded the rifle, pressed the butt into his shoulder and aimed at Kimmen.

'Lee Enfield .303. Eight and a half pounds weight; more than three and a half feet long; two thousand yards' range; clip-loaded and a deady weapon – aimed at your head.' He waved the barrel slightly. 'Tell these men to throw down their guns.'

Kimmen froze for a moment, then realising the odds, looked beyond the rail. The derrick had stopped as gears were changed for the last load to swing out over the cutter and be lowered on to her now crowded deck. He grinned wolfishly, gaining confidence from the nonchalance of the Afrikaners near him, aware of their superior abilities in the face of these unarmed civilians.

'Mr Jackson, we are too many! I have seen you shoot! You hit nothing!'

'I'm better with a rifle,' Jackson replied slowly, his unwavering aim causing consternation and indeed taking all attention, allowing both Cornelia and Stanley Grace, who had inched towards the shadow of the saloon door, to slip away.

'You're bluffing,' shouted Kimmen.

'You can find out if you don't put down your guns,' Jackson challenged him. 'Two of my men are dead.'

Kimmen hesitated, hearing the distant gears change. He looked round, to see the derrick operator begin to swing the load, now out over the rail of *Otranto* and above the waiting cutter. He walked several paces nearer the overhanging flying bridge. 'Mr Jackson, that is enough. We are going.'

'Nowhere, Kimmen, not with weapons to kill our

men,' he replied, licking his lips. He tasted salt and suppressed his fear. He knew he *was* better with a rifle.

Cornelia and Stanley Grace in the saloon had rushed to the mahogany and glass cabinet where the shotguns were kept, broken open the doors, hastily loaded as many as were possible, grabbed cartridges and run back to the shadows of the doorway to the terrace. Marsh and Meyer saw them first and immediately accepted the weapons, unseen in the shadows beneath the awning. Only when one of the Afrikaners spotted the double barrels in their hands was it all up. Pointing the shotguns, Grace and Cornelia stepped out to join the two trembling journalists. All four pointed their weapons.

'We're here!' sang out Stanley Grace, and Jackson heard the welcome voice clearly. Stunned and caught with their own guns slung over their shoulders, the Afrikaners remained where they were, eyes now fixed on the passengers lining the tea table. The man at the derrick gears, it was generally argued later, tripped not only oiled machinery to let out the load, but the whole incident which followed.

'Now!' cried Jackson. Immediately bells rang in the wheelhouse and a moment later the thunder of *Otranto*'s waiting engines was heard. Jackson changed his aim and fired.

The Afrikaner at the derrick saw the flash, but it was the last message his brain received as a .303 bullet exploded, destroying the delicate tissue. His hands fell from the gear stick, causing the brake to be applied, grinding the chain on the davit arm. The load jerked to a halt, then it swung out over the cutter with men up from the hold now and clinging on to be deposited below, shouting in alarm. Jackson reloaded fast as Kimmen, on the terrace deck, raised his Mauser. Both men fired simultaneously. The German rifle was accurate as the Dutchman had stated and the bullet travelled exactly where it was intended, but Jackson, no longer standing rigid, had crouched slightly, and as the shot whistled over his head he saw his own .303 hit hard in the upper chest of the Dutchman, who was knocked off his feet and sprawled backwards on to the deck. Egerton, impeded by the case of gold on his wrist, ran to him, picked him up awkwardly, and propped him against the rail. He reached down to seize the Mauser. Jackson fired again – twice, the first shot staggering the black giant, who shot wildly; the second bringing him to his knees, where he slumped against the bulwarks.

Jackson now knew these men were representing the revolutionary Boers, military trained and dangerous. He was determined to deal with them accordingly. He guessed also that his stand against them would prompt the tougher sailors amongst the crew to fight back. *Otranto* was already making smoke and underway as the Boers opposite the tea table, who Jackson could see as he bolted quickly, had unslung their rifles and were pointing them at the passengers as each frantically pressed a round into their breech.

Two shotgun blasts rang out, then a third, and two of the burly men were blown back against the rail, one thrown right over to fall into the sea. A third fired, hitting Meyer, whose enthusiasm had brought him out into the sunlight. Blood spattered over white suits and dresses as the man catapulted on to the table and fell across it, taking crockery and all ornaments on the embroidered tablecloth on to the deck, to screams from the women.

Cornelia ignored him and fired her shotgun a second time, the pellets, in close formation at such short range, ripping into the Boer's stomach. With a scream, he disappeared through the open gate at the top of the stairwell down to the foredeck. Boers elsewhere ran to the rails in confusion. Several shots rang out, bullets smacking against the ironwork rails around Jackson, who fired and reloaded until his clip was empty. He replaced it quickly, then he again shot accurately, dropping two of the distant men. Immediately they began to crawl to the for'ard scuppers – the sea was now their only way to avoid capture.

On the terrace, Stanley Grace had seized one of the Lee Enfields and joined Jackson in picking off and harassing the Boers. Surprise had turned the tables and created a rout, but the Afrikaners could see all too clearly their biggest problem – escape, in the form of the cutter being snatched from them. Tied securely to *Otranto*, even as desperate crew aboard tried to cut the lines, the vessel was being dragged along with the steamship.

Jackson threw down his rifle and seized the chance. He shinned down the stair rails to the terrace, past cowering figures at the table, across to the gate and leapt the last metal rungs of the inclined ladder to the foredeck. Kimmen shouted to Egerton, who dragged himself to his feet and helped his master up to the rail. Kimmen cursing heavily, rolled over and fell into the sea, immediately trying to swim for the stern of the cutter and crying out for help. Egerton hesitated, then jumped. The black giant screamed as he felt the true weight of the gold. He plummeted into the sea leaving a great swirl of foam and although he fought desperately to tear the handcuff from his wrist, the gold's weight took him into the depths where he slowly drowned.

Skirting the open hold, reaching the derrick, Jackson pushed the dead Boer out of the seat, slammed the gears to neutral and released the brake. Helpless cries from the Boers swinging on the heavy load of guns and ammunition sounded out as some of the more brave jumped, despite the fact few of them could swim. The contraband followed fast – the derrick chain slackened, then with a grinding of links on runners as it played out, the load dropped. It hit the cutter at its centre, smashing open the deck, breaking through the hold, then tearing a hole in the keel's plating. Jackson engaged gears and slammed them into reverse. The davit arm actually bent before the chain snapped with a crack as the broken links whipped up and back across the deck. They whirled above Jackson's head and drew sparks from the davit before swinging free.

Jackson looked up to the flying bridge, where the Captain, no longer threatened, was directing armed sailors towards the remaining Afrikaners aboard, who, rather than face incarceration, leapt overboard. Other crew severed the lines of the striken cutter as another detail rolled the dead and wounded off the ship into the sea.

Jackson climbed back to the terrace deck, noting the crouching passengers who only now realised it was over. He stopped beside the tea table, seeing Meyer, groaning in pain, being lifted gently on to an improvised stretcher, supervised by his colleague Marsh. The ship's doctor would be put to good use if the wound was to be properly dressed; although it looked bad, it did not appear mortal. 'Afrikaners,' stated Jackson. 'Boers out from South Africa, at war with the British Army – an unpleasant bunch. Where's Kimmen?'

Cornelia, noticing for the first time the bloodstains on her dress, pointed with the muzzle of her shotgun – before it was politely taken from her by Stanley Grace – 'Swimming, I believe.'

Jackson stepped to the rail and saw the cutter, broken in two and sinking, surrounded by struggling men, some clinging to the flotsam, others treading water and waiting for the small dory hastily thrown into the sea. Already shark fins had appeared and were circling with wary curiosity.

'How awful,' murmured Cornelia.

'So are corpses in British uniforms,' Jackson replied grimly.

'Like the old days, eh, Lucifer,' winked Grace, exhilarated by the dangerous action.

'You do realise,' coughed Marsh, 'I shall have to report fully the jeopardy in which you put us all, Mr Jackson!'

'It's my ship,' was the growled reply.

'What "old days"?' asked Cornelia inquisitively.

'Well,' began Grace, 'I was a sergeant up the coast a ways from ol' Shanghai and young Hollis, as he was then, an' none too strict honest, helped us out of a spot o' bother.'

'With a few Chinese,' snapped Jackson, hoping to end the conversation.

'A few!' exclaimed Stanley Grace. 'Why, my boys counted more'n fifty! An' you was . . .' Jackson walked away, suddenly exhausted. He stood at the rail, looking towards the landfall which they would no longer explore. The Captain was already going about, *Otranto*'s wake forming a great crescent in the shimmering sea around the wreckage of the cutter. Zanzibar would soon be far behind them as they travelled northeast, back to their original course for the Red Sea – 'and all this for gold,' thought Jackson privately, 'lives at risk, men dead. What a waste,' he muttered to himself.

'What was that?' asked Cornelia as she came to his side, leaving Stanley Grace to regale a willing audience at the tea table, which the stewards were already trying to rectify, with his military exploits years before on the China coast when he had encountered Lucifer.

'You have a lot of grit,' Jackson smiled at the woman he at once respected and despised – loved.

'And you, Mr Jackson, are full of surprises.'

'Thank God we were lucky,' he grunted.

'Ask Mr Meyer,' said Cornelia softly. Jackson

413

nodded in agreement as the voice of Mr Marsh sounded loudly.

'Mr Jackson, I say! Miss Morgan!'

'What is it now!' snarled Jackson, turning around on Cornelia's arm . . . which is why with a flash and snap the photograph of the couple shows Jackson's sour expression captured for posterity, and reveals the woman on his arm looking tenderly up into his face to be more than a mere amoureuse; closely examined, the picture reveals her to be nearer a real lady falling, or perhaps already fallen, in love.

28

Evening sunlight had found its way into Silas Hayes'
cabin on *Vesper* as the ship languished in the heat of
the South Atlantic on the equator. The oval porthole
above the framed pictures on the wall seemed to pour
sunbeams between the Captain and his son and, having
discovered a vignette in a brass oval, danced on the
fading photogravure, illuminating years past and
refreshing the memories of Silas and Jamie.

Cornelia Morgan, on the arm of her new husband,
stared out breathlessly with shining eyes and a
generous smile for the world as 'Mr Hayes' concealed
joy beneath an expression of responsibility. The beard
and moustache made him look older but his eyes
conveyed more than he wished; on his arm was the
woman he loved. Jamie had found the picture hidden
in a drawer of Silas' cabin and insisted, to his father's
annoyance, it be put up. The boy often glanced at it,
polished it and straightened it when weather turned it
on the nail he himself had hammered into the panelling.

'Do you ever . . . miss her, Father?' he asked quietly.

Silas, eyes closed, spread on his bunk, merely
grunted. Outside, he could hear his men singing lazily
the shanty, 'Not for All the Tea in China', which
reminded him of old glories and adventures.

'Father, do you?'

Silas opened one eye. 'There's always something to
miss about anyone we've known, laddie. Your mother's
no exception.'

'But – ' began the boy.

Silas interrupted. 'She always had a mind of her
own, and I didn't want big city so-ci-et-y.'

'Why did you not stay together?'

Silas looked at his son's earnest expression and smiled kindly. 'When you were born, we loved each other, be sure of that, boy.'

'But I love you both still,' the boy stated with conviction, staring at the clear features in the framed vignette. His father saw the mother in his son's eyes and full lips, and for a moment there was regret in his heart. 'Do you think, sir, that we'll – ever – all – be together again?'

Silas sat up on his bunk and stared at his son, who was sitting on the steps up to the quarter deck. 'Life teaches, boy, as life takes away. Time makes history just by being there, but it never stays the same. You've all of your life ahead of you, so perhaps it's difficult to understand. But people change, too – sometimes grow apart. Most of us start out with good intentions which are not always easy to maintain. Your mother and I are no longer the couple you see in that picture.' Silas paused and spoke for himself softly. 'Perhaps we never really were. . . .'

'Do you still love her?' asked the boy.

Silas looked long at the vignette. Already the sunlight was slipping away, the contours of the picture lost in the gloom. The father turned to his son. 'I love *you*, laddie,' he replied quietly, with conviction.

The boy's eyes became anxious. 'Will *we* ever grow apart, Father?' he said.

Silas stood up, buttoning the loose shirt, feeling the heat as he moved across the cabin to kneel before his son. He took the boy gently by the shoulders. Twilight and first stars in a darkening sky framed the child's pleasant features, his tan and tousled hair emphasising his pale grey-blue eyes.

'You and I, boy?' smiled Silas Hayes. 'You and I will only ever grow old together.'

Jamie hugged his father, and in that moment Silas

416

felt the warm breeze on his face and silently thanked the God he had privately discovered.

'We're out of the doldrums, laddie,' he said, and as the boy's hair ruffled in the wind, knew for sure at last they were indeed.

Top sails unfurled, crew running, swarming aloft, hurricane lights lit, the gusting breeze lapping flags, cracking canvas, shouted orders, compass readings checked, stars found by professional eyes and foam at the bows of both *Vesper* and *Chantril*, and the clippers were off, briskly before a building south-easterly wind, into the night.

Several days later, both ships were still in sight of each other and only four days south of the Cape Verde Islands. The wind remained constant within several points and all canvas was up. On *Chantril*'s decks, the women's alarm at foam surging along the water-line and over the rails as Eli leaned his ship into the sea, hard pressing her on the wished-for wind in the magnificent weather, caused him to order out oil-bags, slung either side of the figurehead so it slicked the length of the clipper from bow to stern and into the wake. Crew forced from the fairleads by flying spray could then go back to work in safety as the passengers returned to the protection of the deck-houses to observe a speedy passage.

Lewis Ellory lost not a moment of the good weather, recording crew in the shrouds, on the yard and at more mundane tasks on deck as the clipper ploughed ahead.

On *Vesper* there were other problems.

'Water's got into the rice, sir!' shouted Hughie Sutherland above the noise of wind and sea.

'Damn!' exclaimed Silas, and the men, followed by Jamie and Polly, went below. In the hold several crewmen stood by the locks of a door obviously under strain from within. The rice having expanded with absorbed water was forcing itself out of the hold compartment. Silas knew he must release the pressure but was equally aware of the mess it would make. He saw expectation in his son's face.

'This was where you stowed yourself was it not boy?'

'Yes, sir!' grinned Jamie.

'Then you'd better stand back, laddie,' snapped *Vesper*'s captain, and he nodded to the crewmen, who released the locks. White rice exploded out of the door, falling about them all to roars of laughter from those who had seen the effect for the first time. They were smothered in what appeared to be, lit by the lamps in the gloom below decks – to Jamie at least, like

'Snow!'

Palm trees in a sea of white sand shimmered as if a mirage as the hazy silhouette of *Otranto*'s superstructure moved slowly, engines at half, cruising by curious Arabs on the banks at Suez, the beginning of the Gulf of Suez towards Lesseps' Great Egyptian Canal. With the noise of dull thunder, the steamship passed out of the blistering heat of the Red Sea on its way north to the Mediterranean.

Having rounded the Horn of Africa, Mr Meyer, who was making a good recovery, began to make dissertations on the various Arab dhows seen in passing, and with the expected sympathy for his gallant wound – his arm and shoulder stayed ostentatiously in a large sling – he kept the attention of the ladies and, even after days of his 'special study', continued to force courtesy from the gentlemen. All had tired of recounting their adventure at sea with the Boer pirates, thus 'the dhow' became *the* topic which Jackson assured himself would make them all experts by the time they had completed the one thousand, four hundred miles from Aden to Port Said.

The reward, of course, was that the dhows were a fact, frequently seen, and on calm days with pleasant winds blowing, made a pretty sight as they plied their mysterious trades throughout inconstant waters. Most of the first-class passengers saw them merely as daily cabaret, largely unaware of the dangerous worlds from which they came or the difficult business they were to sail in any lively weather.

By the time *Otranto* was through the Great Bitter Lake and into the final part of the canal, Mr Meyer's bandage was smaller, consideration for his obviously improved condition less, patience short and conviviality amongst them all – now far too long together, as regular arguments, stretched to the very borderlines of politeness, proved – became cursory exchanges without substances.

In cottons and silks beneath the awning, the passengers, much acquainted and now long accustomed to the tropics, enjoyed what little breeze there was as officers joined them for lunch to convey the latest information, avidly sought, of the ever shortening voyage home. Lunch was served on a memorable day for them all, as diaries later attested. Cornelia, as was often the case, led the conversation with a society woman's instinct, attempting where others failed even to try, to elicit interest in even trivia. When in doubt, she reverted to her own background, having dug into the very foundations of the others to find mostly silage and clay.

'My son is enjoying that most important of pleasant sufferings, as you know, in San Francisco, as I have mentioned before.' She paused for the acknowledgement, lazily given by all. 'Which is necessary in becoming a gentleman. The word is "grooming".'

Stanley Grace, hot, overdressed and irritated, having drunk too much, grinned before sipping wine and speaking out, 'An' 'ow do we detect a gentleman – "groomed"?'

'It results in an appearance, Mr Grace,' she replied

with some obvious distaste, 'an attitude – a behaviour, acknowledged by ladies.'

'Ah!' began Grace, 'but 'ow do we know 'oo's a lady, might I ask?'

Protestations from the men and some bored women at the table were stifled by Cornelia's hand waving for silence.

'I will answer!' she smiled patronisingly. 'A lady,' she emphasised, 'for those who need to be told,' she said pointedly, 'is a woman who may elicit from *any* man those qualities to which *he* must *aspire* – to *become* a gentleman.' Approval at the lunch table was instant. Murmurs from the women, some applause from the men. Jackson smiled as more barely chilled wine was poured into the cut-glass wine goblets.

'You married a sea captain,' he stated. 'Was Silas an exception?'

Cornelia wafted a fan, feeling a film of sweat form on her brow. She grimaced at the man for whom her feelings were not yet settled. 'Some men,' she said slowly, 'are incapable of finer behaviour and are therefore,' she paused, 'expendable – Mr Jackson.'

Jackson sipped the wine from a new bottle and nodded approval. 'Presumption always has its pitfalls,' he said.

Cornelia blushed. 'Presumption, Mr Jackson, is almost always a man's indication of obvious inadequacies.'

'And how does a woman illustrate her own inadequacies?' Jackson asked, finishing, 'By criticism of those she discoveres in others?'

'Are you suggesting I criticise on occasion without reason?'

'No madam, I am saying you criticise without reason regularly!'

Cornelia stood up immediately, her blush deepening.

The table was now completely stilled, most astonished at the exchange.

'Are you standing, madam, because I have spoken a fact, or invented a lie?' Jackson's voice had a laconic timbre.

'Because you are no gentleman, *Mr* Jackson,' she hissed.

'Then I must seek for *a lady* who is able to bring out those qualities you find I am so sadly lacking.' He smiled affably.

Cornelia suppressed a scream of frustration. She reached across the table, deliberately selecting an almost full glass of untouched red wine, seized the stem and threw it at Hollis Jackson, spattering his whites with vintage claret. She raised her head, spun on her heels and stormed off. Jackson licked his lips as eyes, averted from the scene for a moment, returned to him. He spoke to the table in appreciation of the fact that he was finally eliciting real emotion from this cultured pearl.

'Robust,' he stated, but only Stanley Grace laughed.

Otranto's horn sounded out loud and long, and all heads turned.

'Port Said!' exclaimed Marsh.

Jackson stood up, feeling a fresh wind in his face. He smiled. 'And the Mediterranean,' he murmured.

Bedraggled passengers emerged from the protecting shadows on the open deck of *Otranto*'s steerage section, where the many poor wretches who were travelling in an altogether different fashion from first-class POSH saw the thin line of distant blue water and smelt the ozone and brine on a breeze blown from a new sea. Some managed a cheer, others remained glum and uncomfortable after the tedious journey up the canal, but all agreed that they were now within striking distance, as they would now count the days, to home.

Elation for Hollis Jackson was short-lived. Joining other elegantly presented ladies and gentlemen pressed to the rail, through hats and parasols he could see not only the shabby port basking in the sun but an Admiralty cutter lazily holding position with minimum effort from a small engine chugging quietly. Jackson's eyes narrowed as the small vessel hooted. Marsh took a photograph, Meyer began to write furiously, but awkwardly, holding his pad against his bandages, arm propped on the gleaming brass rail. Stanley Grace saw the morse flashes and read them accurately.

''Allo, 'allo, what 'ave we got 'ere then? As the policeman said to the cat burglar. Cats, is it? Well, Lucifer, here's one out o' the bag all right!' He shook his head, bemused.

'What is it?' he asked. The reply came from Captain Tom Wallis, who had joined the group at the rail. Jackson felt the slow progress of *Otranto* slow even more. Distantly bells from the wheelhouse sounded and the regular dull thunder of her engines changed pitch.

'Tom?' Jackson questioned, looking into his captain's eyes, squinting to read more of the repeated message. Like the entertainer, he too shook his head. 'They want us impounded for a full search,' he said quietly.

'What!' exploded Jackson.

The Captain indicated the cutter now almost below at the lowered gangway. 'A British Marine officer, it looks like to me,' he murmured.

'I don't understand,' growled Jackson.

'Well, we'll soon find out,' muttered the Captain as the sprightly, well-built young man left his colleagues, jumped out on to the small platform, ran up the steps and was led to the terrace deck by a sailor. Salutes and a smile from the pleasant, tanned face were the prelude. The wire solved part of the mystery as the Captain read it and handed it to Jackson, coughing as he did so, anticipating his owner's reaction.

'Who the hell are you?' snapped Jackson.

'Lieutenant Robson, sir. British Marines, Suez station, sir. Currently Port Said based. I'm sorry, sir, but I've had my orders from Headquarters in Alexandria, direct from the officer in charge of investigation of shipping.'

'And who the hell is he?'

'Captain Lubbock, sir,' said the Lieutenant innocently.

Hollis Jackson stepped back a pace as if he had caught himself walking on a grave and read his own name inscribed on the tombstone. He stared at the young officer in disbelief, then said slowly and deliberately, enunciating each word, 'Does he have a brother out East?'

Lieutenant Robson frowned for a moment. 'I believe he does, sir.'

Jackson shook his head. 'God damn him then,' he growled, turned on his heel and strode away.

The Captain coughed and led the young officer to one side, away from the curious group.

'We have an incident to report to the British authorities here. I have written it up in full. Two of my men died; we buried them at sea. Perhaps if you would come to my cabin we can discuss details.'

'Yes, sir,' replied the Marine officer courteously.

The two men left the group, who were largely unaware of what was taking place. As they walked to the stairway leading up to the flying bridge, they fell into conversation.

'Always wanted to go to Shanghai,' said Robson, 'sounds so exotic.' He smiled at the older seaman. 'I didn't know they made guns there, though.'

'I didn't know we were carrying them,' muttered Tom Wallis.

'Were?' repeated the Lieutenant.

'Yes,' sighed Captain Wallis. 'I'll tell you about it over a sherry.'

'For soup at sea,' began Eli Lubbock, 'three things are essential as most of you have, or will discover.' He smiled and nodded to the Chinese steward, who began to serve the first course of dinner aboard *Chantril*, half-way between the Cape Verde Islands and the Azores in a breaking sea but before a steady blow. The passengers in the dining saloon watched as their soup dishes were filled with practised skill, while the ship rolled then pitched. Each of them grabbed a dish full of ladled soup and attempted to add to it from other dishes containing hot vegetables and sliced bread.

Prayers was spoken by Emily and the business of eating began in earnest.

'Three things,' Eli repeated, catching the decanter almost as an afterthought as it appeared to be about to disappear off the table. Hurricane lamps swung above the heads of the diners, as did circular glass-holders where water and wine could be deposited in comparative safety. 'A utensil,' stated Eli and dipped his spoon as the angle of his soup changed alarmingly. 'And bread,' he went on, holding and lifting the plate slightly at one edge between two fingers, the bread secure beneath his thumb. He sipped expertly. Adèle watched her hot broth pour to starboard from the dish she had seized, putting the hot liquid over her hand and on to the table. In a temper, she reached back to the open cupboard behind her, where mugs swung on hooks. She took one and held it for the steward to pour again from the ladle. Smiling at Eli's quizzical expression, she sipped from the filled mug – twice, then a wave hit *Chantril*'s bow and a shudder went through the ship. Soup splashed into Adèle's face. She swore loudly, which courteously was ignored by all at the table. 'And a napkin,' Eli finished. 'Mugs have drawbacks.' He offered his own napkin and, amused, watched the young woman wipe her face.

Impatiently, she glared at him. 'Why must we have soup?'

Eli smiled and was about to speak when Lewis Ellory suddenly leaned to one side and vomited on to the floor.

'Like the sawdust,' said Captain Lubbock, 'it is necessary. Soup warms the body – for we are going further north each day into bitter cold. A sharp contrast to what we have experienced to date, I assure you.'

The steward had begun to mop up as Ellory attempted apologies, whilst Emily wiped his grey face with almost motherly concern.

Awan gazed on, trying to ignore her son Cha'ze, who hovered at the doorway awaiting instructions to remove the soup tureen.

'And you, Miss Emily,' said Eli, covering the awkward moment with a voice of mock admonishment, 'must eat for two until we get in, or Silas will have my hide as well as yours. . . .'

The meal continued with a cut of chicken, newly dispatched, appetising and nutritious to all but Mr Ellory, who insisted on remaining – but only for the coffee, which Cha'ze finally brought in from the spray-filled walk in the night, announcing with a wide grin that the cook had declared the galley was now closed.

Above on the quarter deck a shout brought Eli to his feet. He excused himself and went up. Cold and dark and bleak, the poop was already the sharp contrast Eli had described. Warm weather was over for all aboard *Chantril*. Hurricane lamps were masked by spray as Eli squinted against the chill water, buttoning his oilskins, examining the sail plan in his mind as Billy Williams told him what was up, feeling the wind, seeking instinct for orders to issue, checking the compass and following his mate's pointing finger to where, distantly, amber lights appeared and disappeared to port, diffused by the dark rising waves, the curling foam and lacy spindrift.

'They'll be the Portugee whalers out from the Azores,' he grunted, hearing watch bells ring the length of his plunging clipper. It was his turn to relieve his mate for hours on end, and at this hour, when he would have enjoyed at least a half hour of his own with a pipe, he felt it almost an imposition.

'They've a hard life in those small boats, Billy,' he said, taking the wheel.

'And we haven't?' said his exhausted mate, accepting hot grog from the small Chinese boy, Cha'ze, who – still grinning – ran off, enjoying every moment of his great adventure.

Both men stared into the darkness, seeing the long dorys, out to hunt whale, rise and crash into the waves, lost in the wind-whipped foam, each one containing tough little fishermen wrapped against the elements. Rain on the gusting blow finally obscured even their lights as the clippers' moaning rigging became background for Eli Lubbock's private, isolated thoughts.

'So the sea is all romance, is it?' he murmured and shook rain from his face. 'December,' he growled softly.

Emily, despite her condition – 'fragile' as Adèle had declared privately several times – had escorted Mr Ellory from the dining table and back to his cabin, then helped him lie flat on his bunk. Adèle arrived, and both women tucked in the hapless young cameraman, then they repaired to Emily's small room space, where she too lay heavily on her bunk and conceded the pain and sickness as Adèle leant over her, murmuring pleasantries.

'Oh, Silas,' whispered Emily, and her shed tears confirmed not only the celestial, everlasting love of poets but the immediate need for strong arms around her body, tender words whispered into her ear, gentle caresses and soft kisses upon her wet cheeks. She shut her eyes tight as *Chantril* rose up, only to crash heavily into the night sea, sending more shudders through the ship. Amelia bit her lips against the stabbing pains, feeling bile in her throat but conjuring a picture in her imagination of her man . . . her captain, smiling and telling her that no matter what, not to fear, all would be well, all would be. . . . Only when Emily slumbered did Adèle turn down the lamp's wick and secure the door's latch, leaving her friend loosely strapped into her bunk, to the ravaging nightmares of her fertile imagination.

Silas Hayes' pipe glowed as he puffed it in cupped hands, tobacco tight packed, holding it inverted against the rain and wind. Lying back in his canvas chair on the poop deck of *Vesper* he glanced at his mate, Hughie Sutherland, trimming the wheel, expertly holding course to the compass bearing.

'How far ahead is he?'

'Two leagues, I'd say,' replied Hughie. 'Maybe less. He's got Portugee whalers to starboard and more canvas up than us.'

Glowing lamps rose and fell in the lifting sea rolling in cross-waves showing to Silas' sharp eyes the position of the small dorys.

'We'll have him soon,' Silas murmured, sucking on his pipe. 'Just a question of when. . . .'

Jamie arrived on deck with bread, cheese and flip-top glass bottles of beer for his father and the Mate. 'A puff more wind,' continued Silas, 'and he'll lose his sky sails – even to' gallants.' He took a beer and prised off the top; upending it, he swallowed greedily and wiped his mouth. 'I know our Eli well enough,' he said, and ruffled his son's wet hair.

'Look!' exclaimed the boy. To port in the distance,

lights showed, not amber and bobbing amidst rolling waves but regular in lines, as if a floating building. It was, as Silas immediately identified, an ocean liner. For several minutes the two men and boy watched the distant steamship, occasionally lost in flurries of rain but eventually seen falling behind the clipper. Jamie grinned proudly and the two men exchanged a look, equally pleased. Spray cascaded over the wheel, causing Hughie to seize the brass handles and steady *Vesper* as she bucked against a rogue wave. He consulted the compass again. Silas stood up and joined him as the boy clung to the binnacle.

'We've held to a north-west course since the Cape Verde Islands. If we turn due north and are off the Azores in a day or so – we'll make our run in from there, east-north-east into the Channel.'

'And winter sir,' Hughie reminded him. A shout from the for'ard watch sounded out and Hughie spun the wheel, hearing the warning. Silas tapped his son's shoulder and pointed where huge whales were breaching, blowing fountains of water from the centre of swirling foam. Jamie, in awe, saw the white water picked out by the moon showing between scudding clouds.

'They're so big!' he exclaimed. 'Could they sink us, Father?'

'They've their own lives to lead, laddie,' replied Silas. 'They don't bother none about ships. They talk to each other.'

Jamie looked up at his father in wonder. 'Talk?' he whispered.

Silas nodded. 'And if we could understand them, they might tell us where we could find Hollis Jackson.' He winked at Hughie Sutherland. Jamie stared out into the darkness, seeing again fountains of water erupting from the surfaced whales, caught in the moonlight for a moment, then cold spray, sea salt and rain lashed across the deck, blinding him so that he shivered and winced.

Dessert was served in *Otranto*'s warm dining saloon at the Captain's table soon after nine o'clock at the end of the third week of the last month of the nineteenth century.

Outside, the cold Mediterranean tossed and churned angrily in the night, as if affronted that passengers aboard an ocean liner could be so oblivious of a small but all the same mighty sea. The steamship, tried, tested and now hardened to weather and ocean, cruised forward confidently on a course set to pass through the ancient Pillars of Hercules on the Straits of Gibraltar.

Alexandria had been tiresome for some, a relief to be ashore again for others; in all, the Captain's full report of the Dutch arms incident satisfied suspicious officials.

Once at sea and way behind schedule, Jackson had ordered the Captain to force the engines to make up time. His daily preoccupation had now become the race and the bet he had made with Hayes and Lubbock. He became unpredictable as his moods fluctuated between pleasant consideration and impatient aggression. His relationship with Cornelia suffered, as did his dealings with his captain and, indeed, anyone who crossed his path. He was morose, it seemed to those with whom he did converse, and brooding upon the past, which was unusual for a man who had for so long been preoccupied with the future – as Cornelia had remarked on several occasions.

She was determined not to allow him to upset either herself or those around her, especially at meal times. As a result, Jackson became more isolated from the group, so she became increasingly more brittle and acid.

429

Champagne was poured by the sommelier and the diners sipped it with appreciation of its quality.

'Hollis, really,' Cornelia began, 'the champagne is not sufficiently chilled.'

'Neither was Egypt, madam!' he snapped, and gestured to the steward to bring more ice and another bottle.

Marsh coughed, adjusted his bow tie and made a big thing of it, deliberately looking out of one of the long windows at lights sparkling far up into the night.

'Gibraltar, isn't it?' he said, knowing it was. No one replied.

'So now we must turn north, I believe, and, ahem, bucket our way across the Bay of Biscay until we're directly off Brittany, then....' Meyer wafted an arm in the direction of his friend Marsh, but grimaced at the pain, having only just taken off his bandage.

'Home,' stated Marsh simply.

'The weather,' said the Captain, 'will dictate if we bucket, as you put it, Mr Meyer, not this ship.' Meyer nodded, referring to the deep thunder from below. Ice and champagne arrived, creating a diversion from the atmosphere building up. Ostentatiously, Jackson took the bottle from the sommelier and offered it to Cornelia, who felt the obvious cold moisture on the glass.

'Does this meet with your approval, madam?'

'*It*,' she said pointedly, 'does.'

'Ne'er you mind, ma'am,' grinned Stanley Grace, the only one of the group in a maroon smoking jacket, 'you'll be able to stick yer bottles in the snow when we get back to ole Blighty!'

'You, Mr Grace, may be familiar with privation. I am not. I am truly astonished that in these modern times one has to put up with so much aboard a passenger liner.

'Baths with insufficient hot water,' she continued, 'beds that feel as solid as rock, no matter how many mattresses one may use. Bland food, and *warm* wine.' She put down her glass and surveyed the table. 'After ten weeks at sea and more than four in various filthy ports along the way, I shall be relieved to return to a civilised life, in London, at Claridges.'

Jackson leaned forward, fixing Cornelia Morgan with an unsettling stare.

'Claridges?' he asked, but it was more statement.

'Then, madam, I shall be pleased to escort you in a carriage and pair from the dockside, through the East End, up west to your Mayfair hotel. For the greater part of the journey, you will be surrounded by people less fortunate than yourself.'

'Really, Mr Jackson!' Her expression was icy. 'I have other things to consider than the lives of those with whom I am not acquainted.' She sipped the champagne again, now with obvious distaste.

'You are wrong as you are acquainted with me,' Jackson continued. 'En route up west I will show you where I was born.'

'How interesting,' said Marsh, pausing in his writing.

'It wasn't,' said Jackson gruffly, remembering.

'Oh, come on, me ole' China,' said Stanley Grace genially. 'Limehouse? You wouldn't 'ave missed it for the world – would you?'

Jackson looked him in the eye, aware he knew the truth. 'I almost missed the world because of Limehouse,' he said quietly, 'and so did you.'

'Nah look 'ere, Lucifer,' began Grace, but Cornelia, sensing the growing danger in the atmosphere, interrupted.

'None of us selects the place from which we came, that is influenced only by our heritage. Some of us who are more fortunate are far beyond the daily preoccupations of those poor wretches living in squalor.'

Jackson's eyes seemed to tear the imperious veneer

from Cornelia as he indicated the luxuriously appointed dining saloon. 'This is only one of numerous ships that belong to me. You have travelled almost half the world in *Otranto* and she is *mine*.' He finished vehemently. 'Do you know what that means to me?' Jackson's emotion held the table silent.

'I – can imagine it . . . understand – of course . . .' faltered Cornelia.

'How dare you!' he exclaimed. 'When I was a boy I only ever dreamed of a substantial meal – what you see around you here would have been, to that child, an impossible lie! I say that because *that* boy could not *even imagine* all this.' He gestured again. 'It is *my* thrill *I* offer to share, which you might *understand* after seeing the place from which I come.' His last words, filled with so much recalled, came out as if laced with poison. He stood up, buttoned his coat, nodded goodbyes and left the gathering frozen; only Marsh scribbled on furiously. Stanley Grace offered Cornelia more champagne, but she shook her head, eyes filled with tears.

Hollis Jackson stepped into the kitchen to see bustling chefs and assistants not only clearing up but preparing long tables of food, groaning platters laden with everything possible to celebrate the season – hams, chickens, pies, turkeys. . . . The head chef approached and bowed slightly to the owner, gazing in some wonder at the vast array.

'For the festivities,' he said, by way of explanation.

Jackson merely nodded, then began to smile. Suddenly he burst into laughter and, roaring, he slapped the chef about the shoulder and began to rap out instructions. The man was left astonished as the owner turned on his heels and went back into the dining room.

'It's almost Christmas,' Hollis Jackson announced, to the consternation of the group lingering at the Captain's table.

'Is that supposed to be a surprise, Hollis?' asked Cornelia, attempting to hide her tears.

'For you – yes,' he replied. 'Come with me.'

'Where?' she asked.

He held out a hand. 'Come,' he said more kindly, and nodded to Stanley Grace. The three of them, the two men escorting the woman, strode from the dining room together, leaving a very curious audience.

Descending almost into the bowels of the ship was an unpleasant experience, even for Stanley Grace, who had grown accustomed to the comfort of the upper decks. For Cornelia it was another world, to Hollis Jackson it was merely a familiar reminder of other times. Second-class seamen, less well presented than those from above decks, led the way to a doorway which earmarked the gateway to the alternative form of ocean travel. They threw bolts and cantilevered an arm to reveal the great hold where, dimly illuminated by dull inset lights and hurricane lamps swinging with the sea swell, huddled figures crowded about an accordion player, voices raised in a carol.

> Good King Wenceslas looked out,
> On the feast of Stephen . . .
> Brightly shone the moon that night,
> Though the frost was cruel.
> When a poor man came in sight,
> Gath'ring winter fuel . . .

The chorus faded away as faces turned towards the arrivals silhouetted in the strong light from the corridor behind them. The three, Jackson, Cornelia and Stanley Grace, took the short flight of stairs to the greasy deck. The smell caused them all an intake of breath as they approached the first almost bare table, on it bare plates, wiped clean of their contents. The massed faces stared about and mouths whispered but there was only hesitation and no singing. The owner of *Otranto* looked into the eyes of Cornelia Morgan and indicated the tables.

'A substantial meal,' he murmured.

Cornelia, unable to control herself seeing so many haunted and gaunt expressions gazing at her, slowly broke into tears of compassion. 'I didn't know,' she began, but then the carol started up again and her words, for the first time – certainly at sea – were drowned.

Devouring huge morsels torn from laden platters spread over many of the tables in steerage, hungry passengers washed down the food with generous gulps of wine, whilst throughout the hold candles added dimly to the gloom, and interspersed laughter sustained the carol singing led by Stanley Grace. Cornelia and the owner of *Otranto* were helping waiters serve food and drink to scolded children, grateful mothers, proud fathers and bemused riff-raff, who, although greedily consuming the generous fare, retained a certain measure of suspicion that it might have to be paid for by some manner or means they would not enjoy.

''Ere, guvnor,' said one of them, 'Wa's all this for?'

'Let me say,' shouted Jackson in reply, the noise of the party becoming good-humouredly raucous, 'it's a long time since I was where you are now – and I used to dream. . . .'

'You was 'ere?' exclaimed another of the shabby group, a soldier with dull buttons and a dirty tunic. ''Ow did you get all this, then?'

'I sold matches,' Jackson said simply, and the immediate audience roared with laughter of disbelief.

'Get on wiv ya!' exclaimed one of the riff-raff. 'There ain't that many matches in the world!'

'You may 'ave started wiv a tray,' interrupted the soldier, swallowing with a grin. 'But you 'as to 'ave done other things – 'owd it come about?'

Jackson raised a glass and winked. 'That, my friend, is a very long story. . . .'

'Compliments of the season, Hollis,' said Cornelia in his ear.

Jackson surveyed the crowded hold and turned to her. They chinked glasses.

'Claridges,' he said, and for just that moment, two worlds met and she understood the fullness in his heart.

29

Watch bells caused Eli to stir in the Captain's cabin of *Chantril*. He awoke feeling the confident movement of his ship, then rolled from his bunk. Although it was already light outside, he turned up the wick of the lamp swinging over his charts, checked his pocket watch and examined the new course he had plotted. Calculating from notes placed beside a mug of steaming tea, he re-estimated time and position, taking a rule and pencil to trace progress logged, and potential for the day. Concentration and addition of figures shut off his mind even to the gentle knock at the door.

Adèle entered and put down hot bread and confiture. Eli Lubbock ignored her until she began to fidget with protractor and set square.

'Well?' he asked.

'Merry Christmas,' she said.

He looked at her and grunted. 'Is it?' he mumbled, and continued with his figures.

'Emily,' she began, 'is . . . not well . . . I believe – '

Eli Lubbock finished his calculations, made the sum, drew the line, smiled and slammed down his pencil.

'Billy!' he roared. Taking his tea, he gulped it down, plunged bread into the confiture and began chewing, donning his coat and buttoning up against the cold he knew he would feel up top.

'Eli, please,' Adèle began again.

'You haven't washed,' he said, picking his teeth.

Affronted, the young woman glared at him. 'There's only salt water for – '

'Then use it,' he cut in. 'Fresh is precious.'

Billy Williams put his head through the door; tired, wet and cold, he still managed a smile.

'Wind's backing, sir.'

'We're turning for the Channel,' snapped Eli. 'All hands.'

'But, sir,' blurted the Mate.

'Aloft, Mr Williams!' ordered Eli. 'That is a command! I'll take the wheel!'

'Aye, aye, sir,' Billy responded reluctantly. The two men stepped up, leaving Adèle angry and frustrated with an empty mug in her hands. Alone, she smelt herself and, realising Eli was right, smashed the mug on the floor of the cabin in a temper.

The first thing *Chantril*'s captain saw astern was *Vesper* with filled canvas closing fast. He took the wheel, listening to the two crew at the knot line singing out until speed was declared and the chip log reeled in.

'Fifteen knots, sir,' said Billy, jubilant. 'Present course due north.'

Eli checked the compass, musing to himself.

'Sir,' said Billy, 'on the turn we'll have the wind directly behind us – we must reef some canvas or – '

'East-north-east, mister!' interposed Eli, 'and *all* sail!'

Billy nodded, dubious, but accepting orders as Eli began to spin the wheel, slowly at first. The crew ran to halyards, braces, the foot-ropes to climb the shrouds, told that even reefed canvas was to be unfurled and clewed in. *Chantril* turned into cresting waves as Eli spun the wheel, now hard over.

'We'll have lost him by midday,' grinned Eli, glancing behind at *Vesper* and, as *Chantril*'s sails grew taut, straining at the yards, it seemed certain he was right. She surged forward, striking hard into the running sea, and as minutes went by, *Vesper* began to fall away. An hour passed and the elements appeared to favour *Chantril*, her captain's judgement and crew's competence. Ever the gambler, Eli Lubbock had decided on this long run in to the Downs to throw for victory – *if* they had successfully put Hollis Jackson's *Otranto* behind them through calculated delays. He forever scoured the horizon, seeing only unfamiliar ocean vessels bound for unknown destinations, and became agitated, wanting, willing, a sighting of Jackson's *Otranto*, to *know* he could win. Hoping, as he had often said, was only 'wishing'. She could be miles ahead, already docked, or, with luck for the two clippers, far behind.

Vesper was almost lost over the distant horizon astern when the first sail ripped and was torn to shreds on the wind, which then sought a second canvas – and found it. With the main royal fluttering, royal stuns shredded and the sky sail went. This left pressure on the main to' gallant, and with strained braces the top mast slipped off its setting and sagged awkwardly.

Eli Lubbock exploded with anger and, ignoring Billy's protestations about 'only bad luck', he stripped off his coat, threw the revolver at his waistband to Billy – who caught it one-handed, as he fought to readjust the wheel – and began to run. In shirt and waistcoat, Eli Lubbock jumped for the rat-lines to go up to the main shrouds and beyond the main cap to the cross-trees above. Seeing several of his crew ahead of him moving slowly, he bellowed for them to make way as, hand over hand, he ascended quickly.

Spinning around the dead-eyes Eli looked up to the exposed hell of the top mast and began to climb again, now higher than he had been for years, feeling the strength of wind behind him, he clung on and examined the damage. Swearing above the roar of wind, he decided to make the best of it and indicated to several crew that:

'It'll hold! Metal braces! Bring them from below – it ain't so bad . . . Tell Mr Williams!'

'Aye aye, sir,' replied the men, and descended gingerly as Eli continued to check the straining hemp braces and wire stays. The view was undeniably magnificent, he admitted to himself, riding out the waves like an old hand, his only thought being for the safety of his ship and her continuing forward passage.

Vesper's fast approach astern came at first as a shock, when he turned to see the billowing clipper close. He swore again, knowing his falling speed, as other sails were reefed to allow repair, would lose him the advantage. He could already see the plunging figurehead even though he could not see his own helm as the filled sails obscured a clear sight-line. For a moment, so far aloft, after so much time, he felt not vertigo or fear but apprehension – of what he could not determine, and so discounted instinct, which had always stood him in good stead.

The two Chinamen appearing from below were initially a surprise to him. They were not immediately recognisable, but with a sudden chill in his blood, Eli did realise he knew the cloth bands they had bound about their heads and, feeling welling fear, he understood the power and patience of men such as these. 'After so long at sea,' he thought, 'it is impossible.' But it was not. The two ascending crewmen with Malay kris' – serpent knives – in their mouths were not out to aid and repair. They were approaching, in their Triad headscarves, with the worst intentions, as ordered by their master so far away – Kin Sang.

Eli grasped at his waistband for his revolver, always there but now on this one occasion with his mate at the helm.

'Jesus Christ!' he hissed, but there was no answer to the plea. Heaven merely smiled and waited – as it does – always.

Aboard *Vesper*, Jamie's curiosity was prodigious. That

was accepted, fostered, indulged and affectionately known by many different words, depending upon which crew member discussed 'the Captain's nipper'. On the quarter deck with a telescope, as *Vesper* closed on *Chantril*, he was hawk-eyed relaying to his father, who lay in a canvas chair, smoking, each last yard which passed before they were alongside in their bid to better the now stricken clipper.

'Eli's above the main cap!' shouted Jamie excitedly.

'The top mast's off its heel,' said Hughie Sutherland, pointing.

Silas smiled to himself and puffed away at the tobacco. 'We have him,' he murmured.

'He has two crew with him,' went on Jamie. 'Chinese.'

Silas grunted but frowned a moment, knowing Billy would have sent up some of the old hands, all of whom he knew. He glanced over his shoulder. 'Chinese?' he asked.

'Yes,' exclaimed Jamie. 'And, Father! They have knives!'

Silas was on his feet immediately. He snatched the telescope and saw for himself. 'God Almighty,' he growled. 'Triads. Get me a Winchester, Jamie – fast.'

'Yes, sir.' The boy went quickly, eyes wide.

'Hard over, Mr Mate,' snapped Silas. 'They're Triads – up after him and out for revenge.'

'Where's the others?!'

'They're all below and can't see him, Hughie, for his damn canvas!'

Already aboard *Vesper*, passengers and some crew were lining the rail and waving at *Chantril*, as the two vessels bent to the wind, now almost parallel, less than one hundred yards apart. Jamie leapt up on to the poop, thrusting a rifle at his father, who took it, loaded the breech and, locking the .44 to his shoulder, aimed high into the shrouds of *Chantril*. The range and accuracy of 'the yellow boy' in Silas Hayes' hands was exceptional. He knew it well and had always been a fine shot, but between two moving ships, with his friend already almost a target himself as the two Triads reached the cross-trees . . . He squinted, knowing there would be only seconds as *Vesper*'s poop ran beside *Chantril*'s main mast where, high above the billowed canvas, unknown to all aboard, their captain was about to fight desperately against men sworn to kill him.

'Come on,' growled Silas as yard by yard *Vesper* slid past *Chantril* to cheers carried on the wind from both ships' passengers, oblivious of the drama in the upper shrouds.

'We're too close, sir. It ain't safe,' Hughie Sutherland began apprehensively.

'Hold it steady, Mr Sutherland,' commanded Silas, 'and sheer off when *I* say.' He'd lost a clear sight of Eli, canvas obscuring the men, but his confidence remained in the cold wood and metal against his cheek. Only seconds more. . . . 'Now, Mr Mate!' he bellowed, and Hughie began spinning the great wheel as Jamie's mouth fell open from both excitement and fear.

The first Triad lunged at Eli through the open cross-trees, causing him to step back against the mast-cap, his boot sliced clean across. He knew the deadly Malay kris was designed and honed to decapitate with a sweep of the arm, and in no way underestimated the skills of these men. Sunlight burst through from clouds and for a moment Eli was blinded. The second man was hauling himself up against the braces. Eli kicked out. The man moved instantly, seized the kris in his hand and grinned at Eli, seeing his companion pull up on to the cross-trees. The ship lurched, causing all three men to cling on tight.

'They'll know!' Eli pointed below, shouting against the wind at the men. 'Don't be fools!'

'Mr Lubbock, your body will be in the sea – what will they know? The facts will be our secret.'

'We have waited, Captain,' said the other man, and shifted closer – within striking range. 'Now is the time. You are cursed – and now you are dead!' He swung his arm in a scything movement; Eli had no option but to step back. He slipped off the edge of the cross-trees and grabbed for a stay as the man lunged at him. Eli kicked hard, connecting solidly, causing the Triad to grimace with pain. Like a two-pronged fork, the cross-trees extended from the cap, holding the to' gallant royal and sky sail backstays, which Eli edged out to until there was nowhere to go.

The first man, grasping the mizzen royal stay, stared in hate at Eli for a moment, then stepped from the fairlead plank and edged out to follow his victim. Eli glanced below to see the stern of *Vesper* across a short stretch of water, churning a wake as she sheered off, her voluminous sails almost a part of his own ship. He had time only to identify faces on her quarter deck, peering up, then *Chantril* plunged again into cresting waves and he lost his footing, clinging desperately to the two backstays, legs flailing, boots scraping against the oiled wire leading one hundred feet down to the deck.

The second Triad raised his arm to throw the kris into Eli's back, and Eli knew then that he was finished; wild-eyed, he was about to plead with the man when an astonishing thing happened; to Eli it was a miracle. Blood exploded from the man's chest and he was thrown forward across the stay into the rat-lines, where he crumpled and slipped away from the cross-trees, plunging below.

The Triad now almost on Eli turned in shock to see his companion's fate, giving Eli a chance to pull up hard. Using all his might he managed to get one foot back on to the cross-trees and looked up at a glinting kris rushing towards him. With a cry he thrust out an arm and felt immediately the pain as the honed metal slashed through the shirt, slicing into his forearm. Blood spattered all over him, which he ignored, as in amazement he saw the Triad's face disappear in a welter of bone and tissue. The man tumbled away.

Now Eli guessed what had happened and craned his neck. The bullet from Silas' rifle had entered the back of the Triad's head, blowing his face apart. He saw his friend on the stern of his ship as it moved away. Hughie was still spinning the wheel, Jamie was waving wildly. Eli grinned and waved his thanks, grimacing at the pain he could now feel acutely in his forearm. Silas raised the rifle and fired one shot into the air, the wind whipping away the smoke from the barrel. Eli shook his head, disbelieving for a moment his good fortune, then faced the more immediate task of descending safely to the deck.

Helped from the rat-lines by horrified crew, he made quite a sight. His white shirt and brown waistcoat, face and arm, bloodied and stained with mucous and tissue. He rapped out orders for braces to be set above, then retired to his cabin to clean up – whilst the broken body of one of the Triads who had not fallen into the sea was dragged from the roof of the aft deck-house. Hughie, leaving the wheel to the noon watch, was dumbfounded, until Eli began to explain while Adèle washed his wound and bound it tightly. She pointed to the bowl of bloody water. 'The water is fresh,' she stated wickedly.

Chantril's captain drew the young woman to him and kissed her tenderly.

'Merry Christmas,' he whispered.

Snow flurries danced with the foam off dark waves in the fading light of late afternoon, under a slate sky lowering over *Vesper* as she ploughed into the seas

443

surrounding the Western Isles. Silas, hunched at the wheel, shivered, watching as the chip log was pulled, proving they were maintaining a steady speed before a prevailing south-westerly.

Hughie continually scanned the horizon's three hundred and sixty degrees with the telescope. Jamie, huddled beside Polly, searched the sea with a smaller telescope, knowing it was a nervous time for his father.

Silas had told his son of the scheme he and Eli had concocted in an attempt to delay Hollis Jackson's steamship, but they had no way of knowing if it had worked. If it had, and the gods favoured them, then it was just possible, if they were not already beaten, that they could expect a sighting of *Otranto* soon. Silas had calculated the delays at maximum and minimum, and concluded that any time from the Western Isles would be when they might best their competition – even *Chantril*, 'if old Eli can keep up', Silas had said, to roars of laughter from Hughie and Jamie. But the mood on board was more nervous than humorous.

'Several westbound ships, sir,' murmured Hughie for the log book. 'We've outrun everything plying east-north-east.' He slid the telescope closed, replaced it in the binnacle and took the wheel to allow Silas a stretch and to light his pipe.

Inverting the packed tobacco, Silas crouched and lit a match in cupped hands, bent against the wind and puffed expertly until a heathy glow appeared in the bowl. He stood and glanced at the compass, now illuminated by hurricane lamps. A momentary showing of the setting sun on the horizon flooded the sails above with orange light and Silas pointed out to his son the will-o'-the-wisps darting about, snow and spray combined, giving rise to the myths and legends of days gone by. Tasting salt, Silas glanced over his shoulder to see the sun sink beneath a troubled sea. Puffing his pipe he nodded to Hughie Sutherland.

'We've the wind behind us now but we'll double clew the to' gallants before we hit the Channel, south of the Western Isles once they're sighted. If we encounter an easterly blowing out of France, we've lost our royals and sky sails – straight off.'

'I'll see to it, sir.'

'Leave the wheel to the watch, Hughie,' said Silas. 'You've been fourteen hours up top. Come below and have some grog after our passengers have been fed.'

'Aye, sir.' The Mate grinned at the very thought.

Silas watched Jamie playing with the terrier. 'It wasn't much of a Yuletide for you, was it, laddie?'

Jamie smiled broadly. 'It was the best, Father.'

Silas chucked the boy's chin. 'Are you stayin' above?'

'I want to find one of the ships,' replied Jamie. Polly whined agreement.

'Have a care then, laddie,' Silas warned, and went below.

The meal over, with an increasing roll, a building sea and a bucking ship, most of the passengers retired early. James Collins lingered to be pleasant and drink the Captain's port, but left soon after certain opinions he had aired were curtly dismissed by Silas Hayes, who immediately turned down the lamps and closed the doors. Settling against the wall, he sprawled in a corner chair, listened to the moaning wind outside and watched the swinging glass holder, with several candles guttering, throw strange shadows around the room. Jamie and Polly had retreated to the saloon, smelling food and seeking warmth, and they too sprawled, both dozing beside a glowing fire in a contained grate. Silas yawned, checking his pocket watch as Hughie sipped more port.

'Dog watch for me,' he said.

'Then you'll be the first to sight the Lizard,' Hughie pointed out.

'Aye,' Silas agreed. 'We'll tack due east off that shore. Them wreckers would like us to go down on the Cornish cliffs as you well know. There's been enough in the past, and no doubt more to come, but it ain't going to be us.' Silas puffed on his pipe. 'Remember *Flying Spur?*'

Hughie grunted. 'She went in on the Martin Baz Rocks in the eighties . . . an' not the only one. So many 'ave gone, Silas, I wonder 'ow *we've* lasted.'

Silas realised his pipe was out and lit up again as Jamie woke and slipped out of the cabin, followed by Polly. Hughie poured more port, the decanter sliding across the table back to Silas Hayes, and they reminisced about the relative merits of the great ships they had sailed.

Hughie grinned. 'The two most beautiful sights in the world are a woman in love and a ship under sail. If you treat 'em hard they'll serve you well – if you treat 'em with ease – they'll send you to Hell. . . . How does it finish?'

Silas puffed on his tobacco, hearing watch bells rung above. He was about to speak when the door burst open.

'*Chantril!*' shouted Jamie. 'Half a league astern.'

Silas slammed his fist and was on his feet immediately. 'Damn you, Eli Lubbock – how the devil . . . ? Now we've a race, Hughie!' He took his coat and began buttoning it tight. The Mate, slower, also stood up.

'An',' he started, 'an' . . . ? How did it end, sir?'

Silas knocked out tobacco from his pipe, which he put in his pocket, and almost spat out the words.

> An' if your fate's the gates of Hell,
> Leave the woman and take the sail!

Hughie smiled, remembering, as Silas stepped up to

take his turn at the dog watch from midnight to the early hours.

Light and shadow leaping about the woman's face seemed to gouge at her features, distorting her beauty into ugliness, which complemented the agony she so obviously showed when the hurricane lamp was held steady above her bed.

Awan, in tears of compassion, began again to wipe her mistress's forehead, murmuring in Chinese. Again *Chantril* plunged heavily, and the jolt as her bow fell into a trough to surge streaming from the immediately following wave, caused the whole ship to shudder.

Billy Williams standing respectfully with his hat off, looked across at Emily's tense face, her eyes staring back at him, full of accusation. He coughed and stepped out of the compartment, walking to the first stairway up to the main deck. Spray washed over the bulwarks but, secure in his oilskins, he walked back to the poop briskly, checking crew were in position and at their watch stations.

Eli Lubbock, intent on the dim lights ahead, nodded forward, grasping the wheel tightly together with one of the crew to port.

'He's there, Billy. By God, we have him!' he cried jubilantly. 'Do you see him?'

'Aye, sir!'

'We'll take him on the lee! Are the crew up?'

'Goin', sir. But, if I may be so bold. . . .' He hesitated, knowing Eli of old, and in such a mood, to be tricky to convince. 'With all up, we'll 'ave to hope that jury-rig will hold. Them braces is tight, but metal'll go like anything else if we 'as more'n a puff more.'

'Take him, Billy!' snapped Eli, ignoring the advice. 'The Western Isles have shown lights far to our port quarter, so we've a game now that I ain't losin'.'

'Sir,' Billy began, reaching for the wheel Eli relin-

447

quished, 'the woman, Eli, Miss Emily, she ain't feelin' too well. It's our speed – we're pitchin' heavily.'

'She'll bear up till we get in,' Eli told him, rubbing chafed fingers and blowing on them.

'But she's started them pains, sir, that women 'ave afore they – '

Eli spun on Billy, eyes full of anger, cutting off further conversation. 'Take him, Mr Mate, and that is an order.'

Billy knew better than to argue, so he merely nodded and fixed his gaze ahead, where *Vesper*'s lights were already much closer.

'Hold the course . . . and on the lee, Mr Williams!'

'Aye aye, sir,' growled Billy.

Eli Lubbock went below to plot and plan the run in. In his cabin, he removed his wet skins, undid his damp top coat, unbuttoned his waistcoat, took out his pistol and put it in the first drawer beneath his pull-out desk, supported by twin arms which took his weight as he slumped forward, exhausted. For a moment he remained gratefully still, eyes closed, examining with body, mind and ears the ship around him which had brought them so far across the world. As he heard the creaks and groans of timber, the whistling of the shrouds, moaning of the wind and roaring sea outside, he thought he detected amongst it all a distant scream as if the soul of the ship was in pain. He opened his eyes and stared at the flame in the swinging hurricane lamp; at least that was familiar, and a cigar. . . . He smiled grimly and took one out of a box; few left from the many he had brought indicated imminent arrival. He lit up from the flame, moving with the ship as she rolled and plunged, confident now that she was going forward at a lick which would put him where he intended to be, ahead, in front, first in.

'Eli.' Adèle's voice came quietly. He blew out smoke but said nothing. She had taken time to understand the privations inflicted on a sea captain by the known elements and unknown forces in combination. If nothing else, she had learned to dispense with the notion of romance and had accepted that something else existed in the blood of a true sailor whose courage was challenged daily. Only now had her affections for Eli become strained, because of his single-mindedness and lack of concern for Emily's increasingly critical condition.

'Eli,' she said again, and sat on the bunk, turning his chair so that he faced her. 'You may have reason to be as you are. Perhaps you can live with this on your conscience, but how will you face Silas when he learns what you have done?'

'I have done nothing – madam.'

'But you must! Eli, I plead with you. She will die, and so will her child if you do not stop!'

The clipper plunged forward, jarring the entire frame of the ship and causing Adèle to cling on and the hurricane lamp to swing erratically. Eli merely puffed his cigar and stared at her, knowing what he had decided and determined to be unmoved.

'Eli, if it is the wager – please.' Adèle's eyes were moist. She leaned close – no women's wiles but sincere desire to impress upon the ship's captain the urgency of her request.

'Eli,' she whispered, 'you shall have so much more from me. Please see her, look upon her face, then decide – for yourself.'

Eli pursed his lips as if about to speak but said nothing. The hard expression in his eyes changed and he stood up. 'Take me to her,' he said. Immediately, Adèle was on the move. In the long corridor running the length of the ship, sea legs were necessary. Adèle clung to the wall but Eli in the centre strode down to midships, where the passengers' compartments were laid out. Hurricane lamps swung crazily from their hooks, throwing light into great pools of shadow where cargo sections and additional crew's quarters, stewards and the cook were bedded down.

Outside Emily's quarters, he stopped and waited for Adèle, who was thrown across the corridor into his arms. For a moment, holding her, his resolve weakened and there was nothing in the world but the two of them. Nothing else in life could matter. What of a ship? What of a journey? What of ambition? Then Emily screamed as the clipper bucked and crashed, and the noise cut through Eli even more than he had imagined, above the shrill wind and roaring sea – the elemental became secondary in that sound of human pain.

'Look on her face, Eli,' said Adèle, seeing him hesitate. 'Look on her!' she commanded, seizing him. Emily screamed again, and it died to a whimper. 'Eli, have compassion – stop, I beg you!'

'If we wallow, she will suffer still and I will be endangering all aboard this ship,' he argued.

Chantril rose up, pitching and rolling to port. Both Adèle and Eli were thrown to one side against stacked cargo. Eli recovered first, turned and began to walk back to his quarters. Adèle grasped him, thrusting him against a compartment wall. 'Eli, have a mind!'

He shook his head. 'We'll be in sooner under full sail and I will not furl it now! She deceived me when we embarked and she will take her chance now, as we all must. She boarded this ship with child, and, by God! that is how she will leave it!' He pulled away, and began to walk to his cabin.

'You have always been alone, Eli Lubbock!' shouted Adèle, tears falling from her eyes. 'That is what makes you cruel. You have no reason to – '

Eli spun round.

'Reason!' he bellowed, 'Listen to me! This China run will never happen again. When we are in the Thames and have ended what is the last race, an era will be finished and my world of the winds and blue water is then over forever! Even as a boy 'prentice, I dreamed of my own command and one hundred days to England. Only now have I been given the chance to become a part of that tradition – of history.' His voice became vehement. 'I will win because that is what I set out to do!' He pulled her face inches from his own, holding her tightly as the pitch and roll threatened to pluck them apart. 'It may be only a moment of glory,' he hissed, 'but *that* is enough to live with for the rest of *my* life!'

'Oh, Eli,' sobbed Adèle, 'I will give you everything – anything.'

'You do not sell self-respect, madam!' He released her and she sagged against the corridor wall. 'Take your money, and buy elsewhere!' He left her and strode confidently back to his cabin and the charts for England.

Furnace doors swung open, revealing roaring flames to the stokers who, under orders, shovelled coal faster than they had ever been required to before, even during the cyclone, when *Otranto* had been at maximum danger. The thunder of engines and the sound of racing pistons gave rise to many anxious looks amongst old hands. Mr Reinhardt had been to the furnaces on several occasions, equally concerned but outwardly trying to convey confidence to men fully aware of their increasing jeopardy. Only locked, watertight doors muffled the sound representing a single man's ambition, but the continuing bells rung between wheel-house and engine room illustrated the increasing tension.

'She just won't take no more, Mr Jackson,' said Captain Wallis soberly, staring out at the dawn light through the spray-lashed glass of the wheelhouse.

'Once it was all a matter of reputation,' Jackson said

quietly. 'Do you think it really possible that they could still do the run in one hundred days, Tom?'

'Well, we're more'n ninety days out ourselves.' He paused, ruminating, ''Course I was never on a crack clipper like yourself, and those was different times. I'd guarantee we'll be home long before they're in the Downs. They'll not make more'n three knots – takin' port and starboard they'll see more of France than England. It's just that for me' – he caught Jackson's eye – 'I just don't want to strain our engines, sir. Look, without the delays ashore we'd be – if I was a bettin' man I'd say we'll be housed and fed and bedded long 'afore they even sight the Lizard.'

Jackson squinted to the north-west, where light spreading from the coast picked out something on the horizon. He took up binoculars and focused.

'That'll be landfall, Mr Jackson,' said the Captain. 'England.'

Jackson traversed the distant horizon slowly and found only sea and sky – then land. He nodded. 'England,' he confirmed, and offered the binoculars to Captain Wallis, who refocused and reversed his sighting from east to west, light into darkness, until he found, lit against the dull clouds, bright canvas; he lowered the binoculars, disbelieving, then looked again. Not one but two, leagues away but clearly picked out by the strengthening sunlight.

'Lo and behold,' he muttered, and with his face a mask handed the binoculars back to Jackson.

'God Almighty!' exclaimed the owner of *Otranto*.

'Yes, sir,' muttered Captain Wallis as a buzz of speculation started amongst the others in the wheel-house. 'Both of 'em – *Chantril* and *Vesper*.'

Jackson lowered the glasses and ground his teeth. 'I'm a bettin' man, Tom, who's racin' – an' I ain't losin'!'

The Captain sucked his pipe and took time to light it

– unusual so early but then so were the circumstances. 'Someone racin',' he said, philosophically, 'always 'as to lose.' He blew out smoke with a wry and resigned expression on his face – but Hollis Jackson was already gone.

Cornelia Morgan, wrapped against the cold in a large fur-lined mink coat with dark hat to match, leaned on the rail of the Terrace Deck, already up and out for morning air before breakfast. Jackson joined her, and neither spoke for several minutes, lost in their own thoughts. Then Cornelia saw the distant clippers, canvas caught in the sunlight, clearly illuminated against the low dark cloud. She shivered and pulled her coat tight.

'Are they . . . ?' she asked, turning to Jackson.

'It's them,' Jackson admitted quietly.

'Did you not sleep well, Hollis?' she asked. He looked at her; their blossoming affair had cooled during recent days and his own fluctuating moods had allowed him little time to speculate that perhaps *she* might actually be missing *him*.

'Hardly at all,' he answered. 'You?'

'Oh – well,' she replied too quickly, 'always well.'

'I know,' he said, and smiled for the first time. She glanced about her quickly. The affair was hardly a secret but society's veneer had protected her from loose gossip.

'That is hardly gallant, Hollis,' she hissed.

'It is a fact,' murmured Jackson, warming to the conversation.

She looked away from the expression in his eyes and pointed. 'Why are we behind them, Hollis? I had thought we were ahead?'

'We have all day to catch them,' he replied.

'They appear to be moving . . . fast,' she observed.

'So are we.' He took her gently by the shoulders,

pulling her to him. 'What are we to do?' he asked, slowly contemplating the future.

Cornelia was more practical. She smiled and kissed his cheek lightly. 'Have breakfast,' she answered, and laughing coquettishily, led Jackson, reluctant to take his eyes from the two clippers, into the dining saloon.

The Captain's table was full of passengers bubbling with conversation. Wagers, speculated upon for days, now the sightings had been confirmed, were hastily struck. Stanley Grace had quickly established a sweep, against which Marsh, Meyer and numerous others, including the ship's officers, all had their own opinions. But money changed hands and the excitement provided a fillip to the last days at sea.

Jackson and Cornelia were served kedgeree from an ornate polished silver trolley, as was the Captain on his arrival.

'Mr Jackson,' he said formally, 'I have noted in the log that it is against my judgement to drive on, as you have instructed, at such a pace. We must reduce speed, as I am sure we are all aware.' He surveyed the table of attentive faces. 'If we were to lose power in this sea. . . .' He shook his head. 'Too near the shore and we'd be lost. A drifting steamship in a shifting sea is like a tethered goat to a prowling tiger.'

Cornelia sneezed. 'Your years, in India I believe you told us, provided colourful similies. Tell us, do – when shall this "tethered goat" arrive and put an end to all our sufferings?'

Captain Wallis, fork laden with kedgeree, mused for a moment. 'We could be in the Thames Estuary soon after dusk – depending on prevailing weather.

The Captain was silent until a sailor hovering behind him ventured to speak. Tom Wallis listened and only then smiled.

'Ladies and gentlemen,' he announced, 'the wind has veered round – to the east – force six.'

'And what does that mean, Captain?' asked Cornelia innocently.

Jackson, triumph in his every word, answered, 'We have engines!'

Cornelia took out a scented handkerchief and sneezed again. There was courteous concern at the table. 'It is of no consequence,' she said with a small gesture of approval. 'Claridges has wonderful hot broth and their mattresses are so soft.' She glanced quickly at Hollis Jackson, who was already in conversation with the Captain, jubilant that the clippers' progress would now be effectively halted by the strong head-wind. So she sneezed again; loudly.

30

A signal rocket soared up from *Chantril*'s deck and exploded far above her top canvas in a shower of red stars. On the quarter deck Eli pointed out to his mate numerous pilot ships – small, fast vessels, once all sail, now with engines – chugging out from the distant shore, smoke trailing from their tall stacks.

'We'll take the first pilot that can keep up, Billy.'

'But sir – '

'I'll not lose way,' Eli snapped. 'Put the gig on a line and they can jump for their guineas.'

'Sir, the wind's backing.'

'It won't last,' Eli replied, staring above at the canvas and wafting away the very suggestion. 'We'll tack it out until it veers in our favour.' His excitement and sheer will for victory disturbed Billy, but he complied with orders as always, noting the shifting wind with a curse as he did so.

The Captain's gig was released from the deck-house roof and lowered over the side on two lines securing it to the bulwarks. A fast steam pinnace, seeing this, approached rapidly at an angle, having gained way on its competition. Coming in from the port bow, the vessel suddenly gunned its engines and spun around, drifting stern first as it slid to touch the bouncing gig. At the very moment before impact, a wiry little man leapt from pilot boat to gig, immediately clinging on with an expertise all who witnessed the sight admired.

'They must be gettin' hungry,' suggested Billy.

Eli nodded. 'It'll improve the price.'

As the pinnace fell away, riding out the foam-flecked sea, it hooted rapidly, answered by morse light flashed to acknowledge the pilot's arrival. The little man scrambled up a rope-ladder and was over the bulwarks and on to the main deck to be escorted to the poop seconds later. He saluted the helm.

'Welcome, Captain Lubbock. We have been informed of your imminent arrival.' He grinned a gap-toothed smile, looking in his drab clothes and tall old-fashioned hat more like an undertaker come to indicate the way to the hereafter than the life-saver aboard to show the three masters the way in. 'All of London seems to be talkin' of the race – you an' them other two. . . . It's just like the great days, sir,' he said, addressing Eli. 'Now then,' he coughed, 'to make it official – may I congratulate you as the first in from China, sir – a feat I will be pleased to confirm.' He paused, equally pleased with himself, it seemed. 'You know I ain't had occasion to say that in years.'

Captain Lubbock nodded. 'And you've none to say it now,' he snapped. 'We've a deal of a way to go and' – he pointed – 'what is that, mister?' *Vesper* was certainly a good league astern, but she was holding her position, as, indeed, was the further distant *Otranto* – a mere smudge on the horizon, but there still. The pilot squinted to identify the other clipper. 'Why sir,' he replied slowly, 'that is the *second* in from China.'

Eli shook his head. 'No, it is the last in,' he said soberly. 'We've no room to boast yet – mister. The wager was to the Thames.'

'An' there's money aplenty staked on it too, sir, I assure you of that, indeed I do.' The man pulled his thick top coat about his sparse body, feeling the bite of the stiffening wind. 'In gentlemen's clubs, sir – all the rage since the telegraph's arrived from Shanghai – as to who's to do it!' He stared at Eli. 'For myself, I confess astonishment as to 'ow the steamship ain't already docked.' The pilot, already the professional, gauged the wind, checked spread canvas and suggested a held course until the charts had been examined. Eli and the man went below, leaving Billy at the wheel controlling *Chantril* in a blow on a heaving sea. He didn't have to look, he knew *Vesper* was behind – still there.

A tall, sharp-featured man presented himself to Silas Hayes and with little formality, sniffing the wind, absorbing general conditions aboard, having already surveyed the canvas set, ordered rather than suggested.

'Tack to port; the wind is gusting, but we'll find it stronger inshore. *Then* you shall be the first into the Thames. We'll take him' – he pointed ahead, where those at the wheel could just make out *Chantril* riding the green water caught intermittently in shafting sunlight. 'We'll take him,' he repeated, 'before the Downs.' He was referring to the waters off England's southern shores. The man readjusted an old ex-naval cap and his tongue wetted thin lips. 'A deal of money has been wagered, I gather.'

'You've good ears,' growled Silas Hayes.

'But a small balance in the bank,' replied the pilot.

Silas Hayes had been waiting for it and smiled, 'What would a man like you do with fifty pounds?'

'A lot less than with fifty guineas,' came the prompt reply from a stoic face.

'Why, sir,' said Silas in mock admonishment, 'that is fifty shillings over the fair price.'

'It is *the* price, which is fair.'

'To the Thames?' asked Silas, detecting a Scottish burr in the man's voice.

'To Gravesend,' said the pilot, his pale face twitching.

'Then you must board your pinnace again, sir,' Silas told him. 'It is fifty pounds – and that is all or nothing for us to enter with the tide before' – he paused – 'the others.' He held out a hand, watching the pilot hesitate, glancing at his pinnace running parallel, smoke streaming from her stack, waiting for approval from the Captain aboard *Vesper*. The pilot calculated and made his decision – it was a wet trip back and here was money, and after all they had the rest of the day and with luck, a decanter of port.

He shook hands with Captain Silas Hayes. 'You'll be the first in, sir,' he said. 'I'll warrant that!'

'I hope so,' replied Silas quietly, then assumed the face of geniality designed to encourage. 'Port?' he asked but already knew the answer.

As the day waned, Eli was proved right, his prediction more of a wish than Silas' nose had told him, but both men had separately come to the same conclusion. The strong easterly having provided so much elation aboard the steamship *Otranto*, allowing her to gain a league on the two clippers, putting her so much closer, abated, sprang up again, gusted, veered, backed and behaved in a generally baffling way. Coupled with the confused sea and the gloom of the lowering sky, dispensing squall, icy rain or harsh sleet, the inconstant wind drew from each captain all their reserves and skills to ply forward and maintain distance from the ever approaching threat of Jackson's *Otranto*. Late afternoon was so dark, the Needles' fixed light showed first white then, as the clippers scudded through the waves, barely a league apart, to a position south-east-half south, it appeared red. Both pilots confirmed good progress, now aided by a building south westerly veering often to the west but never so far south as to cause either Eli or Silas over-concern. Their eyes were on each other but both became increasingly disturbed by the speed of the closing steamer.

Beyond Portsmouth, the clippers had each made out Nelson's monument painted red and white at Spithead. St Catherine's and The Nab lights showed intermit-

459

tently, obscured often by the swirling sleet and, by four-thirty, rapidly falling darkness. Arundel, New Shoreham and the Owers light vessel were sighted and identified, first by Eli, then Silas, who was making no way against *Chantril*'s consistent speed. For the first time, *Vesper*'s captain felt uneasy at the prospect of losing what he had determined, especially seeing *Otranto* still behind, would be *his* race. In his cabin, Silas and the pilot, well lubricated with port, examined yet again the chart to Beachy Head from the Brighton and Newhaven shorelines, illuminated by the ever swinging hurricane lamp.

'We'll see the cliffs with a glass,' observed the pilot. 'That is, if we glimpse the moon. It's a sight all right, especially for the man too long abroad.'

Silas nodded, knowing the feeling of old. The steep, white chalk cliffs, seven in all, to the west of the telegraph and watch-house were always a remarkable sight before the Eastbourne Beach Town, two and a half miles to the north-east.

'How long to Dungeness?' questioned Silas Hayes, pouring more port for them both.

'Hard to say,' began the pilot. 'We've chips at the log telling us a constant twelve knots, and I'd make a guess but for this damn gusting sleet. I believe it's more important for the watch to keep a keen eye than worry some about headway – we've enough.'

Silas grunted. 'So 'as he.' He indicated ahead, where *Chantril* still plunged forward, outstripping her competition.

'It's red you might remember,' said the pilot, 'which we'll not see but it's worth remarking on.' He paused then explained. 'The lighthouse – it's a fixed light with excellent argand lamps and reflectors, an' we'll see them all right for a good six leagues from the shore, then we'll be well on our way to the Dover roads.' He grinned and gulped his liquor as watch bells rang above. Each man consulted his pocket watch. 'Then we must bear to starboard to make our tack to port, and north then north-west and west, so we must all pray for a windshift long before midnight. If we was to pick up an easterly blowing up our stern we could wave as we pass him.' The pilot indicated the heel of Kent and the curve into the Thames Estuary.

'And if he turns first?' asked Silas gruffly.

'Well, sir, then, ahem, I've lost my fifty guineas.'

'Pounds.'

The pilot smiled weakly. 'Ah yes,' he said, 'I was forgetting.'

Although the pain was not hers, Adèle winced as Emily threw her head to one side, her face lost in shadow as her scream was muted by the rushing elements all about as *Chantril* ploughed towards the final leg at the Straits of Dover. Awan leant towards her mistress, her son Cha-ze standing beside her, watching the vain attempts to feed soup to the suffering woman. The small Chinese boy had been bringing nourishment for more than a week, especially concocted by the cook from the best available for the pregnant 'Lady of Mr Hayes'. White-faced and clearly exhausted, Emily stared up at the lamps above her, feeling every shudder of the thrusting clipper surging into the night sea off England.

'We are almost there,' whispered Awan. Emily sipped soup from the spoon and, despite the cold, sweat showed on her forehead. She said nothing.

Lewis Ellory put his head in the compartment, hat doffed out of respect, enquiring silently if he could help. Adèle shook her head, then *Chantril* hit a big one and, as the soup emptied from the bowl over the bed, each of those standing had to cling on tight. Emily's scream rent the air and burned its way into Adèle's heart. Her

461

face became grim and her wide eyes hardened with conviction and decision.

'All our remaining drinking water,' she ordered of the hesitant, stunned Ellory – 'heat it *now!*' She stepped to the doorway, removing her apron.

'Where are you going?' asked the young cameraman anxiously.

'Real life, Mr Ellory, must be faced and lived, not merely photographed!' She strode unsteadily down the corridor.

Adèle stopped at the door to the Captain's cabin, leaning against the narrow corridor's panelling. She cautiously reached out for the handle and opening the door, stepped in quickly. The cabin was empty, save for ghosts of the past which seemed to moan and groan in answer to the wailing shrouds above. Timbers, plates and braces strained to their limits for so long were the real source of the exhausted sounds of the tired ship in a wild sea. Gingerly, Adèle moved across the small space to the desk and ducked beneath the swinging lamps, wicks turned low to save oil. She held her breath and prayed as she slowly pulled open the drawer. Next to the unused bible lay a rimfire pistol – Eli's. She took it out, checked the cartridges and pushed the drawer closed. Grasping the gun tightly, she left the cabin and looked up at the steps leading to the poop deck. Water sluiced about above and dripped through every open crack. She shivered, but resolution drove her on. Grimly she ascended.

'These bafflin' airs 'as cost us 'alf a day, Eli,' shouted Billy Williams above the roar of wind. 'We can't tack to port or we'll become part of the white cliffs of Dover!' The pilot glanced up from the compass, wiping water from his face, and nodded agreement. Icy spray whipped across the deck and together with the sleet flurries, as Eli had already stated, they were all having 'a wonderful blow' as plump shipowners often referred to heavy weather on comfortable nights in pleasant surroundings after an excellent dinner, over port, brandy and cigars.

'The wind's veering, by God!' cried the pilot, now certain that bearing and direction were correct.

'When do we turn north?' shouted Eli. 'How many miles?'

'Fifteen!' answered the pilot. 'We could squeeze it to ten if we're well out in the Channel – you'll need men at the braces and the sky sails reefed.'

'I know my business, mister!' snarled Eli. 'Do yours!'

The pilot grimaced then grinned, thinking of his money – in his mind already spent. 'When we hit the estuary with a full-blow easter directly astern, we'll be the fastest ship on the river!'

Eli spun the man around. Tired and tense, he pointed to the lights of *Vesper*, seen briefly between the spray and sleet, but there for certain upon the dark sea and distantly but not distant enough, the great array of lights from *Otranto*.

'Count your sovereigns slowly, mister. We've a way to go and we ain't lost 'em yet.'

'Eli!' screamed Adèle. He turned to see the young woman, hair streaming in the wind, her small figure framed by the door to his cabin. She wore only a dress and with no top coat was already shivering.

'Go below – you'll catch your death of cold,' shouted Eli. She shook her head and her features, etched by the hurricane lamps about the quarter deck, seemed to Eli strangely determined. Her arms hung down, her hands concealed in the folds of her dress. The shawl about her shoulders was whirled away with the icy spray gusting across the ship, but she made no attempt to stop it. She raised a hand and pointed Eli's Remington, her thumb on the hammer, directly at the captain of *Chantril*. Instinctively Eli touched his waistband, swore under his breath and grimaced.

'I will fire,' Adèle announced, 'if you do not now stop.'

Eli made to move – immediately, she cocked the hammer of the revolver.

He hesitated, angry now. 'You are in British waters. If I am shot you will be hanged.'

Adèle smiled wryly. 'I have no need to shoot if you stop.'

'I said *hanged*, madam!' bellowed Eli, embarrassed in front of his mate and the pilot, but noted they had no intention of approaching an obviously loaded gun, aimed with clear intention. Again spray swirled across the deck and sleet patterned Adèle's dress, but the revolver remained steady, now held in both hands; even as the clipper pitched heavily she rode out the movement with expert balance.

'Shoot and be damned!' snapped Eli.

'The bullet would only find a cold heart,' replied Adèle. 'Stop,' she finished, her voice suddenly hard. Eli's eyes narrowed and he stepped towards her. Instantly she took a pace back and felt the closed cabin door behind when she leant heavily, breathing deeply, her chest heaving – dangerous.

'Enough – furl the sails!'

Chantril rose up, throwing spray the length of the ship as thunder rumbled, crackling across the black night suddenly illuminated by forked lightning. Adèle remained resolute.

'Sir!' warned Billy and made to stop Eli, who threw off the Mate's hand and took another pace. Adèle fired effectively, transfixing Eli, who felt blood spurt, then course down his cheek. He touched the wound and grinned menacingly. 'You're bluffing!'

Adèle shook her head. 'I was aiming at your heart. You shall not murder an innocent woman!'

'If I am to stop now,' shouted Eli, above the wind, 'you will be killing me without bullets!'

'Do not think of yourself, Eli,' Adèle pleaded, 'or even of the woman, think of the child, I beg you!'

Eli held out a hand for the gun.

She hesitated. 'Your word,' she said.

'You have it,' growled Eli Lubbock reluctantly. She offered him the gun. A sleet flurry caused both of them to squint against the icy flakes as Eli took the revolver and adjusted his grip from barrel to handle, which he grasped in one hand. Then he seized Adèle's dress at the throat and swung her, screaming, across the deck to the stern rail. He arched her back over the dull brass and, leaning towards the frightened eyes, his face inches from hers, he thrust the muzzle of the gun into her neck, anger exploding from him.

'I am the master of this ship!' he snarled, 'and you are threatening the security of all on board. I can shoot you now and have you thrown into the sea – within the law!'

'Do so – but save the child,' cried Adèle, tears wet on her cheeks. Eli stared into the eyes appealing to him with the very soul that commanded their expression. 'They will die,' she whispered. Thunder drowned Billy's shouts for caution as lightning flooded Adèle's face for a second, creating an image in Eli's mind that he would never forget and might have remained indelibly on his conscience.

'That is blackmail,' he hissed, relaxing his grip.

'It is life,' said Adèle softly. She reached up and touched his still bleeding wound tenderly. 'Please Eli,' she murmured, 'I want to love you.'

'Sir!' said Billy Williams, now at Eli's side. 'Sir?' he repeated.

Eli relinquished his grip on Adèle and released the revolver to his mate. He stood erect and turned to survey his canvas glowing in the lamplight, shadows jumping across the obediently taut sails straining as commanded to capture the wind and bear away all in

465

their charge as directed by the captain of the ship. *Chantril* pitched again, heavily, and foam broke across even the quarter deck as she rolled to port, inundating those at the helm, causing Adèle to cling to Eli, who was facing the most difficult decision of his life. After ninety-nine days . . . Eli swore under his breath.

Adèle reached up and turned his face to look down upon her own. She could not have heard the scream of frustrated ambition inside him as he closed his eyes, knowing – accepting finally – that he had no choice.

Unscheduled watch bells were rung and crew given rapid instructions by incredulous mates ranking directly beneath First Mate, Billy Williams. They mounted towards the shrouds with consoling shouts to each other, knowing that the course of events might now deny them the bonus promised at the commencement of the voyage. The consensus of opinion was that the wily captain must have a plan. It was a comforting thought as, in the adverse conditions, they went about the task of reef and furl at sea.

For Eli Lubbock it was all over. There was no plan – even for his future – now. Walking the length of his ship along the corridor between stacked cargo compartments and quarters for extra crew and paid passengers, seeing the swinging lamps throw shadows all about as if mocking apparitions come to taunt him, he realised his world of hope, expectation and a life ahead, based upon the present race – was finished. For a full half-hour he had lingered above at the helm, ensuring that Billy Williams brought *Chantril* hove to in safety. Satisfied, he had gone below and re-plotted, then followed Adèle's footsteps to Emily's small room.

The thunder and lightning had eased as the Channel storm rolled on in the night to the south-west. Clouds had parted and Eli had even seen some stars. It was undeniably cold and the sea continued to heave about

Chantril but with a lessening forward speed, she settled into the water more and rode out the waves with elegance.

The Mate had become dejected and would not speak. The pilot looked anxiously towards the approaching *Vesper* and, beyond, *Otranto*, as if at any moment Eli Lubbock would change his mind, up sail, continue the race, finish and win.

Eli's footsteps revealed his despondency – heavy and paced out. With the changing conditions and slower headway of his ship they were also disturbingly – to the Captain – sure. Lights flickered from the gloom ahead and voices spoke urgently as Eli approached. He stopped and leant against the compartment wall, hesitant to enter. His face was a mask, hearing the moans and cries within as he detected also the unmistakable sound outside of rushing water from another vessel. It was *Vesper* passing close. He pressed fingers to the bridge of his nose, closed his eyes and felt his heart sink. Everything he'd aspired to achieve, become, inherit, pass on, at this very moment, he knew now, was lost.

The fast-clearing weather and intermittent moon had shown all at the helm of *Vesper*, exchanging the glass, that something was up aboard *Chantril*, less than half a league distant.

Hughie was, as always, sceptical. 'He's takin' in sail, sir,' he said, as if it was not already a proven fact but obvious lie.

'Well, Captain,' the pilot had suggested quickly, knowing his guineas were safe in consequence, '*whatever* – he's the poorer . . . we'll be past him in minutes.'

Silas Hayes was unconvinced and with fixed gaze had watched *Chantril*'s advantage diminish until they were almost side by side. There was nothing in his experience or knowledge of his friend to explain what was now taking place, so as others speculated loudly, Silas remained silent, merely an observer of an unfathomable mystery.

Morse lights as the ships came abreast exchanged information. Questions and answers.

'What trouble – why stopping?' *Vesper* sent.

'No trouble,' came the reply, 'just fishing.'

Silas recognised Billy at *Chantril*'s helm as her brass rail passed swiftly, his eyes were narrowed, his mind suspicious, aware but not a part of the jubilation aboard as his crew and passengers, relieved at the increasingly clement weather, cheered and waved.

'What have you caught?' sent Hughie Sutherland, watching the crewman flash the morse light. Jamie, and Polly, whining piteously, came up to the poop, joining Silas, who fondled the dog after greeting his son.

'What is it, Father?'

'Look,' said Silas.

'Why are they taking in canvas?'

'I don't know,' grunted Silas Hayes.

'Mermaid?' laughed Hughie Sutherland.

'What?' asked Silas.

'That's what they sent, sir.'

'Are there mermaids, Father?' asked Jamie.

'No,' was the answer, as Silas continued to stare at *Chantril*. ' . . . with child,' declared Hughie, reading still from *Chantril*'s flashing light. 'What does that mean? I thought mermaids 'ad fish.'

Polly whined irritatingly and Silas looked down at his son, who had already understood but, having promised, was reluctant to reveal what he knew to be the truth.

'Your lady,' he began hesitantly, 'Miss Emily, is aboard *Chantril*.'

Silas seized his son, roughly hauling him into the air with both hands so they were face to face. 'What did you say boy?'

'She made me promise not to . . .' hesitated Jamie, 'but she was very big.' He indicated his stomach.

'She is on board . . . ?' said Silas slowly – both question and answer.

'Yes, sir,' murmured Jamie. His father remained transfixed, slowly accepting the impossible.

'The stupid bitch,' growled Silas, and lowered his son to the deck. 'Congratulations, Captain,' babbled the pilot, beaming from ear to ear. 'You have won!' and as *Vesper* passed beyond *Chantril*'s bow and forged away into the night, the statement seemed indisputable. . . .

With a final scream of pain a life was born and all the efforts of Adèle, Awan and Mr Ellory, were rewarded. Adèle cut the umbilical cord and held up the child. As Eli Lubbock summoned the courage to step into the cramped quarters, the young woman slapped the baby and heard it cry out. Flushed and tired but exhilarated, she looked at Eli and smiled.

'This, Captain Lubbock,' she said quietly, 'is winning.' And at that moment, who was Eli to disagree? He knew she was right and smiled back.

Dressed and cleaned, the baby was placed in the mother's arms and agony became ecstasy as the small face sought succour in the welcoming embrace. Eli returned to his cabin to write up the log, Adèle busied herself with Awan, and Mr Ellory sank down gratefully on to his own bed, astonished still at the prowess of women; their instincts and abilities tested and proved.

The Captain drank rum. *Chantril*'s helm, secure in good hands, Eli began to write even as he poured from the decanter best dark Lamb's liquor. The pilot joined him.

'And where is "the future"?' asked Eli facetiously.

'Coming,' said the pilot glumly, knowing *Otranto* was fast approaching.

469

'Jackson will crow about this for the rest of our days,' Eli said harshly.

'It was your decision,' replied the pilot, sipping rum.

'It was,' stated Eli, 'necessary.'

'But *he* doesn't know that,' said the pilot.

'No,' answered Eli, and smiled wryly, 'but *I* do.'

The cabin door burst open and Billy entered, inarticulate and emotional.

'Eli. . . .'

'What is it?' snapped *Chantril*'s captain as the pilot glanced up.

'Come and see,' mumbled Billy Williams. The three men went up to the quarter deck together. Stars showed and the moon had emerged from behind breaking cloud. The night was clearing, the wind abating and the sea had ceased its efforts to inundate and destroy, becoming, instead, a moving ally to *Chantril*, allowing the moonlight to shine a beacon glittering on the waves, indicating the pathway home. And ahead was *Vesper*. Eli made no sound. His eyes said it all.

'My God,' muttered the pilot, and Billy Williams wiped tears from his cheeks. Reefing and furling all but the essential sails, Silas Hayes was coming to. Eli shook his head and put an arm around his mate's shoulders. 'We'll still be in by midnight, Billy,' he said.

Minutes later, the two ships were alongside and hellos and hurrahs were exchanged loudly.

'Good evening!' shouted Eli Lubbock.

'How is she?' came the bellowed reply from Silas. Eli grinned, '*She's* bonny!' he revealed, but could not hear his friend whisper 'bonny' to himself, or indeed see the tears of joy in his eyes. But everyone heard the terrier, Polly, barking wildly – even Emily below, cherishing the child of her love, knowing now that the secret was out.

'Oh, Silas,' she murmured, and felt indescribable happiness.

*

A magnum of champagne, opened with a loud report, heralded a spume of froth as it was immediately poured into numerous glasses for the Captain's table aboard steamship *Otranto*. Hollis Jackson had seldom been seen in better spirits by the company around him. Removing a cigar from his mouth, he indicated to port through the long dining room window. 'Observe, ladies and gentlemen – where you see the past. . . .' Clearly in view were the two clipper ships moving slowly, ghost-like in the moonlight. 'Let us all drink to the future!' he said and raised a glass for the toast to be joined by Marsh, Meyer, Grace, Cornelia and the Captain, who, feeling the vibration of his thundering engines, drank quickly, excused himself from the resulting babble of conversation and retired to the bridge to discuss final instructions from the pilot they too had now taken on.

Beyond North Foreland and the Goodwin Sands, where the light vessel, exhibiting the familiar three-point triangle, had been observed, and the gong heard as the mist of evening demanded for wary seamen, *Otranto* moved at speed towards the Thames Estuary. Recycling steam and maintaining pressure as ordered at maximum for days had caused Mr Reinhardt nightmares. Repeated requests to ease up and rest the pistons had been accepted by the Captain but rejected by Hollis Jackson, who had pushed on until first sighting of the clippers. After that it was impossible to reason with him, and anxious faces at the wheelhouse and in the engine room had replaced words. Only now, as *Otranto* bested her competition ninety-nine days out of Shanghai, did Jackson, in full view of his opposition, knowing victory in that agreed race was his, allow that perhaps speed could be reduced. But it was already too late.

'What are they playing at?' grunted the Captain in *Otranto*'s wheelhouse, lowering his binoculars.

The two clippers, moving slowly side by side along

471

a moonlit sea road, seemed oblivious of the great steamship passing so close. Tom Wallis shook his head, muttering, 'In all my days.' Then the telegraph rang loudly and immediate and insurmountable problems presented themselves. 'Mr Reinhardt requests, sir, that we must reduce speed!' the First Officer relayed loudly.

'What's the problem?' asked Captain Wallis.

'Pressure, sir,' answered the young officer.

'To half then, mister – now!'

'Sir!'

The telegraph rang again – urgently, gauges below were dictating action with or without orders. Safety valves wide open, steam built up over so many days had proved too much and justified Mr Reinhardt's fears.

'Shut them down!' he ordered, as if an unseen hand would provide a solution to the obvious danger. Searing steam swirled about the boilers, forcing the men to back away. The thundering pistons had begun to slow, but arrows on the gauges indicated into the red and beyond the last figures.

'Clear the hold!' Reinhardt decided, and not a moment too soon. The bulkhead door, closed and secured, saved his life. Seconds later, the explosion that took place could have torn the side out of a lesser ship.

'Ladies and gentlemen,' Stanley Grace began, responding in the dining salon to Hollis Jackson's genial humour, 'may I propose a toast.' He stood up and smiled. 'To the turn of the century!' Some applause and raised glasses proved Grace's suggestion popular, the booming noise deep in *Otranto*'s hull and resulting shudder that went through the entire ship were not. Movable objects were thrown about, people fell, cried out, screamed in alarm, and to add to the confusion aboard *Otranto*, the lights flickered, then all of them, as one, went out.

At the rails of the two clipper ships the sight of an

ocean liner passing close at night was a modern wonder. A city of lights glowing in the dark, majestic and in the knowledge it was man-made, awe-inspiring. The fact it was Hollis Jackson's, made it less than a welcome sight to Eli and Silas, and each man cursed loudly, which some more superstitious than others later contended had prompted fate to intervene. All the lights suddenly disappeared – swept away, leaving *Otranto* duly invisible, only the sound of her engines revealing she was still in the water. Shouts of astonishment became genuine concern until what had happened was understood and explained to the majority. Silas Hayes began to roar with laughter, now making out *Otranto*, from emergency lights, slowing rapidly, her bow wave diminishing.

'By God, she's blowed her stack!' declared Hughie Sutherland. Lewis Ellory appeared on *Chantril*'s deck, setting up his camera clumsily in an attempt to capture the moonlit incident at sea.

'Who'll go in first?' shouted Eli over the water to his friend. Already familiar beacons and buoys had been noted by both pilots as the two ships, gliding forward, entered safe channels into the Thames, now to everyone's elation well ahead of *Otranto*.

'We'll dock together!' replied Silas, waving hugely. The shore was in sight and the rails of *Chantril* and *Vesper* were crowded by eager faces with glistening eyes.

'England!' someone said, which brought tears, and patriotic hurrahs were loudly exchanged between each ship.

Only on *Otranto* was there gloom. The Captain had accepted the situation and rectified it as much as was possible. His unheeded warnings had been acknowledged by Hollis Jackson, having sought an explanation for the initial chaos aboard. Now they were limping in but at least it was home and they were out of danger.

'We might still catch them,' grunted Jackson, shivering on the terrace deck beside the fur-clad Cornelia.

'You have only one engine remaining; at half ahead slow, Hollis . . . please don't be a bad loser.' She pulled her coat about her warm body. 'For myself, I can only hope that you are able to recommend something better than this ship for my voyage to New York.' She sighed affectedly, but there was a twinkle in her eyes. 'Can you Hollis?' she asked quietly.

'Yes, my dear,' he replied. 'Fly!' At the ridiculous suggestion she began to laugh and, accepting defeat, he joined her then kissed willing lips as rockets began to soar from the shores and, faintly at first, church bells began pealing from every hamlet village and town glowing distantly in the night.

'Welcome to the twentieth century, Mr Jackson,' she whispered. He checked his pocket watch, seeing the hour approaching, and nodded. 'Soon,' he murmured, 'and not before time.'

Cannons boomed from darkness as small tugs took the two clippers in tow and, side by side, some passengers leaning far out and reaching across the brass rails to shake hands for the first time, in jubilant celebration, the ships moved up the estuary together.

'Jamie!' shouted Silas and, shaking a halyard free, he jumped up on to the bulwarks. The boy hesitated, then leapt up into his father's arms.

Hughie shook his head. 'Silas,' he began.

'You think I'm too old for it?' grinned the Captain of *Vesper*. 'Hold me, boy,' he said, then shouted for attention. 'Eli!' Polly scampered around on deck, barking excitedly. Seizing the hemp firmly in both hands, illuminated by exploding rockets and a curious moon, Silas hoisted himself and his son up, and with a shout of warning swung across to *Chantril*'s poop, grimacing at the effort but determined. He landed heavily, caught by Eli, and the two men tumbled to the deck. Jamie, releasing himself, found his feet, and looked down quizzically at the fallen captains.

'We used to land on our feet,' grinned Silas.

'New technique,' confirmed Eli, standing awkwardly. The two old friends embraced.

'Shipowners at last,' laughed Eli.

'And not before time,' agreed Silas.

'Do you think Hollis is saying that . . . ?'

'He should,' answered Captain Hayes.

Running wildly the length of the ship, Adèle burst into Emily's room.

'Silas!' she exclaimed. The child began to cry as her mother's eyes opened wide with both fear and pleasure. The two women began fussing over themselves, Adèle primping Emily's hair and wiping her features clean with a flannel. Silas coughed, knocked and, bidden, entered, removing his dark peaked cap. He stared at Emily and, smiling, shook his head in happy disbelief.

'Lassie,' he began.

'Silas, please,' she murmured, 'hold her.' She held up the baby and Silas took her gently as Jamie put his head around the door. The little girl stopped crying and tried to focus upon the giant holding her up to the light.

'Bonny,' whispered Silas, and clasped the child securely in his arms.

Eli Lubbock waited for the watch bells of midnight to sound, seeing Billy checking his own timepiece. Adèle took his arm and pulled herself close.

'Thank you,' she said, 'for stopping.'

'You gave me no alternative,' Eli answered.

'Do you regret it?'

Eli smiled, appreciating the expression in the young woman's face. 'You are a remarkable lady, Miss Morgan, and are more than reward for an old sea dog. I regret nothing.'

She closed her eyes and he kissed them both tenderly before finding her lips.

Silas Hayes watched his son return the small child to her mother's arms as he stroked Emily's forehead, wondering at her courage and proven love for him, then, with a hug for Awan, he took Jamie back along the corridor to the Captain's cabin, where the door led above to the poop.

The sounds of an excited nation greeting a new century were more than apparent, even below decks. Silas paused before stepping up, in his mind reliving the adventures of the ninety-nine days before landfall and destination.

'Have we arrived, Father?' asked Jamie.

Silas nodded. 'Aye, laddie – together.'

'And will this be our home now?'

Silas knelt before the boy and looked into his eyes. 'For a sailor, Jamie, only the sea is home. Arrival,' he paused, 'is an end. It is the voyage that gives you life.' He looked at his son's open face as he tried desperately to fathom the words of years of wisdom. 'Always hope that your journey is long. Do you understand?'

Jamie shook his head. 'You will, my son,' said Silas, touching his boy's cheeks. 'One day you will. Come.' He stood up, and the two of them stepped to the helm as watch bells rang loudly – ragamuffin and father together to face the future.

When Jamie saw his mother on the deck of *Otranto* as the steamship came abreast of the clippers, he waved wildly. She, hearing a familiar voice, looked below, but didn't recognise him.

'If you had to choose between . . .' Jackson started.

Cornelia glanced at him, her eyes sure. 'I have already chosen, Hollis,' she replied.

He held her firmly and turned to the clippers. 'Where will you go, now the ships are yours?' shouted Hollis Jackson to both Silas and Eli.

476

'The Pacific!' bellowed Silas.

'Hawaii!' countered Eli.

'I'll race you!' declared Jackson.

'Jamie!' exclaimed Cornelia. Finally realising that the urchin beneath her was indeed the velvet and ruff child supposedly safely ensconced in a San Francisco preparatory school, she fainted dead away into Hollis Jackson's arms.

Bells, rockets, cannons and cheers heralded the first moments of Queen Victoria's last years on the throne of England, and a new age. Polly seemed to understand, and contributed with his usual enthusiastic barking. Lewis Ellory was the only seemingly sober man aboard any of the ships from the steamship steerage rails to poop deck's celebrations. Oblivious of his light problems, hoping for the best, he was cranking his camera, using up the last of his film.

The night sky revealed its wealth of stars and the moon shone encouragingly upon the travellers from afar as rockets burst everywhere, obscuring constellations. England received the ships into her bosom with great display.

Jamie looked up and privately whispered, 'Thank you, Ben,' and thought for just one moment that he heard his friend's quiet reply. Silas ruffled his son's hair as choruses of, 'Should auld aquaintance be forgot' began.

'Happy New Year, laddie,' he said. 'Well, you're a sailor now. You have experience of the blue waters of the world's oceans. Would you have missed it?'

Jamie grinned as Lewis Ellory finally captured them all: a vignette of people soon to become lost in time.

'No, sir,' answered the boy. 'Not for all the tea in China.'